GOOD DOG

"After 15 years working Homicide," I told the Sheriff as I unhooked Ginger from the leash, "you develop a nose for murder. If you think she died of natural causes, that's fine with me. But there is one other thing, Sheriff. How many women do you know in the state of Maine who run around the house this time of year in their bare feet? I mean, think about it. Where are Allison's slippers?"

Before anyone could look at Allison DeMarco's bare feet, Ginger slipped out of my grasp and bolted up the stairs to the second floor. A few seconds later she came bounding back into the kitchen. It was quite a sight—a curly-haired black and tan dog with sparkling brown eyes, wearing a denim jacket and holding a fuzzy pair of pink bedroom slippers in her slobbery peanut buttery mouth. She stopped in front of me and dropped the slippers at my feet. It seems that Allison—with my help—had done a nice job of training Ginger to fetch.

I bent down to hook Ginger up. As I did, I noticed a brown stain on one of the slippers.

"What's this?" I said, picking it up. "Blood?"

LEE CHARLES KELLEY

A NOSE FOR MURDER

AVON BOOKS

An Imprint of HarperCollinsPublishers

This is a work of fiction. Names, characters, places, and incidents are products of the author's imagination or are used fictitiously and are not to be construed as real. Any resemblance to actual events, locales, organizations, or persons, living or dead, is entirely coincidental.

AVON BOOKS
An Imprint of HarperCollins*Publishers*
10 East 53rd Street
New York, New York 10022-5299

Copyright © 2003 by Lee Charles Kelley
ISBN: 0-06-052493-6
www.avonmystery.com

First Avon Books paperback printing: March 2003

Avon Trademark Reg. U.S. Pat. Off. and in Other Countries, Marca Registrada, Hecho en U.S.A.
HarperCollins® is a registered trademark of HarperCollins Publishers Inc.

Printed in the U.S.A.

10 9 8 7 6 5 4 3 2 1

Dedicated to my mother
and
to the memory of my brother, Frank.

Acknowledgments

First I want to thank all the dogs that I have ever met. The list begins with Charley and Puck and goes on to include Otis, Achille, Trudy, Lucy and Lotte, Mack, Mickey, Maggie, Guiness, Cassie, Satchmo, Roark, Breezely, Baron, Caroline, Cassie, Fluffy, Jane Russell, Lex, Pal and Spike, Rocky, Shadow, Buddy, Chili, Elsa, Risa, Samantha, Sasha, Amanda, Stella, Sophie, Shadow, Sammy, Max, Txai and Shango, Buttons, Claude, Margo, Ophie, Priscilla, Senator and Grendel, Tyrone, Zelda, Sunny, Tasha and Saul, Freckles, Daisybelle, Sophie and Phoebe, Tiffy, Buckwheat, Brodie and Shelby, Cairo, Pooh, Scarlet, Mocha, Chance, Tess, Gizmo, Otto, Electra, and many more too numerous to mention by name.

I also want to give special thanks to my favorite client, Kate Hughes, and to my other favorite clients, Thomas and Mareane, Joel and Marcia, Patty and Michael, Kirstin and Tom, Dorianne Elliot, Jane Marino, Helen Burguiere, and Paul Faust. You have all been a big help in this book getting done. Thanks, too, to my sister Sue for financial support and my brother Del and my neighbor Melanie Weiss for technical advice.

Thanks also to Kevin Behan, whose book *Natural Dog Training* totally changed the way I look at dogs and dog training. Thanks also, Kevin, for your personal encouragement and positive feedback.

Thanks to Jason Herman, the second best dog trainer in New York City, and to Kelly Reilly, the best dogwalker in the entire Big Apple. Thanks to Ricoh for help with my computer.

Acknowledgements definitely need go to Paul Escoll, my screenwriting agent and manager (and my biggest fan for the past eighteen years), and to Frances Kuffel, my literary agent, without whose determination, dedication, and vision this book might not have ever been published. She's simply the greatest.

Thanks to Jennifer Fisher and Erin Richnow, my editors at Avon, and to all the staff at Avon and at the Maria Carvainis Agency.

Special thanks also to Dana, my constant muse. Oh, yeah—and an extra special thanks (and a big bone) to a dog named Fred. Good boy!

Author's Note

The training techniques used by Jack in this book are based on the methods found in *Natural Dog Training* by Kevin Behan. These techniques are based on the simple idea that a dog's social instincts are not about a power struggle or a conflict over who's most dominant—it's actually an instinct for group cooperation and harmony, which is inextricably tied to the canine prey drive. In fact, a dog or wolf's social instincts exist only to enable them to hunt and kill large prey, as provable by the fact that those canids who live in social units called packs also tend to hunt large prey, while those who don't never do. Knowing this, training becomes a matter of stimulating and then satisfying a dog's prey drive. This makes learning fun, easy, and in some cases, instantaneous.

For more information visit Kevin Behan's website: *dogman@naturaldogtraining.com*, or e-mail me at *thekelleymethod@aol.com*.

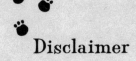

Disclaimer

The following is a work of fiction. All of the characters and situations are imaginary. Any similarities to any persons, living or dead, is purely coincidental. In fact, even some of the locations (such as Rockland County and the town of Perseverance) are entirely made up.

Only the dogs are real.

"The more I see of men, the more I admire dogs."

Mme. De Staël

A NOSE FOR
MURDER

1.

I was about to pay the check at O'Neal's, a cozy Italian joint on Bayview Street, when Jamie's beeper went off.

"It's probably Uncle Horace," she said, taking the device from her purse and glancing at the digital read-out.

"Why do you still call him that?" I said, looking over the bill and almost regretting the nice bottle of Barolo—almost, but not quite. "After all, he's not *your* uncle."

"I know." She leaned across the table to kiss me. "But I love him almost as much as I love you. In a different way, of course."

That was said to satisfy me and it did. For a second. "Yeah? So where does that leave his nephew?"

She swung her legs sideways and got up from the table in one graceful motion. The curve of one naked knee peeked out from a hole in her faded jeans. "Who?" she said, innocently.

"Your husband, Oren? Remember him?"

"You mean *ex*-husband," she said, "or soon-to-be. And the funny thing is, Jack, when I'm with you every other man in the world seems to disappear."

I jerked a thumb at the waiter, who was hovering over my right shoulder. "Then what's *he* doing here?"

She smiled, leaned over and kissed me again. "He's the waiter, sweetie. He's waiting for you to pay the check." With that she was on her way to the pay phone to call the sheriff.

I paid the waiter but he just stood there looking at me with anxious eyes. He had short rat-brown hair, wore a nose ring, and had a red and white striped plastic candy cane pinned to the pocket of his pale blue oxford-cloth shirt.

"Um, are you Jack Field?" he asked finally.

"'Fraid so. Who'd I piss off this time?"

"Huh?" he said. "No, I've got a problem with my dog and I was wondering if you could—um—give me some advice."

"Does this mean I don't have to pay the tip?" He hemmed, so I let him off the hook: "Just kidding. What's the trouble?"

His name was Tim Berry. He was a young kid about twenty or so and had been a pre-law student at Bowdoin College but funds were tight so he was back home in Camden for a semester or two to try to earn tuition by waiting tables. He told me what was bothering him: a simple problem—if basset hounds are ever simple—but not one that could be solved or even explained properly over coffee and dessert, so I gave him my card.

"Thanks," he said and took it, looking at both sides before putting it in his pocket. He turned to go, then stopped and said: "A friend and I went to a lecture you gave in Belfast last year. What you said made a lot of sense."

"Thanks. I've got another one coming up in Boothbay on Saturday. Maybe you could come."

"I work Saturdays." He frowned, then went to take care of the check. Jamie returned just as I was pocketing the change.

"What's wrong?" She seemed a trifle upset.

She sighed as she put the beeper in her purse. "One of Horace's deputies found a body in a cabin out by Hobb's Pond. I have to go out there. I don't suppose you'd want to come along?" She took her yellow parka from the back of her chair and began putting it on.

"Not especially. I gave up all interest in corpses a long time ago." Still, I got up and put on my Levi's jacket. "Why do they call it Hobb's *Pond*, by the way? I mean, it's clearly a *lake*, isn't it? I've even seen fishing boats and waterskiers out there in the summertime."

She was having trouble getting her left arm into the proper sleeve, so I did the gentlemanly thing and she let me. "Well," she said, "you'd have to ask the original settlers. And the thing is, Jack, you knew the deceased. It's Allison DeMarco."

She flipped her dark brown hair over the hood, then shook her head twice to make it fall pretty, which it did.

"Oh, that's a shame. What did she die of?"

She gave me a pointed look. "That's probably why Uncle Horace called *me*, don't you think?"

"Of course," I said, a little embarrassed. "Well, maybe I *should* go out there with you, just to check on Ginger. Did Flynn say anything about her?"

"Yes. She's been barking nonstop since early this afternoon. That's how Quentin Peck found the body in the first place. Several of the neighbors called to complain."

We went to the front door and as I held it open a tall, leggy blonde, eighteen or nineteen, did a little sideways waltz between us, then stood in the entrance, scanning the room as if expecting to meet someone. She had a cute turned-up nose with a gold nose ring in it, just like our waiter. Of course, since I was with Jamie, I didn't really look at her that closely.

"That's what I like about you, Jack," she said as we stepped out into the chilly December night, "when we're out together you never ogle the competition."

"You don't have any competition, sweetheart."

She hugged my arm and it occurred to me that the blonde looked familiar but I couldn't place where from, so I took another glance as we passed by the window and saw that she was now engaged in an animated conversation with my new pal, Tim Berry. I couldn't be sure, but it looked to me as if they shared more than a common interest in facial disfigurement.

"Besides, the really cute ones hang out at Gilbert's," I said with a nod to the public house across the street.

She punched my arm with her free hand. The cold salt air nipped at our ears and she frowned at my fleece-lined denim jacket as we walked to the parking lot around the corner.

"Aren't you cold in that thing?"

"It's Christmas in Maine, sweetheart. You're *supposed* to be cold." Then I nodded at her parka and the jeans with the ripped right knee and said, "How about you?"

She brrred and said, "I'm *freezing*."

"Well, then?"

As we got to her car—a green Jaguar sedan her father had

given her for graduation from medical school—a faint swell of voices came wafting from inside the First Congregational Church, where the choir was rehearsing for the upcoming Christmas concert. The holiday decorations were up all along Bayview, Elm, and Main: holly garlands, plastic Santas, and twinkling lights. The restaurant and shop windows were spray-painted with semitoxic frosting proclaiming, "Peace on Earth, Good Will toward Men," and "All Major Credit Cards Accepted." Another eight days and it would all be over with. Hallelujah.

I walked Jamie to the driver's side, gave her a quick kiss, and said: "You know, it's funny. Ginger's not usually much of a barker."

"Yes," she said, digging for her keys, "but then, it's not like Allison DeMarco to lie dead on her kitchen floor, is it?"

I got in, settled into the leather seat, and hooked up the seat belt, feeling that glow you get from good food, good wine, and good company. Jamie backed the car out of the parking lot onto Bayview, turned left onto Washington, and soon the soft burr of the tires, the gentle hum of the engine, and the warm purr of the heater lulled me into a feeling of quiet contentment. I cracked my window just enough to let some cold air blow across my right temple.

I thought it funny that the British manufacturer of this automobile called it a sedan. It had four doors but there was practically no room for anyone to sit in the back seat. Still, when Jamie and I had first started seeing each other, which was back in early summer, we'd gone on a lot of picnics together—everywhere from Wiscasset to Bar Harbor. We often took her car, though I usually drove, and it had been nice to have that back seat, small as it is, so we could take Frankie along.

I had worried a little about Jamie's reaction the first time I'd suggested we include him. We were going to the lighthouse at Pemaquid Point and when I showed up with the dog Jamie gave me one of her patented smiles. (I've since made a mental catalogue of most of them—there are over two dozen. This is the one that means, "Do you have any idea how *lucky* you are that I put up with you?" Though all she actually said was, "You and that dog.")

We had a great time, though, and she and Frankie got

along quite well, especially considering the fact that English
setters tend to be aloof with strangers. It was overcast that
day, and when we got to the point, it started to rain, so we
ended up having our meal in the parking lot—a rough grass,
gravel, and dirt affair about forty yards away from the tumble
of huge rocks and boulders that keeps the ocean and the
tourists entertained.

We sat in the car listening to the splatter of raindrops on
the roof and windshield and the car was immediately inun-
dated with the scent of cold rain falling on warm pine needles
and hot stone and gravel. Since the windows were closed I
guess the smell must've gotten in through the ventilation system. Once in a while, as we talked, Jamie would break off a
piece of sandwich and hand it to Frankie. She did this without taking her eyes off me or losing the thread of our conversation—a very charming and a very feminine behavior.

Afterward, on the drive home, Frankie scooched up tight
against the back of Jamie's seat and rested his chin on her
shoulder. I think that was the exact moment I first fell in love
with her.

"So, Jack," she curled her left arm around Frankie's head
and scratched his ear, "who comes first with you, your girlfriends or your dog?"

"Well, chronologically speaking, *he* does." She hit me
lightly with the back of her hand. "Hey," I defended myself,
"I've known him for almost five years. And this is only our
third date, so . . ." She pouted a little, or pretended to, and I
explained: "Honey, I think I may be falling in love with you,
and I'd do almost anything to make you happy, but let's get
one thing straight—that dog is like more than family to me."
Her eyes softened. "So if you're thinking about asking me to
choose between you—"

"—Don't worry, I'm not," she said and stroked Frankie's
head some more. She had another smile on her face—the
one that means, "I think you're wonderful," or words to that
effect.

We took Washington to 105 and soon the well-ordered
houses of town, with their manicured hedges and small
lawns, gave way to the tall pines and overgrown shrubs

which line the rambling gravel drives of local farmhouses and lake cabins. As we hit the state road, my quiet reverie gave way to feelings of nervous apprehension. There were two reasons for this: first of all, I was about to meet Jamie's "Uncle Horace," who, I'd been led to believe, might be just a little prickly on the subject of my relationship with Jamie and her impending divorce from his nephew, Oren Pritchett (his sister's son). Second—once she gets on the open road, Jamie is a terrible driver.

"Sorry about this," she said, after a bit.

"Sorry about what?" I thought she'd meant her driving.

"About how the evening is ending. I'm sure you had another outcome in mind. I know *I* did."

It's true. I had, in fact, been fantasizing about taking her back to my place. I'd even had enough wine to imagine throwing her over my shoulder and carrying her upstairs, not unlike Rhett Butler. Now, that was a *real* fantasy: Jamie—though blessed with a slender, yet very feminine physique—is nearly as tall as I am (I'm six-one), and there's no way I could throw her over my shoulder, let alone carry her up a full flight of stairs. It's a shame, too, since Jamie is the type of girl who *should* be carried up the stairs once in a while. (I made a mental note to start doing more push-ups every morning.)

Jamie, meanwhile, had moved on to another subject:

"Uncle Horace thinks he's doing me a favor when he calls me on these things. The state pays sixty-five dollars a corpse and twelve cents a mile and I end up losing money every time. Not to mention potential boyfriends." She gave me a shy look, her face lit by the blue dashboard light and the green radio dial, which was tuned to a listener-sponsored station in Blue Hill. They were playing some sort of Irish Christmas music.

"Hey, don't look at me," I said. "I *like* the fact that you're a career woman. It's one of the things I find most appealing about you."

"Thanks," she said, somewhat skeptically, "but most guys find what I do sort of disgusting. You know, messing around with dead bodies."

"You get no argument from me there. But you know, a lot of people find what *I* do disgusting, too."

"Training people's dogs? That's disgusting?"

"Not the training part. But I also run a kennel, remember, so I spend half my time cleaning up dog shit. Now, that's—"

"—Disgusting," she laughed. "You're right. I guess that makes us even. What are you laughing at?"

She seemed so pleased that we were "even" that I had to laugh. It just tickled me that she liked to keep score.

"Nothing. So, does Uncle Horace know about us?"

She didn't take her eyes off the road, just angled her head in my direction to let me know she'd heard me. We came to a curve, she leaned sideways in her leather seat and took it at full speed—no braking or downshifting, her rear wheels skidding into the territory of oncoming traffic. Luckily there aren't many cars on 105 on a Saturday night. The road straightened out, I began to breathe again, and she finally answered my question: "He's in denial. He doesn't even want to admit that Oren and I have separated."

Another curve. This time there actually *was* a car coming—a gray, shapeless Ford or Toyota or something. I closed my eyes and braced for the crash, then heard his horn dopplering behind us as we raced deeper into the night.

Jamie looked in the rear-view. "What's *his* problem?"

"I don't know, sweetheart. I guess some people don't like being forced to drive in the drainage ditch."

She glared at me for half a second, then sighed. "Do you really care what Horace Flynn thinks?"

"Sure," I said. "He's a fairly big man and he's been authorized by the county to carry a gun. Besides, I'm very fond of Sheriff Flynn. He's been like an uncle to me."

She laughed. "You idiot. You've never even met him."

"I feel like I have. I see him and his mustache in the papers all the time. Besides, he's crazy about you, isn't he? That makes him a-okay in my book."

She took my hand but another curve was coming, so I let go, closed my eyes, and said a silent prayer.

"You know," I said, as we shimmied back onto the straight-away, "don't most cars nowadays come equipped with *brakes*?"

She gave me a defensive look. "You want to drive?"

I put my hands up in surrender. "I'm the one who drank most of the wine at dinner, remember?"

"Anyway," she said, "I was always taught that you're not *supposed* to slow down when you go around a curve."

"No, sweetheart," I explained, "you're supposed to slow down when you go *into* a curve and accelerate slightly when you come *out*. You ought to try it sometime. It's kind of fun."

She thought it over. "But then I might have to downshift."

"Now, there's an idea."

She shook her head sadly. "I hate this car," she said, mostly to herself. "*I* wanted a Cherokee, but noooo—my father insisted—a doctor *has* to drive a Jaguar or Mercedes. And it *has* to be a stick."

We drove on a bit and were suddenly passed from behind by a Camden police car, its siren going. It reminded us that we were on our way to a possible murder scene. This goes to show you how dumb I am: after moving to Maine to get away from police work—not the whole reason, but a major part of it—I fall in love with a woman who works part-time as a medical examiner.

After the police car disappeared around a few curves ahead of us, Jamie said: "So how much do you know about Mrs. DeMarco?"

"Allison? That's an interesting question. I know practically everything there is to know about her temperament, or personality, you might say, but very little about her life in general. In fact, I didn't even know she was married."

"Divorced. She and I have the same divorce attorney. Or had. Her ex-husband Richard is an endocrinologist up in Bangor. And if you didn't know she was married, then how do you know so much about her personality?"

As she was saying this a jogger was coming toward us on the right, with a big German shepherd running next to her on her left, away from traffic.

"Hey, there's Satch and Dorianne," I said, turning to look over my shoulder as we passed. "God, he's a beautiful dog, isn't he?"

"Jack, I'm trying to have a conversation with you."

"Sorry. What were we—? Oh, yeah, how do I know so much about Allison? Well, I trained her dog." She gave me a

look. "It's true. You can read a person's complete psychological profile that way. I've often thought that if Sigmund Freud
had allowed his patients to talk only about their pooches, instead of free-associating about their mommies and their potty
training, they would have all been cured a lot faster."

She laughed. "Interesting theory. Now prove it. Tell me
what Allison DeMarco was like."

So I told her.

Allison DeMarco had been an attractive woman in her
mid-thirties: medium height, kind of skinny, but with a nice
figure, dark blue eyes, black hair, and a surprisingly direct
manner, designed—from what I could tell—to make men
find her fascinating. It had even worked on me at first.

"You had a thing for her?" Jamie asked teasingly.

"Well, maybe a little crush at first, nothing more. But then
I met you, darling, and suddenly lost all interest in other
women."

She shot me a suspicious look. "Yeah, right."

"It's true. I mean, why go on looking for zircons when
you've just found a diamond mine."

"Awww," she sighed. "That is one of the sweetest
things—"

"—Oops, honey," another curve was coming, "both hands
on the wheel." She bit her bottom lip, looked at the road
ahead, then touched the brakes lightly, downshifted, came
into the cradle of the curve, and as we came onto the
straight-away, she hit the gas and shifted back into third. It
was perfect.

"Nicely done, James."

"Thanks. And you're right," she smiled, "it *was* fun.

"So, Jack," she said after a bit, "what makes you such an
expert on Freud?"

"You'd be surprised."

"That's true. You're full of surprises, which is a good
thing, I guess." She sighed again. "It just bothers me that you
won't talk about yourself more."

I shook my head. "The past is past, sweetheart. It happened to two different people."

"You say that a lot but I still don't know what it means."

We passed one of the mountain roads that lead to my kennel. I glanced at the carved wooden sign with white letters:

'DOG HILL' KENNEL—7 miles
Pet Supplies / Boarding / Training
Jack Field, Dog Trainer

"It means you've got the present Jack Field—the one on that sign—and if that's not enough for you—"

"—Well, it's not. I mean, it is and it isn't. There's so much I don't know about you. And I don't understand why you won't let me in."

I sighed again. She had such a sad look on her face, like I was deliberately holding back my feelings in order to hurt her, which wasn't the case at all. Still, I didn't know how much longer I could skate by on just my wit and charm—as irresistible as those qualities might be—without finally making a stab at some kind of real intimacy.

"Okay," I said. "What do you want to know?"

"Really?" She smiled, happy again. I nodded. "Okay, for starters, what made you switch careers at your age?" (My age? I'm forty-one, Jamie is thirty-two.)

"Let's just say I love dogs and I hate cops and corpses."

She shook her head. "Very adroit, Jack, but not very forthcoming."

She was right. "Okay, I guess I just wasn't very good at being a homicide detective." She mulled it over and so did I. "Well, that isn't true, exactly. I was *good* at it—at least the mental chess part of it. I just wasn't cut out for the politics, all the plea bargains, and the toll it takes on you personally. You've really got to have a thick skin to work homicide in New York."

Then I told her how, about ten years ago, I had worked a case with a K-9 unit—a building collapse we suspected was due to an arson fire that had burned down the building next door. We were there looking for witnesses, for victims, and, with luck, for any survivors that might still be under the rubble. The minute I started working around those dogs—a couple of Labrador retrievers and some German shepherds—I felt my spirits lifting, as if I hadn't really been fully alive until then. I started hanging out with the K-9 guys on weekends, and they taught me a lot about dog training. I became fascinated and it turned out, even though I was just an amateur, I was really good at it.

"So then what happened? I mean, how did you decide to become a dog trainer and stop being a detective?"

I was silent, trying to figure out a way to put it. "Well, I was moonlighting, training dogs part-time, and I even asked my watch commander if I could be reassigned to the K-9 unit."

"Really? What did he say?"

"She. And she didn't say anything at first—she just laughed. Then she said I was too valuable as a detective. She told me if I loved dogs so much, I should get my own dog. Which I finally did, five years after the building collapse."

"What took you so long?"

I shrugged. "I didn't have time to take care of a dog properly. Not until I moved closer to the precinct house. Then I figured, if I got a dog, I could walk him during my lunch hours. Shortly after that, I found Frankie in a pet store on Second Avenue."

"Then what happened? Why did you quit the police force?"

"Oh, I don't know. Things came to a head, I got caught between a dog and a hard place, and in the end the dog won."

"You're being vague again, Jack. Colorful, but—"

"I know, honey, but that's all you get from me for now. I promise to tell you the rest some other time."

"Jack . . ."

"Sorry, that's all you get for one night."

I wasn't ready to tell her about the incident that had gotten me fired—or rather, forced to take early retirement. It was just a stupid thing—silly, really—but it was too embarrassing to talk about.

I also didn't want to explain the situation with my foster son Leon (or Duke, as he likes to be called). His grandmother and I agreed that it would be healthier for him to leave Manhattan and not testify against the scumbags who had killed

the rest of his family, so I took him with me when I bought
the kennel and moved to Maine. He lives in the guest house
and helps out with the dogs. The trouble is, the Manhattan
DA's office still has a material witness warrant out for him
and if I were to tell Jamie about it and the authorities found
out that she knew Duke's whereabouts and didn't report it,
she could lose her job and maybe her medical license. So I
stopped talking.

Jamie sighed. "It's like prying teeth with you . . ."

"I'll explain it to you later, I promise."

She shook her head, then slowed down as we approached
the little town of Hope, which was closed up tight for the
night. We stopped briefly at the intersection to wait for an approaching green Cadillac to pass us going south, then made
the left turn onto 235.

"Jack?"

"Mm-hmm?"

"Do you think Allison DeMarco might have been murdered? I mean, from what you know about her, was there
anyone who wanted to kill her?"

"That's an interesting question. I've never known anyone
who didn't at one time or another want to kill *somebody*.
Still, it's one thing to want to kill someone, but quite another
to actually go through with it. That's why I prefer dogs to
people. In a way they're more civilized. When a dog attacks
it's out of pure instinct, not jealousy or revenge or because he
got left out of the will.

"But you know"—I remembered something—"Allison
did say she was being stalked by someone."

"Really? Did she say who?"

"No. And she didn't actually use the term 'stalking.' I
think she said someone was 'watching' her. That's why she
got a dog in the first place—for protection."

"That's interesting. Tell me more about her."

"Well, she was a lot like you—smart, pretty, independent,
though she was a little more spoiled, I'd say."

Her neck tensed up. "You think I'm spoiled?"

The music was getting jumpy so I turned the radio down.

"I didn't say you were spoiled, I said that you and Allison
were alike except for the fact *she* was spoiled."

"No you didn't. You said that she was *more* spoiled, implying that I am, too."

"Okay, okay, I apologize. It's just that I come from a blue collar background, so I tend to think of anyone with rich parents as being spoiled." Then I explained that the technical term is "overnarcissized," which refers to someone whose internal mirroring is overdeveloped during early childhood, which creates a libidinal dynamism in the individual, making them incapable of identifying or empathizing with the needs and/or experiences of others. Or in layman's terms, they become self-absorbed jerks, and—in extreme cases—sociopaths.

"Libidinal dynamism?" She whistled. "I can't even say it, let alone understand it. So I guess you *do* know a thing or two about Freud. But that still doesn't sound like me. If anything, it sounds more like *you*—"

"—touché—"

"—or my father."

"Really? The famous Dr. Jonas Cutter doesn't have any empathy for his patients?"

"His patients, yes, just not for the rest of us." She slowed down for a left turn, then pulled off 235 and over a dip onto Hobb's Pond Road. "So what makes you say that Allison was overnarcissized?"

"Oh, I don't know, the way she sometimes forgot to feed Ginger for days at a time, or left her tied up out back without quite knowing she was there. She rarely left water in her bowl so Ginger was always drinking out of the downstairs toilet. She also had the attitude that the dog should just naturally obey her." To me it was a tribute to the wonderful nature of dogs how much Ginger loved Allison, even though she'd been ignored like this.

Jamie shook her head. "If she treated the people in her life that way they'd probably *all* want to kill her."

"Not necessarily. An undernarcissized person would turn the anger inward and become depressed or self-destructive. Someone who's properly narcissized wouldn't let it bother them."

"I thought narcissism was a *bad* thing."

"Not necessarily. Think of it as being analogous to self-esteem. Too much and you've got a narcissist. Too little, and you've got a doormat. At any rate if Allison *was* murdered, I'd say it was more likely to have been done by someone with the same personality type."

"Now you sound like a profiler."

I shrugged. "I spent a little time studying the subject. I've even profiled a few cases. But it's really just common sense. Murder is the ultimate act of narcissism. I would say that most murderers—except for some who commit crimes of passion, and of course serial killers, who have a far different and a far scarier pathology—I would say that most murderers are by definition highly narcissistic in nature."

"I never thought about it, but you're right."

"In fact, many psychologists believe there's a link between severe narcissism and sociopathic behavior."

As we got closer to the lake the tall pines got taller and the night seemed to be getting progressively darker.

"As for Allison, I think she was also using the dog to work out emotional issues she had with her parents. It's not that uncommon. The owner engages in a kind of psychodrama, with the dog playing the role of the owner's inner child and the owner in the role of a parent or authority figure. That's where most of this stuff about dominance and being alpha comes from. From what I've observed, dogs don't care who's alpha and who's not. Only emotionally dysfunctional owners and trainers do."

"What? Wait a second, I thought the canine pack was considered a prime example of a dominance hierarchy."

"Most scientists think it *is*, or used to. Some are now starting to question that idea. Personally, I see the pack more as a self-emergent cooperative heterarchy, based on the need to hunt large prey. You see, in order for the pack to—ow!"

We'd just hit a rough patch of road, causing me to bump my head on the ceiling. Jamie smiled her crooked knowing smile. "Got another lecture coming up, Jack?"

I held onto the dashboard. "On Saturday, in Boothbay. Why? You want to come . . . or am I boring you?"

"A little."

The road smoothed out and her smile softened. Her face was framed by her long fall of dark hair. "Don't get me wrong, Jack, I love the fact that you work with dogs. It means you're the steady, reliable type. Someone a girl can count on. As long as the dogs don't get in the way. I just think that sometimes you get a little too involved with the subject."

"Yeah, I know," I sighed, "it's just that—"

"—What?"

"—well, that dogs are wonderful and people are—for the most part—pretty awful."

It was her turn to sigh. "You live in a wretched and lonely world, Jack Field."

"I used to. But then I moved to Maine and met you."

"Well," she smiled—sweetly this time, "I'm glad you did. And I'm glad I came along to save you."

"So am I, sweetheart. So am I."

"And I'm glad we talked. Even if you wouldn't tell me everything. At least I understand you a little better now than I did before." She shivered. "Although I still don't know why you always have to have your window cracked open, even on a night like this. I'm freezing."

"Sorry," I said and ran the glass up tight.

We both heard the barking at the same time. We came around a curve and saw two sheriff's jeeps, a Camden police car, and an old black Dodge Ram Prospector parked by the side of the road. Jamie made a quick left turn onto the gravel drive of a large gray saltbox-style house I recognized as Allison DeMarco's. She jammed on the brakes, knocking my head against the windshield. I groaned.

"Are you okay?" She put a hand on my shoulder.

"I'll be fine, I think," I said, feeling my forehead for contusions.

"Sorry," she said, then put the car in reverse. "I've got to go up to my mom's and get my kit and the Polaroid." (She'd moved back in with her mother as part of her legal separation agreement with Oren.) "Tell Uncle Horace I'll be back in about ten minutes. And try not to cause any trouble while I'm gone? Remember, I have to work with these people."

"Yeah, yeah," I said and got out of the car.

She leaned toward the passenger side and said: "So, Jack, if everyone wants to murder somebody, who do you want to kill?"

"That's easy," I said. "Whoever taught you to drive."

"Funny," she said, rolling up the window, "because it was Uncle Horace."

"Liar," I said. "And he's not your uncle."

But she just laughed at me from behind the glass.

As Jamie backed the car out onto the road I became aware
of the potent scent of pine and fir needles which permeated
the December chill, and—even more overpowering—the
sound of Ginger's barking. No wonder the neighbors—the
nearest of whom lived at least a couple of football fields
away—had called the sheriff's office to complain. It didn't
sound like barking so much as a constant cry of pain—the
way a wolf sounds when his leg is caught in a trap.

I followed the gravel driveway around to the back and saw
that Allison's blood-red Escalade was parked behind the
large unscreened back porch. A light was on inside the
kitchen and the storm door was standing wide open. From
where I stood in the darkness I could see Sheriff Horace
Flynn—with his big mustache and pot-belly—along with a
short deputy, a Camden police officer, and another man, very
tall—not in uniform but probably a deputy as well—milling
around in the yellow light.

The proper protocol would have been for me to go up
there, introduce myself, and ask permission to take care of
the animal. I didn't, though. The pain in Ginger's voice made
me anxious to check on her first, then—after I'd made sure
she was okay—to go up to the house and deal with the human beings.

As I went past Allison's SUV the light of a crescent moon,
glimmering low over the lake, revealed that Ginger was
hooked up to a tie-line—a metal cable stretched between one

corner of a woodshed to my left and a bare sugar maple on the other side of the driveway, with a ten-foot yellow polyurethane cord running from the cable down to the dog's collar. Tie-lines are very popular in the state of Maine. They're designed to keep a dog under control while giving her about twenty yards or so of imaginary freedom. And Allison, like a lot of Mainers, has no fence around her yard to keep a dog in: her property begins with a flower bed at the edge of the highway and ends where the waters of the lake lap up against an old, unused wooden dock.

The first time I'd met Allison was in early summer. She was in the garden, wearing gloves and overalls, her dark hair tied back under a red bandanna. The blue delphiniums and pink hollyhocks that clung to the side of the house were all in bloom, though not yet at full height, and the air was thick with no-see-ums and mosquitoes: one of the problems with living so close to a lake, I guess.

I came up behind her while she was busy, kneeling over what looked to me like a bed of tulips, only shaped like stars instead of upside-down bells. She turned, saw me, caught her breath, and for a moment I thought I'd gotten the date or time wrong, she seemed that surprised.

"Mr. Field," she said, "I uh I'm sorry I was—I guess I was sort of lost in thought." She stood up.

"That's quite all right. And call me Jack."

I sensed an air of sadness about her—not of present troubles but of some deep, long-standing sorrow. I didn't find out until later—until after she'd died—exactly what that sorrow was. I just remember catching a brief, vague glimpse of it that day in the garden.

Her dark mood didn't last long, though. She smiled suddenly—a gorgeous smile—and it was like the sun had come out, even though it already *was*. She took off her gardening gloves and shook my hand. "Let's go up to the house," she smiled again, "I want you to meet the devil dog."

I laughed and nodded to the red and yellow blossoms she'd been laboring over. "Nice flowers. What are they?"

"They're amaryllis," she said with a glint of satisfaction in her eye. "And they're *gorgeous*."

I agreed.

As we walked up to the house she told me that she'd ordered a tie-line and it had just arrived via UPS—would I mind helping her hook it up? I told her that a tie-line wasn't a good idea: that being left out in the open would constantly stimulate Ginger's hunting instincts, but because she was tied up she'd be unable to act on them successfully. As a result she might become frustrated, aggressive, or just plain depressed. I said that if she didn't want the dog inside the house she should build a kennel outside—there was a perfect spot for it next to the shed. Kenneling a dog, when done properly, stimulates the den instinct, inducing calm, focused behavior.

Allison didn't mind having the dog in the house, she said, as we reached the steps. One reason she'd got Ginger was for protection. She said she'd had the feeling recently of someone watching her. She thought that having the dog locked in a kennel wouldn't be much of a deterrent.

"Have you called the police?"

"Oh, it's probably nothing," she shrugged it off, "just an old boyfriend who can't get over me. Why is it that they don't show any passion or gumption until after I've broken up with them?" I said I didn't know. She looked me over. "Hmm . . . strong, tall with curly hair and a beard . . . maybe I should give *you* a try."

I laughed good-naturedly but said, "Let's see what we can do with your dog first before we start down that road."

She shrugged and said, "It's my own damn fault, really. I always go for the mousy, innocuous type. Not like you. I don't know why. Of course, it could be my money. I do have a little, you know. So it could be someone out to rob me. You know, casing the joint?"

I realized she was talking about her stalker again.

"I inherited a couple of valuable pieces of art—a Picasso drawing and a Matisse print. I wouldn't mind donating the Picasso to some museum, but I'd hate like hell to lose that Matisse, though it *is* insured for three million."

We got to the stairs by the side of the house and she led me up them. I could hear Ginger, anxiously whining inside, aware of our presence and unable to contain herself for very much longer.

As soon as I stepped inside the kitchen I realized that the

view of the house from the road had been deceptive. It seemed a rather bland, nondescript sort of structure from out there. But that's because the main feature of the property was the view of the lake. And this side of the house was designed to use that view to full effect. There was a simple yet elegant flow of open space from kitchen to dining room to living room. Each room had a large picture window facing the lake, and each was decorated and painted in light sky, lake, and earth tones. The ceiling in the living room was two stories tall, as was the picture window. And the furnishings and appliances were quite simply the best that money could buy. I realized Allison had been understating things when she'd said she had "a little money."

My appreciation of the decor was cut short when Allison opened the puppy gate on the door to the guest bathroom next to the stairs. Ginger came bolting into the room like a runaway train, her paws slipping and skittering across the light blue tile of the kitchen floor.

Like most of her breed, Ginger had a dense wiry black and tan coat, groomed in such a way that she seemed to have a short Scotsman's beard growing beneath her chin. Her tail was docked, about six inches in length, and looked like the curved handle on a blueberry rake (the strange-looking, dustpan-like implement that's used to harvest wild blueberries during the late summers in Maine).

"This is the thing," Allison said with a wave of her hand, "my dog has way too much energy. See what I mean? I can never relax when she's around. I thought if she were tied up part of the time, we'd both be a lot happier. So let me just get the tie-line and then you can help me hook it up." She seemed very determined to have her own way about things, and was quite charming about it, too (as overnarcissized people *can* be—just look at me), so I nearly gave in, but there was something about the way Ginger greeted me when we came in that changed my mind.

She was so happy to see us, jumping up and twisting around in midair—I just had to laugh. She seemed to be saying, "I don't want to be tied up. I want to run and play and bite something. Please? I'm a dog, I *need* to *bite* something!"

So instead of following Allison into the dining room,

where the brown UPS box sat leaning against her cluttered computer desk, I stayed just inside the kitchen door, said hello to Ginger, patted my thigh, and invited her to jump up on me, holding my left arm out for her to take. She jumped up and grabbed my arm with her jaws.

Allison turned, saw Ginger "attacking" me, and shouted: "No! Bad girl! Get down!" as if that would mean something to an exuberant four-month-old puppy who (luckily) hadn't been trained yet to respond to those words.

I calmed Allison. "It's all right. She's just saying hello to me in Airedale. It's actually a form of affection."

Allison nodded. "Yeah, I went to one of your lectures once. You have some strange ideas about dogs, I must say. But don't most people think that jumping up is a sign of dominance?"

I smacked Ginger playfully, encouraging her to nip at my hands. She was happy to oblige. "Yeah, well, some people think *everything* a dog does is a sign of dominance. But technically speaking, I think dominance is a purely sexual behavior and can only take place between two males or two females, and never between a dog and a human being."

"Okay, fine, whatever," she said, getting a little miffed, "but seriously, I don't *want* my dog jumping up on my friends and biting them whenever she feels like it—"

"—She's not biting me, she's gripping my arm. From a dog's emotional point of view, there's a huge difference." I explained the five ways a puppy uses its teeth and jaws, then said, "And don't worry, I promise I'll train her not to jump up on people. But I'm sneaky. I start out by teaching her to jump up on command, and then I teach her she can only do it when she hears the command first. I also teach her to channel the original impulse to jump up on me into a very focused 'sit' or 'heel.' "

To illustrate I turned sideways, and in an inviting tone of voice, said, "Okay, Ginger, off!" She immediately jumped down, assumed a sitting position, and looked up at me as if awaiting further instructions. Her wild, uncontrolled energy was now totally focused on me.

"Wow, she's sitting," said Allison. "That is so cool."

"Thanks, but it's all just a matter of channeling her instincts rather than repressing them."

I thought Allison, like a lot of people, especially many dog trainers, would have trouble understanding this. But she didn't. She tilted her head, smiled, and said, "Where were you when I was a kid? You could have done wonders training my parents. They were very fond of repressing *my* instincts, as I recall."

We had a laugh over that and then began our first training session: basic puppy stuff; housebreaking, how to deal with mouthing of the hands and chewing on the furniture. Of course Allison, like a lot of my clients, wanted to start right in on basic commands—"sit" and "stay" and all the rest. I told her that since I always work with a dog's hunting drive as the focal point for training, I don't like to start obedience work until the dog reaches emotional maturity, at about nine to twelve months of age. This is the way they train search-and-rescue dogs, attack dogs (I prefer the old term "attack dog" to the newer, more Orwellian "protection dog"), and drug enforcement dogs. A lot of the popular trainers say you should start obedience as early as possible—even at two months—but to me that's like putting a five-year-old kid into a college algebra class. I say let a puppy be a puppy. Give its little canine brain time to develop naturally, without imposing too much structure and discipline from the outside. All you need to do with a puppy is teach her how to play a few simple games such as fetch, tug-of-war, and hide-and-seek and the rest of the training process falls into place much quicker.

"Can you teach her to bring me my slippers?"

I laughed—of course the first thing she would want from a dog is to have her slippers fetched. I said, "Sure, after she's finished teething. Right now, she might think they're some kind of a toy and rip them up." I told her we could start the ball rolling, though, with a puppy game called "find," which I showed her how to do, first with a piece of food, then with a real toy.

When I showed up for the next session a week later, Allison admitted that Ginger was much more responsive and easier to control after she'd learned to play these simple games.

"I thought you were saying I should just let her do whatever she wanted, but now I realize that when you play games with her she starts to listen and pay attention to you. It's really amazing. Where did you come up with this—?"

"Oh, I didn't. A guy named Max von Stephanitz did."

"Max von who?"

"Never mind. He's just a guy who invented a form of dog training where the first rule is, 'Before you teach a dog to obey any command, you must first teach it to play.' Or words to that effect. And it works."

"It sure does."

At that second session I noticed that the tie-line had been put up in the backyard. Allison had gotten someone else to do it. She was not a woman who was willing to have her desires thwarted.

The last time I had seen her had been in early December. Ginger had turned nine months and we'd started her strict training regimen—sit, stay, heel, down at a distance, down while running full speed, coming when called—pretty heady stuff. Oh, and fetching Allison's slippers. And she was great at all of it. So good, in fact, that Allison no longer needed to keep Ginger tied up outside, or so she'd said. She'd even promised to take the tie-line down and get rid of it.

After that day's session, Allison and I had coffee, sitting in her living room with its two-story picture window looking out over the lake. Ginger had her head in her mommy's lap, an unusual behavior for her. As for me, I was gazing at a portrait of a woman in a flower print dress, lounging languorously on a red and white striped salon chair—Allison's treasured Matisse.

She seemed different that day, Allison did. A little like the woman in the painting—happy, content, and complete—and I told her as much.

"Thanks for noticing," she said. "I certainly *feel* different. I don't know, maybe it's the dog. She's calmed down and so have I. Or maybe it's my biological clock. I'm thinking I might be finally ready to have a baby." My face must have registered surprise or something because she said, "Oh, it's nothing definite. Just a feeling I have." She sighed and looked out at the lake and said, "I had a chance at motherhood once,

a long time ago, and I blew it. I think this feeling is God or
Fate or Ginger . . . ," she petted the dog's head, "giving me
my second chance at being a mom, and I'm going to do it
right this time."

I remember that I'd wished her luck and finished my coffee. Then we'd made vague arrangements for the next session
to take place sometime after the holidays. She was planning a
good old-fashioned Maine Christmas, she'd said, and had invited all her friends and family to come celebrate. And now
here it was, just a few weeks later, and she was lying dead on
her kitchen floor, surrounded by strange men in uniform.

4

I chose my steps carefully as I made my way past the red Cadillac to where Ginger was tied up. The ground was cold and hard. It hadn't snowed since the day before Thanksgiving, but it rained the next Thursday, and then on Friday the temperature had dipped into the mid-twenties and stayed there, which left small but treacherous patches of ice in unexpected places.

The instant Ginger saw me she stopped barking. There was a brief moment of pristine silence—which I knew would cause the men inside the house to stop whatever they were doing and wonder what was going on with the dog. Then she began to whine and bounce high in the air—the way Airedales do—expressing how happy she felt to see me. Her jaws were dripping with saliva and the tan-colored fur on her chest was covered with small slobbery icicles. Her mouth was open in a canine "stress smile" and she was panting heavily.

I could tell she was thirsty, so I looked around for her metal water bowl, but she'd knocked it over. It would have been filled with solid ice anyway. She was also shivering terribly, poor thing. I looked back toward the house, knowing I ought to go up there and announce my presence before doing anything further with the dog, but I couldn't just leave her shivering like that, so I took off my Levi's jacket, draped it over her back and helped her front paws through the arm holes. Then I took a six-foot cotton leash from inside the jacket pocket, took hold of her leather collar, and made a handling error: I unhooked her from the tie-line before attaching her to the cotton leash. That's when I heard the crunch of large boots on cold gravel.

A young male voice from behind me said, "Can I help you?"

I hate when people do that. It's such a disingenuous thing to say. "Can I help you?" he'd said, when what he'd really meant was, "Who the hell are you and what are you doing here?"

I tried not to get too annoyed, though, because I'd promised Jamie I wouldn't cause any trouble. So I ignored him. Besides, I still had my hands full with the dog who, from the first moment she'd heard his voice, had begun to snarl and pull. She weighed nearly sixty pounds and her collar was icy cold and wet with slobber and it was all I could do to keep her from going after him, let alone to try and get her hooked up to the leash.

Most experts say that when a dog is acting aggressive you need to act tough, take control, show them who's boss. So of course I did the exact opposite—I softly praised her instead: "Good girl, easy, easy," I said and she calmed down. It's a sad commentary, I think, that most so-called experts on dogs actually don't know the first thing about them.

The guy tried again, louder. "Sir? I said, 'Can I *help* you?' "

I sighed, unable to contain myself. "Yeah, I'm sorry. My name is Jack Field. I'm this dog's trainer. I'm trying to get her under control. So if you really want to help me, could you just go back inside the house, please?"

"Excuse me?" he said.

"I said, 'Could you please go back inside the house?' You know, get lost? Disappear? Bug off? Can't you see this dog wants to *kill* you? Just let me get her under control first and *then* we can talk—okay?"

Instead of listening to me, he actually took a few steps closer, which caused Ginger to erupt again. My hands were numb with cold and I almost lost my grip.

I heard a soft click, turned my head, and was blinded by the cold blue-white glare of a flashlight stabbing my eyes.

Looking at his silhouette, I could see that he was the tall, husky guy I'd noticed in the kitchen earlier—the one not wearing a uniform. I could see too that he was a good six inches taller than I, and that he spent a lot of time at the gym lifting weights. Heavy ones.

He said, "All right, sir, I'm going to have to ask you to show me your hands and step away from the animal."

I couldn't help myself. I had to chuckle.

"You think this is funny?"

"Of course it is. You talk like law enforcement but you're not wearing a uniform and you haven't identified yourself. How do I know you're not some jerk who just wandered in off the street? How do I know that *you* didn't kill Allison DeMarco?"

Come to think of it, maybe he *had*. That would certainly explain Ginger's explosive reaction to him.

He was shocked. "Yeah? And how do *you* know she's *dead*?"

"I know a lot of things, Ace. Maybe some other time I can explain a few of them to you. And I know that Allison's dead because I was with Dr. Cutter when Sheriff Flynn called her to come examine the body, okay?"

"Dr. Cutter?"

"Yeah. Dr. Jamie Cutter?" (Jamie had kept her father's name when she got married because it was the name on her diploma and on her medical license.) "We were having dinner in Camden and we drove up here together."

"Nice try, buddy," he shook his head, "but Dr. Jamie ain't arrived at the scene yet. You just slipped up big time."

I sighed—it was hopeless. "That's because she dropped me off, then went home to get her medical kit. Look," I said, still struggling with the dog, "I know you're just trying to do your job, but I'm freezing my ass off in order to keep *yours* from getting bit, okay? If you can just get that-one-little-fact-through-your-skull, then I can explain everything."

He wasn't interested in explanations, though, only in compliance—the standard cop M.O. Fact is, I'd danced this dance myself once or twice when dealing with a suspect.

"Okay, sir," he said, "my name is Sam Kirby. I'm a deputy with the Rockland County Sheriff's Office." He unsnapped the safety strap on his holster. "Now, I'm going to need you to show me your hands and step away from the animal."

I sighed, wondering briefly why he was wearing a gun when he wasn't in uniform, but then a lot of strange things take place in the state of Maine, so I chalked it off and made one last try at communicating. "Look—do you really want to get bit? Because as soon as I—"

"Show me your hands, sir!" he snapped. "Now!"

I put my hands up in the air, which meant I had to let go of Ginger's collar. She immediately went for his throat.

He stepped back, twisted sideways, and drew his weapon, but was unable to get off a shot because he slipped on a patch of ice, lost his balance, and fell hard to the ground. As he fell, his gun arm was flung straight up in the air and the weapon went off, sending a bullet sailing high over the lake. His flashlight flew up in the air too, flipping end over end, scattering weird lights and shadows in the dark pines and the naked oaks and maples. As he hit the ground, his right elbow landed hard, knocking the gun a few inches from his hand.

By this time Ginger had jumped on top of him, planting her front paws—and her full weight—on his sternum. Her lips curled back so that her teeth were bared (Dogs don't do this to communicate aggression, as is commonly supposed—to me it seems more like a survival reflex—a way to get the soft flesh of the lips out of the way of the teeth when a dog has a strong urge to bite). She was also growling—releasing primal emotions through her throat.

Meanwhile, Kirby's face was strained in a mask of fear. A dark stain appeared in the crotch of his chinos and spread across his hips and down his right pant leg.

There are degrees of aggression. Ginger, though not at the lowest level, was a still a few notches below the highest. If she'd been at the top I would have had to step in and take physical control by grabbing her back legs and pulling her off the guy. This can be risky and may sometimes even escalate a dog's aggression.

"Just lie perfectly still," I told Kirby, "and nothing will happen. She's not going to bite, trust me."

He gave me some unwanted anatomical advice. The anger in his voice caused Ginger to growl even louder.

"Shut up and don't move! Don't even breathe!" To Ginger I said: "Good girl, easy, easy. Gooooooood!" She started to calm down. "Who wants kisses?" I said in a silly, happy voice. Her docked tail wiggled a little. "Huh? Who's the great big kissy girl?" Her tail wagged even more and she turned her head to look at me, de-bared her teeth and began licking her chops.

Aha—the licking reflex. I had her now. "Gooooood! Good little kissy girl. Kisses and kisses." Her little rump was wiggling and she looked at me expectantly. "Ready?" I said, as if about to play a game, then I turned my back, and over my shoulder, said, "Okay, Ginger *come*!" and ran away.

She jumped off Kirby's chest and ran after me. I stopped, turned to her, and let her jump up and give me a big hug and lots of canine kisses and nibbles on my nose and beard. While she was doing this I hooked her up to the leash (finally), then looked back to see what Kirby was doing.

The stupid sonovabitch was up on his hands and knees, crawling toward his gun.

"This guy never learns," I thought.

"I'm gonna kill that fucking dog," he muttered.

"Like hell," I said, then ran toward him with Ginger in a tight heel. I got there just as he reached his weapon. I quickly kicked it out of his hand. Ginger gripped the left sleeve of his down parka. Feathers flew.

"Get her off me! Get her off me!"

He flailed around with his left arm and reached up with his free hand and grabbed my sweater, twisting the fabric. Even on his knees he came up to my chest.

I'd had enough. I planted my feet and gave him a good hard right cross to the jaw—just below his left ear—and felt something crack. He looked at me awkwardly for a moment, as if trying to say something, then his eyes retreated into the back of his skull and he decided to roll over on his back for a while and take a nap.

Ginger immediately jumped on his chest again and did something very odd: she began frantically licking his face, as if trying to wake him up. (I realized she was just releasing the tension she felt in her mouth and jaws.) While she was doing this I knelt down, checked Kirby's jaw to see if it was broken (it wasn't), then used his flashlight to examine his pupils. They were equal and reactive to light, which meant he only had a slight concussion and would be up and around and causing more trouble in just a few minutes.

I picked up his gun for safekeeping, then called Ginger over and had her jump up on me. She grabbed my right arm with her teeth and clamped down hard (another way of relieving tension). And as her teeth dug gently yet firmly into my arm I felt a sudden flush of pleasure prickling down the backs of my arms and flowing in a hot rush down my spine, through my legs, and into the frozen earth. I lifted my head to the sky and took a deep breath of night air—which tasted of pine shadows and deeply etched starlight—and felt as if I should howl at the moon, what little moon there was—but I heard voices coming from the back porch—Flynn and the others, who had no doubt heard the gunshot and were on their way to investigate—so I sighed and told Ginger, "Okay, off!" and she jumped down and it was time again for me to try and explain myself to people who don't understand the raptures of dogs.

5

"You did what?" said Sheriff Flynn.

"Well, he wasn't in uniform and he didn't identify himself." I handed the sheriff Kirby's gun, "Plus, he tried to shoot my dog."

"Since when did this become *your* dog?"

Ginger was sitting next to me at the bottom of the steps, still panting. But at least she was wagging her docked tail. I had the leash in one hand and her water bowl in the other. Sheriff Flynn stood just outside the kitchen door with two uniforms—a tan one and a blue one—beside him. The tan was a sheriff's deputy: short, with tobacco hair and a quick, easy smile, roughly the same color. The blue one was a Camden cop: about my size, though a lot younger, with a few thin wisps of premature gray running through his curly black locks. Both were skinny. At least they looked skinny next to Flynn.

"Figure of speech, Sheriff. It refers to any dog attached to the end of my leash."

"Yeah, well, I'm about at the end of *mine*. You haven't explained who you are or what you're doing here."

Flynn's big face was a little sunburned, and though his gruff voice was lyrical, it had that hard-edged Yankee cut hiding beneath the charm. I introduced myself, told him how Jamie had dropped me off, then apologized for any mistakes I might've made in how I'd handled things.

Flynn said that was all right—it was straightened out now, more or less. The Camden cop said, "I was just sayin' we ought to call you anyways, Jack. The barking was driving us nuts."

"Hey, Carl. I didn't know it was you. How's Sasha?"

"Fine."

"Who the hell is Sasha?" Flynn wanted to know.

I explained that Sasha was a cocker spaniel I'd trained. She belonged to Gina Staub, Carl's sister, who runs a T-shirt and souvenir shop on Main Street.

"Gina says you're originally from New York," Carl said.

"That's right. I moved here about a year ago."

Flynn said, "And Carl was telling me you used to be some kind of homicide detective." He looked me over. "You don't look old enough to be retired."

"Who said I was retired?"

"So what'd you do? Quit or get fired?"

"Maybe neither, maybe both. Maybe none of your business." I said it with a smile, but Flynn remained uncharmed.

"Smart guy, huh?" he said.

"It's my only flaw." I smiled again—still no luck. "Okay, look, Sheriff, I don't want to get off on the wrong foot here—"

"A little late for that, isn't it?"

"You're right. I apologize. I just came out here to see if I could help you with the dog. She knows me. If you want, I can keep her at my kennel until the courts or any surviving family members decide what to do. It's up to you. I just—"

"Fine," he hmmphed, then wiggled his mustache twice, as if scratching an itch, turned to his deputy, handed him Kirby's gun, and said: "Quent, go check on Sam, willya?"

Quent danced down the steps, flashed me a quick nicotine grin, and went out to the yard.

Flynn squinted at me. "He gonna need an ambulance?"

"No, I think he'll be okay." I told him how I'd checked on Kirby's condition. "Am I gonna need a lawyer?"

He was still giving me his hard look, but then he shook his head. "Nah. I can handle Sam. It may actually do him some good to get himself conked once in a while."

"Hey, anytime you need me, Sheriff, I'm happy to oblige."

Carl laughed nervously and ran his fingers through his hair. Flynn said, "Don't push it."

"That's my other only flaw. Is it okay if I come inside and get the dog some water and make a quick phone call?"

"Well, I guess *you* can come in for a bit, as long as you don't disturb anything. I'd like to pick your brain on this, anyway. We don't get as many bodies around here as you fellas in the big city do. But the dog's gotta stay outside."

"Aw, come on, Sheriff, it's *cold* out here." He looked at the freezing Airedale, who was still wearing my jacket. "I'll keep her out of your hair until my ride comes."

"Oh, all right. Just keep her out of the way."

I said I would and followed Flynn and Carl up the steps, with Ginger in tow. Flynn gave me a pair of latex gloves and some paper booties to put on, then looked down at Ginger.

"What about her paws?"

I shrugged. "She *lives* here, Sheriff. Her paw prints are all over the place. Besides, I'll tie her up in the other room. The thing is," I gestured with the water bowl, "she really needs to be hydrated or she could go into shock."

"Fine. Just do it."

I tried to walk Ginger past Allison's body but the poor dog had to stop and sniff. She didn't understand why Allison didn't get up off the floor. She even pushed at the body with her nose to try to make her move. Meanwhile, I could feel Flynn getting hot under the collar, so I said, "Okay, Ginger, let's go. And don't worry, honey, that isn't Allison anymore."

Flynn wiggled his mustache again and muttered, "Talkin' to the damn dog like it's a damn human being."

I led Ginger to the foot of the stairs in the hallway and tied her to the banister. Then I went back to the kitchen and ran some water into her bowl, took it to her, set it down, and let her lap it up, which she did with a lot of gusto. Then I went back to the kitchen again to use the phone.

I called the kennel and Duke answered. I asked him if Sloan was still there. He said she was and asked why. I told him I needed her to come out to Ginger's house and pick me up.

"I thought you was on a date with Jamie."

I briefly explained the situation and he expressed his sadness at the news of Allison's death, then volunteered to come over. "Not likely, Duke. I know I've been teaching you to drive, but you don't have your license yet."

"Yo," he said, "I ain't tryin' to hear that. I'm a good driver. I mean, Sloan don't even know where Ginger lives at and whatnot."

"Well, put her on and I'll give her the directions."

"Ah, mannn . . ."

"Leon," I used his real name to let him know I was serious, "I need you to stay there and take care of the dogs. Besides," I lowered my voice, "there aren't any reporters or photographers here yet, but there might be some by the time you arrive. It wouldn't be a good idea for you to get your picture in the papers, now, would it?"

"No," he said sadly. "I'm sick o' hiding out, though."

"I know. I'm working on it. Now put Sloan on."

He grudgingly agreed. While I was waiting I took a look at the body.

Allison seemed to have gained a little weight since I'd seen her last. She was lying face down on the light blue tile of her kitchen floor, the fingers of her right hand clutching a long, sharp-steel butcher's knife. Her left hand was stuffed into the pocket of a pink calico apron—almost casually, it seemed, as if she'd been preparing a meal and had died so suddenly she hadn't had time to take the recipe out of her pocket. The knife was clean—there was no blood visible on it. There was no blood anywhere else that I could see, and no obvious sign of trauma to the body. But then, it hadn't been turned over yet.

The kitchen looked nice and tidy, too. No cutlery scattered about, no windows broken, no drawers ransacked. There was a single tomato on the cutting board, sliced in half.

I looked at the back door and it showed no obvious signs of forced entry, though I wasn't close enough to get a really good look at the latch. But it had been open the whole time I'd been there so I guessed that Quentin Peck had found it that way when he'd come to see about the barking and that Flynn had told him to leave it open until Jamie got some Polaroids and had a chance to take the room temperature.

There was a Macintosh computer with its own phone and modem on the desk in the dining room. The computer was turned on but a screen saver of flying toasters was all you could see. There was a desk lamp next to the computer but it was turned off. On the other side of the dining room was the foot of the stairs, where Ginger had finished her water and was lying on the carpet, with her chin resting on her front paws, staring at me.

I looked back at Allison. She had on gray sweatpants and a lime-green T-shirt under the calico apron. Her feet were bare: no shoes, no slippers. The skin around her ankles was starting to turn purple, or cyanotic, as Dr. Jamie would put it.

Sloan came on the line and I gave her directions, then hung up the phone, and turned to see Flynn watching me.

"So, what do you think?" he said.

"She should be here in about ten minutes."

"I mean about the body," he said.

"I don't think anything about the body."

"I saw you looking her over. You're a detective."

"Used to be. Now I run a kennel. Oh, there is *one* thing. Allison DeMarco was left-handed. So why is she holding a knife in her right hand?" Flynn looked down at the body. "Do you mind if I look around to see if she had any vitamins in the house?"

"You sure she was a lefty?"

"Positive. So about those vitamins?"

"You think someone poisoned her vitamins?"

"No, I mean vitamins for the dog. She's been under a lot of stress. Her adrenal glands are overworked. She needs some zinc, B2, B6, pantothenic acid, and maybe some vitamin C."

He looked at me with a blank expression. "You're going to give vitamins to the frickin' dog?"

"Why not? Dogs need vitamins same as humans."

He shook his head. "Okay, but then get the hell outta here." He turned away. "Lotta help you turned out to be."

"Sheriff, I'll be glad to help you out any way I can once I get the dog squared away." He turned to look at me. "I mean, that's the only reason I'm here, really."

"Fine. Get your frickin' vitamins." He looked back down at the body. "So, she was left-handed, huh?"

I was starting to like Flynn, though I could tell he wasn't too thrilled with me. I wondered if he had picked up on the fact that Jamie and I had been out on a date together when he'd called.

I looked through the cabinets and found a lot of dishes and glassware and pots and pans and baking soda and cans of tuna and boxes of Minute Rice, but no vitamins. Then I opened a drawer and found some nice silverware and some napkins and sandwich bags, but no vitamins. I could almost feel Flynn breathing on me. Finally I found a drawer with old prescription bottles, thyroid medication, Tylenol, Advil, prescription eyedrops, vitamin C, kelp tablets, calcium (100 mg.), and a multi-B.

I took out a C and a multi-B and put the bottles away and shut the drawer.

"If it weren't for the frickin' knife, you'd almost think she died of natural causes," Flynn said.

His thoughts were interrupted by the sound of Quentin Peck coming up the steps, trying to placate Sam Kirby.

"Take it easy, now, Sam," he said.

"Where is he?" Kirby said. "I'm gonna kill him."

I heard Ginger growl and turned to see her standing up, with her shoulders high and her hackles raised.

"Good girl, easy, girl," I said, and she relaxed a little.

Kirby came barreling through the open doorway and in one clumsy motion tried to take a lunging roundhouse swing at me. I stepped aside easily but was nearly knocked over by the reek of urine coming from his crotch: his pants were soaked in it. Ginger began barking and growling, straining at the leash.

Flynn stepped between us and stood toe-to-toe—though not eye-to-eye—with Kirby. "Back off, Sam," he said. "And can somebody shut up that frickin' *dog*?"

I went over to calm Ginger down. She stopped barking but continued doing her little Airedale dance—bouncing up and down a little, and twisting her back end around in half-circles.

"That's right, easy, girl. It's all right." I stroked her back.

"But, Horace," Kirby said, "that sneaky bastard. One minute I'm standing there talking to him, and the next thing I know I'm out cold in the dirt. He musta had an accomplice standing behind me the whole time."

Flynn said, "Don't call me Horace," then looked at me. "That true? You got somebody else hiding outside?"

"No," I laughed and walked over to where Flynn and Kirby stood, "it happened just like I told you. But I understand why Sam might think that."

"Why?"

"Because there's always some short-term memory loss—about thirty seconds' to five minutes'—when the brain suffers a concussion. That's why he doesn't remember being attacked by the dog and then trying to shoot her."

"I did *what*?" Kirby was indignant. "No *way*!"

"You sayin' he doesn't remember *any* of that?"

"That's right. There's no way he could."

"Bullshit, Horace—I mean, Sheriff," Kirby sputtered, "he's lyin' through his teeth."

To Flynn I said: "You know those murder stories where the private eye gets sapped, and describes the whole thing in gory detail? 'A black pool suddenly spread at my feet . . .' It could never happen like that. No one *ever* remembers getting knocked out. It's a medical impossibility. Ask Jamie when she gets here. Besides, you all heard the gunshot, right?"

"Ask me what?" Jamie said. She was coming through the open doorway of the kitchen, holding the black handle of her gray medical examiner's kit with both hands. "And what gunshot?"

I briefly explained what I'd just told Flynn.

"Jack's right," she said, as she put her kit on the kitchen counter, opened it, and began putting on her latex gloves and paper booties. "There's always a certain amount of short-term memory loss after any concussion. Why?" She had a puzzled look on her face. "Was Mrs. DeMarco knocked out before she died?"

"No," Quentin Peck said, "Sam was."

The sheriff said, "Sam, go on home and get cleaned up. Then put your uniform on and get back out here. I'm gonna need you to keep the press and any lookie-lous off the property. And how many times do I have to tell you to identify yourself before you start going around telling people what to do."

Jamie—ever the doctor—asked Kirby, "Are you all right, Sam? Do you want me to take a look at you?"

Kirby grunted an embarrassed grunt. "No, I'm all right." He shook his leg twice, pulled a toothpick out of his big forest-green parka, jammed it in his face, then stepped around Flynn and towered over me. "I'll be seeing *you* around," he said, then he went past me giving me an "accidental" shoulder shove.

After he'd gone, Carl and Quent shook their heads. Quent said, "Sorry it took so long, Sheriff, but Sam and me had to search the whole back yard there, lookin' for Mr. Field's phantom accomplice."

He and Carl had a good laugh over that.

"Call me Jack," I said.

Flynn muttered something about how if only Sam were married like them, or if he at least for chrissakes got laid once in a while, he wouldn't be such a headache. Quent and Carl agreed, then Quent said, "But Sheriff, *you're* not married."

Flynn hesitated, then said, "Yeah, well that's differ'nt."

"So, Jack, how's the dog?" Jamie asked.

"She's doing a little better now. You want to say hello?" I pointed to where Ginger stood tied to the banister.

She looked at the dog, shook her head. "You idiot. You put your jacket on her!?"

"She was cold."

She laughed. "Well, I would say hello, honey, but I have things to do." She took some things out of her kit—a meat thermometer among them. "So who knocked out Sam Kirby?" I was flexing my fingers. I hadn't realized how cold and numb my hand had been or how hard Kirby's jaw was. Jamie shook her head, sighed. "As if I didn't know."

Flynn and I both said, "I'll tell you about it later."

"Okay, what about the gunshot? Who shot at whom?"

Flynn gave me the skunk-eye and did the same for Jamie. He was starting to catch on. After all, she'd just called me 'honey.' Jamie averted her eyes and may have even blushed a little. "Well, what about this gunshot? Who shot at whom?"

"Sam Kirby tried to shoot Ginger."

"And that's why you knocked him out?"

"It's a long story."

Flynn looked back over at me. "You know, I'm starting to not like you, Field."

"Yeah, join the club," I said.

"Oh, he's a pain in the ass, Uncle Horace. Especially when there are dogs around. And he's impossible to talk to. But it's only because he was overnarcissized as a child."

"Very funny," I said.

"But you'll really like him once you get to know him, Uncle Horace. I know you will."

"I doubt it," Flynn said.

"Oh, yes you will. You two are exactly alike." Then she went over to look at the body.

I went to the refrigerator and began foraging around.

"What the hell are you doing now? Looking for snacks?"

"Peanut butter. For the dog. To put the vitamins in so she'll swallow them. Besides, it's high in potassium."

"I don't believe this."

Jamie looked at us, sighed and cleared her throat at the same time, then knelt down next to the body and got to work. "Okay, Carl, Quentin: the mini-recorder isn't working, so I'll need one of you to take notes. The other can take pictures." To Flynn she said, "Who's coming for the body?"

"We thought you oughta make the call on that."

She checked her watch. Carl got out a pen and pad while Jamie handed Quentin the Polaroid camera. "Okay," she said to Flynn, "call Rockland Memorial for an ambulance. We can take her up to Augusta in the morning, if necessary."

Quent started taking pictures of the body. Flynn went over to the phone, saw what Quent was doing, and said, "Shoot the door first, Quent, so we can close it. It's like a meat locker in—"

"—No, leave it open," Jamie said, shining a penlight into Allison's left eye. "I need to get a reading of the room temperature." To Carl she said, "Left eye fixed and dilated." She shone the penlight in the right eye and said: "Jesus, she's got a blown right pupil."

"Should I write that down?" Carl said.

"Yes, write it down."

"What does it mean?" asked Flynn.

I said, "It means she probably died from a sharp blow to the head."

Flynn looked to Jamie for corroboration.

She nodded and said, "Possibly. It's a key indicator, but that doesn't necessarily mean—" She began palpating Allison's skull, looking for bone fragments or bits of blood.

"It could be an accident then, right?" Flynn said. "She slips, falls down, and cracks her melon."

"—No blood or discernible cephalic damage," Jamie said, and Carl wrote it down. "We'll have to wait for the X rays." To Carl she said, "You don't have to write that part down."

I thought of something and went to the cutting board.

Jamie looked at her watch and said to Carl, "Official time of death is ten forty-seven on the seventeenth of December."

"And the *actual* time of death?" said Flynn, who'd just finished his call to the hospital.

"You got *me*," Jamie said as she lifted Allison's right arm, or tried to, then said to Carl, "Rigor has set in the extremities." She pressed the skin on the underside of the arm. It was dark purple and didn't change color when she applied pressure to it. "Fixed lividity in the right forearm." Carl wrote it down. She said to Flynn, "I'd say she died somewhere between noon and four-thirty."

"That's the closest you can come?"

She laughed at him. "Are you in some kind of hurry here, Horace? I haven't taken her liver temperature yet. Or the room temperature, for that matter. Even with that information, we won't be able to narrow it down any further until after Dr. Reiner or Dr. Feeney does the autopsy. For the time being, though, I think we can call it a potential homicide." She was very thorough and efficient and I stood staring at her, admiring her terribly.

Flynn fortunately didn't notice. He nodded sadly and held the phone out for Carl Staub. "I guess you'd better call the boys in Camden, Carl. It's their baby now." (In the State of Maine homicides are investigated by the local police, the state police, or both—never by county sheriffs.)

Carl went to make the call.

Meanwhile I scooped some peanut butter onto a knife, squished the vitamins into it, and gave it to Ginger to eat.

She gulped it down, but got some of it stuck to the roof of her mouth, causing her tongue to go into convulsions as she tried to lick it off.

I laughed at her antics, then heard a horn honking from out on the road—three short toots followed by a long one, which was the signal I had given Sloan for when she came to pick me up.

"There's my ride," I said.

"So, you got any ideas you want to pass along before you go?" Flynn said.

I looked at Jamie. She nodded at me, urging me to say something.

"Well, a few things, I guess. First of all, Allison was left-handed, like I said, so I have to wonder why she's holding the knife in her right hand . . ." They all looked at the body. "Another thing," I said, with a nod toward the cutting board. "That tomato has slight indentations on the left half, indicating that it was sliced by someone who's right-handed. That fits in with the knife being planted in her right hand."

"Wait. You're saying the knife was *planted* there?"

"Well, it *had* to have been, Sheriff. There'd be no reason for Allison to hold a knife in the wrong hand. You know, you might even be able to lift some prints from that tomato and run them through BCI—"

"—You gotta be kidding," Flynn said. "You can't tell anything from lookin' at a frickin' tomato."

"After 15 years working homicide," I told the sheriff, as I unhooked Ginger from the leash, "you develop a nose for murder. If you think she died of natural causes that's fine with me. But there is one other thing, Sheriff—how many women do you know in the State of Maine who run around the house this time of year in their bare feet? I mean, think about it: where are Allison's slippers?"

Before Flynn or Jamie or Quent or Carl could look at Allison DeMarco's bare feet, Ginger slipped out of my grasp and bolted up the stairs to the second floor. A few seconds later she came bounding back into the kitchen. It was quite a sight—a curly-haired black and tan dog with sparkling brown eyes, wearing a denim jacket and holding a fuzzy pair of pink bedroom slippers in her slobbery peanut-buttery mouth. She stopped in front of me and dropped the slippers at my feet. It seems that Allison—with my help—had done a nice job of training Ginger to fetch her slippers for her.

From out on the road the horn sounded again.

Flynn's face was red. "I thought that was your ride."

"It is," I said, and bent down to hook Ginger up. As I did I noticed a brown stain on one of the slippers.

"What's this—blood?" I picked it up.

Jamie came over. "Could be," she said, looking it over. "I'd better do a presumptive." She took the slipper back over to her kit, which still sat on the kitchen counter.

Flynn was puzzled. He wiggled his mustache, then looked over at Carl and Quent. "It don't exactly figure. No blood anyplace else." He looked at me. "Maybe it's an old stain?"

"Maybe. Though my guess would be that it's the killer's blood. That's why she wasn't wearing the slippers when the body was discovered. He'd hidden them somewhere."

"It's definitely human blood," Jamie said, after daubing some chemicals onto a swab she'd made of the stain. "We'll have to type it to see if it's Allison's or someone else's. There's probably enough that we could even run a DNA sample."

The horn sounded again and I headed for the door with Ginger in tow. "Well, it was nice to meet you, Sheriff." I dug into my wallet and handed him one of my cards. "I'll take good care of the dog. Call me if you need anything."

"Wait. You just taking the dog with you? Just like that?"

I stopped. "I was under the impression that that's what you wanted me to do. If not, well—"

He thought it over, looked at Carl Staub. "You vouch for this guy?"

Carl hesitated a little. "Well, sure, I guess. I mean, we could call animal control, but if it was *my* dog I'd rather have Jack take her."

They both looked down at Allison's body as if trying to get a sense of what *she* would have wanted. Flynn looked over at Jamie. "You seem to know this guy pretty well. Maybe too well, considering. What do you think?"

"Oh, Horace, come on." She just pointed to the dog. "This is a man who's willing to freeze to death in order to keep the dog warm. How could she possibly be in better hands?"

Flynn looked at me grudgingly. "Okay, you can go."

"Thanks, Sheriff," I said. As I passed by Jamie I said, "I'll call you later."

She shook her head. "I'll be up pretty late with this." Then Flynn came over to look at the slipper. The last thing I heard as I headed down the steps was Flynn asking her, "So, what's with you and this guy Field?"

As I came outside I saw my midnight blue Chevy Suburban parked in the driveway behind Allison's red Escalade. I came around the front of the car, heard a squeal of tires, and saw a silver Volvo pull out of the shadows across the road, fishtail onto the pavement, and drive off at high speed. I couldn't see who was driving or get the license number, but I *did* notice that the left taillight had apparently been broken in an accident and had been replaced with red acetate.

I put Ginger in the crate I keep in the back, then got behind the wheel and asked Sloan—early twenties, long-limbed, and slender, with hair and eyes the color of wet sand—if she'd seen the Volvo. She had, but couldn't tell me anything more than what I'd already seen. I made a mental note to tell Flynn about it, or better yet, Carl Staub, since the Camden police were now in charge—but Ginger started whining, so I asked Sloan to get me a tennis ball from the glove compartment. Then I got out, went around to the back, and gave the ball to Ginger for her to chew on. She stopped whining and we drove home.

6

The next morning I was in the play yard (a squarish grassy fenced-in area roughly the size of the infield at Fenway Park), nursing the hand I'd bruised on Kirby's jaw and throwing a couple of tennis balls around for Frankie and Ginger to chase when the bell over the kennel door rang a few times, then stopped. A moment later Mrs. Murtaugh came out the front door. "Telephone!" she shouted.

"If it's the sheriff again, tell him I moved to Chicago."

"It's not the sheriff, it's some young man."

I left the dogs in the play area, latched the gate behind me, then went up the hill to where Mrs. Murtaugh—wearing overalls and a corduroy car coat—stood outside the kennel building. It's actually an old barn, rebuilt on the inside with concrete blocks and a cement floor, heated from underneath by a system of PVC hot-water pipes.

Mrs. Murtaugh was standing by the front door watching Frankie and Ginger play. Her breath made little clouds in the foggy morning air. Ginger had the tennis ball in her mouth, tempting Frankie to make a grab for it, all the while knowing that if he *did*, she'd just run away and make him chase her.

"It's such a shame about Allison," Mrs. Murtaugh said as I reached the top of the hill. She knew Allison fairly well since she'd groomed Ginger every six weeks or so from the time Allison had first gotten her. I say "groomed" even though Airedales shouldn't be clipped and scissored, the way most other breeds are. Their fur is plucked, which is more time-consuming, and therefore more costly. This is why you sometimes see an Airedale or wire-haired fox terrier with a badly "faded" coat. All the vibrant color they once had as a puppy is gone. It's because their coats have been clipped, not plucked.

We looked down at the dogs and were about to go inside when Frankie froze in the classic setter stance. It was as if Ginger were some prey that he was suddenly stalking. We froze as well. When a true field setter sets, it's almost impossible not to watch.

Even Ginger was impressed—so much so that, without quite meaning to, she dropped the ball. In an instant Frankie ran in, scooped it up with his jaws, and ran away. Ginger went bounding after him, but he was too fast and tricky for her. He would stop, fake right, and go left. Then he would stop, fake right, and then *go* right. He has quite an arsenal of moves, this dog. To Ginger he must have seemed like a white streak with black flecks and patches, zipping and zooming around the play yard, laughing and running away, while she—the frustrated Airedale—chased and barked at him, all to no avail.

"They really love each other," sighed Mrs. Murtaugh.

"Tell me about it. I got practically no sleep last night."

"Well," she said, with a slight scolding tone in her voice, "everyone knows you're not supposed to let a dog sleep in the bed with you, let alone *two*."

"There's a lot of things you're not supposed to do that end up being the best thing you *can* do once you do them."

"I'm not sure I understand what that means."

"Well," I explained, "if you were Ginger, and your owner had just been murdered, would you rather spend your first night without her, alone in a kennel, or sleeping on a comfortable bed with someone you know and like?" With that, I ushered her inside, leaving the dogs to play on their own for a bit.

"She does like you a lot," she said, closing the door. "So I guess you're right, Jack. Having her sleep in bed with you *was* the right thing to do."

"Hey—I thought you knew—when it comes to dogs I'm *always* right."

"Of course you are, dear." She patted my hand. "But you don't really think Allison was murdered, do you?"

I said I did indeed.

She sighed, shook her head, then went into the grooming room and started up one of the blow-dryers to finish a bichon cut she was doing on a miniature poodle named Max, whose hair was as white and poofy as hers.

I closed the grooming room door, took off my gloves, put them in the pocket of my down vest, went behind the counter to my desk, sat down, and picked up the phone.

It turned out to be Tim Berry, the waiter from O'Neal's. He was calling to find out if he could come out to see me about his basset hound, the subject we'd discussed the night before.

"It'll be better if I can come out there."

He said that was okay—and, in fact, sounded rather pleased about the idea of me coming to see him—and I told him my fee and he said that was okay, too—though he sounded less pleased about *that*—and then he gave me his address and I said I'd see him in about an hour.

I poked my head into the grooming room to remind Mrs. Murtaugh about Frankie's regular Monday morning bath. As usual she didn't ask me why he needs a bath every Monday morning, and as usual, I didn't tell her.

I went back outside and played with the dogs for another ten minutes or so then put Ginger in her kennel for a nap—she'd spent all day Sunday barking, after all. Then I took Frankie to my office and left him on his cedar bed with a vanilla rawhide to chew on if he felt like it.

I went up to the house and found Duke at the kitchen table eating a bowl of Sugar Pops. I asked him to keep an eye on the dogs, especially Ginger, telling him I'd pay him extra, and he said, "That's cool. I got nothin' to do today but lie around my room and watch TV until my regular shift starts anyway."

"You could always study for your GED."

He laughed. "Christmas vacation."

I shook my head. "Don't make me call your grandma on you, Duke. And you realize that as soon as I get the Manhattan DA's office off your tail you're going back to school full-time."

"I'd like to see you make me," he grinned, his mouth full of sweet honey-and-corn goodness (along with a lot of milk). "That's what *I'm* sayin'."

I flipped up the bill of the Yankees cap he always wore backward, so that the back of it slid down over his eyes. He screamed, "Hey!" pushed it back up, got out of his chair, and we slap-boxed a little, just for fun, though Duke kept saying, "I'll kick your ass," as if he meant it. I knew he didn't, though. To me it was no different from the way a dog growls at you when playing tug-of-war.

After I finished fooling around with Duke—which was almost as much fun as playing with the dogs had been, maybe more—I grabbed my keys, got in the woody, and drove over to Tim Berry's house, making one stop along the way.

7

On the drive over to Jamie's mom's place—to drop off some Christmas presents and say a quick hello—my detective's brain slipped into gear again and I began thinking about Allison's murder—puzzling over the clues, trying to think of a possible motive, getting out the old mental chess board and dusting off the pieces. It wasn't until I'd gotten to the bottom of the mountain road and heard myself saying out loud that this was silly, that I ought to wait for the autopsy results before going any further, that I realized what I was doing. Old habits die hard.

I sighed, switched my attention back to my kennel and the dogs, and immediately felt the tension in my neck and shoulders disappear. I enjoyed the rest of the drive, untroubled by any more thoughts of violence, intrigue, and murder.

Laura Cutter's home, a nineteenth-century farmhouse painted bone white with robin's egg trim, sits on a hill surrounded by white pines, sugar maples, linden, alder, and blue spruce trees. It overlooks an old mill pond fed by a trout stream that winds through the town of New Hope, which consists basically of a few scattered farmhouses, a post office, a general store, a gas station, two white clapboard churches, and a grange hall. It sounds picturesque as hell, and it is. But it's also just another hardscrabble New England farm town.

New Hope, along with the nearby villages of Hope, Union, Freedom, and Perseverance, make up what in the State of

Maine is called a plantation—a loosely knit political body with governing power somewhere between that of a city and county. (I'm not sure I understand it either, but I like telling people that while I used to reside in Hell's Kitchen, I now live halfway between Hope and Perseverance. I think it's funny, but Jamie got tired of hearing me say it a long time ago.)

Laura had used the money from her divorce settlement with Jonas—which wasn't a lot, he had just graduated from Harvard at the time—to start her own real estate business, which kept her afloat through some hard times, raising two children—Jamie and her older brother Jason—on her own. So while the kids were in school every day, and while Jonas was starting to make a name for himself as a rising young neurosurgeon in Boston and as an adjunct professor of medicine at Harvard (now professor emeritus), Laura was driving up and down the back roads of Rockland County showing properties to prospective clients and keeping an eye out for any new "For Sale" signs that might have sprouted up along her route overnight.

As I came up the gravel drive I honked the horn and Laura came out the kitchen door onto the wide back porch and waved. A slim woman with an easy, graceful gait and a face like a 1940s movie star, she was wearing sharply creased navy slacks, shiny penny loafers, and a bright canary cardigan over a pewter silk blouse, She always dresses as if expecting company.

I started to open the car door but she kept walking straight to the window and leaned in from the waist, hugging herself to keep warm. I rolled down the window.

"Hi, Jack," she smiled. "Nice to see you."

I don't know what it was exactly about Jamie's mom that made me feel this way, but she had an uncanny knack, with just a smile or a touch of her hand, of always putting me in a good mood. Maybe she reminded me of the way my own mother behaved on those rare occasions when her medications were working. I remember how my kid sister Annabelle and I used to tiptoe through the house after school, day after day, when Mom was lying in bed with a "sick headache."

I know better now, what with all we've learned about brain chemistry, but as a kid I always had the feeling—or at least, a kind of vague suspicion—that my mother's headaches were just her way of avoiding the responsibilities of being a mom, responsibilities that Laura Cutter seemed to relish.

Maybe she enjoyed them too much sometimes; as far as *Jamie* was concerned she did. But to my mind, Laura Cutter was the perfect mom—the kind of mother *I* only knew on those rare and glorious days when Annie and I came home from school and found the bedroom door standing wide open, and there was mom—smiling, asking us about our day, or playing Chopin and Mozart on the spinet piano (her glasses perched on the end of her nose), or whistling happily in the kitchen while whipping up a batch of peanut butter, or oatmeal and raisin, or chocolate chip cookies (all equally good, in my estimation).

"Hi, Laura," I said, almost blushing a little in a schoolboy kind of way. "Jamie isn't here, I hope?"

"No, she's at the hospital."

"Good." I handed a half-dozen gift-wrapped items to her through the window. "You can hide these for me."

She took them and said, "Don't you want to come in for a cup of coffee? I just made some fresh cranberry muffins. They're still warm . . ."

"I can't," I said, "I've got a meeting with a client." She seemed disappointed, so I thought, what the hell—Tim Berry could stand to wait a few minutes. "Come to think of it," I opened the car door, "I could really use a good cup of coffee . . ."

She smiled and we walked up to the house together. She hugged the gifts and said, "I certainly will not hide these, Jack. They're going right under the tree. Did you wrap them?"

I laughed. "No, I conned Mrs. Murtaugh into doing it."

She shook her head. "And how, pray tell, did you do that?"

"It was a snap. I just pretended I wanted to do it myself, but did such a sloppy job that she naturally took the scissors and ribbons and paper and scotch tape away from me."

"Very clever, Jack." She sighed. "It's such a rotten shame about Allison DeMarco, isn't it?"

"Yes. Did you know her?"

"No. Though I did know her father, Samuel Davies. Or at least, *of* him."

The name sounded familiar. I thought a minute. "Wait. Is he the guy they named the park after in Augusta?"

"You know it?"

"Sure. Samuel L. Davies Park. It's right across from the office building where I got my kennel license. I spent quite a few hours there last summer, cooling my heels, feeding the squirrels, and wondering who the hell Samuel L. Davies was. Now I know. He was Allison DeMarco's father. Small world, huh?"

"Not really," she shrugged, "it's just the way things are in Maine." We got to the door and I held it open for her. "Thank you. I do hope you're still planning to come over for Christmas."

I told her I was and we went inside to the smell of coffee and muffins. I sat on a stool at the kitchen counter. Laura put the Christmas presents on a table just inside the door, then went to the pot and poured two cups of coffee. She put some two percent and Sweet'N Low in one, then said, "Black, isn't that right?" I said it was, thanks for remembering, and she handed it to me and I blew over the rim while she got the muffins out of the oven, placed one on a saucer, set it in front of me, then got a butter tray from the refrigerator and placed that and a butter knife next to the saucer. I cut open the muffin and a little steam rose from the surface of each half. I buttered them, watched the butter start to melt, then took a bite and wondered where she'd been all my life. Even at sixty-four she was as pretty as Jamie, which is saying a lot. *And* she could cook.

"Delicious," I said, my mouth full.

"Thank you."

"Where'd you get the fresh cranberries? They're quite tangy."

"At the general store. They always have them in stock this time of year. Where do you do *your* shopping?"

"I don't," I said. "Mrs. Murtaugh does it for me. Among other things."

"Like your gift wrapping?" She laughed. "I guess she takes pretty good care of you."

"I know," I blushed again. "But the thing is, she *likes* doing it. I can't stop her. It would hurt her feelings. Plus, I have an open-door policy in my kitchen for all my clients and employees: free soda, coffee, fresh fruit, pretzels, cookies, potato chips. Mrs. Murtaugh keeps it well stocked."

She said that sounded like a nice policy. I said I thought so, and then we chatted about nothing and everything for a while. I asked how Jason was and she said he was doing fine, though she'd like to see him and Carla and the baby more often—he's so busy down in Boston, following in his father's shadow. And I said, don't you mean footsteps, and she said yes, what did I say? And I told her and she laughed and said, yes, Jonas does cast quite a shadow—not just for Jason, but for all of us.

Then she asked me about *my* family, what my mother and father were like, did I have any brothers or sisters, and I told her what life in the Field house was like when I was a kid. I explained my mother's condition, then said, "I ended up looking after my kid sister Annabelle a lot because of that. And sometimes, on days when Dad was home late from work, I even ended up making dinner, doing the dishes and all the rest."

"Quite a lot for a ten-year-old to handle. What kind of work did your father do?"

"He was a police officer in San Diego. We lived in a little suburb on the outskirts called Lemon Grove."

She stirred her coffee. "I guess Jason's not the only one to follow in his father's shadow then, is he? And what made you decide you had to take care of your sister?"

"What do you mean?"

"Did your mother or father tell you to do it? Or maybe an aunt or an uncle? Or a clergyman?"

"No, nobody *told* me to do it. I just did it because I *had* to. She was only six. *Someone* had to take care of her."

"I don't buy that. Would you like some more coffee?"

"No thanks," I said, puzzled by her previous comment.

She poured herself another cup, sat back down, and saw the puzzled look on my face. "You and Annabelle are roughly the same age difference as Jason and Jamie. The last thing *he* wanted when he was ten was to have anything to do with his little sister. He just wanted to have fun and play with his friends."

"Yeah, I remember thinking that way. A lot." As I said this I was captured by a sudden memory—something I hadn't thought of in years which explained what she was talking about.

As I was leaving school one day, the school nurse caught up with me and told me she'd just sent my sister home with a fever. She'd called the house to speak to my mother about it but no one had answered. (My mother often kept the phone in her bedroom under a pile of pillows so the ringing wouldn't disturb her sleep.) She was worried, the nurse was. And she wanted me to go right home and see if everything was okay.

I wasn't in the mood to do it, but I lied and told her I would. I was on my way home anyway, to pick up my bat and glove, so I could've easily stuck my head into Annabelle's room and then gone off to play baseball with my friends. Someone had just dug up one of the lemon groves near our block. Some kids had heard they were going to put in a car dealership there, but they hadn't started construction yet or even put up a fence. All they'd done was steamroller the lot, leveling the irrigation ditches, and leaving an almost perfect baseball field. We could have played on the diamonds at the elementary school, of course. And *they* had grass. But it was much *cooler* to have your own field, one that nobody else knew about. Then there was the fact that we didn't know how much longer we'd be able to play there every day. A fence might go up tomorrow.

I got home, got my bat and glove out of my bedroom closet, and got to the front door before I remembered about my sister. I went back to check on her and that's when my life changed.

It wasn't that Annabelle was all that sick or anything, or that I was afraid she might die if I didn't stay home and take care of her. It was just that there was this look she had in her eyes when she saw me come through the door: a mixture of sheer happiness to see me, followed by guilt—like it was her fault that she was sick and I had to take care of her, then fear that I *wouldn't* stick around and take care of her, and she'd be left alone, and finally a look of abandonment, like Mom wasn't available when she needed her the most. It was the fear and loneliness that got to me. I'd felt them both so often myself, even though I would never admit it.

"I threw up on the floor," she said. "I tried to clean it up but I got dizzy and had to go back to bed. Don't tell Mom?"

"I won't," I said. "Do you need a glass of water or something?"

She nodded. "I'm very thirsty."

So I got her some water, cleaned the mess on the floor, then sat next to her on the bed, and held a cold washcloth on her forehead until she fell asleep. I refilled the water glass and left it on the nightstand in case she got thirsty again. Then I tried to leave, to see how the game was going, but I couldn't. I got halfway down the driveway but had to come back. That look in my sister's eyes kept haunting me. (In some ways, I guess, it still does.)

I didn't tell Laura any of this. It took me less than a second to remember it. It's funny how a whole afternoon can be encapsulated in just a single flash like that. Especially an afternoon that has such an impact on your life.

"What's wrong, Jack? Are you crying?"

"No," I said, finishing my coffee. "I just forgot to take my allergy medication."

"Really? What are you allergic to?"

I wanted to tell her, "The past," but I said, "Dog dander," which was also true. "Ironic, huh? By the way," I took a pen from my pocket, "I wonder if you could tell me a few things . . ."

"I suppose. What things?"

"Well," I said, writing them down, "there are four or five things every man should know about the woman he loves. I don't know, I think I read it somewhere, but he's supposed to know her dress size, her shoe size, her ring size, whether she wears pierced or clip-on earrings, and also, does she prefer gold to silver, rubies to sapphires, pearls to emeralds, etc. Oh, and her favorite perfume."

"Jamie's allergic to perfume. She likes to wear men's cologne, though. Halston is her favorite, I think." I gave her the list. She smiled at me. "I guess you really love her, don't you?"

I shrugged.

She scratched off the information I'd requested and handed me back the slip of paper. I got up, went to the door, and stopped. "By the way," I said, "Allison had quite a lot of money. I got the impression she inherited most of it. Do you have any idea what her father did for a living?"

"Yes," she came to the door, "he was in commercial real estate. Property in Portland and Augusta. In fact, that park you spoke of? No one named it after Sam Davies. He donated the land and named it after himself."

"Must have had quite an ego."

"So it would seem. He owned some property in Camden and a portion of Owl's Head, as well."

"Really? That's Rachel Carson territory, isn't it? *Silent Spring* and all that? The birthplace of ecology?"

"Yes. It's also the home of the Winslow Homer Museum."

"Really? Maybe you could show it to me sometime."

"I'd be delighted to. Let me walk you to your car." We went outside. "And perhaps sometime you can tell me more about your sister, and why you—"

"It's a long story. Did Allison DeMarco have any siblings that you know of?"

She laughed. "You really were a cop, weren't you?"

"What do you mean?"

"Oh, I don't know." She smiled and it reminded me of one of Jamie's smiles. "It's just this way you have of asking questions but never answering them. I hope you're not like that with my daughter. It would really drive her crazy."

"I know. It *does*. So, about Allison's siblings?"

We got to the woody and stopped and she touched me lightly on the back. "Yes, as I recall she had an older sister, or half-sister, from Sam Davies's first marriage."

She looked off into the distance.

"What?" I said.

"I don't know. I just . . . I can't quite remember the details but I think there was some sort of scandal. It involved Allison's half-sister and her marriage to someone in local politics, but I just can't recall what it was about. I know that it was the husband who was implicated in something illegal, not the half-sister. . . . Oh, I just can't remember what it *was*!

Or the sister's name." She sighed. "I guess I'm getting old."

"We should all grow old as gracefully as you, Laura."

She smiled and kissed my cheek. "Thank you, Jack. My daughter told me you were quite the silver-tongued devil."

I almost blushed again. "Jamie never said that."

"Well, perhaps not those words exactly. But she does think you're charming. And so do I."

"Good," I said, getting into the car. "That makes three of us. Now if we can only convince the rest of Rockland County . . ."

8

I drove to Alden Street—which dissects one of the highest points, geographically speaking, of Camden proper—and pulled up to Tim Berry's house, a pale green three-story Queen Anne. On a clear day you could probably look out any window and count the dozens of blue islands that litter Penobscot Bay.

A beat-up yellow '72 Firebird TransAm stood in the driveway so I parked the woody on the street. Berry must have been keeping an eye out for me, because he immediately came out onto the front porch dragging a wiggly tricolor basset hound—about four months old—on a skinny red leather leash. The poor pup's ears were so long that he was practically tripping over them.

"Mr. Field," Berry called out, holding the screen door open with one foot, "glad you could make it. This is Thurston."

"Call me Jack," I said closing the door and locking it.

"Um, okay," he said, then whistled at the woody. "Wicked cool car." He eyed the cream paint job and the oak and cherrywood side panels. "What kind is it?"

"It's a thirty-eight Ford and they call it a woody." He seemed unaware that I was paraphrasing the opening line of an old Jan and Dean song—"Surf City"—but then he didn't grow up in southern California in the sixties, like I did.

He whistled again and said, "It must've cost a lot."

I shrugged and came up the steps and crouched down next

to Thurston. He tried to roll over on his back and made a tiny puddle on the floorboards. Berry grabbed him by the neck, picked him up, and shook him, yelling "No!" in his face.

I stifled an urge to grab *Berry* by the neck and shake *him*. Instead I said, "Hey, hey, hey! What are you doing?"

He let go of the dog, who scrabbled underneath a nearby chair. "I read about it in a book. It's what a mother dog does to her pups. It's supposed to be the natural way."

"Well, some people believe that, but not me. Besides, a mother dog does a lot of other things you wouldn't even think of doing to your puppy. Like eating its feces." Berry made a face. "Although you're right: it *is* natural when a mother dog does it, but not at all natural when a human does, is it?"

"I guess not," he grimaced.

"Besides, how would you feel if you had to pee real bad and you were afraid someone would shake *you* like that?"

"I don't know. I'd probably pee even harder."

"Exactly." I crouched down to Thurston's level again and enticed him out from under the furniture with a piece of cheese. He came out slowly and took the bait. Then I grabbed his leash, handed it to Berry, and said, "Let's go inside."

We went in. There were lace curtains on the windows and antimacassars on the maroon velvet couch and armchairs, and an old amber oak upright piano against one wall with a brass floor lamp next to it. It had an emerald shade, fringed with tired red silk. The Oriental carpet was ancient, although there were no bare spots visible. As I took in the décor I realized that Tim Berry lived with his grandparents.

"Would you like some tea or coffee?" he asked.

I said no thanks and settled into a velvet armchair while Berry sat on the floor with Thurston in his lap. He stroked the dog with his right hand and wrote down everything I said on a yellow legal pad with his left.

I said the first step in housebreaking a basset hound is to lower your expectations: "Realistically? He may be a year old before he gets it."

"Oh, man," he sighed, "my grandma's gonna kill me."

"She'll get over it. So you live with your grandparents?"

"Yeah," he frowned. "My mother's dead and my father's

in prison. We've got a great family. Stephen King gets all his best material from us."

It sounded more like Faulkner to me but I said nothing, except that I was sorry to hear it.

I watched him writing furiously on his yellow pad and thought of Allison DeMarco for some reason. What was it she'd said about the type of men she attracted—mousy and innocuous? That was Tim Berry to a tee.

He was finishing writing what I'd just said, and was mouthing it as he wrote: "He might be a year old before he's housebroken," then he looked up at me, confused and apologetic. "But—um—I don't mean to disagree with you but—um—the thing is, my uncle has a basset hound that was totally housebroken at eight weeks. So . . ."

I shook my head. "That's way too early. A puppy needs to go through certain stages of emotional development before he's really ready to go to the bathroom outside on his own. And I'll bet you anything that your uncle's dog has developed some sort of strange behavioral quirks as a result."

Berry thought it over and gave me a chagrined smile. "You're right. She *does* tend to hide under the furniture a lot. In fact, she only comes out from under the couch when she has to eat or go to the bathroom." He laughed a little nervously and looked down at Thurston, who was happily chewing on a stuffed toy. "I guess I'm making my dog neurotic too, huh?"

"Not necessarily. Just cool it with all the dominance crap you've read about. And start teaching Thurston *how* to behave properly rather than punishing him when he makes mistakes. Puppies don't understand punishment. At his age you're painting his map of the world. If he's always getting yelled at and punished, when he grows up he'll naturally feel the world is a scary and threatening place and act accordingly."

"Just like Molly," he said, writing it all down.

"Your uncle's dog?"

"Yep. That's probably why she hides under the couch."

"Probably," I said, then gave him a housebreaking schedule and taught him how to tell when a dog needs to eliminate.

He wrote it all down, then said, "What about chewing the furniture and biting my hands and stuff?"

Thurston had lost interest in his chew toy and was now attempting to chew Berry's legal pad. Berry's response was to pull it away and say, "No!" which only made Thurston more interested in it.

"Those are two very good questions," I said. "And you're giving a perfect demonstration of doing exactly the wrong thing to keep him from chewing your legal pad right now."

"I am?"

"Sure. Anytime you take something away from a puppy, or even move it away from him while he's focused on it or interested in it, you're only making it even *more* interesting. That's because his hunting instinct is hard wired to go after anything that's moving away from him."

"So what do I do?" He was helplessly holding the legal pad high up in the air while Thurston was jumping all over him, trying to get at it. I resisted the urge to laugh and said:

"Watch this . . ." I clapped my hands and made a loud, hearty laughing sound, straight from the diaphragm. Thurston was startled and looked at me. "Good dog! Good *boy*!" I said, very enthusiastically, and he immediately came running over to me. I leaned over and picked up his chew toy off the floor, began teasing him with it, and when he was just as crazy for it as he had been for Berry's legal pad, I gave it to him.

He took it back over to his spot on the floor next to Berry and chewed on it happily, just as he'd been doing before.

"That is so cool. My ex-girlfriend said you were a genius."

I laughed. "Thanks, but I didn't make up this exercise. I stole it from a guy named William Campbell. And who's your ex-girlfriend, if I may ask? Sounds like I might know her."

"Of course you know her. It's Allison DeMarco. You trained her Airedale, Ginger."

I was stunned. "That's right. I did." How in the hell had I known earlier that Tim Berry and Allison DeMarco had been an item? Certainly he was the mousy, innocuous type, but still—was I psychic all of a sudden, or was this just a coincidence?

"Remember? I told you I'd been to one of your seminars with a friend of mine?"

Aha. So I wasn't psychic after all. I'd probably just seen them together at the seminar and that information had been stored somewhere in my subconscious. Nor was it a coincidence: Berry would've never asked for my advice at the restaurant if he hadn't been to that seminar. And I'm not the type of guy who notices or pays attention to waiters. (With waitresses it's a different story, but don't tell Jamie that.)

"How well did you know her?"

He sighed—I assumed because he'd heard about her murder—and said, "Pretty well. At least, until things got complicated."

Before I could ask more about Allison, Thurston stopped chewing the toy, got up, and began sniffing the carpet, looking for a place to pee.

"Uh-oh," I said. "See what he's doing? That's one of the signs that he needs to go. Better take him outside."

Berry picked him up and went to the backyard. When they came back a few minutes later, I was standing in front of an end table, looking at a framed photograph of an imposing, multigabled three-story Victorian house. It had a nice vista of pine trees, and a wooden dock leading to a rocky beach.

Berry said proudly, "That's my Aunt Rachel's house on Monhegan Island. It's going to be mine someday, I hope."

"Well, it's a great house. So you were about to tell me more about you and Allison . . ."

"Was I? I don't know." He sat back down on the floor and picked up his legal pad. "We was pretty close, I guess. I mean, I was kinda crazy about her and stuff, but then something happened to screw things up. Now it's hopeless."

"Hopeless? I guess that's one way of looking at it."

Thurston got bored with his chew toy and went for Berry's legal pad again. I repeated the routine I'd done earlier and in no time he was back chewing on the stuffed toy.

"I can't get over how cool that is. And what do you mean that's one way of looking at it? Does Allison talk to you about me? Do you know something that could help me get her back?"

My God, I thought. He hasn't heard about her murder. I was about to tell him about it when a flash of light caught my eye and I looked outside and saw a silver Volvo pull up behind the TransAm. I watched as the blond teenager I'd seen at O'Neal's the night before came up the front steps.

"Mr. Field? Do you know something?"

I jerked a thumb at the window. "You've got a visitor."

He came to the window and looked out. "Tara? Oh, God. That's one of the problems with me and Allison, see? Though it's not my fault. I didn't know that she was—" Whatever it was that he didn't know was muffled by the sound of the doorbell. Then he shouted, "Come on in, Tare. It's open."

She came through the door and was about to say something but stopped cold when she saw me. Her face had that raw look of someone who's been crying for hours and has just stopped.

Berry went to her. "What's wrong?"

She looked at me uncertainly.

"This is Jack Field. He's helping me train Thurston."

She turned around and ran back outside.

Berry turned to me, made an impotent gesture, and said,

"She's been bugging out lately." We heard the sound of her car starting. "I'd better go after her and see what's the matter." He grabbed his keys and his coat. "Can you do me a favor and put Thurston in the kitchen before you go? And can I pay you later?"

I said that was fine and he ran outside.

I picked up the basset pup and we watched through the curtains as Tara backed her silver Volvo into the street. I noticed that her left taillight was taped on with red acetate.

Then, as Tim Berry got in his TransAm to follow her, I realized what it was that had made Tara seem so familiar to me, even though I'd never seen her before last night: She bore a striking resemblance to Allison DeMarco. Tara had light hair and green eyes, as opposed to Allison's dark hair and blue eyes, but there was definitely some shared DNA in their backgrounds—as if they were sisters or something.

9

I put Thurston in the kitchen, gave him a biscuit, put down some water, turned on the radio to keep him company, and left him behind his puppy gate. Then I used the phone in the living room to call Mrs. Murtaugh to see if there were any messages.

"Yes, Sheriff Flynn called again. Twice."

"Tell him I moved to Nebraska."

"You said Chicago before."

"Apparently that's not outside his jurisdiction."

She laughed. "And Jamie called. She said she wishes you'd get a beeper or a cell phone. Oh, and what's a Luddite?"

I chuckled. "Never mind. Just tell Jamie she's lucky I have any kind of phone at all."

"Tell her yourself. She's at the hospital doing an autopsy on that poor Mrs. DeMarco. She wants you to come for lunch."

"At the morgue? Sounds like a fun lunch."

I hung up, locked up the Berry house and drove back to the kennel to pick up Frankie for our Monday morning madness in the pediatric ward. We arrived a little early so we wandered around, looking for the morgue. I pretended I was a basset hound and followed my nose. Frankie followed me.

Jamie and her assistant, Nikki, a young woman about Jamie's age but shorter and with dishwater-blond hair, were in the autopsy room, about to start the postmortem. The smells of alcohol and formaldehyde filled the air and my nostrils, and I was feeling a little cold. Not as cold as Allison De-Marco, whose naked body lay face down under the green fluorescent lights on a steel examination table.

"Hey, Jack." Jamie was dressed in hospital greens and her hands were encased in latex gloves. "You're a little ahead of schedule. What's Frankie doing here?"

"Don't worry. He has a pass."

She shook her head. "Yeah, right. And even if he *had*, which I'm sure he hasn't, he doesn't belong in here." To Nikki she said, "That dog is like a fifth appendage for this guy. He takes him everywhere."

"Technically, he would have to be a *sixth* appendage, since I already have five."

She laughed. "I wouldn't call what you're referring to as an appendage, exactly. And just get the dog out of here before he contaminates things, okay?"

"Fine," I said and took Frankie to the door. I opened it and told him to go out in the hall and stay there, which he did. I closed the door, turned and saw Jamie staring daggers at me.

"What an amazing dog," said Nikki. "He really listens."

"Jack, you can't just leave him out there all by—"

The door opened and a young male doctor, pale, blond, with a slight build and a face that was all forehead and cheekbones, said, "Whose dog is this?" He seemed terribly irritated.

"Mine," I said, walking toward him. "His name is Frankie, and he has a hospital pass." I took Frankie's pass out of my wallet and showed it to him.

He examined it and said, "I see. Still, the animal shouldn't be left unsupervised. It even says so right here: 'The dog is allowed off-lead when under supervision only.' "

"He *is* under supervision," I said. "I've told him to stay and he'll do it all day and all night if he has to."

"Really?" He seemed impressed. He looked down at Frankie and stroked his head. "What a good boy! What is he, part Dalmatian?" I went through the usual routine, explaining that, no, he was an English setter. "Well, so long, Frankie." The dog never took his eyes off me. "He sure is focused on you, isn't he? Well, have a nice day."

"You stay, Frankie," I said, and let the door close.

Jamie had her hands on her hips. "Let me see that pass." I showed it to her. "Since when does this hospital give out—" She looked up at me. "He's a canine therapy dog!"

I nodded. "We come by every Monday to wreak havoc in the pediatric ward. Frankie really likes the kids."

She handed back the card. "Why didn't you tell me this?"

"Why would I?" She huffed at me. "Look, there are just some things you don't go around telling people about, okay? You just *do* them. If you start *talking* about them, well—"

"—I think it's sweet he didn't tell you," Nikki said. "It's very old-school, very charming."

Jamie thought it over. "Maybe you're right. Jack *is* kind of old school—aren't you, cowboy?" She smiled at me. "Come to think of it, I guess it *is* kind of sweet of you to do this every week and not tell anyone about it."

They were both beaming at me as if I'd just scored a major point on *Oprah*. "Oh, please. You guys are gonna give me a yeast in—"

"Shut up, Jack," she said and kissed me. To Nikki she said, "Can you get started on the fingernail scrapings and take them and the blood and tissue samples up to the lab? I can get Jack to help me with the body."

Nikki said okay, and I said, "You can get me to do what?"

Jamie took hold of Allison's right thigh and grunted and said, "Help me turn her over, please."

"Oh, Jesus, okay. Wait a sec." I looked around for the latex glove dispenser, found it on a counter under a glass cabinet, put on a pair of gloves, then came back and took hold of Allison's shoulder and tried to lift it up. "Ow!"

I'd forgotten that my hand was still tender from last night. I shook it a few times to get the blood flowing.

"What happened to your hand?"

"Sam Kirby's jaw. And listen, Frankie and I have to get up to the pediatric ward in about ten minutes, so . . ."

"That's fine. Let me see it." She came over and examined my bruised knuckles. She palpated the bones on both sides of the joints and told me to make a fist. "Well, I don't feel a fracture, but since you're already here you should get it x-rayed."

"I'll be fine."

"Jack, I'm a doctor. You need to have an X ray."

"Yeah, yeah. If it's not any better tomorrow, I'll think about it. Now, let's just get this over with, okay?"

She shook her head, sighed, said okay, and went back to the other side of the examination table. As she did I noticed that there were no visible signs of trauma to the back, or what Dr. Jamie would call the posterior region of the body. We got her turned over, which wasn't easy—she'd gone into rigor. Then once she was on her back I averted my eyes and took off my gloves and went to the sink to wash up.

I told Jamie how Flynn had been calling me since seven A.M., pestering me with questions about the case, testing out a dozen different theories as to how Allison might've died without it being foul play. Nikki began scraping under Allison's fingernails. She was smiling at what I was saying, as if in response to some secret joke.

I dried my hands and sat on a metal stool. Jamie said, "I wouldn't worry about it, Jack. Uncle Horace tends to be a little sentimental when it comes to murder. He doesn't want anyone in his jurisdiction dying of anything other than natural causes. Especially not during the holidays."

"Yeah, but why does he have to keep pestering me? And by the way, murder is *not* his jurisdiction."

"No, but Rockland County is. And you should take it as a compliment, him asking you questions. It shows that he admires your detecting skills."

"He doesn't know squat about my detecting skills," I huffed, "or if I *have* any. He's just keeping me under glass."

"What are you talking about?"

"I went through something like this once myself. There was this guy on the squad. I was convinced he was boffing this exotic dancer I had a thing for."

She and Nikki exchanged glances. "I'm not sure I want to hear this," Jamie said. Nikki was still carefully scraping under Allison's fingernails with what looked like an Exacto knife, collecting the detritus in a small brown paper bag.

"It was a long time ago. Anyway, this detective I knew caught a murder case and I wangled myself onto the detail to keep an eye on him and this dancer. That's exactly what Flynn is doing."

She laughed. "You're saying he's jealous?"

"Sure. Jealous by proxy. For his nephew, Oren."

She shook her head. "That's the most ridiculous thing I've—" Her beeper went off and she unhooked it from her belt and glanced at the read-out. "Speak of the devil—"

"That's Flynn?"

"No, Wade Pierce, my divorce attorney." She reholstered the beeper. "Well, he'll just have to wait."

Nikki finished what she was doing and said, "So far no evidence of skin or blood, though there are some fibers. They look like cotton."

"Maybe from her apron?" Jamie and I said in unison.

Nikki said they could be and that she'd take them up to the lab and get started. After she left, Jamie said, "And by the way, Uncle Horace knows a lot more about your detecting skills than you think. He's been checking into your background."

"Oh, that's just peachy. Well, I guess I could open a kennel somewhere up in Alaska . . ."

"I don't know why you say that. He's found out about the honors you've won for your work with the major crimes unit."

"And why I'm no longer on the force?"

She was setting out her instruments of torture. She set down a scalpel and looked at me. "What you did was right, Jack. I don't know all the details—you're very stingy with facts sometimes—but I know if you refused to turn over one of your informers to the Manhattan DA's office, you probably—"

"The word is 'informant.' And he was just a kid who saw his whole family get murdered, that's all. And I'll be damned if I'm gonna let the prosecutor force him to take the stand and have the same thing happen to him three days later."

"See what I mean? I'm sure if you gave Uncle Horace a chance to hear your side he might agree with you."

I just grunted, then said, "I hope he hasn't found out who the witness is. Has he?"

"He didn't say anything to me about it if he did." She looked at the door, then at me. Quietly, even though Nikki was gone, she said, "Now I understand why you wouldn't tell me more about this last night. You're still protecting him, aren't you? Duke, I mean."

I shook my head. "I told you, I can't talk about it."

"Gotcha," she said, then eyed the table to be sure everything was in place. Then she changed the subject. "You know what I think would be great? If we worked together to solve this murder."

"Get serious."

She stopped and looked at me. "I *am* serious. I'm a pathologist, you're a detective—"

"—Ex-detective."

"We'd make a great team. Uncle Horace could hire you as a consultant, or something. Are you sure Frankie's okay?"

"Don't worry, he's fine. By the way, remember the teenage girl we saw at O'Neal's last night?"

"You mean the cute blonde you didn't stare at?"

"Was she cute? I didn't notice. Anyway, I thought I knew her. That is, she seemed sort of familiar, you know? I think she might be Allison's sister."

We both stopped and looked at the body, realizing for a moment, in the midst of our casual chatter, that this had been a woman with a family and friends who would probably miss her.

"Do you know where she lives?" Jamie asked.

"The sister? No, but I can find out, I think."

"Good. We need someone to ID the body. Allison didn't have any other family that we know of. Her ex-husband is on vacation in the Virgin Islands." She sighed. "Seems like everyone's on vacation but me." She put a blank tape in her portable cassette recorder.

I looked at my watch. "Wait a minute," I said, "she has another sister somewhere. Your mother told me about her."

She began examining Allison's skin. "Really? When did you speak to my mother?"

"This morning. I drove by and dropped off some Christmas presents."

"That's nice. So, the blonde," she went on, "is that why you snuck that second look at her?"

"Sneaked. And I didn't think you noticed. As I recall, you said you *liked* the fact that I didn't look at other women."

"I know. I said that to train you. That's what you do with dogs, isn't it? Positive reinforcement?"

I chuckled. "Yes, but what you're talking about is called 'successive approximation.' If you reinforce a dog for doing something similar to what you *want* him to do, he'll eventually learn to do the actual behavior on his own."

"See how smart I am?" She tapped the miniature microphone on the cassette recorder and said, "Test, test," and the record-level light flashed red. She put the recorder in the pocket of her surgical scrubs and clipped the mike to her V-neck. "So what happened with you and that dancer?"

"Who? Oh, yeah. Well, the detective I was jealous of happened to be gay and the dancer turned out to be not that exotic. And if you don't think Flynn is jealous, then why is he poking around? Homicide is not his responsibility."

"Yes, but it won't officially *be* a homicide until I finish the autopsy, now, will it?"

She had me there. "It's still a suspicious death. He should let the Camden PD handle it and leave me alone."

She ignored my comment and went to the supply cabinet and got out a pair of Plexiglas goggles. While she was doing that, I took a look at Allison's personal effects, piled neatly on a side table. Not much there: clothing, underwear, and a small scrap of paper with some writing on it. "What's this?"

"It's a website," Jamie said. "They give legal advice about wills and probate. It was in her apron." She switched on the circular saw to make sure it was working. An involuntary twinge ran up and down my spine in both directions at once.

"You're about to do that 'V' thing, aren't you?" I had to shout to be heard above the buzz.

"What 'V' thing?" she shouted back.

"You know, where you cut the body open?"

"It's called a 'Y incision' and it's usually done with a scalpel, not a saw. This is for cutting open the skull."

"Question is," I tried to breathe, "what am I doing here?"

"Keeping me company? This is my first official autopsy for the state and I'm a little nervous."

"You'll be fine. Besides, Frankie and I need to—"

"Don't tell me you've never been to an autopsy before."

I leaned over, switched off the saw, waited till it slowed down, and said, "You really like this, don't you."

"Like what?"

"Cutting people up, digging around inside."

"It's a medical procedure, Jack—to determine the cause and manner of death. And this is a rare opportunity for me. Most autopsies are done by the state medical examiner in Augusta or his assistant. But he's on vacation and she's overworked. And yes, I *do* like it. I like finding a tiny bit of scar tissue that shouldn't be there, or a slight discoloration in a vital organ. Anything I come across during an autopsy is pure discovery, and quite frankly, it's thrilling in a way."

"Good. But the thing is, you have beautiful hands, honey—"

"Oh, I get it." Her eyes almost twinkled. "You don't want to see my 'beautiful hands' pulling messy organs out of someone's dead body?" She laughed at me. "And here I thought you were a tough guy. You're not. You're just a big mush. You and Uncle Horace are almost exactly alike."

"I doubt it."

"You are. You're both a couple of blustering softies." She put on her Plexiglas goggles.

"If you say so. Now, if you don't mind, Frankie and I need to get upstairs before the room starts vibrating."

"What are you talking about?"

"Hey, at every autopsy *I've* ever been to, at some point the room starts vibrating and I have to go lie down somewhere."

"Like I said," she laughed, "you're nothing but a big softy."

"That's me," I said, then leaned in close and kissed the back of her neck. It was the only part of her body not covered in surgical scrubs, latex, or Plexiglass.

A little over an hour later I heard the door to the autopsy room open and Jamie came out. She was still dressed in scrubs, though she'd taken off the gloves and goggles. Frankie was lying at my feet. He looked up at her and wagged his tail.

"All done?" I said.

"Not quite. How was your visit to the pediatric ward?"

I told her it had gone quite well. There had been one kid in particular who'd really come out of his shell as soon as Frankie arrived. She said it sounded like Frankie was very good at his job, then pulled up a chair and sat with her back to me, pulling her long hair up on top of her head, exposing her neck for me to massage. I put down my paperback and obliged.

After a while I said, "I'm hungry." Frankie looked up and wagged his tail. (He always does that when he hears the word "hungry.") "I thought this was a lunch date."

"Sorry, I can't. I've got work piling up like crazy."

I kneaded her neck some more. A lovely sound came from deep in her throat. She was obviously enjoying the massage. "Do you think we could go someplace warm for Christmas?"

"That's a tough one," I lied.

"If it's the money, I'll pay. Oren wasn't able to spend *all* of it on coke. Did I tell you he sold our house and that he's now living on his boat? With that bimbo from Texas?"

"You did tell me. Anyway, it's not the money—though thanks for the offer—it's just that the kennel is usually full this time of year. And I don't think I can take off and leave Mrs. Murtaugh and Duke to handle things on their own."

She grunted. "You need more employees. Why don't you hire that guy with the beagles?"

"Who, Farrell Woods?" I laughed.

"What's so funny? He's always coming around asking you for a job. And he seems like he's really good with dogs."

"Oh, he is. Better than me, even. In fact, he was a dog handler with the K-9 corps in Vietnam. But he's also a pothead. Didn't you ever smell it on him?"

She shrugged. "As long as he's not high while he's at work, though . . ."

"Knowing him, he would be. Plus, I'm pretty sure he deals the stuff as well. Whenever he comes by, he and D'Linda spend a little time alone in his truck." (D'Linda is Mrs. Murtaugh's assistant groomer.) "But you know, I could talk to Sloan and D'Linda and see if they want some extra hours so maybe we *could* go to the Caribbean or something after New Year's." I told her all this knowing I had already booked us for a weekend in New York and a week in the Bahamas—Jamie's Christmas present—and that Sloan and D'Linda were already expecting to work all that week.

"Besides," I said, "I thought I was invited to spend the holidays with you and your mom."

She sighed, leaning into the massage. "You are, but . . . I don't know, I just need to get away from everything."

"We'll go in January," I said, then stopped the massage, but kept my hands on her shoulders. "I should take off. I'm supposed to meet a Lieutenant Coletti at the Camden PD."

She turned to look at me. "Danny Coletti?"

"You know him?"

She hesitated. "I know a lot of people." I gave her a look. "I thought you said you were over your jealous phase."

"I did, I am. You're just acting strange."

She sighed. "Oh, all right. He's had a crush on me since we were in high school together. We were friends for a while, or tried to be, but he really wanted to . . . *you* know . . . and it got weird." She seemed to feel guilty about it.

"It's not your fault. I'd be surprised if there was one guy in this whole state—hell, the whole world—who wouldn't want to '*you* know' with you if he had the chance."

She leaned her cheek against my left hand, which was still on her shoulder, and kissed it. "Don't say anything to him about us, okay?"

"Why would I? I'm old-school, remember?"

She smiled. "And speaking of jealousy, what was her name?"

"Whose name?"

"The stripper you told me about."

"Oh," I laughed. "Tatiana, I think. At least, that was her stage name. Her real name was Vicki or Debbie or something."

"I'll bet she's still in New York, pining for you."

"Actually, I think she married a dentist from New Jersey." I got up and so did Frankie. "So, Dr. Cutter, did you find out what killed Allison DeMarco?"

She stood up, sighed, and said, "Cardiac arrest, brought on by ventricular tachycardia."

"She had a heart attack?" She nodded. I said, "So Flynn was right after all. It was natural causes."

"Not necessarily."

"Why not?"

"I don't know. It just doesn't look right to me. There's no sign of degenerative heart disease. No scarring of the heart muscle or atherosclerosis. There was some tissue damage, but it was all recent."

"What about the blown pupil?"

"That's what really puzzles me. There's no skull fracture, no subdural hematoma, no brain damage, nothing."

"That's odd."

"If nothing shows up on the tox screen I may have to call Dr. Reiner in Florida and ruin his vacation." She yawned, stretched her arms, then turned her back and went to the autopsy room door. Over her shoulder she said, "One thing's for sure: even though I haven't figured out yet what killed her? If she *was* murdered, it's a double homicide. Maybe not legally speaking, but . . ." She turned to look at me. "Allison DeMarco was three months pregnant."

10

An affable redhead wearing a sharkskin jacket, a tan shirt, a green tie, and black wool pants stood behind a black and chrome desk and waved me into his office. He apparently had great taste in women (he was smitten with Jamie, after all) but it clearly didn't carry over to his taste in clothes. He pointed to a chair in front of and a little to the left of his desk.

"Come in and have a seat, Mr. Field. I'm Dan Coletti. Can I get you something to drink? Some coffee or soda?"

"I'm good." I showed him a brown paper bag I was holding. "Okay if I eat while we talk? I haven't had lunch yet."

"That's fine. Would you mind closing the door?"

I closed the walnut veneer door and saw that Sheriff Flynn was sitting behind it. He was twirling his big sheriff's hat around in his big lap.

"Hello, Field," he said. "I heard you moved to Chicago."

"I'm thinking about it. Or maybe Tahiti."

I sat down and so did Coletti. Flynn said, "So anyway, the priest says to the rabbi, 'Good Lord, Rabbi Silverstein, what did you say to him?' And the rabbi says, 'I told him *we* were married.'" Flynn laughed heartily and slapped his knee.

Coletti chuckled, then looked at the bagel I was taking out of my bag. "What have you got there?"

I shrugged. "I don't know, it's from that bagel place around the corner. Probably not very good, but . . ." To Flynn I said, "The one about the priest and the rabbi in the gay bar?"

Flynn gave me a sour look. "You heard it, huh?"

Coletti said, "From what I hear, they make great bagels."

"Maybe so, but the people that say it have probably never been to H & H or Zabar's. I only got this because I was starving and it was close by."

There was nothing on Coletti's desk but a beige telephone, a brass nameplate, and a manila file folder, so I put my bagel on the edge of his desk and unwrapped it. Then I got a carton of orange juice from inside my down vest and opened that. I looked around the room. It was the cleanest police station I'd ever been in and I told Coletti as much.

"Thanks, I guess. Can we get down to business?"

"Sure," I said and picked up my bagel to take a bite.

Coletti opened the folder. Inside was a police report, along with some Polaroids, and curled fax paper. Coletti said, "I understand you were acquainted with the deceased, Allison DeMarco, and that you've got her dog at your kennel."

"That's right." I took a bite of the bagel and chewed it. It was good. "Hey, this ain't bad," I said and took another bite. "Matter of fact, this is pretty damn tasty!"

Amused, Coletti asked, "What kind'dja get?"

"Onion with cream cheese and chives," I said, taking a bite. "Hey, this is really good." I grinned at the two men.

"Almost as good as the ones at Zorba's, huh?" Coletti said, then referred to the file. "I also understand you used to work homicide in New York."

"Zabar's," I corrected him, taking a swig of orange juice. "And I didn't actually work just homicide. I worked major crimes. And, since I have a background in psychology, I was also what you might call a criminal psychologist. And you know what? These are better than the ones at Zabar's."

"You were a shrink for perps," said Flynn.

"I guess you could call it that."

"I just did."

"Or criminal profiling," I said.

Flynn snorted and shook his head in disgust.

"Well, I hope you don't have any ideas about profiling anybody in our little investigation here," Coletti said.

"Me? Furthest thing from my mind. I'm happy running a

kennel." I pointed to Flynn. "I told the sheriff that." I sat back and used a napkin to wipe some cream cheese off my beard.

Coletti relaxed in his swivel chair and his warm smile warmed even more. "Long as we're on the same page."

I told him I thought we were, then went on to tell him what I knew about Allison, Tim Berry, Tara, and how I'd seen her, or her car at least, driving away from Allison's house the night of the murder. "She and Allison look a lot alike, so they may be related. That's about all I can tell you."

Coletti tapped a pencil on his desk for a bit, shook his head, and said, "Thanks for the background. I'm just curious about one thing. Are you investigating this on your own?"

"Me? No, not at all. In fact, just the opposite."

"Well, the thing is, Sheriff Flynn says you're convinced that Allison DeMarco was murdered. And it seems like you're kinda pushing that angle."

"I'm not 'pushing' anything," I said. "I'm just stating the facts. She *was* murdered. That much should be obvious."

He frowned. "How so?"

I made a frustrated sound. "You mean besides the blown pupil, the fact that she was barefoot, that there was blood on her slippers, that the knife was placed in the wrong hand, and that the back door was left wide open? What more do you need?"

"I don't know. We just got faxed the preliminary autopsy report. Dr. Cutter says she died of cardiac arrest."

"Oh, come on, that's what all preliminary reports say. You must know that: 'Victim was stabbed: cause of death, cardiac arrest. Victim was shot in the head with a shotgun: cause of death, cardiac arrest.'" I bit off some more bagel and chewed it. "Exactly how many homicides have you investigated?"

He looked at Flynn. They both shrugged. "Well, you're right. This is the first one we've had in about ten years or so. All I know is, it doesn't look that suspicious so far. Maybe her heart just stopped. It happens sometimes, you know."

"Sure," I nodded, "if there's a blow to the chest. It doesn't even have to be that hard. It's called *commotio cordis*. There was a famous case of a twelve-year old kid who got killed playing softball in a New York schoolyard. Got hit in the chest with a soft line drive. But if that's what killed Allison DeMarco, there would be no evidence of ventricular tachycardia, no damage to the heart muscle, and no blown pupil."

"Hunh. You sound a little like a coroner yourself."

"Yeah, well, don't mind me. I spend a lot of time read—"

"—I understand you dropped out of Harvard medical school. Is that right?"

"I don't know if it's right, but yes, I dropped out. I was thinking of becoming a psychiatrist and lost the calling." I looked at Flynn. "You've really been checking up on me, haven't you? I could've saved you the trouble and faxed you my CV and resume. I think I may have copies of my high school report cards, too." I turned back to Coletti. "I get the feeling Sheriff Flynn doesn't like me very much."

"They're still married," Flynn said hotly.

Coletti stared at me, then at Flynn, then he realized what Flynn had meant. "You're *doing* Jamie Cutter?"

I stared back at him for a moment, then got up to go. "Give me a call when you actually start your investigation."

"Sit down," Coletti said. I just stood there. His face was both red and apologetic. "Look, I'm sorry. That was inappropriate of me. Please, sit down. It's just that—"

"I know. She told me."

He blushed some more. There was a knock on the door and Carl Staub came in, holding a curled fax paper in his hand.

"This just came in from the Virgin Islands," he said. "It seems that Allison's ex-husband, Richard DeMarco, has been murdered."

Coletti stood up, took the fax in his left hand and looked it over. "Died of a knife wound," he read from the report. "Around ten this morning." He sat down and looked at me.

"Gosh," I grinned, "seems suspicious, don't it?"

Coletti didn't find that amusing. "You wanna stop being cute for a minute and maybe help us connect the dots here?"

"You're the one who said for me not to get involved."

Coletti sighed. "Fine, but you've been acting like a real smartass, okay? Like you know more than all us small-town hicks. I think maybe it's time for you to put your money where your mouth is, Field. Who knows—we might all learn something from the great wise-cracking detective from the big city."

Flynn snorted and shook his head again.

What could I say: the man had a point. "Well, I guess I could give you a thumbnail profile of your killer if you like, but I should warn you—it's not gonna stop me from being cute."

Flynn looked like he wanted to belt me. Carl Staub suppressed a smile. Coletti just shook his head.

Me? I didn't want to be inside a police station, talking with men whose job is to track down a killer. I'd done that and gotten tired of it. So tired, in fact, that I'd moved to Maine, at least partly to get away from it. I glanced out the window. Across the parking lot I could see the mill stream that runs through the center of town. I pictured myself walking along its banks, with Frankie and Ginger frisking in the fallow grass. I was reminded of how Ginger used to follow Allison from room to room and I wondered what it was like for her now that there was no more Allison to follow around.

"Okay," I sighed, "the two deaths are probably related. Now, this is just a thumbnail sketch, okay? But from what I know of Allison's personal life and the details of the crime scene, I'd say you should look for a well-educated white male, middle-aged or a little younger, definitely right-handed, someone who was well known to the deceased, who comes from an upper income bracket, and is originally from a warmer climate. Oh, and he has what's called an overnarcissized personality."

They all just looked at me. "Aren't you going to write any of this down, Lieutenant? The NYPD used to pay me a lot of money for this kind of bullshit. They still do, in a way." I smiled at Flynn. "Pension and disability benefits."

Coletti sat down. "Yeah, but isn't profiling really just a bunch of bullshit? I mean, you just said so yourself."

"Sorry, that was me being cute again. Although that is *one* view of profiling. And it's certainly a popular view among certain law enforcement personnel." I looked pointedly at Flynn.

"Yeah? And what's your view?" Coletti asked.

I told him I thought that profiling was a valid scientific discipline based on a knowledge of psychology, statistical analysis, and an awareness and understanding of past cases.

"Yeah, speaking of past cases," Coletti said, then went on to tell the story of a multiple homicide that took place in Boston and how a profiler from the FBI was brought in to help with the case. The profiler's explanation for how and why the murders took place ended up being totally off the mark and the case was eventually solved through routine police work.

"Yeah, I heard that story," I said. "Or saw it. But it didn't take place in Boston, it was in New York. And it didn't actually happen. It was an episode of *NYPD Blue*."

"It was? Jeez, I heard it from a guy who knows a guy worked the case. Maybe they based it on the real story."

"Sure they did," I said. "The same way they based—I don't know—*I Dream of Jeannie* on a real astronaut who found a woman in a bottle? Come on, Lieutenant. I'm sure whoever wrote that episode is good at what he does. But his job, basically, is to kill time between car commercials."

Flynn shook his head. "You know what gripes me about this profiling crap? You got this dead little girl out in Colorado and you got two different profilers working the case—one says the parents fit the profile of the killer perfectly while the other says the parents couldn't a possibly done it."

I shook my head. "The problem *there* is that it's just one murder. You can't do a proper profile without at least three separate crimes that are somehow linked together. It's like triangulating someone's position geographically. You need three points on the map in order to do it. Same with profiling. But I have to tell you, when it works, it's almost like looking your killer up in the phone book. It's that accurate."

Coletti sighed, opened his middle desk drawer, took out a steno pad, and got ready to write. "Okay. Explain."

"Explain what?"

"Why you think what you just said. All that crap."

"All right," I said. I explained that I thought the killer was probably well educated because he wanted to make the death appear to be due to natural causes and had been successful, at least so far. "You're still not convinced that it was murder. And Dr. Cutter hasn't found anything yet to prove that it was. You've gotta be pretty smart to fool her."

I explained that my theory that the killer was white and middle-aged was based mostly on statistical probabilities. "Most crimes of this type are committed by men—nearly ninety percent of them, in fact. As far as the killer's age is concerned, the crime was deliberate and fairly well thought out, though not very well executed. A younger man would have been more impulsive, an older man less so. The fact that the killer was probably white—well, this is Maine, folks. Not a lot of ethnic diversity in these parts.

"You sure you want me to explain all this? I have dogs I gotta get back to." I *did* have dogs to get back to, but I was also starting to get tired of the sound of my own voice.

Coletti shrugged. "I don't put much stock in this crap, as you're well aware. But anything that might help out . . ."

I sighed. "All right." I went on to explain my second and third points—that the killer was right-handed and that Allison probably knew him. I repeated what I'd already said about the knife and pointed out that there was no sign of forced entry. I also reiterated that she'd gotten the dog for protection.

"A lot of good it did her," Flynn said.

I sighed and agreed with him. "Fourth point: . . . what was my fourth point?"

Coletti said, "Upper income bracket."

"Oh, right. Statistics again. Allison had money, ergo, if the killer was someone she was on intimate terms with, he would probably come from a similar economic stratum. Also, Allison had some valuable artwork that wasn't stolen, so we know it wasn't a burglary. What was my next point? I forget."

Coletti looked up in the air, trying to remember. Carl Staub said, "You told us the killer came from a warmer climate."

Coletti said, "Now in the hell do you figure that?"

"The slippers," I said. "She had to have been wearing something on her feet—shoes, slippers, socks, *something*.

No woman goes around the house barefoot in the state of Maine this time of year, unless she's got heated floors in her house."

"Who the hell has heated floors?" Flynn wanted to know.

"The dogs in my kennel do. But that's beside the point. If the killer had grown up in this climate he would have replaced the slippers she was wearing with another pair."

"That's a stretch," said Coletti. "But let's say you're right. Let's say she *was* wearing the slippers with the bloodstains, and that the bloodstains happened during the murder." He looked at Flynn. "If there *was* a murder. Why wasn't there any blood anywhere else?"

"Who says there wasn't?" I said. "You won't know that for sure unless you luminol the kitchen. Or you could use phenolthaline . . ."

"Yeah, I'm familiar with the various chemicals used to detect hidden bloodstains, Mr. Field. But since there were no wounds on the body, where do these bloodstains come from?"

"From the killer," I explained patiently. "He must've been injured during the murder. Maybe she stabbed him. Why else would he hide her slippers?"

Coletti thought it over, looked at Flynn. "You seem to have given this a lot of thought."

I shrugged. "It's just a reflex. Sort of like a bad habit that's hard to break. By the way, the girl I mentioned? Tara something or other? She may be Allison's sister."

Coletti looked at Flynn. "She had a younger sister?"

"Well, I don't know for sure," I shrugged. "Though I *do* know she had an older sister. I also know her sister's husband was involved in some sort of local political scandal."

Flynn stared hotly at me for a moment and seemed about to say something but didn't. Coletti looked at Flynn but didn't say anything either. I'd touched on a hot topic, although I had no idea what it was. Maybe it explained Flynn's interest in the case—some personal angle I knew nothing about yet.

"I thought you said you weren't investigating this case."

I put my hands up. "I'm not. Can I help it if people tell me things? Oh," I remembered something, "I don't know if it's in the prelim, but Dr. Cutter told me that Allison was three months pregnant, so the father is another angle to consider."

"Interesting," said Coletti, writing it down.

"One other thing," Carl Staub interjected, "Richard De-Marco had connections with the mafia."

I found that hard to believe and said as much. "Since when do endocrinologists fool around with the mob?"

"Well, his father is Victor 'Slick Vic' DeMarco from Buffalo. He owns a carting and hauling business."

On hearing Buffalo mentioned, Flynn stared down at his lap. Coletti looked at him, bit his lip, and shook his head as if saying no to a stray thought that had wandered into his head.

Carl went on, "The story goes that Slick Vic didn't want his son mixed up in the family business, so he sent him to medical school on mob money. The two later became estranged. There might still be a connection with the murder, though."

"I doubt it," I said. "Hit-men use .22s, not knives. No, I'd say that money, not mob ties, is the angle to look at." I tried a friendly smile on Coletti. "I mean, you know what they say, 'Follow the money'—that's where you'll find your killer."

I stood up to go.

Coletti said "You think you've got this thing all figured out, don't you?"

"Hey, you're the one who asked me what I thought. Can I help it if I have strong opinions?" I looked at Flynn. "Another bad habit."

"You're just chock full of 'em, ain't ya?"

"Maybe. And maybe I'm wrong about everything I just said." I picked up my sandwich bag. "After all, I was wrong about these bagels. Now, if you gentlemen will excuse me, I've really got to get back to my dogs, though I may grab another bagel on the way home. I'm telling you, these are really *good*."

"Thanks for your input." Coletti stood up and shook my hand. "I don't know if your ideas are gonna pan out, exactly, but I appreciate it. That said, any other thoughts you have about the case, I'd appreciate it if you bring them to me first. No press, no personal investigations of your own, okay?"

I put my hand up. "Believe me, the last thing I want to do is get involved in another murder investigation. And I especially don't want any press on this. I'm a dog trainer now, not a detective." I went to the door.

Carl Staub stopped me. "You were wrong about one other thing there, Jack. It's true that Allison DeMarco had quite a lot of money. Ten million dollars, in fact."

We were all impressed.

"But I don't think following the money, as you put it, is going to help us find her killer. Not unless the dog did it."

We waited for the other shoe to drop.

"They found her will on the computer. She left everything she had to her Airedale."

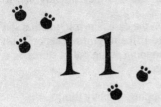

11.

They let me keep Ginger at the kennel instead of carting her off to Animal Control. There was a fair amount of paperwork involved but I didn't mind. Frankie and I had kind of gotten used to having her around. They made one concession, which I also didn't mind: they assigned a detail to watch my place in case whoever had killed Allison also decided to try and kill her canine "heiress." There was a radio car parked in shifts on the ridge above my property, about forty yards from where the county road and my driveway intersect. Mrs. Murtaugh— bless her—kept them supplied with hot coffee and blueberry muffins.

The toxicology report came back the next day and it turned out negative. There were no drugs, chemicals, poisons, or any other foreign substances in Allison's body. Actually, there was *one* thing: a trace amount of atropine from some prescription eyedrops. Not enough to kill her, just a normal dose. Jamie called me late Tuesday night to tell me this.

I was in bed at the time, nursing a nightcap of twelve-year-old Glenmorangie and trying to put myself to sleep by reading a book of essays by Jacques Lacan. His views on the mirror phase and its effects on narcissistic personality disorders seemed germane for some reason. Meanwhile, Frankie and Ginger were lying half-on and half-off Frankie's bed, each one chewing on a rawhide retriever and occasionally casting suspicious glances at the other dog's bone, as if it might somehow be better than the one they already had in their possession.

After Jamie caught me up on the case, she told me that she had Wednesday off, and would I like to go to Freeport with her and do some Christmas shopping at the outlet stores.

"Not on your life," I told her.

"Why not?"

"Because men don't go shopping, we buy things."

Miffed, she said, "What's the difference?"

I explained: "When a man needs or wants something, he goes into the store, finds what he's looking for, buys it, and walks out. A woman can't do that—or *won't*. She has to *look* at everything. She has to *talk* about everything. She has to spend hours *comparing* and *deciding* on every possible purchase. It drives men crazy."

"You mean it drives *you* crazy."

"Well, I'm a man . . ."

"You certainly are." She didn't sound pleased. We compromised. I told her that I'd be happy to accompany her to Freeport and even stroll through a couple of shops if she insisted, but as soon as she came up to me with something in her hand and said, "What do you think of this?" I had her permission to run to the nearest bar and stay there until she was through for the day. That wasn't quite the end of it, though: "You know, Jack, it wouldn't hurt you to get in touch with your feminine side once in a while."

"I'm already in touch with my feminine side. It's what I use to train dogs with. Have they found that Tara girl yet?"

"No, they've got warrants out for her and the waiter. And I always had the idea that animal trainers were all tough, macho guys with big boots and safari hats."

"A lot of them are like that. Mostly closet sadists who like hurting animals and rationalize it with all this nonsense about proving you're the alpha dog. Personally, I'm not sure there is such a thing, at least as far as a dog is concerned."

"So you keep telling me."

I took a sip of Scotch. "But you know what? Two of the best animal trainers in the world—and we're talking lions and tigers here, not helpless puppy dogs—are an effeminate gay couple living in Las Vegas. Talk about your feminine side."

"I wish you hadn't said that. Now when we make love I won't be able to stop thinking of Siegfried and Roy."

"Yes, you will. Trust me. So do they really think this Tara girl and our waiter are the killers?"

"That's the theory. How's your hand?"

I flexed it unconsciously. "A little better. Did they luminol the kitchen?"

"No. Danny said it's not worth the expense. It's tough to get the results admitted in court these days because it doesn't definitively prove the presence of blood, just protein."

I sighed. "I don't understand these local cops of yours. First they insist that I mind my own business, then they insist that I give them a profile, and then when I do, they ignore it. Tim Berry is left-handed! He shouldn't even be a *suspect* in this case, let alone have a warrant out for his arrest!"

"Well, he was seen by a witness having several very heated arguments with the deceased."

"What witness? And if Berry killed her, how did he do it? You still don't have a manner of death, do you?"

She sighed. "No, we don't. But we did a presumptive on the knife and found blood on the blade. It might not be enough for a DNA test, but this girl Tara's fingerprints are on the handle. Oh, and Dr. Reiner is back from Florida. I was a little worried that they were going to insist on doing another post in Augusta but I guess they trust me. And listen, I'll promise not to pester you with 'female' shopping questions if you promise not to go on and on about dogs anymore, okay?" There was a long silence from my end. "Jack?"

"Do you mean at all—ever? Or just on this trip?"

She sighed. "Okay. Just on this trip."

"It's a deal," I said. "And the fingerprints don't mean a damn thing because the knife wasn't the murder weapon."

Around eight the next morning Jamie showed up with a couple of girlfriends in tow: Eve and Arden I think their names were. They drove up as I was hosing off the woody on a little patch of grass to the left of the kennel between the Suburban and the willow in front of the house. Ginger was acting as my assistant: chasing the water from the hose and trying to bite it. Frankie just lay on the tailgate, licking himself.

Jamie parked her Jag in the gravel parking area to the left, and she and the girls—one a bottle blonde, the other a bottle redhead—got out. I dried off and came over and shook hands and invited them to look around while I went inside and got cleaned up. One of the girls—the redhead—asked, "You sure you don't mind if we come along?"

"To Freeport? Hell, no," I said. "It takes some of the pressure off me."

The other one said: "Can we say hello to the dogs?"

"Sure. Just don't get them too riled up."

"Do you have to keep them in cages, though?" the first one said, scrunching her face.

"No, I just do that 'cause I like being mean."

She acted like I'd just insulted her, which maybe I had. I shrugged it off and the two dogs and I started up to the house.

I heard Jamie say, "He's just kidding. He even lets some of the dogs sleep in bed with him."

"I bet you must love that." The two girls sniggled (a cross between a snort and a giggle).

Jamie said, "Let's just go look at the dogs, okay?"

When Frankie and Ginger and I came back out a few minutes later, Jamie and the girls were still inside the kennel and Tim Berry was parking his yellow TransAm next to Jamie's Jag.

"Mr. Field," he said, getting out. "I have to leave town for a while and I was wondering if you could board Thurston for me?" He took the basset pup from the car and handed him to me. I looked around for Jamie. Being a part-time medical examiner made her an officer of the court, meaning that if she saw Tim Berry it would be her duty to turn him in.

I scruffed Thurston's ears. "No problem," I said.

Berry looked at Frankie, who was trying to sniff Thurston's wiggly little butt. "Wicked cool dog," he said of Frankie. "What is he, part Dalmatian or something?"

"No, he's an English setter, though I think there's probably some Dalmatian blood somewhere in the breed's history."

"He sure looks like one. Only with long hair."

"Luckily he doesn't act like one." I lowered my voice. "Listen, the cops have warrants out for you and Tara, so—"

"I know. I guess that's why you was asking me all those questions about Allison, huh?" He hung his head. "I've screwed up everything. I'm turning out just like my dad. By the way, I want to pay you for the training session and the boarding."

He handed me a wad of money. Just then we heard the siren from the patrol car, followed by the squeal of tires as the on-duty officer peeled rubber on the county road and started to make the quick left-hand turn onto my long down-hill driveway.

Berry turned, startled, then with his left hand he pulled a .38 revolver out of his parka. The hairs on the back of my neck stood up. All three of the dogs started barking at once—either at Berry, or at the siren, or at each other.

"Look, don't be stupid," I told him.

"You don't understand. She didn't kill her mom, Mr. Field!" He waved the gun aimlessly. "But they'll never believe her like I do. Besides, it's all my fault anyway."

My feet seemed to be stuck in quicksand and my mouth was dry as burnt toast. "Call me Jack," I croaked, "and *I* believe you. Just put the gun down before someone gets hurt."

"No, I gotta get outta here . . ." He fired at the cop car but it kept coming down the driveway at a fairly good clip. Berry fired off another shot then ran to his car. Frankie ran up to the front porch of the house, taking the high ground. Ginger stayed behind my leg where she felt safer.

Jamie and her two friends, along with Mrs. Murtaugh, came running outside to see what was going on. When Mrs. Murtaugh saw Berry getting in his car, waving the gun around, she said: "Oh, my . . ." I handed Thurston to her and told her to take him inside. She got hold of the squealing little worm and did as I'd asked. When Jamie saw what was happening she said, "Uh-oh," and I told her to take her friends inside and she did. I probably should have gone with them, but didn't.

The police vehicle careened into the parking area, throwing up a big wave of gravel. Berry backed his yellow TransAm in a wide arc—just missing the woody and me by

inches—then fired his pistol again with his left hand, while
steering with his right. A bullet shattered the police car's
windshield. The Camden officer jammed on the brakes,
opened his door, got out, knelt down, and used the car door as
a shield to return fire.

He missed Berry and I felt someone tap me on the shoulder. Berry gunned his car around the police vehicle and up toward the county road. Frankie jumped off the porch and
began chasing Berry's car, barking and carrying on as if he'd
successfully chased him away. I gave him his recall signal,
"Heyo!" and he turned on a dime and came running back to
me.

The Camden officer jumped back in his car, ground it into
reverse, spun around wildly for a few seconds, then finally
took off after the determined young waiter. After his siren
faded in the distance, Jamie and the others came back outside.

Jamie looked at me in shock. "Jack, you've been shot."

I followed her gaze and saw that she was right. Blood was
dripping from the left sleeve of my Levi's jacket.

"I didn't even feel it," I said stupidly.

"Do you have a first-aid kit?" she asked.

"Sure, it's in the, uh . . . it's in the . . ."

"Alice!" Jamie barked at Mrs. Murtaugh, "I need your
first-aid kit, now! He's going into shock."

"Oh," said Mrs. Murtaugh. She seemed to be going into
shock herself, but then she snapped to. "Oh, yes, I'll . . . right
away." She turned and ran back inside.

Frankie was licking my hand, which was dripping with
blood. I told him to leave it and he did, but there were also
splotches on the gravel. Ginger was licking them and Frankie
joined her.

Eve or Arden—I'm not clear which—looked at the dogs
and said, "Can't you stop them from doing that? It's disgusting!"

"Sorry, these are real live dogs, princess, not Disney car-
toons. They happen to like the taste of blood. It's a part of
their natural instincts." I felt lightheaded as I said it.

She glared at me, then turned to her friend—the blonde—
and made a disagreeable face.

Jamie led me over to the woody and sat me down on the

tail-gate, though I insisted on covering it with a towel first. (I love that car.) Mrs. Murtaugh brought out the first-aid kit. Jamie helped me take off my Levi's jacket and flannel shirt. She used some gauze and a lot of pressure to slow the bleeding. The bullet had gone through the left deltoid muscle, just above the collar bone, and had grazed an artery. I was feeling more and more lightheaded, still I told Mrs. Murtaugh to keep Thurston separate from the older dogs—he hadn't had all his shots yet—and to have Duke start him on a house-breaking schedule, and to make sure he got only puppy food, not the adult kind, since he needs the extra protein. She said she would.

"Yo, what's all the ruckus?" Duke had just woken up and came walking around the front of the woody, tucking in his shirt and rubbing his eyes. When he came around the back and saw me and all the blood, his knees buckled. "Oh, no," was all he could say. "Oh, no, oh, no."

"I'm okay, Duke. It's just a scratch."

"Oh, no," he repeated. The blood must have reminded him of the night his family was murdered. He kept saying it over and over: "Oh, no . . . oh, no . . ."

Jamie said, "He's going to be all right, Duke. I'm taking him to the hospital right now."

Duke said, "A'ght. I'm comin' too."

I said, "No, you've got to stay here and help Mrs. Murtaugh with the dogs. I'll be okay. I'm in good hands."

He just stood there looking at me with the saddest, most helpless eyes.

Then, as Jamie and her friends were helping me into the car, the redhead said, "Shouldn't we call the police?"

"Why," I said, "so they can come shoot me again?"

Under her breath the other one said, "Not a bad idea."

I ignored them. To Jamie I said, "Come on, honey, don't make me go to the hospital. It doesn't even hurt. Really."

"That's because you're in shock," she said.

"No, it isn't. It's because I'm getting in touch with my masculine side," I said. Then I passed out.

I was in a bed with too many pillows. Jamie was there and so was a man with a big hat. Jamie was sitting next to me. The man was standing by the door, twitching his mustache and twirling his big hat. I wanted him to leave. Leave me alone with Jamie, I wanted to say, but all I said was, "Big hat."

Jamie looked over at the hat and agreed with me. Then she brushed the hair back from my forehead. It felt nice. She said, "I guess the drugs are working, huh, Jack?"

"Feel good," I said. "What happened . . . Eve Arden?"

"Who?" she asked.

"Your friends, Eve Arden. Go shopping without you?"

"You mean Evelyn and Ardyth?"

"That them?" I licked my lips. My mouth was dry.

"That's them. We're going on Friday. I had a patient to take care of," she patted my knee, "so I switched shifts." I licked my lips again and she poured me a glass of water. "Lift your head up a little." She helped me take a sip.

I sipped the water, then said, "Maybe I'll come, too."

"Un-huh," she said sarcastically. "And maybe you'll stay in bed, mister. You just got shot, remember?"

I feel fine, I wanted to say. But the bed was warm and comfortable and I *was* a little sleepy, so I agreed with her. Time enough to argue about it later.

13.

Mrs. Murtaugh called around noon and told me that her granddaughter, Audrey Stafford, was home for the holidays. She and her husband were students at Boston College and she'd done a little dog walking to make ends meet. She wondered if it would be okay for her to help out while I was in the hospital, and how much could I pay her? I mentioned an hourly rate.

"That's a lot more than you pay Duke, isn't it?"

"Not that much more. Besides, Duke lives in the guest house rent free and eats his meals out of my kitchen. And by the way? I won't actually be in the hospital much longer."

"Really? Did Jamie say you could come home?"

"No. But I feel fine. How's Duke holding up?"

She sighed. "He's terribly worried about you but he won't talk about it. You know how he is."

"Well, tell him I'll be home soon. When can Audrey start?"

"She's here now. She's playing with Ginger."

"Really? I like her already."

I was about to hang up when she said, "Oh, by the way, there was a lawyer who came by. What was his name? Let me see if I can find . . . he gave me his card . . ."

"A lawyer? What does he want? To sue the Camden Police for shooting me?"

"No, it was about Ginger."

"Oh, yeah, I almost forgot," I said, "she's a millionaire now. She's going to *need* a lawyer."

Mrs. Murtaugh laughed. "Not a lawyer *for* the dog, you idiot. He said it was *about* the dog. Custody and the like. Oh, here it is: Wade Pierce." I recognized the name of Jamie's divorce attorney. "Do you want his telephone number?"

"No thanks. If it's really important he'll be in touch."

Sure enough, an hour later, while I was arguing with a big matron of a nurse about whether or not I could leave the hospital without Dr. Jamie's permission, there was a quick knock at the door and a wire-haired young attorney with wire-frame glasses and a wiry build came in the room. He was wearing a black nylon sweatsuit with purple and orange trim and a dark blue cotton headband, and was carrying a black squash bag with a shiny orange racquet sticking out. He was sweating.

"Mr. Field? Uh, my name is Wade Pierce. I was, uh, Allison DeMarco's attorney. I need to speak, uh, speak to you about her dog?"

That's nice, I thought. I'm lying in a hospital bed after being shot by the police and this guy doesn't even ask me how I'm feeling? Or express sorrow over Allison's death?

"Don't try anything funny," the nurse said, taking my jeans out of the tiny closet next to the bathroom. "Just to be on the safe side, I'm gonna take these to the nurse's station. You can have 'em back as soon as Dr. Jamie says it's okay." She brushed past Pierce, taking my Levi's with her.

"Hey!" I complained to Pierce, "she stole my pants! That's against the law, isn't it?"

"I don't know. I think they have to follow certain protocols, you know, based on a patient's, uh, well-being and—"

"Bullshit. What kind of lawyer are you? Any patient has the right to leave a hospital AMA, don't they?"

"AMA?"

"Against medical advice."

"Well, yes, now that you, uh, I suppose that, under certain circum—uh—stances, yes, the patient does have the right—"

"Hey, are you all right? You look like you could use a towel or something." He was really sweating.

"Oh, that." He produced a handkerchief and wiped his brow. "No, I, just, uh, just finished playing squash with a client at the Samoset and, uh, I didn't have time to shower. I wanted to see you as soon as possible. Okay if I come in?"

"Sure, why not." I fluffed up a couple of pillows, leaned back in the bed, and put one arm behind my head. The other one was too sore. "What's all this about the dog? I thought you were Allison's divorce attorney."

He came in and sat down, somewhat gingerly, favoring his right side. "I think I threw my back out," he laughed, "you know, on the, uh, the courts. And around these parts you tend to, uh, wear a number of hats. I'm also the executor of her will." He unzipped a compartment in his bag and pulled out a file folder. "The *original*, uh, that is. The will that the police found probably won't—" he coughed "—hold up in court."

"Dogs can't inherit money in the State of Maine, huh?"

"No, it isn't that. It is a bit unusual, but it's, uh, perfectly legal. No, the problem is that the newer will wasn't witnessed or notarized. Technically, uh, it may, it, uh, it may be invalid."

I was starting to be hypnotized by his self-interrupting manner of speech. Still, I told him it was my understanding that if a will isn't witnessed or notarized it's *automatically* invalid: not "technically" and not "maybe." He nodded yes, but explained that he'd received a certified letter from Allison two days before her death, notifying him of her intention to change the will and appoint a new executor. The letter also detailed explicit changes she wanted made in the new will. Pierce explained that this fact made the matter a little, uh, sticky—that the letter may have possibly constituted legal intent.

"I guess I can see that. So who's the new executor?"

"A law student by the name of Tim Berry. Are you all right? Should I ring for a nurse?"

"No, I'm okay. I'm uh, I'm just, uh, just a little surprised." Great. Now he had *me* doing it. "Do you have any, uh, any idea why Allison named him executor?"

"Not, uh, no, not really. I understand that he's the one, uh, the one that shot you? Or . . . ?"

"No it was a Camden Police officer. He tried to shoot Berry but got me instead. You can sue them for me if you like. That's a joke. So why do you need to see me?"

"Uh, well," he opened a file folder and pulled out what

looked like a legal document of some kind, then uncapped a pen and said he needed me to sign an agreement—meaning, I supposed, the document in his hand—giving up any and all legal claims to Ginger; that I was her temporary custodian, nothing more.

I told him I had no problem with that, unless he thought I was taking care of Ginger just so I could weasel my way into Allison's will.

"Uh, no, no, of course not," he lied. "I'm a dog lover myself. I'm just, uh, looking out for my client's interests. You know, uh," he smiled, or tried to seem like he was smiling, "Ginger's a great dog. She and I used to take walks together around the, uh, around the lake. She was really responsive to me. Very obedient, you know?"

"Of course I know," I was about to say, "I *trained* her," but Jamie walked in, before I could say anything. "I hear you've been giving my nurses a hard time." She glowered at me.

I smiled sweetly. "Tell them it's nothing personal, sweetheart. I give everyone a hard time."

"I know, I told them." She saw Wade Pierce. "Oh, hello, Wade. What are you—"

"Hi, Jamie. Uh, we were just, uh, discussing the legal, points about Mr. Field's, uh, custody of Allison's dog. Have you, uh, found out how she, uh, you know, how she died yet?"

"I can't comment on that, Wade. You know that. At any rate, I'll let you two get back to whatever you were discussing." She turned back to me, "But you're not leaving this hospital until I say so. You got that, mister?"

"Yes, Mommy."

"Uh, Jamie," Pierce stopped her, "don't go on my account. This should only take a second. Really."

She stayed. He got up and brought his pen and his legal document over to the bed, stood over me and put them in my hands—the pen in my left hand and the document in my right. I got sensible for once, handed them right back and said, "Tell you what, why don't you fax a copy to my lawyer? Let her look it over, and if she says it's okay, I'll be happy to sign it. She'd kill me if I signed anything without letting her read it first—you know how lawyers are." He gave me a

slightly murderous look. Jamie looked up at the ceiling and
shook her head. "Hey." I defended myself. "I'm just
saying . . ."

"Well, you know, the thing is," Pierce said in his usual in-
direct fashion, "I, uh, I'm going to be out of town tomorrow
and I, uh, I really do need to get this cleared up right away."

"Fine. Then you'd better fax it to her as soon as possible."
I gave him Jill Krempetz's name and was about to give him
her fax number but he said he knew Jill. Then he packed his
bag and I stopped him from going: "Let me ask *you* something: who stood to inherit under Allison's *old* will?"

He hesitated, taking the opportunity to wipe his brow
again. "I'm really not at, uh, liberty to, uh, discuss that."

"Oh, sure, I understand," I said as he turned to go. "It's
okay to come down here and try to get me to sign something
while I'm high on morphine, but—"

"Actually," Jamie said, "it's Demerol."

"Demerol?" I looked at Jamie. "Now you know what to
get me for Christmas." She chuckled and shook her head.

Pierce sighed. "It's kind of, uh, complicated, but suffice it
to say that the, uh, the bulk of her estate would have gone to
Richard, her, uh, her ex-husband." We must have looked surprised, because Pierce shrugged. "I can't explain. I guess she
still loved him in a way. Family was important to her, and
other than an older sister who's somewhat incapacitated and,
uh, not, you know, capable of handling her, uh, her own af-
fairs, I guess Richard DeMarco was her only family."

I nodded, turned to Jamie and said, "Don't you need someone to ID the body?" She said yes and I said, "Is it still in the
basement?" She said it was. "Who better than her attorney?"

Jamie looked at Pierce. He looked at his watch, then
sighed and said to make it quick. Jamie asked him if he could
wait in the hall for a moment or two while we talked in private. He sulked but said okay and got out his cell phone and
left.

Jamie came over and sat next to me on the bed. "Let's add
a few things up, shall we?"

"Sure, sweetheart, glad to. I'm not sure I like that look on
your face, though. What things, for instance?"

"Well, for instance, you antagonized my Uncle Horace,

who's one of my favorite people in the world, no matter what form of skunk his nephew turned out to be as a husband. Then you upset my best friends Evelyn and Ardyth, and nearly get them killed—"

"Now wait a second, that wasn't my—"

"Let me finish. And now you seem to be deliberately trying to ruin my relationship with my divorce attorney?"

"Honey, I'm telling you, there's something screwy about that guy. Have you listened to him talk? It's like he's reading his lines off a very slow Teleprompter. I don't know, maybe he's drunk and trying to hide it—my friend Lou Kelso used to talk and sweat like that when he was drinking a lot. Or maybe he has some minor form of aphasia. If he were nervous or shy that would be one thing, I mean it might explain his strange locutions. But this guy, he's not shy at all, he's cold and arrogant and—"

"—His strange what?"

"Strange locutions, his manner of speech. You know, the Ally McBeal sort of way he, uh, uh, uh, you know, *talks*?"

"Oh, that. Well, he's a lawyer. Maybe he's just overly careful in how he chooses his words. Or it may be that he's distracted, you know? He has a lot on his mind right now, what with his marina project at Owl's Head being on the rocks, and then this whole thing with Allison. They were very close."

"Really?"

"No, not like that."

"No, I mean about his marina project being on the rocks."

"Oh, no, don't even think about it. You think Wade—?"

"Hey, at this point everyone who *knew* her is a suspect. Unless they have an alibi. Where is Pierce from?"

"He's lived in Camden all his life."

"Oh, well," I said, remembering my theory that the killer came from a warmer climate, "I guess that lets him off the hook. Maybe."

"God, I hope so. The thing is, Jack—what I'm trying to say is, please try not to antagonize people. Just as a favor to me? And try to make it up to Flynn and Eve Arden."

"Okay, I promise."

"And apologize to Wade Pierce."

"Oh, all right," I huffed. "But I'll bet you anything he doesn't really play squash." She gave me a dangerous look. "Okay, okay. I'll apologize. Besides, I may need his help to figure out who killed Allison DeMarco."

She smiled. "You're going to find out who killed her?"

"Well, I know for sure it wasn't Tim Berry."

"I don't know, Jack. Uncle Horace told me they found a spare key to Allison's house on top of the back porch light. And Tim Berry's fingerprints are all over it."

"That's interesting. Have they found him yet?"

"No, he and his girlfriend got away."

"Hmmm. Good for them. Or not so good. So that's how they think the killer got in, the spare key?" She nodded. I said: "Well it wasn't him, though I would like to get my pants back so I can go have a look at that porch light."

"Try to get it through your head, Jack: you're not going anywhere until—wait a minute. Who do *you* think killed her?"

"If I tell you will you give me my pants back?"

"No."

"It doesn't matter. I can't tell you who the killer is until I know for sure myself. But it wasn't Tim Berry and it wasn't his girlfriend. Oh, by the way, she's Allison's daughter, not her sister like I thought." I repeated what Tim Berry had told me outside the kennel, then said, "How would you feel about running some more lab tests?"

"The ones we ran were conclusive, Jack. I *told* you that. There were no foreign substances in her system."

"Yes, but what if she was killed by an abnormal amount of something *not* foreign? You know, an indigenous substance?"

"You mean en*dog*enous, like a hormone?" She got an aha look in her eye and said, "You know what, you may be onto something! Adrenaline, thyroxin, or any number of hormones in the right combination could cause a heart attack. And Richard DeMarco was an endocrinologist! You think he killed her?"

I added it up. "He died of a knife wound, and if what Pierce said is true—that he would've inherited most of Allison's money under her old will—that would certainly give him a motive for killing her. That is, *if* he knew she was planning to change it. Otherwise, I don't know. Let's wait and see what the new tests show."

"I'll run them right away." She smiled and kissed me. "So I guess we're going to be a detective team after all."

"Well, it would be nice if *someone* around here knew what the hell they were doing. Besides, I feel bad for our waiter. And I promise I'll try to make it up with Flynn and Eve Arden."

"You mean, Evelyn and Ardyth."

"Them too. I guess I'm kind of hard-headed sometimes."

"I guess you are."

"And stubborn."

"That too."

"It's because I was overnarcissized as a child."

She laughed. "I could've guessed."

"But you still love me, don't you?"

She stroked my forehead. "Yes, though I don't know why."

"Me neither. Now, can I have my pants back?"

"No."

14

Duke came to visit and brought me a new pair of jeans—which I'd asked him to do—and we sneaked out the back way while Jamie was busy in the lab. We drove out of the lot and parked across the street, then I sent Duke back inside to get my wallet and keys. Since I was now off the hospital grounds the nurses gave in and let him have everything.

We drove over to Allison's house with Duke at the wheel—my shoulder was too sore to steer properly—but halfway there I had second thoughts about leaving the hospital. The drugs were starting to wear off and I was sweating through my clothes.

"You okay?" Duke asked. "How's your shoulder?"

"It hurts."

He nodded and looked back at the road, his chin trembling a little. "I shoulda been there," he said.

"Why? So you could get shot, too?"

"I just shoulda been there, that's all."

I let him drive a bit, struggling with his emotions, then I said: "You're getting to be pretty good behind the wheel."

He seemed surprised and happy. "You think so?"

"Yep. You've got a knack for it. We may have to get you a real driver's license one of these days."

He smiled again. "That'd be a'ight."

"So, how's Audrey doing with the dogs?"

"Mrs. Murtaugh's granddaughter? She's cool. She says 'No!' a lot, though. Scully and Mulder are scared of her."

"They're scared of everybody. It's the Toland kids—they torture those poor little Pomeranians. When we get back I'll teach her how to use the Distract-Praise-Focus formula."

"I already taught it to her."

"Really? That's great, Duke."

It was good to see him smiling and happy again. I'd been waiting for the right time to get him to open up about his family's murder. His mother and father, an older sister, and an older brother were all gunned down in their apartment on Manhattan Avenue by drug-dealing gang members. The older brother had been peripherally involved in a dispute between two rival gangs. One of the gangs took vengeance. When my partner and I arrived at the scene, I found Duke hiding in a closet, trembling, in tears. He was thirteen at the time. He said something to me then, similar to what he just said in the car: "I shouldn'ta been hiding. I shoulda died with 'em."

It's called "survivor's guilt," I wanted to tell him. It's perfectly normal to feel that way, but it isn't real. I've tried to broach the subject with him a number of times since then, but he always shuts down when I bring it up. You can't force a kid to deal with something he's not ready to deal with. So instead I teach him things, like how to drive, and I praise him when he does it well. When he struggles, I patiently teach him how to do it better. It's sort of like dog training.

"Yo, Jack? What's a knack mean?"

"A knack?"

"You said I had a knack for driving. What's it mean?"

"It means a natural ability, or talent. Like, you know, Tiger Woods has a knack for playing golf."

He nodded his head. "Yeah, that's a'ight. I got a knack for drivin', just like Tiger Woods got a knack for playin' golf." He looked at me. "Just like you got a knack for pissin' people off." I let him have that one. It was good to see him smiling as he drove us the rest of the way to the murder scene.

15

When we got to Allison's house Duke helped me out of the car. He was very attentive, like a natural-born orderly. I went up the back steps to look at the porch light, where the spare key had been found. I told Duke to stay in the yard as my lookout. Another old habit: you don't want civilians wandering around, accidentally destroying evidence.

The concrete steps were already scuffed and dirty from all the activity at the scene. Allison had painted them slate blue a week or so before the murder. It had rained a few days afterward, then the weather had been clear and dry ever since.

The porch light was brass-plated, with beveled glass panes. Unlike most, it was not situated directly over the kitchen door, but a little to the left, out of the way of the main traffic. I noticed that the blue surface of that portion of the concrete right underneath the porch light wasn't scuffed at all, though it was still covered with the dusty film you get after wet weather. I got down and scanned it from a horizontal angle.

"Whatcha lookin' for?" Duke asked.

"I don't know. Footprints?"

"Yeah? Find any?"

"A couple. About a size fourteen too, I'd say. I struggled to my feet—my injured shoulder and hand weren't helping me any—and looked up at the porch light. If I stood on my tippie-toes I might be able to stash a key behind it, but most likely not. And Tim Berry was six inches shorter than I.

I came down the steps and Duke followed me back to the car.

"Where to, boss? I kinda like driving you around. Maybe I could move to Hollywood and get me a job as a limo driver. What do they call that in French?"

"A chauffeur," I said. "Let's go to town."

As we pulled onto the road I saw an empty black Dodge Ram Prospector in the driveway of a neighboring cabin, just sitting there with its motor running. A white cloud of exhaust gave it away. I tried to get a look inside the cab but couldn't see anyone. Maybe they were in the house, letting the car warm up first. Then, a few miles down the road, I happened to glance in my side-view mirror and saw the same black Dodge truck—or another one just like it—a couple of yards behind us.

We got to town and I had Duke drop me off in front of Peter Ott's tavern. I gave him my credit card and a list of books I wanted him to pick up for me at The Owl and the Turtle.

"You crazy? A black kid with a white man's credit card?"

I laughed. "Don't worry. Talk to Tom or Margot. They know me—I clean out their inventory every couple of months."

"Okay, so what do you want, boss? A copy of each book?"

"No, buy every copy they have. There's a cold front moving in. I feel like building a big fire tonight."

While we were talking, a black Dodge pick-up turned off Elm, drove past, and parked across the street. No one got out.

"When you're done I need you to call Otis Barnes at the *Camden Herald*," I said. Otis Barnes was a good friend of one of my best clients, Kate Hughes. She'd named her Hungarian viszla after him. And she'd been so happy with Otis's (the dog's) training she'd told Otis (the editor) about me and he'd written a nice profile on me for the local paper. He was a good guy.

"Have him meet me at the police station in half an hour. Tell him I've got some background on the murder case.

Then you can head back to the kennel. I'll catch a ride home."

He said okay and I went into Peter Ott's and then into the kitchen and out the back door and out onto Sharp's Wharf, past the docked sailboats. I shocked the hell out of a big pelican who was sitting on the wooden railing near the harbor master's office. Since it was winter I guess he thought he had the place to himself. He jumped up in the air, then took off and swooped down toward one of the stationary mooring docks where he landed and squawked at me from a safe distance. I circled around toward Main Street and into the back door of Gina Staub's shop.

Sasha was happy to see me. She sat down and pushed her front paws at me and wagged her tush, in lieu of her tail. I got down to her level and waved my hands around her jaws, teasing her to bite me, and she grrred and mouthed me playfully.

Tall and slender, with dark hair and brown eyes, Gina Staub, Carl's sister, came over laughing at us. "I still don't understand why you let her do that."

"Let her? I'm encouraging her. As long as she knows it's a game, it's actually quite healthy. If she gets too riled up, tease her with a chew toy and let her champ on that for a while. She hasn't been biting the customers again, has she?"

"No. I don't know why, but it seems to have worked."

Gina's partner, Leslie, with clear blue eyes, short blondish hair, and a stocky frame, came downstairs from the office. There was no one else in the store, so she came over and put her arm around Gina and gave her a kiss on the lips.

"We were just talking about Sasha's biting," Gina said, putting her hand in Leslie's.

"You did a good job with her," Leslie said, her blue eyes flashing. "Although she did bark at Sam Kirby the other day."

"Well," I said, "if she growled at Kirby she's only being sensible. That's my opinion."

"True. But then, none of us has had the kind of soap opera upbringing Sam Kirby had. Or so the rumor goes."

This rumor was news to me, but as they gazed at one another I felt awkward about asking Leslie for more information. They looked like they wanted to be alone. I asked Gina if she'd do me a quick favor and have Carl tell Dan

Coletti I'd like to see him in about a half-hour, and for Carl to meet me at the Camden Deli right away. She said she would and I left, going out the front door and up the block where I got a table and a menu and waited for Carl Staub to arrive.

It only took him five minutes.

16

"When Gina called I thought it was something serious."

"It *is* serious," I said, blowing on a spoonful of clam chowder. "It's a murder investigation. Have a seat."

The waitress came by with another menu. Carl sat down and said, "Coletti told you not to investigate on your own." The waitress shifted her weight and tapped her pencil on her order pad. Carl opened his menu and said, "I guess I'll have the chowder . . ." The waitress took the menu and walked away.

"That was before I got shot by one of your brothers in blue." I had another spoonful of chowder. "Now it looks like it's up to me to make sure the proper person is arrested."

"You don't think Tim Berry and his girlfriend did it?"

"Not even close," I laughed. "By the way, where did Sam Kirby say he found the spare key to Allison's house?"

"On the porch light, out back. But why did Berry run, then? Doesn't that show he's got a guilty conscience?"

"Maybe. Or maybe he's just stupid," I said and stood up. "How about giving me a ride home?"

"Uh, okay. My car's over at the police lot, though."

"Good. You told Coletti I need to talk to him?"

He nodded. Just then the waitress arrived with Carl's chowder. He sat there looking at it longingly. I put some money on the table.

"Let's go," I said. "We're losing daylight."

We left and walked up Main Street to the bend in the highway. I asked Carl about his ambitions with the Camden PD.

"What do you mean?"

"I mean do you want to move up through the ranks? Maybe become a detective someday?"

"Sure," he sighed, "but it'll never happen."

"Why not?" We waited at the light, crossed the highway, and walked down a back street toward the police station.

"You know why not. Because of my sister." His face burned a little as he said it. When he saw that I didn't believe him, he said, "This isn't New York. People around here tend to be more prejudiced. Maybe they don't come out and say it, but . . ."

"You're full of it, Carl. Your sister is a respected businesswoman. No one on the force is going to pass you up because Gina has a same-sex life partner. Grow up."

"It's pretty obvious you're not from around here."

"It's pretty obvious that you're letting your own feelings ruin your chances at advancement. Remember I asked you where Kirby found the spare key? I already knew where the key was *found* when I asked you that question."

"Then how did you know it was Kirby who found it?"

"I didn't. I just had a hunch it was Kirby, and you told me—unintentionally—that my hunch was correct."

He made a disgusted sound. "Me and my big mouth."

"Exactly. For future reference—if you ever want to become a real detective—that's a good way to get information. Or I should say, confirmation. Act like you already know the answer to part of the question.

"I'll let you in on another little secret: the reason I had a hunch it was Sam is because I think he planted the key there."

"Huh," he said, "I wouldn't put it past him."

"Look, Carl, I think you could be a good detective if you just got over yourself a little and started concentrating on your own abilities instead of what you imagine other people are thinking about you and your sister. I'd be happy to give you some pointers from time to time if you like."

"Why would you do that? I mean, it's awful nice of you—"

"Honestly? I need someone to help me do an end run around the department, and I think you might have the guts."

"I don't like the sound of that."

"Don't worry. I can handle Coletti and the Camden PD. I worked fifteen years in New York, remember? So first of all, what kind of vehicle does Sam Kirby drive?"

"An old black Dodge Prospector," he said. "Why?"

I told him about seeing Kirby's truck near Allison's house and how he'd followed me and Duke into town. Carl laughed a sour laugh. "He's probably still pissed off about how you cold-cocked him the other night." Then, when we got to the station house, he said: "How's your shoulder feel?"

"Except for the fact that it's got a hole in it? Fine."

He said he was sorry about what happened and I told him it wasn't his fault and asked him if he wouldn't mind "borrowing" a few things from the evidence locker. Shocked, he shook his head and said no, quite vehemently. I talked him into it.

When we got to Coletti's office Sheriff Flynn was there in his usual seat, waiting for us.

"You paying rent here now?" I said.

"Cute," he said.

"You wanted to see me?" Coletti asked.

"Yeah." I nodded toward Flynn. "In private."

Coletti sighed and said, "Give us a moment, would you?"

Flynn got up from his chair and he and Carl left. Flynn to wait outside, eavesdropping by the door, Carl Staub to get the things I'd asked him to get from the evidence locker.

I sat down in *my* usual spot. Coletti stood behind his desk. "So, what's on your mind?"

I said nothing.

"You thinking of suing the department over the accident?"

"Accident? You ever been shot?" My shoulder was still pretty painful. I almost wished I'd stayed at the hospital.

He heaved a heavy sigh and sat down. "No, I haven't."

"Well, I'm still considering my options on that score. I might sue, I might not. Depends."

"Depends on what?" He leaned across his desk.

I just sat there, smiling at him.

"Well?" he said.

I took my time, then said: "I bet you Flynn is out there right now, wondering what the hell we're talking about. I hear Otis Barnes is on his way over, too."

"Otis Barnes? From the *Camden Herald?* What are you playing at?"

"Just a little game of chess. Hope you don't mind."

"Well, I'm not sure."

I nodded, took a moment, then slapped a newspaper on top of his desk, hard enough that it could be heard through the door. "No!" I shouted, also loud enough to be heard outside, "I won't do it! You can't pay me enough to work for you, Coletti! I'm not a detective anymore, goddamnit! I told you that before!"

"Are you out of your mind?" he said. "What the hell are you—oh, I get it."

"No! No way!" I shouted. Then, after a pause I said, still loud enough to be heard: "Well, as long as you put it that way I'll do it. But only if nobody else knows about it."

He laughed. "You're a crafty bastard. And just what good do you think this little act of yours is gonna do you?"

"The question is, what good do you think it'll do *you?*"

He laughed. "That's a point to consider."

"Like it or not, I'm gonna find out who killed Allison De-Marco, and what Sheriff Flynn's personal stake is in this case, and why he's still involved."

"Flynn is not involved in the investigation."

"Yeah, tell me another one."

"He's not. Not officially."

"Then what is he doing here? Shouldn't he be polishing his belt buckle for the Fourth of July? That's his real job, isn't it? To ride a white horse and look pretty for the voters?"

"You are such a pain in the—"

"And why is Sam Kirby planting evidence?"

That stopped him cold. "What evidence?"

"The house key, for one thing. Maybe the fingerprints on the butcher knife. I bet Kirby found those too, didn't he?"

He leaned back in his chair. "That's a lucky guess."

I leaned back in *my* chair. "Maybe you're in on it with

them. Why else would you be pushing to arrest Tim Berry and his girlfriend when you know they're innocent?"

"I could have you up for obstruction." He seemed amused.

"Oh, you have no idea what kind of obstruction charges I could lay on you, not to mention Flynn and Kirby at this point. So what's going on with those two?"

He shook his head. "I'll make you a deal. None of this goes to the press. You go ahead with your little snooping operation and just trust me that Flynn is totally aboveboard."

"Is he?"

"Yeah, he is."

"Except where Sam Kirby is concerned."

He clucked his tongue. I was starting to like him. I didn't trust him a hundred percent, but I was starting to like him. "You do what you gotta do," he said, "but you get nothing from me on Sam Kirby and Sheriff Flynn."

"So there *is* something to get? Just not from *you*?"

He said nothing. He did smile, though. Then he said, "I see now why you got all those commendations from the job in New York. I also see why they threw your ass off the force."

"Yeah, and what's going on with your Virgin Islands investigation?"

"They're keeping in touch, keeping us apprised."

"Apprised? You haven't sent one of your own men down there to investigate?"

He scoffed. "We're not running a Club Med for our personnel here, Field."

"What *are* you running?" I explained how Allison's ex-husband looked good for the murder. "Better than Berry. That alone should get you to stay the warrant on him."

"Sorry, that's not up to me. It's up to the DA."

"Bullshit. You could tell him your case is iffy. That you've got another possible suspect."

He thought it over. "That's not gonna happen. Tim Berry shot at a Camden Police officer."

"Oh, really," I said, sarcastically. "Which one? The one that shot me?"

"Fine," he laughed, "file your lawsuit. It isn't going to change the way I run my investigation."

"Nor the way I run mine."

He smiled and raised his hands in a magnanimous gesture. "Fine, Field. You go ahead and do what you gotta do."

"Thanks, I will." I got up and went to the door; when I got it open I said: "Okay, Dan, I'll keep you apprised . . ."

Coletti laughed a long, deep, hearty laugh. Flynn watched me go, as did Otis Barnes, who had just arrived. Flynn went into Coletti's office and I heard him say: "So, he's working for you now, is he?" Coletti just kept laughing.

Otis Barnes—tall, lanky, sixty or so, with limp hair the color of French bread, wearing a shiny black suit, a white shirt and Stuart tartan tie—followed me outside, asking me a lot of questions, to which I had no comment.

Finally, in the parking lot, he grabbed my sleeve. "No comment? Then why the hell did you ask me to meet you here?"

I stopped and looked him in the eye. "Sorry about that, Otis. I needed some leverage with Coletti. You got elected."

He didn't like that much and made his feelings clear.

"Look," I said, hoping to sway him over to my side, "what is the key element in all this? What's the most important thing for all concerned? Selling papers? Protecting Coletti's career, or mine, or yours? No, it's finding the killer."

He chewed on his lower lip. "I'm listening."

"I'm working on something, but I need your help."

"Like I'm gonna help you now? After you waste my—"

"You gotta let that go, Otis. Believe me, it'll pay off in the end. Now, here's what I can tell you, but it's strictly background. You'll have to corroborate it on your own."

He shook his head and looked at me like I was an idiot. "Where did you go to journalism school, Jack?"

"Me? I didn't."

"Really?" There was a heavy dose of sarcasm in his voice. "I mean, do you seriously think I would print a story based on one source, no matter how reliable? Of *course* I'm going to corroborate what you tell me. I mean, Jesus, who do you think you're dealing with here?"

Chagrined, I apologized, then went out on a limb and gave him everything I knew, including my precarious legal position with Duke, knowing that he'd keep that under wraps. I also voiced my suspicions about how the case was being mis-handled by the Camden PD and the Rockland County Sher-iff's Office. I gave him a list of people whose backgrounds needed looking into, then I asked him not to publish any of it for the time being.

"Are you crazy? This is a gold mine!"

"Yeah, well, people have been known to die in gold mines. You get that? And trust me, that may include you. I have a feeling we've gotta wrap this up tight—with Christmas rib-bons—before we show our hand."

He thought it over, then gave me a deadline: I had until the next edition went to press to have the whole thing wrapped up tight—with Christmas ribbons—or he'd publish it on his own. I wasn't worried—the *Camden Herald* only comes out once a week.

A few minutes after he left, Carl showed up to meet me. He had the camera equipment—one of the things I'd asked him to "borrow." I'd also asked him to walk off with a copy of the police report and Allison's will on floppy disk.

As we got into his cruiser he said, "I'm not sure if this is going to help me get a promotion or get me fired." Then he started the car and we pulled out onto Washington.

"Don't worry, Carl," I said. "I guarantee you won't lose your job over this. Let's drop by Allison DeMarco's house."

"I thought I was taking you home."

"It's on the way," I lied.

When we pulled into Allison's driveway the sun was go-ing down and the front yard was in deep shadow. We came around back and I showed him what I'd found earlier. The slanting rays of the setting sun brought the faint impressions of footprints into clear focus. Then I pointed out how high the porch light was.

"If Tim Berry put a key up there then Shaquille O'Neal had better watch out."

Carl scratched his head. "Well, he could've used a ladder or a box or something to stand on."

"He could have. But then the surface of the porch would show that. There'd be scuff marks, or ladder marks, or box marks. It's totally clear except for some very big footprints."

"But why would Kirby plant the key there?"

"You tell me. For now, let's just get a picture of this baby quick before the sun goes down."

Carl nodded and set up the camera and took some photos. When he was done we went back to the patrol car and I said, "Another thing that bothers me: Kirby wasn't in uniform the night of the murder, yet he had a gun and a flashlight."

"He always carries those around." He started up the car. "I hope you're not suggesting that *he* killed her."

"I doubt it. But he may know who *did*. What's the story with him and the sheriff?"

"What do you mean?"

"I'm not sure. I keep getting glimmers of something that's not right between them. I'd like the whole picture."

"That's a whole can of worms I don't want to get into."

"Why was Kirby at the scene, but not in uniform?"

"Maybe he came with the sheriff from the airport."

"The airport?"

He nodded. "Flynn flies up to Buffalo every other weekend. Kirby usually drops him off and picks him up."

"You don't think that's strange? And isn't Buffalo where Richard DeMarco's Mafioso father lives?"

"Yeah . . ." He thought about it. "You don't think?"

I shook my head. "It would be too neat a coincidence. But why does he go to Buffalo so often?"

"I have no idea. I mean, I always got the impression that he visits family up there. But I don't know that for sure."

We drove for a while. I let him think things over.

"Listen, Carl, how would you like to take some lost time, maybe call in sick for a few days, and help me solve this case?"

"You have got to be kidding."

"I'm deadly serious. I'll even pay your expenses."

He chuckled nervously. "What expenses?"

"Well, your travel accommodations, for one thing."

"Travel accommodations?"

I smiled and patted him on the back. "Have you ever been to the Virgin Islands?"

17.

It snowed that night. I was sitting on the big leather sofa in my living room with Frankie sound asleep, twitching and whining from some doggie dream, his head in my lap, the two of us in front of a blazing fire.

There was a big Christmas tree in the corner, to the right of the granite hearth. It was decorated with strings of popcorn and cranberries, multicolored lights, sparkling tinsel, and shiny red, blue, green, silver, and gold ornaments. It was Mrs. Murtaugh's idea. I told her she had her own tree at home, but she insisted I get one, so I bought it at the lot in West Rockport, and then she, along with her son-in-law Tom Stafford and a nephew named Mike (I think), put it up, decorated it and insisted that I get into the Christmas feeling. I had an impulse to tell her that Field is a Jewish name (it is, sort of) but instead gave in to the Yuletide spirit (sort of).

Besides, I liked the way it made the house smell.

My shoulder was still throbbing and I had been medicating myself with some cocktails. I wasn't alone: I had a little help from Audrey Stafford, a champagne blonde, five-six, with a round, freckled face, skinny arms and legs, and a nicely rounded figure. She had finished work at the kennel several hours earlier but couldn't tear herself away to go home because she and Ginger had fallen madly in love.

They were sitting on the rug by the far end of the couch: Ginger with her head on Audrey's black denim jeans and Audrey stroking Ginger's brow and scruffing her ears. Every once in a while, if I needed more medication, Audrey would get up and mix me another Kelso Christmas cocktail, bring it back to the sofa, then go back and sit on the floor with the love-hungry Airedale. All I had to do was lounge in my gray sweat pants and T-shirt, sip my medicine, stroke Frankie, stare into the flames, and once in a while throw another dog training book onto the fire.

The dogs pricked up their ears, and a moment later I heard a car pull up out front. A car door opened and I heard Duke say, "He's up in the house, Jamie. You can go on up." A few seconds later Jamie came through the front door. The dogs roused themselves and went to greet her, wagging their tails happily.

"I'm very upset with you," I heard her say in a loud, stern voice as she took off her loden coat and matching wool hat. She shook the snow off before hanging them on a couple of wooden hooks in the entryway, or mudroom, as it's called.

"Hi, sweetheart," I called out, my voice a little rich with whiskey. "It's nice to see you. Hey, I bet it's really snowing out there, isn't it?"

"Oh, sure, change the subject. Hi, Frankie! Hi, Ginger! Good dogs!" She came into the living room and said, "Wow! Nice tree, Jack," then, "Oh, I didn't see you," to Audrey."

"Dr. Jamie Carter, this is Mrs. Murtaugh's granddaughter, Audrey Stafford. She's helping out while I'm convalescing."

"It's *Cutter*, not Carter," she said to Audrey. "Nice to meet you." She came around the sofa, looking marvelous in chinos and a knobby sweater. "And convalescing my ass."

"Now there's an idea," I said, grabbing at her.

Audrey laughed nervously and got up to leave. "I think I'd better be going home," she said.

"Don't go. Jamie may need a cocktail or two."

Jamie said: "No, I don't—well, what the hell." She sat sideways next to me on top of her left leg and took a sip of my drink. She made a pleasant face. "It's good! What is it?"

Audrey said, "It's called a Kelso Christmas cocktail. It was invented by a friend of his from New York. It's a sad story, kind of."

"You've been telling Audrey stories, Jack?"

"It *is* a sad story," I said, missing her point, "but it's an amazing little sonovabitch of a cocktail. Perfect for the holiday blues. Care to try one?"

Jamie shrugged and said, "Fire away," and Audrey went over to the bar near the kitchen door to mix another batch. The dogs followed her. Audrey had that effect on them. Her arms and legs were skinny, but there was something about the rest of her that seemed rounder than she really was. Or maybe it was just the three or five Kelsos I'd had.

"How's your shoulder feel?" Jamie said, stroking my arm.

"I don't actually know. I haven't felt much of anything for the past couple of hours, so, fine I guess." I started to take a sip of my drink but she took the glass away from me.

"Let me taste that again." She took another sip. "It's delicious," she said. "What's it made with?"

"Irish whiskey, cinnamon schnapps, and Dr. Pepper on ice."

She took another sip. "It tastes better than it sounds."

"If you have time later, I'll tell you the story behind the origin of this cunning little Christmas classic."

"Oh, I've got all night," she said, "but first we need to talk about your recent carefree behavior."

"Yeah, yeah. Kick off your shoes, though, and help me throw a couple more training books on the fire before it goes out." I handed her a copy of one of the worst of the lot. "By the way, did the lab results come back yet?"

"Not yet." She kicked off her Timberlands. "You're burning books? Isn't that a little fascistic?"

"Probably, but turn to page forty-four of that book in your hand there. Halfway down, read what it says."

She opened the book, found the page in question and read: "How hard should you hit your dog? If she doesn't yelp in pain, you haven't hit her hard enough." She looked up at me in disbelief, then at the cover of the book and said: "How to be your dog's best friend? Jesus, how to be your dog's worst enemy!" She was about to throw the book on the fire but couldn't bring herself to do it. "You can burn these if you want to, Jack, but I'm not going to be a party to this."

"A party? A party to what?"

"I don't know. This! You may disagree with the way these other trainers do things—let me finish—they may seem cruel and medieval, but it doesn't do any good to sit here burning books. Write your own damn book! Teach people the right way, if there *is* one. Don't just get drunk and stew in your own negativity."

"Do you know the kind of damage done to dogs every day because of stupid books like this? Hitting a dog is training?"

"Of course not. But the type of people who'll do it are the type of people who'll probably do it anyway. And I'll bet you anything that if you sat down and wrote your *own* book and told people everything you know about dogs and all your little pet theories, most of these other trainers—" she pointed to the pile waiting to be incinerated "—would read it and not one of them would burn *your* book. They might even learn something, if they're smart enough, and in the long run, they might even modify their approach to training, if yours is better. Now, that's the way to really change things."

"You're probably right," I said, feeling very foolish.

Audrey brought us each a cocktail and Jamie had one and I had the other and we stared into the fire and didn't say much. After a while the phone rang. Jamie was closer so she picked it up. "Hello?" she said, with a puzzled look on her face. She looked at me, made a facial shrug and said: "They hung up."

"Who was it?"

"I don't know. As soon as I picked it up I heard a woman's voice say, 'At ease, General,' then she hung up."

I started to laugh. "It was my sister, Annie. That's her favorite line from *White Christmas*, where Danny Kaye says that to the general. She calls me every Christmas and says that."

Jamie shook her head. "You have a strange family."

"Doesn't everybody? And don't worry, she'll call back."

Sure enough, the phone rang again a few seconds later. This time Jamie handed it to me and I spoke to Ann for a bit and we wished each other a Merry Christmas and all the rest. While we were talking, Jamie sipped her cocktail and Audrey got up and got ready to really go this time.

After I hung up the phone Audrey said, kind of sadly: "I wish I could take her home, you know?" She put on her brown and orange parka, not taking her eyes off the doting Airedale.

"Maybe you can adopt her," I said. "She's crazy about you. We'll have to see how things work out." She smiled as she threw her scarf around her collar. I said: "You did good work today."

"Thanks," she said, "it was fun. See you tomorrow."

Jamie said, "Drive careful in the snow."

"I will," she said and started toward the door, but she turned, knelt down, and hugged Ginger's neck. "I'll see you tomorrow, too, you big goofy girl." Ginger whined and wagged her stub of a tail. Audrey kissed her ear and then left.

Ginger stood watching the door until she heard Audrey's car start up and drive off. Then she came over and lay down next to Frankie, who was on the floor. A few moments later Duke knocked on the front door and came inside. Two Pomeranians peeped out from inside his plaid wool jacket. Scully was the red one and Mulder was the black.

"Yo, Jack. I was wonderin'—"

"—If Scully and Mulder can sleep with you tonight?"

"Is it okay?"

"Sure," I yawned. "Just be careful they don't fall off the bed. Did you check on Thurston?"

"Yeah, I put him in the grooming room with some newspapers, like you told me. And don't worry, they won't fall off. They likes to crawl under the covers wif me."

I chuckled. "Okay, see you in the morning."

After Duke and the Pomeranians left, Jamie got up, threw another log on the fire, then fiddled with the stereo until the listener-sponsored station in Blue Hill came through: they were playing a Townes van Zandt song. Jamie started to switch it off but I told her not to. "You'll get used to his voice," I said. So she came back and snuggled up next to me on the couch, tucking her knees underneath her lovely little fanny, and resting her head against my chest.

"This doesn't hurt, does it?"

"Nope." I stroked her arm and found a loose piece of yarn in her sweater.

"How come you never told me you went to Harvard?"

"You've been talking to Flynn. Want another cocktail?"

"No, answer my question."

"What difference does it make? I dropped out."

"The thing is, now I have to stop thinking I'm smarter than you."

"You *are* smarter, and richer. Although I'm prettier."

She punched me lightly. "All this time," she sighed. "I started college when I was seventeen, then I find out you started when you were *six*teen."

"So what? I got bored with high school."

"Everybody gets bored with high school. Then I find out you have a master's degree in psychology. Is that true?"

"I seem to recall something like that happening a long time ago. So did Flynn show you my SAT scores and my grade-point average as well?" I started picking at the loose stitch in her sweater. "Why do we have to get into all this?"

"Because I want to know everything about you and you don't tell me things."

"Honey, what you have to realize is that there are only two relevant events in my life—that is, my life as it is now. The first was when I adopted Frankie. And the second was the day I met you."

"Awwww."

"Everything else is irrelevant."

"You know you bug the hell out of me sometimes? You are so impossible and then you say something like that . . ." She sighed.

We listened to Townes sing "If I Could Only Fly." Jamie said, "You were right. His voice is rough but it makes the song all that much prettier and sweeter—what are you doing?"

"Your sweater has a flaw in it."

"Well, don't *pick* at it," she said, "you'll only make it worse. Besides, this type of sweater is *supposed* to have flaws. That's what gives it character."

"Just like people, huh?"

She looked up into my eyes. "What do you mean?"

"Well, take me for instance. I have certain flaws, as you've no doubt noticed. But what you don't seem to realize is that it's what gives me character. And picking at them—my flaws, that is—doesn't do any good."

"Do you think I've been picking at you? I'm just—"

"No, you were right about the book burning. But there are other things I do, like leaving the hospital, insulting your friends, just generally making an ass of myself. It's part of who I am. I mean, you can pick at me if you want. It doesn't really bother me, because I know you do it out of love."

"I do. I really do."

"I know that. I just hate for you to be disappointed when you realize that I'm not going to change all that much."

"I don't want to change you, Jack." She put her head on my chest again. "I just worry about you. And I'm not sure I know how to make you happy."

"If you're worried about me now, just wait till you see what I've got planned for tomorrow and the next day."

"Oh, no," she sighed, "what is it?"

"I don't know. But chances are pretty good that sooner or later I'm going to do something you won't like, whether I mean to or not. So is this a new level to our relationship?"

"What do you mean?"

"You just dropping over uninvited like this. You've never done that before."

She giggled. "I'm your doctor, remember? I came over to check on your shoulder."

"Un-huh."

She pinched my arm and snuggled into my chest some more. "So, what if this is a new level? Would you mind?"

"Not at all. You can take us to whatever levels you want."

She sighed and hugged me harder and I put one hand under her sweater and let it slide softly into second base.

She reached up, arching her neck and back, and kissed me hungrily. "Let's go upstairs," she whispered.

"Aha . . ." I said. "You *do* know how to make me happy."

18

"I don't know about you," she said, "but *I'm* happy."

"I know you are."

"How can you tell?"

"I just know. You like being on top, for one thing."

She smiled and punched me softly in the kidney. "You're right. I *do* like it."

The snow was falling and the dogs were curled up and fast asleep on the rug by the side of the bed. Ginger's head was draped across Frankie's neck. Frankie was snoring softly.

"How's your shoulder?"

"Okay, though I was afraid for a second or two that you were going to try to take my stitches out with your teeth."

"Sorry," she laughed, "I got carried away. Oh, I brought you some Tylenol III in case you need it later. It has codeine in it, though, so you really should wait until the alcohol is out of your system before you take any."

She yawned and looked out the window at the snow. I kissed the top of her head. Her hair smelled of shampoo and cologne.

"Your hair smells nice. Are you and Eve Arden still going shopping tomorrow?"

"If I have the time. I have to see the eye doctor."

"What's wrong with your eyes?"

"Nothing. But something's wrong with your theory about the case. A hormone is not something you could just slip into someone's coffee. It would almost have to be injected. And there were no needle marks or puncture wounds on the body."

I thought it over. "What about nasal spray?"

"Yes, the mucous membranes in the nose are thin enough so that the capillaries under the skin could absorb the hormone quickly. Same thing if it were administered sublingually. But you know what I was thinking?" Her eyes were bright. "Eye drops. If she put the drops in one eye and started fibrillating before she was able to administer the drops to the other eye—"

"That would explain the blown pupil. But would the blood vessels in the eyes be able to absorb the hormones fast enough?"

"Absolutely. That's why I have an appointment with Allison's ophthalmologist. To see why she was using prescription eye drops and who else knew about it."

"Did the police find an eye dropper at the scene? I remember seeing one in her kitchen drawer."

She shook her head. "Are you sure you saw it?"

"Yeah. Maybe Sam Kirby glommed it."

"Or maybe the killer did. But if her ex-husband is—"

There was a sudden creaking sound from the bedside stand and it took me a moment to remember that that's where I keep the audio monitor which is hooked up to a microphone in the kennel. I got out of bed and went to the window, which didn't do much good because it faces away from the house and the kennel.

"What is it?" Jamie asked.

"I don't know. I think someone's in the kennel."

Sure enough, a couple of dogs started barking. I heard the sound from the monitor first, and then—with a half-second's time delay—from outside. Frankie and Ginger jumped up and joined in. Before long the whole kennel, in fact, the whole hillside, was alive with frantic canine voices.

I put on my jeans and a T-shirt and grabbed my keys. Jamie started to get out of bed too, but I told her to stay put. I raced down the stairs, through the living room, and into the kitchen, followed by Frankie and Ginger. I stopped at the kitchen door to flip on the yard lights and as I ran out onto the side porch I saw a hulking figure of a man trudging up the side of the hill behind the kennel toward a set of headlights just beyond a thicket of alder saplings along the drainage ditch by the side of the road. He was carrying something in his arms. A few seconds later the Camden cop on night duty came skidding down the long drive in his radio car with the lights flashing. He skated to a stop and got out.

"What's going on?" His eyes still had sleep in them.

Frankie and Ginger were circling around me, barking and howling. Most of the dogs in the kennel were still at it too.

Duke came running out of the guest house, dressed in his robe and pajamas. "Yo, what's up?"

"Someone tried to break into the kennel. You'd better check on the dogs." He just stood there, stupid with sleep. "Quick! Make sure he didn't throw poison into any of the kennels."

Duke really came alive then. He ran to check on the dogs, and slipped going around the corner. He looked a little like Buster Keaton—he kept running, skid or no skid.

To the Camden cop—whose name tag read "Reinking"—I said, "He was parked on the ridge, just behind the kennel." I pointed to the spot. "Made a U-turn and took off north. You think you could catch up with him?"

"Not in this weather." He saw the look on my face. "I guess I could try." He got back in his cruiser and put it in gear, but it didn't do any good—one of his rear wheels had strayed off the gravel and he was stuck in the snow.

Duke came out of the kennel just as Jamie came out of the kitchen and down the walk. She was wearing one of my flannel shirts, her Timberlands, and not much else. I had a brief urge to throw her in a snowbank and make angels, but Duke said, "It's a'ight. The kennels is all locked. Nobody's missing."

"Okay, everybody gets a biscuit."

He nodded and went back inside.

I went around the back, looking at the snowy ground. Jamie followed me. "What are you looking for?"

"Footprints. Not that they'll do me any good."

As we got to back of the kennel I found what I was looking for: a size fourteen footprint. I pointed it out to Jamie. Ginger came over to sniff it, then spraddled her hips over it and soon all that was left was a yellow puddle and some steam. Frankie sniffed and added his two cents worth. Like I said, the footprints wouldn't do me any good. Not because of the dogs but because the falling snow was covering everything anyway.

Jamie said, "Sam Kirby?"

"That would be my guess. No way to prove it, though."

Duke came around the back. His face was sick with what he had to tell me, "It ain't my fault, a'ight? You told me to put him in the grooming room, not in one of the kennels."

"What do you mean? What's wrong?"

"Thurston's missing. He's gone!"

19

I called the sheriff and woke him up. I told him I thought that one of his deputies had kidnapped one of my dogs. I told him what had just happened.

"Yeah? What makes you think it was Sam Kirby?"

"What makes you think *I* think it was Sam Kirby? All I said was that it was one of your deputies."

"Well, Sam's the only one stupid enough and mean enough to do something like this. On top of which, he's been making noise about paying you back for the other night. Goddamnit! I never should have hired him in the first place."

"Why *did* you?"

"None of your business. If it was Sam, just sit tight and don't worry. I'll get you your damn dog back."

I put on some shoes and socks and helped the Camden cop get his radio car out of the driveway. We found a couple of old one-by-twelves in the shed, put them under the back tires, and soon he was on his way back up to the county road for another nap.

Jamie and I were too wired to sleep so we sat in the kitchen at the old pockmarked round oak table. I made some decaf and we sipped at it and held hands. Duke declined our invitation to join us. I think maybe he wanted to go back to his room and hug Scully and Mulder and feel bad.

"It's not your fault, Duke," I said. "And don't worry, we'll get him back. I promise."

Frankie hung around for a minute or two, but no co-

mestibles were forthcoming and there was nothing soft for
him to lie down on, so he went into the living room and
jumped up on the couch. Ginger stood half in the kitchen and
half in the living room and looked at me plaintively.

"What is it?" I asked.

She whined.

"Ginger, what do you want, honey?"

She looked behind her toward the living room.

Jamie laughed and said, "God, you're an idiot sometimes,
Jack. She wants to know if you want her to stay here with us,
or is it okay for her to go and lie down with Frankie."

"Is that what you want?" I said to Ginger.

Jamie laughed at me some more and shook her head.
"She's not going to *answer* you, Jack. Or had you forgotten
that dogs can't talk?"

"Yeah, I know it's silly, but sometimes I *like* having a conversation with dogs like this." To Ginger I said, "Okay, go lie
down with Frankie." Her eyes brightened, her face relaxed,
and she turned and trotted into the living room and curled up
next to her "boyfriend."

Jamie laughed. "Now, was that so hard?"

"Shut up and leave me alone."

"Aww, did I hurt your feelings?" she said, teasingly. She
got up and came around beside me and pinched my cheeks
and shook them, the way you do with a small child. Then she
sat in my lap, stroked my hair and said: "You're just like a little boy, sometimes. You know that?" She kissed me.

"Are you finished having fun? Because I don't think this
chair can stand the weight of both of us for very long."

"Sorry," she got up and went back to her own chair.
"You're not really mad, are you?"

"Yeah, I'm mad. Not at you, at Sam Kirby. What kind of
person steals a harmless little puppy for no other reason than
just being mean."

She sighed, looked toward the window, took another sip
of coffee—or whatever it was we were drinking—and said:
"Do you really think the dog is going to be okay? I mean, you
weren't just saying that to make Duke feel better, were you?"

"No, I try not to lie to him about anything. I really think
the dog is going to be all right. Flynn will take care of it."

She nodded. "We should go back to bed and try to sleep," she said, even though she knew we wouldn't. "Weren't you going to tell me a story?" She put her stockinged feet in my lap and I massaged them and kept them warm. "What are you laughing at?"

"You," I said. "The way you were making fun of me before. You really got a kick out of that, didn't you?"

"Yeah, a little." She smiled a chagrined smile.

"Well, then this story ought to really make you happy. It's not the sad story of Lou Kelso and his Christmas cocktail, it's the story of how I lost my job with the NYPD."

"You were fired? I thought you quit."

"No, I was forced to take early retirement."

"That doesn't sound good. What happened?"

I smiled. "I assaulted a private citizen while off-duty."

She processed this bit of information and gave me a worried look. "I hope you're about to explain yourself."

I nodded and told her the story. "I was coming out of a bar on Columbus Avenue one night, and I saw this guy—this fat jerk in parachute pants—standing on the corner, telling a five-month-old chocolate lab puppy—I think he was a lab mix, I'm not sure. At any rate, he was telling the dog to sit—or I should say, he was yelling, 'Sit, goddamnit! *Sit!* I told you to *sit!*' The puppy was too frightened to obey, so instead of noticing this very important fact, the jerk grabs a newspaper out of a trash bin, rolls it up, and starts hitting the dog with it."

"You're kidding."

I shook my head. "So, of course, I have to poke my nose in and tell this guy to knock it off."

Jamie agreed that that was what *she* would've done.

"So he says, 'Mind your own business—I'm *training* this dog. He thinks he's alpha, and I'm showing him that *I'm* the pack leader.' "

She was skeptical. "Oh, Jack, he didn't say that."

"Yes, he did. Those were his exact words."

"Come on. Alpha? Nobody talks like that."

"You haven't been around hard-core dog people very much."

"I guess not." She shook her head.

"So, anyway, I take the newspaper out of his hand and tell him, 'Oh, yeah? Well, I've got the newspaper *now*, buddy. So I guess that makes *me* the alpha dog.'"

Jamie laughed. "You said you'd just come out of a bar."

I nodded. "Okay, yes, I'd had some Scotch. Not enough to make me drunk, but it *did* loosen my inhibitions somewhat."

"So, I stood there threatening him with the rolled up newspaper and told *him* to sit."

She laughed, almost guiltily. "You didn't."

"I did. And when he didn't sit I started whacking *him* with the newspaper."

She started to take a sip of decaf but began laughing so hard, she had to stop, afraid it might come out her nose.

"So, there I am, like a psychopath, yelling, '*Sit*, goddamnit! I told you to *sit*!'" From the other room I could hear Frankie's tail nervously thumping on the leather couch. "And I'm whacking the guy with the newspaper, I mean really hard, and a crowd gathers. A small crowd, but nonetheless—"

"So did he sit?" she said through tears of laughter.

"No," I sighed, "he slipped and knocked his head against the base of a street light and cut his head pretty bad."

Jamie stopped laughing, as did I.

"There was a lot of blood. The dog was scared shitless. And I had to call 911 for an ambulance."

We sat there for a bit.

"Anyway, he filed a complaint with the Civilian Review Board, hired a lawyer, sued the city, but as it turned out he really *was* training the dog when I interfered."

"What?" she was incredulous. "You have to be kidding."

"Nope. It turns out he's a professional dog trainer, as well as an author on training books. In fact, he wrote a couple of the books I was burning earlier. Of course, he didn't want it getting out that he'd been beating up one of his clients' puppies with a rolled-up newspaper at three hundred dollars an hour. So his attorney settled out of court, the records were sealed, and I retired with three-quarter pension and benefits."

After a while, Jamie shook her head and said, "I hope you learned your lesson, Jack, though the funny thing is, you just basically did what every real dog lover fantasizes about doing in that kind of situation. I mean, I hope you won't ever do anything like it again—I really do—but the fact that you did it at all is actually quite endearing."

"Yeah, I learned my lesson, believe me—it's not worth it. And just ask the City of New York how endearing *they* think it is after they were forced to pay for what I did."

She laughed. "That's true. But in a way I'm glad you're the kind of guy who would do something like that."

"Really?"

She gave me a smile—the one that has a little mischief in it. "What girl wouldn't want a boyfriend who, if she's ever being threatened, will always be there with a rolled-up newspaper to protect her?"

We laughed some more. After a while, she came over and sat in my lap again and brushed the hair out of my eyes. "You are the most interesting guy I've ever known, you know that?"

"If you say so."

We gave up on Flynn and headed back upstairs and that's when he finally rolled up in his Jeep and honked his horn. I went outside and he handed Thurston to me through the car window. The little guy was sound asleep, but his legs were twitching. He was probably having a nightmare about being chased by monster cats. Or bad men in black Dodge pick-ups.

Flynn said, "One of my deputies found this puppy running around in the snow and thought you might know who he belongs to." He tickled the pup's belly with one finger. "He's a cute little fella. What's his name?"

"Thurston," I said. "And you're just gonna let Kirby get away with a stunt like this? No sanctions, no charges brought?"

"Can you prove it was Kirby took him?"

"No. I just know it was. And so do you."

He looked over at Jamie's Jaguar. "Sure. Same as I know whose car that is. But I'm not gonna arrest you for that."

"You *can't* arrest me for that, Sheriff. Sleeping with some-one's ex-niece-in-law is not a crime. Dognapping is."

"They're still married," he said. It was beginning to be his favorite expression. He wiggled his mustache once, then gave me a long, cold stare. "I've been looking into these so-called disability benefits of yours."

I sighed. "Oh, great. Here we go."

"You care to explain to me what it means to retire 'cause of an emotional disability?"

"Not especially. And those records are supposed to be sealed, you know."

He nodded. "What are you, some kind of nut job? That it?"

"That's one way of looking at it."

"What's another?"

"That some people, when they work in the criminal justice system, tend to care too much about what happens to the victims of violent crimes. Especially when those victims are women and children. Maybe I was too sensitive to be a good cop. Maybe life just sucks and people are stupid and ignorant—if not downright evil—and maybe that's why I prefer working with dogs. Now, if you don't mind, Thurston is freezing his tail off."

"They named him Thurston, huh?" He shook his head and put his Jeep in gear. "Whatever happened to people giving regular names to dogs, like Rex and Lassie?"

"Whatever happened to county sheriffs arresting people for breaking the law?"

"Merry Christmas," he said, and drove off in the snow.

The phone woke me up. Jamie was gone. She'd left while I was sleeping. There was a note and a bottle of Tylenol III on the nightstand, and a lingering trace of cologne on my pillows.

"Jack, it's Jill Krempetz. I need to see you right away."

"Sure, okay. What time is it?"

"It's nine o'clock. Did I wake you up?"

"Yeah, but that's all right. We had quite a night here. One of the dogs went missing. I've still got a touch of the Irish flu."

"The Irish flu?"

"Also known as a hangover. Is it still snowing?"

"A little, why?"

"No reason. Do you want to come here or should I come down to Camden?"

"I think you should come down," she said. "Can you drive?"

"Been doing it for years. Why?"

"No, I mean with your shoulder."

"Oh, you heard. Yeah, I should be able to manage it. Do you think we can sue them for negligence or something?"

"Who? The Camden PD? Do you want to?"

"No, I'm just indulging a little fantasy. I'll be over as soon as I can. Just give me a little time to sniff my pillows."

An hour later I walked into her messy little office above The Camden Herald. She was on the phone. Her frizzy red hair was pinned back in a bun and she had two pencils stuck in it. "No!" she shouted into the phone, "we need the first available court date on the calendar. My client has a family to feed. No more stalling." She looked over her reading glasses and saw me standing in the doorway and waved me in. "Okay, call me back," and she hung up. "We've got problems," she said, "or rather, *you* do. But we can't talk here. Have you had coffee yet?"

I told her I had but I wouldn't mind having some more.

"Good. Let's get some. What was that line about sniffing your pillows? Jamie sleep over?"

"You should be a detective. What problems?"

"Problems with Duke," she whispered. She put on a coat and tried the same with her hat. I pointed out that the reason it wouldn't go on properly was because of the pencils. She pulled them out, laughed, and said, "I'm having a bad pencil day."

We went to the Camden Deli and got some take-out cups and bought a couple of newspapers and went up the hill and around the corner and found a park bench by the waterfall and spread our newspapers out and sat down. There was a foot of snow on the embankment surrounding the falls and there was some ice forming on the edges of the pool beneath the deli. I looked out at the mostly empty harbor and an old man in a yellow slicker aboard a twenty-footer saw us and waved. I waved back.

"It sure is beautiful this time of year," Jill said.

"Eh," I said, taking a sip of cappuccino.

"You don't think it's pretty?"

"Cute, maybe. Tranquil, if you like that sort of thing."

"You're a cynical bastard. If you don't like Camden, why did you move here when you left New York?"

"I didn't. I moved to a little spot somewhere between—"

"Hope and Perseverance, I know."

"It was the only kennel up for sale. What about you?"

"That's right. We're both immigrants. I've just been here a lot longer than you." She smiled, shook some Sweet'N Low into her cup, and stirred it with her little plastic stirrer. She looked out at the scene and said, "I came here one summer from Michigan for a friend's wedding. I'd always wanted to come back but I was busy with law school. I got married, moved to Chicago, but I couldn't stop thinking about this little town on the coast of Maine. Then, after about seven years of marriage, my husband started coming home late every night, and guys I trained at the law firm were all getting promoted ahead of me. So one day I got in touch with my soul and it said 'Camden,' and I've been here ever since."

"How wonderful for you," I applauded.

"Screw you. I don't sail, ski, or eat lobster and I love it here." She stuck her chin in the air. "So there."

"That's nice. So what's going on?"

"DHS—that's the Division of Human Services—has gotten notice that you've got an underage juvenile living on your property without parental permission."

"Duke? His parents are dead—how am I going to get their permission? And he's not underage, he's nineteen. 'Underage juvenile' . . . do they really talk like that? That's not only pedantic, it's redundant."

She said, "He looks fifteen to me."

"He's got ID to prove he's not," I said.

"Is it legit? Never mind, don't ans—"

"Objection, Your Honor. Relates to facts not in evidence." She laughed. I said, "Who put a bug up their ass about this, Sheriff Flynn?"

A snowflake landed on her eyebrow. She brushed it off and said, "I have no idea. I just know you're in trouble. Or about to be. God knows they're overworked and underfunded, but they could show up at the kennel at any time with a court order. Do you have any legal grounds for having Duke with you?"

I told her about my verbal agreement with Duke's grandmother, then said, "But if he gets sent back to live with her he'll be dead in three weeks. So will she. These people—excuse me, they're not people, but since I'm an animal lover I can't bring myself to call them animals, that's too good for them—these . . . *maggots* . . . don't discriminate."

"Isn't there anything the police or the DA can do?"

I shrugged and sipped my coffee. "We had the case nailed up tight. We got a search warrant and found the murder weapons, and the ballistics were a perfect match. The fingerprints on the guns found at the stash house and even on the shell casings at the scene were a perfect match. The victim's blood was found on several pairs of sneakers worn by the killers. They were still wearing their bloody sneakers! The DNA was a perfect match. Now here's where it gets suspicious: normally with this kind of evidence, suspects are falling all over themselves to be the first one to make a deal. Not these guys. They were . . ." I took another sip of coffee, narrowed my eyes. ". . . So full of themselves, like they didn't have a care in the world.

"So the defense attorney files a motion to suppress and it's heard by a certain judge—who, if he's not on the take, is being blackmailed by these scumbags, because he lets them go."

"You're kidding."

"Nope."

"On what grounds?"

"Insufficient probable cause for the warrant? Insufficient grounds? I don't remember what it's called. At any rate, the only way we could go back and rearrest these guys is if Duke were to testify. Then all the evidence would be admissible under some legal thing called 'probable discovery.' "

"Inevitable discovery," she corrected me. "Did they offer Duke protection for his testimony?"

"Of course, but the thing is, I'd had a similar case a few years earlier where the DA put a witness into protective custody and the witness and three of the cops protecting her were killed because the ADA in that case was on the take. I was very fond of that particular witness and I wasn't about to have the kind of thing that happened to her happen to Duke.

"On another front, I was dealing with the fallout from some silly . . ." I laughed at my own stupidity ". . . misbehavior of mine that precipitated my early retirement. So I moved up here to Maine, bought a kennel, and brought Duke with me. All aboveboard, with his grandmother's blessing, etc. I just failed to notify the Manhattan DA's office."

She looked at me for a long while, then said, "I don't know. It seems to me you might want to think about all the other potential victims of these scumbags. If Duke testifies, they won't be able to destroy any more lives."

"Yeah, I've heard that speech," I said. "I've even given it

myself a couple of times. Meanwhile, back at the precinct, no one's forgotten this case. They're still going after these guys. And the DA has filed an appeal."

"Yoo hoo, Jack!" a female voice came sailing across the falls from the back door of one of the shops on Main, about a hundred yards away. It was Gina Staub, wearing a long purple coat. She waved at me while Sasha sniffed around in the snow, looking for a place to pee.

"Look, Sasha, it's Uncle Jack!" Gina said to the dog.

Sasha looked up, saw me, and instantly came dashing toward us, leaping over the concrete curb around the parking lot, then splashing through the rocky rill which runs from the waterfall down to the harbor. She finally came zooming up to the bench where Jill and I sat, and leapt straight into my lap, wagging her wet tush and licking my face.

"Too bad she doesn't like you," Jill said, holding her coffee cup away from the frantic dog.

"Occupational hazard," I said. Then, to Sasha, "Okay, off!" She jumped down, turned around, and stared up at me, panting, her tawny fanny shaking with delight.

Gina called Sasha and she looked back over her shoulder at Gina, then back at me. "Go on, Sash. Go to Mommy."

"Sasha, come!" Gina called, very sternly.

"Use the happy voice," I called to Gina. "Remember?"

Gina called the dog, using the "happy voice," and Sasha turned and ran back to her as fast as she could. After they'd gone back inside the store Jill shook her head and said, "Do all the dogs you train love you that much?"

"Well, I train them by stimulating their prey drive. Most dogs tend to like that more than the other stuff, though I probably shouldn't have let her jump on me just now. So what do we do about Duke?"

"Well, I can put some feelers out to see how much time you've got before they take action. We have to be careful, of course, and not tip our hand. Meanwhile, you might want to think about putting yourself in better legal standing—apply to become Duke's foster parent or something."

"I know. I *would*, I just don't want to put him into the system until I get this thing in New York straightened out."

"And how are you going to do that?"

"Oh, I have something in the works."

She sighed. "You're planning something illegal?"

"Well, if extortion is still illegal, then yes. Although, technically, even though it was my idea, I have nothing to do with the actual commission of the alleged crime. It's being handled by a friend of mine, Lou Kelso, a former prosecutor. Matter of fact, he and I worked on that case I told you about where the witness was killed while in protective custody? I'd tell you more but my ass is freezing." I stood up. "Have you heard from Wade Pierce about an agreement he wants me to sign?"

She got up too and we began walking up the hill toward Main Street. "Yes, he dropped it off yesterday but I haven't had a chance to look it over yet." She laughed. "He sure is trying to seem upper crust lately. Probably trying to impress investors in his little marina. He was all sweaty from a squash game he'd been playing. 'With a client,' he'd said."

"At the Samoset?"

"Yes, why?" I told her about seeing Pierce in the hospital. We got to the top of the hill and Jill slipped on a patch of ice and I grabbed her arm and held her steady.

"Thanks, Jack," she said. "It would be too corny if we tumbled down the hill together, wouldn't it?"

I wondered what she meant by that, then I realized she was referring to our names—Jack and Jill. I chuckled.

She said, "I'll take a look at Joel's document as soon as I get upstairs and then give you a call."

I said that was fine with me.

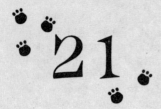

21

Since Jill's office is near the *Camden Herald* I thought I'd take the opportunity, while she was busy being my attorney, to drop in on Otis Barnes, if he was there, and see how his end of the investigation was going.

The receptionist said, "I'm sorry, Mr. Barnes isn't in," then gave me a long look. "Are you Jack Field, by any chance?" I admitted as much and she said, "I thought so. Mr. Barnes said you might be dropping by to see him. He left you this." She handed me a file folder filled with Xeroxed newspaper clippings.

"Thanks," I said. "And how did you know it was *me*?"

"Oh, Mr. Barnes gave me a very detailed description of you—tall, blue eyes, salt-and-pepper hair and beard."

"That's me I guess. Uh, is there a place I can go to—"

The phone rang. She said, "Sure," answered the call, "*Camden Herald*," then pointed me toward an empty desk.

I mouthed a thank-you, sat down, and went through the clippings. The first item was from a paper dated twenty-five years ago. "POLICE CAPTAIN WALTER KIRBY AND WIFE JOAN PROUD PARENTS." It gave the time of birth, the name of the attending obstetrician, and the baby's birth weight: seven pounds, six ounces. Sam Kirby had grown a lot since then. There was a photo of the parents holding the child. Mommy Joan looked tired but radiant. Daddy Walter looked sour and unhappy. Maybe he just took a bad picture.

The next item was dated six months previous to the birth

notice and involved the auction of a sailboat owned jointly by
Walter Kirby and Horace Flynn. The story mentioned that the
boat had won Kirby and Flynn several racing trophies but
that they had dissolved their sailing partnership and were
now auctioning off their beauty. It also mentioned that Flynn,
who had been a protégé of Kirby's on the Camden police
force, had recently quit his job and was now a deputy sheriff
for the Rockland County Sheriff's Department.

The next article was about Flynn's first campaign for
Sheriff, some twelve years later. It mentioned how Flynn had
gotten his start in law enforcement as a protégé of Camden
Police Chief Walter Kirby—who at the time was just a captain—but that Kirby, in this particular election, was throwing
his support behind Flynn's opponent.

The two men had obviously had some sort of falling out,
which had happened six months prior to Sam Kirby's birth.

Interesting. I read on.

There were several more recent items about Kirby's do-
ings as Chief of Police, one of which mentioned in passing
that his wife Joan was in a mental hospital in Buffalo, New
York (a city Flynn now visits twice a month). Then there was
a scandal, involving allegations of years of spousal abuse and
police cover-ups—until a year after the scandal first hit the
papers, Walter M. Kirby was forced to step down as Chief of
Police. Two years later he died of prostate cancer. Joan
Kirby, Sam's mother, is still a mental patient in Buffalo.

I closed the folder and felt tired and dirty and aching with
the Irish flu and with the pain in my shoulder. I almost
wished I hadn't tried to find out anything about Flynn and
Kirby. I got up from the desk and returned the folder to the
pretty young girl who'd given it to me.

"Did you find what you were looking for," she asked.

"Yeah, but I wish I hadn't."

I left, then started to climb the stairs to Jill Krempetz's office. My path was blocked by a tall, gawky man in army fa-
tigues who smelled of marijuana smoke—Farrell Woods.

"Hey, Jackie boy, what's going on?"

I nodded up the stairs. "I'm going to see Jill Krempetz."

"That's cool, man. Hey, I've been meaning to drop by the
kennel, you know, and see if you need anybody . . ."

"Not just now, thanks."

"Okay, man. Well, let me know."

"Sure." I felt bad about turning him down over and over. Plus I like his dogs so I said: "And listen, any time you want to stop by and let your beagles—how many do you have now?"

"Ten."

"Yeah, huh? Well, any time you want to bring them by and, you know, let 'em run around the play yard with the other dogs, I'm totally cool with that. I really like those dogs."

"Yeah, they're great, aren't they?" He tried to give me some kind of cool 1960s handshake, which I successfully avoided, then he danced his way down the rest of the stairs.

When I got to Jill's office—and this is only one flight, mind you—I found myself starting to sweat again, just like I'd done in the car after leaving the hospital. I checked my pockets for the Tylenol III Jamie had left for me.

Jill was on the phone and at least one of the pencils was back in her hair. She waved me in and pointed to a chair (with another pencil) and said into the phone, "Wade, this is Jill Krempetz. I've just gone over your document and my only concern is that there's no provision for my client's out-of-pocket expenses in caring for the dog. I think we should discuss whether that should fall to the county or to Mrs. DeMarco's estate, and how and when Mr. Field is to be reimbursed. Call me as soon as you get this message."

She hung up and said, "I got his machine. You look awful. Do you need some water or something?"

I said I did and she got me some and I drank it and took my Tylenol III and sat in the chair and rested for a bit.

"I don't care about being reimbursed," I said. "I'm concerned that if we get too fancy Ginger will end up at one of the local shelters or in a cage in the back room of some vet's office. Not that they won't take good care of her, but I just think she'll be better off with me."

"Fine," she shook her head, called Pierce's machine again, left another message, and when she was done I said, "By the way, what time did Pierce drop off the document yesterday?"

"I don't know for sure. I could check my book . . ."

"Would you mind?"

She opened her day planner and flipped back a page.

"Around one o'clock," she said. "Why?"

"I don't know. There's something fishy about that guy."

"Oh, that's just Wade. He's arrogant and self-absorbed. Which makes him like you, but without a sense of humor."

"Cute."

"You don't think he's involved in the murder, do you?"

"I don't know. Where's his office located?"

She gave me the address. "But he's out of town."

"Yeah, so you told me," I said. "That's why I want to go over there now. Can I borrow a couple of bobby pins?"

22

The lock was easy to pick, even with bobby-pins. I came inside and looked around. There was a world of difference between this office and the one I'd just left. Where Jill's was cramped and messy, Pierce's was neat and roomy. He had a brand new Gateway, a Xerox machine, and even a couple of healthy house plants on top of his metal filing cabinets and wooden bookcases. There was also a rather large picture of my dog Frankie, hanging on the wall across from his desk. Only it wasn't Frankie. It couldn't have been, because it was an old nineteenth-century English hunting print. It sure looked like Frankie, though.

I spent about twenty minutes going through every drawer, file, folder, and document I could find that wasn't locked up. The trick to doing an illegal search is to not worry how long it takes. It's like training a dog. If you try to go too fast you'll only make mistakes and have to go back and do it all over again later. So I took my time and was very cool and calm and relaxed. Until the phone rang, that is. Then I nearly jumped out of my skin.

The answering machine clicked on. I started to breathe again, but instead of hearing a message being left (as I'd expected), I heard the tape start to rewind: Pierce was retrieving his messages. Out of idle curiosity—or detective's instinct—I looked at the electronic doodads that give you the incoming phone number. I wrote it down. I heard both of Jill's mes-

sages being replayed over the machine, then it clicked off and
that was it. I was safe again.

I scratched my beard and looked again at the two desk
drawers I hadn't looked through, yet—the bottom left-hand
and the middle, or pencil drawer. They were both locked.
Since I hadn't found anything of any interest anywhere
else—meaning anything relating to Allison DeMarco's
murder—I tried the bobby pins again. They didn't work.
The locks on Pierce's desk were better than the one on his
door.

I sat down. The chair was comfortable. I leaned back and
tried to think like a Wade Pierce. If I were he, where would I
keep a spare key hidden, just in case I couldn't find my key-
ring, or in case I wanted to entertain an ex-detective–slash–dog
trainer in absentia on a snowy Thursday morning?

I looked again at the picture of Frankie. There were a few
smaller pictures on the walls as well; all hunting prints fea-
turing setters, pointers, and spaniels flushing out game or
holding dead birds in their jaws. Either Wade Pierce was a
dog lover—as he'd told me he was—or he was a bird hater. I
wasn't getting any closer to finding the spare key, if there was
one, so I tried the usual places, but it wasn't taped under the
desk or under the phone, or hidden inside a lamp, so my eyes
naturally went back to the picture of Frankie's ancestor. I
went over and ran my fingers across the top of the frame and
found it. A nice brass key. I took it back to the desk and tried
it on the bottom drawer. It fit.

I opened the drawer and found a folder full of canceled
checks, drawn on Pierce's account. I still didn't know what I
was looking for exactly, but I found *something*: twenty
checks, each made out to cash in the amount of a hundred
dollars, one every week going back the last five months. I
couldn't be sure—the signature on the back was hard to
read—but it looked to me as if they had all been cashed by
someone named Samuel L. Kirby. I Xeroxed them and put
them back in the desk.

After I was done I tried the key on the middle drawer. It
opened and I found some pencils, candy canes, breath mints,
and a copy of Allison DeMarco's original will, dated five

years ago. There was also a copy of the registered letter she'd sent Pierce two days before she was killed. It stated that she was tired of waiting for him to get around to making the changes she'd requested in her will, which—according to the letter—she'd initially asked him to make back in February. There was also an interesting passage that went something like this:

I understand your feelings, Wade. We've been through a lot together these last few months. I so much appreciate all you've done for me, freeing me from Richard's grasp, and being there for me when I needed you most. And I'm terribly sorry for the trouble you've been having with the project. I think things will work out in the end, so don't lose faith. You'll make it! But still, I do need you to take care of this as soon as possible. My whole life has changed! I have a daughter! And she forgives me for abandoning her. I can't ignore my feelings. Please, please, forgive me if you think that now I'm abandoning you. I'm not, trust me. But I have to go with what my heart is telling me to do. You should understand that more than anyone.

Then she stated her intention to have Tim Berry write the new will and be the new executor.

Interesting. I also found her initial letter, the one she'd written back in February, in which she'd also expressed the desire to change the will so Richard DeMarco wouldn't "get a dime," as she'd put it. Again, interesting. So Wade Pierce had lied about Allison's feelings for her ex. It's true that Richard stood to inherit under the old will, but not because she still loved him: it was because she—or rather, Pierce—hadn't gotten around to changing the will.

I went to the Xerox machine again and had just lifted up the cover and placed the first page of the old will onto the glass when there was a knock at the door. Jesus. I quickly put everything back in place and locked the drawer but accidentally dropped the key. I got down on my hands and knees to retrieve it and banged my head on the underside of the desk as I got back up.

There was another knock.

"Wade? It's Jamie Cutter. Are you there?"

I struggled to my feet, put the key back on top of the picture frame, went to the door, opened it quickly, grabbed Jamie's wrist, and pulled her inside, closing the door behind her.

"Jack! What the—?" She looked around. "Where's Wade?"

"Why, I believe he's out of town, honey. How are you?"

"Oh, no. What are you doing?" Breathless, and without waiting for a reply she suddenly smiled and jabbed my spleen. "You're looking for clues, aren't you? You sneak. How did you get in? Did you find anything?"

I told her I had and she seemed to shiver with excitement.

"This is sooo much fun. Can we look some more together?"

I wanted to stay and make copies of everything connected to the case but I wasn't about to jeopardize Jamie's position with local law enforcement, so I said: "No, I think we'd better get out of here before anyone else shows up."

She was disappointed. "What did you find though, Jack?"

"Nothing, really. Just a few tidbits, which I'll be happy to tell you about somewhere away from here. Okay? And by the way, sweetie, what the hell are you doing here?"

"Oh," she smiled. "I just thought I'd see how my divorce is coming along." She put her hands on my chest. "I've fallen in love, you see, and I want to be totally free from Oren as soon as possible. Plus, I just happened to be across the street at the ophthalmologist's office, remember?"

"I remember."

She went to the window, parted the blinds, and pointed to a building across the parking lot. "It's right next door."

"Well, isn't that handy?" I took a quick look outside, then adjusted the blinds. There were no black Dodge trucks out there that I could see. "Well, look, you know, let's go grab a bagel and you can tell me what you found out. And," I said, going for the door, "I'll tell you what *I* found out."

"Wait, what did you find out? Jack! Wait for me!"

23

"I feel like an idiot," I said. "Everyone in town has been telling me what great bagels they make here, and me, being from New York, I thought I knew better so I just ignored them."

"Jack—!"

"Honey, these are the best bagels I've ever tasted!"

"That's just great, Jack." She pushed a fork into her salad. "Now, what did you find in Wade Pierce's office?"

"You don't understand. I've been feeling like an exile and here's something that reminds me of home and makes life worth living and you don't care." Her head sagged and she sighed and a strand of hair fell across her face. "What's wrong?"

"What do you think? Being in love is supposed to make you feel that way! And now you're telling me that a bagel . . . ?" She angrily tucked the loose strand behind one ear.

I laughed. "You're jealous over a piece of bread?"

"It's not funny."

I laughed again then stopped, knowing I was about to cross the line. "Okay, you're right." (Always tell a woman she's right—that's *my* advice.) "I'm sorry." I took her hand. "You *do* make my life worth living. Much more than a stupid bagel. I just thought you'd know that by now. So, I was just . . . you know, fooling around a little, making a stupid joke."

She stabbed at her salad again. "Yeah, well, Freud says people make jokes in order to mask their true feelings."

"Yeah, or to protect themselves from being hurt, which is what *I* was doing."

She looked up at me. "You think I'm going to hurt you?"

"Of course." She gave me a puzzled look. "I mean, not on purpose but, yeah, falling in love is a scary enterprise, don't you think? You're opening yourself up to all kinds of hurts, disillusions, and disappointments."

"You make it sound so wonderful."

"Well, look at you and Oren. I doubt if you would've married him if you had any idea how things would end up."

"That's for sure."

"So that's what this is all about." I shrugged. "You making fun of me last night, me teasing you about the bagels this afternoon. They really are incredibly good, by the way."

She laughed and shook her head. "Well then, may I have a bite, at least?"

"Sure." I gave her a bite of my bagel—an onion-and-garlic with olive spread and sliced Nova.

"Mmmmm. You're right, they *are* good."

"I *told* you. My theory is, it's the water."

"What does this have to do with our relationship?"

How to put it? Falling in love is fun, sure—but it's also risky. You have to feel your way through certain, I don't know, minefields of experience. You want to test the other person's responses as you open up, so you slowly allow them to see you for who you really are. You do this in small, careful quantum leaps, mind you, leaps that you feel you're in charge of. Meanwhile, they're doing the same thing, in their own way. A way you might not be familiar with, so misunderstandings often occur. Also, both partners are jockeying for position, each one wanting to have at least some amount of control over the other. Freud called this the "unconscious sexual dialectic." (I don't know—it was either Freud or Mae West who said it.) The process can be fun and it can also be fraught with peril. For some, the more peril, the more fun. Go figure.

There are other aspects to the dance. The desire for, and

the need to be with, the other. The hope that s/he will some-how fulfill and satisfy certain emotions in you that have lain dormant or been suppressed. Then there's the way the two of you sort of bump up against each other's strengths and weak-nesses. The way you tend to bring certain of each other's character flaws to the surface, so that you feel as if this per-son has the power to make you a "better person" somehow. Oh, it's all very exciting and wonderful and just a little bit addictive.

I didn't say any of this to Jamie, of course. What I *said* was, "There's always one person in a relationship who's more in love than the other one. In our case, that's me. I need you more than you need me, so in order to protect my-self from being hurt, which I know I will be when you fi-nally realize that you're too good for me, I try to keep my distance and hide my feelings through sarcasm and stupid jokes."

"Oh, Jack." She put down the bagel and took my hand. I think there was even a happy tear forming in one eye. "Is that really how you feel? That I'm too good for you?"

"Of course. I love you more than you can possibly imag-ine. And not just because you percolate my hormones, either."

She laughed. "I what? I percolate your hormones?"

"You sure do. And, I don't know, I guess I'm afraid of los-ing you. Which is also why I love these bagels." I made a grab for it but Jamie was too quick. She snatched it up before I could get it. I sighed. "I mean, who knows how long this place can stay in business—bagels, in Maine?"

"You're such a jerk."

"This is what I've been saying."

She started to make a reply but looked over my shoulder to the front door and her face fell again. "I guess the two of you had to meet sooner or later . . ."

I turned in my chair and saw Oren Pritchett standing in the front door, taking off his scarf. (Jamie had shown me their wedding pictures, which is how I recognized him.)

There was a young woman with him whose make-up skills seemed to have been heavily influenced by Tammy Faye Bakker. Her hair was frizzed and bleached in about ten different shades, none of them found in nature. It actually hurt my eyes to look at her. Jamie must've noticed my reaction, because she said, "And I'll bet you thought I was just being catty when I called her a bimbo."

"I apologize."

Oren saw us at about the same time that his scarf was halfway off his neck. For a second it looked as if he was going to rewrap himself, leave, and go eat somewhere else. But for some reason he decided to tough it out and act friendly.

"Hello, Jamie," he said as he came over. "How are you?"

"Fine, Oren, and you?"

"Never better." He put an arm around the young woman he was with (the bimbo) to punctuate the fact. He was tall, with long greasy hair a kind of reddish-brown color. He was a lot younger than I. He was Jamie's age, in fact, but he looked a lot older.

"You've met Julie," Oren said to Jamie and she nodded, though they didn't air-kiss or shake hands.

To Oren, Jamie said, "This is Jack Field."

"Ah, yes . . . the 'dog person.'"

I grabbed hold of the table to keep myself from belting him one, then took a deep breath, loosened my grip, and smiled.

"Why don't you two join us?" I said.

"Oh, that would be nice," Julie chirped and started to sit down. Oren grabbed her arm. "Ow! You're hurting me!"

"I don't think he was being sincere, sweetie."

She glared at me. "Is that right? You didn't mean it?"

"Sorry," Jamie said. "Jack sometimes has a mean sense of humor when he's around drug addicts."

I clucked my tongue. "Now, Jamie, you know Oren's problem is an illness, not a character flaw."

"I'm sorry," Jamie said.

"Yeah, like you care," Oren snipped. "Oh, by the way? Eddie Cole got released last week on some kind of technicality. Word is? He's been asking around about you."

There was a sharp intake of breath from Jamie. She covered it well with a tilt of her head and an artfully bored look. "Really? Well, isn't that interesting? It was nice to see you again, Oren."

"Fine. I just thought you should know. Come on, Julie." He took her arm.

"Nice to meet you," Julie said as he led her to the door.

"Ta ta," Jamie smiled.

After they'd gone Jamie got depressed.

"Who's Eddie Cole?" I asked.

"Nobody. You know what? This little encounter is going to cost me another three months of negotiations with that—"

"Who's Eddie Cole?"

"I told you, nobody. You know, sometimes I think you don't want me to get divorced."

"Like this is *my* fault?"

"No, you're right. I'm sorry." She sighed. "Now will you tell me what you found out in Wade Pierce's office?"

A waiter came over to see how we were doing. I ordered another bagel—Jamie had eaten most of mine. While they were preparing it I told Jamie what I'd found out. I didn't tell her about the newspaper clippings, or that I knew her Uncle Horace had had an affair with his best friend's wife, Joan Kirby, or the fact that he was Sam Kirby's biological father. I also kept hidden my keen, Freudian analysis that most of Flynn's dislike for me was displaced guilt over his own indiscretion years ago, and all the pain and trouble it had caused. That could wait until Jamie was in a more receptive mood—or better yet, never. I *did* tell her, though, that I thought Sam Kirby had planted evidence.

She pointed out that just because he'd found the spare key didn't necessarily mean he'd planted it.

"You're right. It's circumstantial. But the weather and the condition of the porch *do* prove Tim Berry didn't use that key on the day of the murder. And the question remains: Why is a sheriff's deputy finding evidence two days after the investigation was turned over to the Camden PD?"

She nodded. "It is odd," she said.

"Odd? It's downright peculiar. And what has Wade Pierce been paying Sam Kirby to do for the last five months?"

"A," she said, "you yourself said you couldn't be sure if it really *was* Kirby's signature on those checks—"

"It'll be easy enough to find out—"

"And B—even if it *is* his signature, you don't know that it had anything to do with Allison DeMarco. It could be something to do with the marina project."

"Yes, but Wade Pierce was Allison's attorney and there's definitely something hinky about the will, which is the key to the murder. Plus, he lied about the original will. Look, all I'm saying is, when you put all the lies and discrepancies together, you get a pattern. And it leads away from Tim Berry."

"Maybe he planned it that way."

"Have you talked to him? He's not that smart."

"I thought he was a law student."

"Pre-law. It could just as well have been pre-welding. Have you gotten the lab results back yet?"

"No, I've also been getting flack from Allison's family and from Dr. Reiner to release the body as soon as possible. That's one reason I came by to see Wade: he's representing the family and I wanted him to know why it's taking so long."

"I thought you said she didn't *have* any family."

"She does now. Apparently a nephew turned up. He's related to some sort of half-sister who's institutionalized."

This rang a bell, but my shoulder was throbbing and my second bagel arrived and I couldn't get my thoughts together enough to think of why what she'd just said seemed important.

"Everything's screwy with this case," I said, taking a bite out of the bagel. "What did Dr. Reiner say?"

"He okayed the hormone tests but said if I didn't find anything conclusive soon, I should call it quits."

"What is with these people? Call it quits, even if you don't have an answer for how this woman died?"

She shrugged. "I'm just telling you what he said. I'm starting to feel bad for our waiter."

"Join the club. Though he didn't have to pull a gun on the cops. I have *him* to thank as much if not *more* than the Camden PD for the hole in my shoulder."

"I know, but he's in a terrible jam right now. I just wish there was something more we could do to help him. Oh, by the way, my father called. He wants me to spend Saturday night with him and his new wife Laurie at his place in Christmas Cove."

"Maybe that's it." She gave me a look. "What I mean is, I have to do that seminar in Boothbay on Saturday. You know Dale Summerhays, the crazy woman who runs the Mid-

Coast Animal Rescue League? She's a big fan of mine for some reason and she's organized this shindig at the shelter's thrift shop. Just wait till they hear my opinions on spaying and neutering—though maybe I shouldn't bring the subject up . . ."

"Yeah, maybe not."

"Anyway, we could drive down to your dad's place. He's got some kind of little motorboat, right?"

"You mean the runabout?"

"Is that what you call it?" She nodded. "Well, you could ferry me over to Boothbay and afterward we could both take a little cruise over to Monhegan Island and try to talk Tim Berry into turning himself in." I looked around the restaurant. "You know what I just realized?"

She was stunned. "He's hiding out on Monhegan Island?"

"I think so, though don't quote me on it. This is the first bagel place I've ever seen with Christmas decorations."

"You're such an idiot—the owners here probably aren't Jewish, like in New York." She sighed. "I'll call my father and ask if we can borrow the boat on Saturday."

I munched my bagel. "So what did the eye doctor say?"

"Who? Oh, the ophthalmologist . . . he said that Allison's prescription was for eyestrain. From working on her computer, I guess. What are you doing later?"

"My doctor says I should be convalescing—"

"How intelligent of her—"

"—So I guess I'll go home and take a nap."

"Take two. One for you and one for me." She got up and grabbed her coat. "I've gotta go. I'll see you tonight. By the way, you were right. That was a great bagel."

"Wait. Who's Eddie Cole?" I said, but she was gone.

24

I didn't go straight home and take a nap. Instead, I drove over to Tim Berry's house. There was an unmarked police car parked down the street, sitting on the place. I parked behind it, got out, and walked over to speak to the officer.

"Hi, I'm Jack Field. Anything going on?"

"You're *who*?"

"Jack Field. Coletti knows me. I was on the job in New York. Now I run a kennel up by New Hope." He nodded. "I'm taking care of the suspect's dog for a few days, at least until you guys nab him, and I need to pick up some things."

He thought it over and shrugged. "The grandparents are out of town for the holidays. Place is locked up tight."

"That's okay," I lied, "he left me a key."

I went up the front steps and took out Jill Krempetz's bobbie pins and picked the lock. I looked back at the officer and gave a small wave. He was on the radio, probably checking my story with Coletti. I went inside and made straight for the end table and picked up the photo of the house on Monhegan Island. I took it out of its frame and rolled it up and put it in the inside pocket of my Levi's jacket. Then I put the frame back in place but it looked a little obvious, an empty picture frame sitting out in plain sight, so I took it over to the piano and left it lying face down on top.

I went into the kitchen to look for Thurston's food and dinnerware. I had plenty of such items back at the kennel, I just wanted to be able to walk out the front door with my hands full to make my story look right. I found Thurston's dinner and water bowls and a ten-pound bag of dry food. I picked them up and noticed a door leading to a little room behind the kitchen. I put the puppy things down and went to have a quick look inside.

It had probably been the maid's room once upon a time, but had been converted into Tim Berry's study. There was an iMac computer on his desk, with an external zip drive. I remember thinking that I ought to see if Tim Berry had his own copy of Allison's new will on Zip disk, so I could compare it with the one the police found on Allison's computer. I checked my pockets to see if I had the floppy that Carl Staub had made me. I don't remember if I actually found it or not. The next thing I remember is lying on the living room floor, feeling a blast of cold air hit me. Someone was shaking me and asking if I was all right. It was the officer who'd been watching the house.

"What happened?" he said, kneeling next to me.

"I don't know," I said, feeling the back of my head. "I think I must have slipped on the rug or something."

"Did you see Sam Kirby?"

No, I thought, but his question explained why I had a knot on my head. It also explained my waking up in a prone position, and my sudden short-term memory loss. I checked my pockets. The floppy disk Carl Staub had given me was still there. So was a new disk—a zip disk marked, Allison's will.

The officer helped me up. I thanked him and walked toward the door. He followed me.

"Hey, where are you going? You left your dogfood."

I went back to Jill Krempetz's office to show her the two wills and to get her legal opinion on them. She was smoking a joint when I arrived.

"Don't tell me," I joked, "you've got glaucoma."

She gave me a dirty look, took a long drag, kept it in a while, then let it out. "Cancer," she said, her eyes red and relaxed. "It mitigates the side effects of the chemo."

I sat down. "Jesus. I'm sorry. What kind?"

"Breast cancer. You wouldn't have noticed, since I wear a fake boob, but I'm a trifle less top-heavy than I used to be."

"Now I know why I saw Farrell Woods here earlier."

She shrugged. "Unfortunately, the use of medical marijuana still isn't legal in Maine."

I told her I felt bad and asked if there was anything I could do for her but she wouldn't hear of it. The mastectomy had been successful, if not exactly thrilling, and the chemo was just to be sure there were no traces of the disease left.

"You're not even losing any hair."

"Not yet," she smiled at me. "So, what is it this time? You came back to return my bobby pins?"

"No," I said, then told her why I'd come back.

She held out her hand. "Let's see the disks . . ." I handed them to her. She put the floppy in her computer but it wouldn't open. "Sorry, I have an older operating system. Let's try downstairs. They have a couple of iMacs down at the *Herald*."

We went downstairs, I had a brief but happy reunion with the receptionist, Jill asked if she could borrow one of their computers, the girl said yes, and we sat down at a work station in the back, popped in both disks, and opened the documents. The gist of it was that there were two different wills, sharing some similarities. The one from Allison's computer was well written and professional. Tim Berry had done an excellent job, although there was no mention of his being named the new executor, but it was true: Allison wanted her entire estate left to her dog.

The other will, the one from Tim Berry's computer, seemed to be a rough draft—it was not as well written or polished. It differed in three important points: most of Allison's money was to be left to Tara, her daughter, and not the dog; Tim Berry was to be the new executor; and *I* was asked to take care of Ginger. She'd even left me a little money.

Jill ran through the finer points of all this and then said, "Here's something interesting . . ." She opened the "Get Info" section on the computer's desktop for each file. The sloppily written will, the one leaving Allison's money to Tara and the dog to me, was created on the Friday morning before the murder at exactly 10:23 A.M. and hadn't been modified since then. The will found on Allison's computer showed the same date and time that the file was first created—10:23 A.M. on Friday, but the file had been modified later. In fact, it had

been changed on Sunday afternoon at exactly 3:45 P.M.—
which, according to Jamie's preliminary autopsy report,
would have been roughly around the same time that Allison
had been killed.

"There was another will? An original she wanted
changed?"

"Yeah. According to Wade Pierce she originally left her
entire estate to her ex-husband, though she'd been trying to
get Pierce to rewrite it since last February."

"And Pierce was the executor on that will?"

"I don't know. He *said* he was."

She closed the files and ejected the disks. "It would be
nice to see a copy of the original will, but it might not be necessary. If she was killed for her money, it could've been the
ex-husband or someone close to him, like a family member."

She looked up at me. "You said he was also killed, right?"
I nodded. We got up and began to walk out. "Or it could've
been another of Allison's relatives who wanted to make it
look like her daughter, Tara, was the killer. Or it could've
been . . ."

25

I went home and fell asleep on top of the covers in my jeans and T-shirt. It took a while to get Jill's "or it could've been"s to stop whirling around inside my brain, but I was tired enough to crash, so I did. Around 4:30 I was awakened by a collect call from the Virgin Islands. It was Carl Staub.

"How's the weather?" I asked, looking out at the snow.

"Eighty degrees and sunny," he said cheerfully. "I may not come back."

I laughed. "Hang on a sec." I went into the bathroom and when I was done I came back and sat on the bed, put on a shirt, picked up the phone and said, "So what'd you find out?"

He told me that Richard DeMarco had come to the Virgins on Friday of the previous week, two days before his ex-wife's murder, and that by all reports he'd been there the whole time. He had a female companion with him—a Debbie Sheldon, originally from Florida, now living with him in Bangor—who told the V.I. police that she and Richard ate brunch at about 11:30 on Monday morning and that she'd gone down to the beach alone for a few hours because he said he wasn't feeling well. Then, when she came back to their private cabin on the beach, she found his body in their bed. He'd been stabbed to death.

I was about to ask Carl something when there was a knock at the door and Jamie came in, followed by Frankie and Ginger.

"Guess what?" she said, her face bright with excitement, "we were right." The dogs climbed up on the bed and began jumping up and kissing me. "It *was* hormones!"

"That's great." To Carl I said, "How many times was he stabbed?" Carl said there was just one stab wound.

"Who was stabbed?" Jamie said.

"Richard DeMarco," I told her. Then to Carl I said, "Did they do an autopsy?"

"They said it wasn't necessary. It seems obvious the knife wound did him in. They've even got a suspect."

"Oh, really? Who?" Jamie came over, sat next to me on the bed, and started pulling off my shirt.

"A local grifter," Carl said. "He apparently has a habit of burglarizing these fancy beach cabins."

Jamie got my shirt off and was trying to peel my T-shirt off as well. "What are you doing? I'm on the phone."

"What?" Carl said.

"I need to check your stitches."

"Hang on, Carl." I put the phone down and took off my T-shirt. Mrs. Murtaugh knocked on the door and came in while Jamie looked over my surgery from the day before.

"Have you got a minute?" Mrs. Murtaugh said.

"What does it look like. Why? What's wrong?"

"Lucy just threw up and I was wondering if—"

"Lucy the lab or Lucy the Dalmatian?"

"Lucy the lab."

"She sometimes does that in the afternoons. The vet isn't sure why. Don't worry too much unless she does it again." She nodded and left and I said, "Carl? Are you still there?"

"I'm still here. What's going on?"

"Has he ever stabbed any of his victims before?"

Carl said, "Who, the burglar? Good question."

Jamie said, "Has who stabbed who before?" She found the knot on the back of my head. "And what is this?"

"A Christmas present from Sam Kirby, I think." To Carl I said, "Well, find out if he has. Hang on a sec." Then to Jamie I said, "Did you just say something about hormones?"

"Jack! Sam did this to you?"

"Yeah, I think so. Now about those hormones?"

She sighed and began changing my bandage. "A hormone

cocktail actually—epinephrine, PTH, and an enzyme called renin—all of which could cause an accelerated heart rate. She also had high levels of calcium, which would—"

"—cause the heart muscle to freeze up like a car engine on a cold day without any oil. I know, it's called—"

"Calcium rigor."

"And this was all in her eye drops?"

She shook her head. "Probably just the epinephrine and PTH, or parathyroid hormone, which regulates calcium absorption, among other things. I'm guessing that the renin was a by-product of the PTH. But we found five calcium tablets in her stomach contents as well. Fifteen hundred milligrams each."

"Wow, that's a lot. Look, maybe we should go over this later. I've got to finish this call."

She got up. "Sure. Your stitches look good." She just stood there smiling at me.

"You're not going to yell at me for getting conked?"

She shook her head. "Would you yell at a puppy for doing something wrong? I've finally realized: that's you, Jack. You're just a big overgrown puppy dog. Put some ice on it. I've got to get my nails done then hit the gym. Mom wants to know if you can come over for dinner tonight. Eight o'-clock?"

I said that was fine and she kissed me and left. Mrs. Murtaugh came back in and said, "Quentin Peck is here."

"I love that woman. Who?"

"Quentin Peck. The deputy. He brought his dog with him. Emma. He wants to know if you could give him some pointers."

"Oh, okay. Tell him I'll be right down. I want to find out if he knows who Eddie Cole is . . ."

"And the Stevens family is here, with their boxer, Roarke."

"All right. Have them hang out. Their kids can play with Thurston. That'll keep them occupied. Just make sure Audrey is there to supervise. Oh, and if you have time, ask Sloan and D'Linda if they want to work some extra hours this week."

"I'm sure they will." She started to close the door.

"By the way, the Christmas tree looks great. Thanks."

"You're welcome," she said and smiled. "Come on, kids," she said to the dogs and they followed her outside.

"Okay, Carl," I said into the phone, "where were we—?"

"We were talking about the murder suspect. I just asked the local police if he'd stabbed anybody before. Did I tell you I'm calling from police headquarters?"

"You did not. And what did they say?"

"No. This is the first time. They say maybe DeMarco's the first one who caught him in the act. Anyway, I *did* find something suspicious: there was a Richard DeMarco on the passenger list of a plane that left Portland airport at seven o'clock Sunday night—which would be about three hours before Quentin Peck found the body at Hobb's Pond. The plane from Portland landed at LaGuardia at eight-thirty, and DeMarco was listed on the passenger manifest from a flight out of New York—from Kennedy this time—to the Virgin Islands. The plane left at midnight."

"I thought you said DeMarco had been there the whole time."

"Well, that's what I was told, but it seems—"

"Interesting. Was there a lot of blood?"

"At the airport?"

"No, in the bed, when this Debbie Sheldon found the body."

"Oh, I don't know."

"Didn't you go to the scene and take a look?"

"Yeah, but the hotel staff had already cleaned it up."

"Figures. Did you get a chance to talk to her?"

"No. She flew home Monday night. She lives in Bangor."

"Yeah, I know, with Richard DeMarco. All right, see if you can get a description from the airlines or the flight crews to make sure it really *was* DeMarco on those planes." Then I told him to get copies of all the police reports, photos of the body, etc. "Where is it now, by the way?"

"The body? I don't know. Hang on a sec." I heard a lot of white noise and then Carl came back on the line and said, "It's scheduled to leave for Buffalo, via Kennedy, early tomorrow morning. The funeral's on Monday."

I thanked Carl and hung up and made a few more phone calls, one to Coletti, and one to the State Medical Examiner's

Office in Augusta to tell them I thought it would be a good idea to do a postmortem on Richard DeMarco's body, but no one seemed interested, so I called Carl back. Luckily he was still at the police station in Charlotte Amalie. I asked him to fax me all the shipping information on Richard DeMarco's final journey home and he said he'd get right on it.

I put some shoes on, went downstairs, peeled a banana and called my old pal Lou Kelso in New York and told him I needed a couple of favors. Carl's fax came while I was explaining things, so I read him the flight information and he said he'd take care of the arrangements at Kennedy. He also told me that he'd just made first contact with the judge in Duke's case and that the man seemed nervous.

"Nervous enough to move him on this, you think?"

"We'll see," he said. "Either way, the balance of power has shifted in our favor. I hope."

"Me too." Mrs. Murtaugh came in just as I hung up and said, "Someone from DHS is here looking for Duke."

"Uh-oh." I went to the window, looked out, and turned back to Mrs. Murtaugh. "Where *is* Duke?"

"In the kennel, I think."

I checked my watch. It was after five o'clock. "Okay, these people hate to work past quitting time. Tell the social worker that Duke is out picking up dogs and won't be back until eight or nine. And keep him out of sight until they leave."

She left and I made another quick call to the Virgin Islands. "Carl, I'm gonna need you to meet me at the Portland airport tomorrow afternoon. When are you planning to leave?"

"Tomorrow morning. My wife wants to try this 'sailing-at-sunset' thing they've got down here."

"You took your wife with you?"

"Hey, you said you'd pay my expenses . . ."

26

It had stopped snowing. The clouds were pink and gray and the county road had been plowed and sanded, leaving a big blue plowdrift along the ridge above my property. There were three extra cars in the parking area: Quentin Peck's black Jeep, the Stevens's blue minivan, and Audrey Stafford's red Civic. It seemed that the social worker had gotten tired of waiting around for Duke and had gone home.

According to Mrs. Murtaugh, the youngest of the three Stevens kids were playing with Thurston in the indoor play room, while the third—seven-year-old Joey—was outside making snowballs in the play yard while the family dog—a tawny boxer with floppy ears and a black mask, named Roarke—romped with Quentin Peck and his chocolate lab, Emma, along with Frankie, Ginger, the two Lucys and a blue Dane named Achille (pronounced Ah-*sheel*—one of his owners is originally from Paris).

Joey was having a lot of fun, making snowballs for the big dogs to chase and bite. Sloan was there, too, watching over things. Meanwhile, Ron and Beth Stevens were in the family car, the blue minivan, having what looked like a Christmas squabble. I gave them a happy wave as I walked past on my way to the play yard. They didn't wave back.

As I came down the hill, Joey was about to throw another snowball and started to slip on the ice. Roarke saw this and ran over, sliding his own body under the boy's legs to cushion the fall. Boxers are like that: they live to protect kids.

Frankie and Ginger saw me and got happy. They ran over to meet me at the gate. Frankie did his snake dance and Ginger did her Airedale pogo act. Achille, the blue Dane, got really happy as well. He was about to jump up and put his big paws on my shoulders, but I outmaneuvered him and said, "Sit!" and he quickly sat instead. Then I said, "Paw!" and he gave me his big ham hock of a paw and we shook hands and let it go at that.

Meanwhile, Quentin Peck threw a tennis ball for Emma and she went after it, followed by the two Lucys and the big, lumbering Dane, who wasn't necessarily trying to get the ball, but was just happy to be part of the game. Peck smiled his nicotine smile and said, "You got a great place here."

"Thanks," I said, "have you seen Duke?"

"Who, the kid? Nope. Maybe he's inside."

Quent said he'd dropped by because he was having problems with Emma, his chocolate lab. She had started eating paper clips, newspapers, carpet, etc. As he was explaining this Ron Stevens got out of the mini-van and called to Joey to get the dog. "We're not going on vacation after all," he shouted.

Joey kicked at the snow, sighed, and grabbed Roarke by the collar. "Come on, Roarke," he said and yanked on it, but Roarke didn't want to go so he danced away and the kid's face went all red and he lunged at the dog and yelled, "Bad dog!"

"I don't know what to do," said Quent, "so I was thinkin—"

"—hang on a sec," I told him, then went over to Joey. "Here, Joey," I said, gently. "Let me help you." I went over to the gate and found a nylon leash that matched Roarke's collar, then I showed the boxer a piece of cheese and praised him, hoping he'd come over and take it from me. He didn't trust me so I tossed the cheese in front of him and he scarfed it up. Then I showed him another tidbit which caused Frankie, Ginger, Achille, and the two Lucys to try to get in on the action.

I crouched down and showed Roarke the treat, and he and the other dogs came over. I let Roarke take the cheese. At the same time, I hooked him up to his leash, walked him back over to Joey and said: "He's a good dog. It's not his fault your vacation got called off, is it?"

The kid gave me a skeptical look.

"Come on." I winked at him. "Who loves you no matter what?" I tilted my head toward the dog. "Your dog does, right?"

He thought it over, then leaned down and hugged Roarke's neck. The boxer gave him a big wet kiss on the nose and the kid laughed and said, "Good boy!" Roarke wagged his tush and tried to lick Joey's face some more. Joey giggled and petted his dog's head. I opened the gate for them and they went up the hill, laughing and playing together.

The other dogs were patiently waiting for their treats. I gave them each a piece of cheese, then threw a tennis ball and they all chased it. Emma got to it first, even though she was the chubbiest. "She's fast," I said to Quent, then went toward the gate. "Excuse me. I think Ron Stevens is going to want his deposit back."

He didn't, though. He just got all the kids and the dog together and drove away. I didn't hear any more about them until February, when Beth Stevens's father was found dead in his Cadillac. Roarke was with him at the time. But that's another story.

It was getting dark by this time so Quent and Sloan and I got all the dogs hooked up and took them up to the kennel, where we found Duke sitting behind the front desk reading *People* magazine. Sloan started to put the two Lucys back in their kennels. Duke got up and started making their dinner.

Mrs. Murtaugh was closing up the grooming room. She said, "Dorianne Elliot is on her way over with Satchmo. He's—"

"—Been scavenging a lot, I know. Did you speak to Sloan and D'Linda?"

She nodded. "They could both use the money."

"Good." To Quent I said, "Let's go outside." We went out to the parking area. I had Frankie, Ginger, and Achille (the blue Dane) with me. Quent had the chocolate lab. I asked him about her past training.

"Well, we sent her off to this puppy boot-camp about two months ago." He told me the name.

"Yeah? And when did the pica start?"

"Pica?"

"The ingestion of non-food objects."

"Oh, I don't remember."

"Was it before or after she went to boot-camp?"

"Oh, yeah," he remembered, "it started right afterward."

"Well," I raised the palms of my hands in the air, "did it ever occur to you that there might be a connection?"

"I don't know. I guess I thought about it. But they trained her real good. She listens now, where before—"

"Let me show you something," I said. I turned my back on Emma, who was being held on lead by Quent, then I showed Frankie, Ginger, and Achille a tennis ball and gave them the down command. They all dropped into position instantly, with their tails and ears held high, their eyes bright and clear. I told them to stay, then turned to face Emma and gave her the same command. It was as if I had threatened her. She slowly went down into position, but her ears were pinned back and her tail was tucked between her legs.

"See?" Quentin said, "she's really well trained."

"No she's not. Look at her body language! She's nervous and frightened. She's unhappy. She doesn't want to do this." He looked at Emma and grudgingly nodded. "Now look at these other dogs." He looked at the three of them. "Did you see them? They all went down instantly, they're all calm and relaxed and totally happy and eager to cooperate."

It was true. The setter, the Airedale, and the Dane were all lying in the snow, showing perfect form.

"Yeah, it's like they're waiting to hear what you want them to do next. You've really got that alpha thing going."

I laughed. "There is no alpha thing. That's bullshit."

"What? But everybody says—"

"—Forget what everybody says. I can prove—"

Just then Mrs. Murtaugh came outside and told me that D'Linda would be over as soon as possible. She had to drop off her nephew at her mother's first. I thanked her and she put on her scarf and gloves and started to walk up the long driveway and I asked if I couldn't give her a lift, even though she lives right across the road. She said she'd be all right. "I've lived in this weather all my life," she grumped, "I'm not about to let it slow me down now."

Quentin and I watched her make her way up the hill, both

a little worried she might slip and fall. Audrey came out of the kitchen, onto the side porch. "Has Ginger eaten yet?" she said.

"Not yet."

"Is it okay if I feed her?"

Duke came out the kennel door, "Yo, Jack—"

"Hang on a second—" To Audrey I said, "Sure, in a minute. But first—" I nodded toward her grandmother.

Audrey caught my meaning, called out, "Grandma, wait," then grabbed her coat and ran to catch up with the old woman.

I dropped Ginger's leash and said, "Okay, Ginger," and she ran over to join them. I turned to Duke.

"Yo, you want these animals fed or not?" He was referring to Frankie and Achille. I laughed and told him to go ahead and give them their dinner. He took the two dogs inside.

I turned back to Quent. "What was I saying?"

"You was gonna prove something about being alpha?"

"Oh, yeah. I don't know how familiar you are with the alpha theory, but if I were to lie down on my back and let Emma jump on top of me, wouldn't that make her think *she* was alpha?"

He scratched his head. "That sounds about right. But why would you want—?"

"And if she thought she were alpha, she would be less obedient, correct?"

He said he thought she would, yes.

"Okay, watch this." I showed Emma the tennis ball, teased her with it, then started jumping around, faking left and going right, getting her to chase me. When she was all riled up I put the tennis ball in my pocket and began rough-housing with her instead, lightly slapping my hands and arms around her head and shoulders, stimulating her to bite me. Then I ran away. She came after me and I zigged and zagged some more. Then, when her drive was at its peak, I fell to the ground and said, "Oh, no, you got me! You're the king dog! You got me, you got me!" She jumped on top of me, wagging her tail, play growling at me, and jumping around in happy circles. I immediately stood up, pulled out the tennis ball,

held it high above my head, then made a downward swoop-
ing motion with my ball hand and said, "Go down!"

She instantly dropped into position. Her ears and tail were
up. Her eyes were bright with excitement. She was happy and
eager to do whatever I asked her to. She didn't hold the position for long because I immediately threw the ball for her to
chase, which she did, as if it were the happiest moment of her
life. Then I turned to Quent. "See the difference?"

"No kidding. I mean, I don't believe this."

"Well, it's a well-kept secret but if you do the exact opposite of what most experts tell you to do, you'll usually get
better results."

Emma brought the ball back. I threw it for her again.

Quent said, "That's great, Jack, but what about her eating
all that shit . . . what did you call it?"

"Pica. Look, she only started doing that because the guy
who runs that puppy boot-camp believes in being alpha and
treats or *mistreats* dogs accordingly. I just acted 'submissive'
to Emma, right? I rolled over on my back, which, according
to the alpha theory, means I relinquished my authority.
Therefore, she should not obey me." Emma brought the ball
back again and dropped it in my hand. I made as if to throw
it, then stopped, raised my hand in the air, made that downward motion again, and said, "Go down!" and she instantly
dropped into position, ears and tail up, eyes bright. I threw
the ball.

I turned to Quent. "I rest my case. Don't worry, the pica
will probably go away on its own, as long as you just play
like this with her every day. Oh, and play tug-of-war with her
every day and always let her win and praise her for winning."

"Are you sure that's all it'll take?"

"Well, pretty sure. The pica was probably caused by fear
and a powerful suppression of her hunting drive. It's fairly
common with these boot-camp type trainers—not the pica,
just suppressing the dog's drive. The hunting drive is the key
to the pack instinct and, therefore, to training."

I taught Quent to do the same exercise I'd done, where I
got her to chase me, batted at her face and shoulders, then fell
down in the snow. He did it and she loved it. She was also a

lot more obedient and responsive to him after the game than she had been before.

We played fetch with Emma some more and as we did I began to pump Quent for information: "What time did the first call come in about the barking?"

"What barking?"

"At Allison DeMarco's? The night of the murder?"

"Oh, I don't know. I didn't come on duty until four. You'd have to ask Trudy Compton. She was on the switchboard. But if I was to guess, I'd say it was about two-thirty or so. Here, Emma, give me the ball . . . good girl! Go down!" She did and he threw the tennis ball.

"So when did *you* get there?"

"I'd say about ten, ten-oh-five. Somewhere in there."

"And she'd been barking all that time?"

"I guess. Good girl, gimme the ball." I told him not to give her the down command before throwing the ball *every* time—sometimes you just throw it for free. He threw it for free.

"We get calls like this," he went on as Emma chased the ball again, "where you figure sooner or later the barking is gonna stop, so you just tell the caller you'll look into it and you don't. In this case, she didn't stop until *you* showed up."

We played with Emma some more. "She's gonna drive me nuts with this, now, you know?" He got out a pack of smokes.

I laughed. "Well, you're the one who had to get a lab."

He laughed and nodded his head sheepishly, then shook a cigarette out of the pack. As he lit it, a car came down the drive and I was worried for a second that it might be someone from DHS coming back to check on Duke. It wasn't though. It was Dorianne Elliot in her black Cherokee. Satch, her German shepherd, was in the front seat with her.

Quent took a puff and said, "So, what do I owe you?"

I told him my usual fee, then said, "Tell you what, Quent, if you do what I say, I won't charge you a dime. If you don't, you can pay me double what you paid this boot-camp to screw up your dog in the first place."

He laughed. "It's a deal." He called Emma to him and she came over and he hooked up her leash.

"Don't forget to praise her when she obeys," I reminded him. "She just came when you called her. You have to reward her for it."

He nodded and said to Emma, "Good girl, Emmie, gooood!" and she looked up at him and wagged her tail happily. He started for his car, stopped, and said, "Do I gotta roll around in the snow with her like that every day?"

I laughed. "No, just every once in a while ought to do it. Oh, one other thing—they get a line on this waiter and his girlfriend?"

"Yeah, I don't know, sort of I guess. They found his car— a yellow Firebird. It was in a parking lot over in Rockland. We been checking the motels and stuff, but no luck so far."

Hopefully, I thought, they hadn't checked the ferry to Monhegan Island.

Then Quent thanked me and packed up his dog and left. I had the feeling there was something I had forgotten to ask him about, but Dorianne was waiting for me so I let it go.

27

"Crap," I said, as I watched Quent drive away. "I forgot to ask him about Eddie Cole."

"Who's Eddie Cole?" Dorianne asked.

"That's what *I'd* like to know."

Meanwhile, Audrey and Ginger were just back from walking Mrs. Murtaugh home. She waved to me from over by the back porch, then she and Ginger went into the house.

"So Satch is giving you some problems?" I said.

"He's becoming impossible," Dorianne cried. "He tries to eat everything he sees. I can't run with him anymore. He wants to stop at every garbage can on the way. What am I gonna do?"

We established that she was talking about scavenging, not pica. I told her to stop punishing him, stop scolding him or using a shake-can or any other form of negative reinforcement. And I suggested that she stop taking him jogging with her.

"But he needs his exercise," she moaned.

"I don't disagree, but he needs to run full speed, not lope along next to you. Plus, he needs to chase something he can sink his teeth into when he catches it. You should play fetch with him for at least twenty minutes, twice a day."

"And that's it?"

"No, not quite. Let me show you something . . . you already fed him tonight like I told you? With an extra half a bowl?" She said she had, so I took a firm hold of Satch's leash, grabbed a couple of biscuits from my pocket, threw them on the ground in front of him, and watched him try to go to town, scratching in the snow, working with all his might to get them.

"Well," I said, "this confirms my suspicion that he's not scavenging out of hunger."

"No, it's more like an obsession."

"Okay, now pay attention because what I'm about to show you isn't going to make any sense." I held Satch back with a tight lead, no corrections, just calm, steady tension. He kept scratching forward as he tried and tried to get at the biscuits. As he did, in an exuberant tone, I said, "Good boy! You want those biscuits, don't you? Ooooh, they're so tasty! Ooooh, you've got to get those biscuits. Good boy! You want 'em, you really really want 'em. Good boy! Good dog!"

Meanwhile, I took another biscuit out of my pocket and kept an eye on Satch's body language. Sooner or later, I knew, he'd look away from the biscuits on the ground and look up at me to see what I was so excited about. Sure enough, he did. I showed him the biscuit in my hand and at the same time praised him, using a calmer, more relaxed tone of voice. When he focused on the biscuit in my hand, I used it to bait him past the others—the ones he wanted to scavenge—and once we were past, I let him eat the biscuit from my hand, praising him some more as he ate.

"What the hell?" Dorianne said. "What did you just do?"

"Seems odd, don't it?" I smiled. "You want to try?"

She took Satch's leash. "But this is so opposite of everything I've ever heard before . . ."

"Yeah, well, just give it a shot and see what happens."

I talked her through it, telling her, "Louder, louder, use your diaphragm, make it higher. Come on, give me your loudest, silliest, highest voice! Match his level of enthusiasm!" I had her do it four times and on the fifth go-around Satch was no longer interested in the biscuits on the ground. In fact, I tested him by throwing a biscuit right in front of him. He immediately turned his head and looked up at me instead.

"This is so mysterious," Dorianne said. "I don't get it."

I explained that a dog can't be satisfied when he doesn't feel connected to his pack. The negative training techniques

Dorianne was using created social dissonance, so Satch was looking for satisfaction through scavenging. The exercise made him feel re-connected to her, and he no longer needed to seek satisfaction through food. Dorianne nodded as if she understood, though I don't think she actually did. Still, she promised to do the exercise for at least three days under a different circumstances each time to see if it had a permanent effect (it did) and then I asked her if she'd ever been jogging past Allison DeMarco's place on Hobb's Pond.

"Oh, sure, all the time." She sighed. "It's such a shame, isn't it? Have they found her killer yet?"

"Not yet."

After reading the police report Carl Staub had stolen for me, I noticed that when the uniformed cops had canvassed Allison's neighbors, they'd asked if anyone had seen anything "suspicious or out-of-the-ordinary" on the day she was killed. This prevented Allison's neighbors from reporting or remembering the presence of any people or vehicles that *weren't* "suspicious or out-of-the-ordinary." So I asked Dorianne, who often jogged past Allison's property, what type of cars she'd seen parked in Allison's driveway over the past few months. She had to think about it but she remembered seeing an old yellow sports car parked there a lot. "It was like the one that detective on *The Rockford Files* used to drive, only yellow." She'd also seen a sheriff's Jeep, my woody, and a white BMW.

I thanked her, she thanked *me* for showing her the exercise with Satch—strange as it still seemed to her—then wrote me a check and she and Satch drove off.

I went to the kennel, got Frankie, and we headed up to the house. When we got to the side porch I could see Audrey Stafford through the kitchen window. She was cutting a tomato and some lettuce for a salad. Ginger had finished her dinner and was watching Audrey. As I came in she turned, knife in hand, and so did Ginger, suddenly growling and snarling at me. Frankie didn't like that. He snarled back at her. This set off a chain reaction. Pretty soon the room was aroil with two snarling, growling dogs, and a lot of near-biting and gnashing of teeth.

Audrey made a move, then stopped and looked at me; I

was the expert. I reached over to the stove, grabbed a pot, and dropped it on the floor, then said, "Okay!" in a happy voice. This caused the dogs to stop what they were doing. They both looked at me, kind of dumbly, then in unison, shook themselves.

I said, "Go down!" and they both dropped into position, looking up at me and panting heavily. "Good dogs," I said.

"What was that all about?" asked Audrey. "I thought they *liked* each other."

"They do," I said, then turned my attention back to the animals. I gave the two dogs the "Hup!" command, they both came over and jumped up on me ("Hup!" always stimulates positive social feelings), then I said, "Okay, off!" and they both jumped down. I opened the kitchen door and told the dogs to go out and play and they ran outside where they just *pretended* to kill each other.

"That was close," Audrey said, breathlessly.

"Yeah," I said, then explained what I thought had just happened: "I think Ginger must have been in the kitchen when Allison was killed and she just had a kind of flashback. She saw you with the knife in your hand and heard me coming through the door and for a second she was reminded of Allison's killer. How long have you been pregnant?"

"What?" she said and dropped the knife.

I went over and picked it up. I said, "The way Frankie and Ginger are always following you around. The way Frankie is always sniffing you. The way Ginger is overprotective." I didn't tell her about the feeling I'd had that she seemed "rounder" than she really was. "Does Tom know? That's your husband's name, isn't it?"

"Yes," she looked down at her Doc Martens. "I told him but we're not sure though, if now's the right time to start a family. We haven't told anyone else yet, so please—"

"My lips are sealed. Anyway, I'd better go find a stick or a ball for them to chase. They're still a little hyped up and they're gonna need something besides each other's necks to sink their teeth into. Enjoy your dinner."

I went outside, found a stick, and tossed it around for a while. The dogs bit into it with a little more gusto than usual, and then, when Audrey came outside with her car keys in hand, I asked if she could give me a ride to Glen Cove and she said yes.

I told Duke the coast was clear, at least for the time being. I asked him to take the dogs, and that D'Linda would be coming by to help him keep an eye on things. Then I got into Audrey's car and she drove me down to the Samoset, which is where Jamie was—hopefully—still working out at the gym.

We drove in relative silence for a while, just listening to the whoosh of the defroster and whine of snow tires and Audrey finally said, "What do you think I should do?"

"About the baby? Don't ask me. I've never been pregnant." I examined her softly freckled face in the dim light and realized something I'd sensed for a long time but hadn't really put into words until then: if you want to understand a woman, let her drive. While she's concentrating on the road, you can learn almost everything there is to know about her.

I said, "I've had three or four friends—not *girl*friends— who had it done and not one of them was totally happy about it afterward. Then again, who knows how happy they'd be if they hadn't had it done? I just don't know. And who says their happiness or unhappiness is the relevant issue?"

She thought this over and said, "I just want to do what's right."

"I think you will," I said.

"Sure." She seemed unconvinced. I watched her some more. There was something fine and decent and noble, and even a little courageous about her. I looked back at the road and thought how Tom was a lucky guy.

"Do you really think I'll be able to keep Ginger?"

"Sure, if I have anything to say about it. And I have a feeling I will."

She let out a long, deep breath and her face relaxed a little and I think she even smiled. They say that owning a dog can reduce stress and lower your blood pressure. I've found that sometimes just thinking about a dog can do the same thing.

"Can I ask you something? Why do you get her to jump up on you? Don't most people try to get their dogs not to jump up?"

I laughed a little and said: "Well, first of all I tend to do things backward. For instance, when I first start teaching a dog the sit command, I always give the command after the dog has already obeyed it. Second, have you ever seen Frankie or Ginger jump up on me or anyone else when they weren't asked to?" She said she hadn't. "That's because I've trained them to do it *only* on command. Besides, jumping up is a great training tool. It makes the heel command and the recall much stronger."

"I was always taught to knee them in the chest when they jump up. I guess that's not very nice, though, is it?"

"No, and not very effective in the long run. I've found there are almost always negative side-effects with that kind of training."

She drove quietly for a while and started thinking about her situation again. "Sorry to dump all this on you."

"Hmmm? Oh, that's okay," I said. "I was the one who brought it up, remember? Besides, that little drama we had in the kitchen? I think it just may have helped me figure out how to catch a killer."

"Really? How?"

"I'm gonna sic Ginger on him."

28

Jamie's car was still in the parking lot so I thanked Audrey for the ride and went inside the hotel lobby and down the concrete stairs to the health club. The spandexed girl at the desk wondered if she could help me and I told her she could.

"I'm supposed to meet a Wade Pierce here for a game of squash," I said, looking at my watch. "Could you—"

"The squash court is closed," she said and squinched her face. "Fumes."

"Fumes?"

"They just varnished the floor. They do it every ten years or so. It's been closed for over a week. You know, sanding and varnish and such?"

"But Wade Pierce *is* a member here, isn't he?"

"Oh, I'm sorry, sir." She made an apologetic face. "I can't give out that kind of information. Policy."

I told her I understood, then asked how much it would cost for me to use the gym. She told me and I paid her and we both agreed that I should have a nice workout. I went into the weight room and found Jamie, in a gray sweatsuit, riding an exercycle, her hair up in a ponytail, listening to a Walkman, and reading the latest *New England Journal of Medicine*.

She took off the headphones but kept pedaling. "What are you doing here?" She smiled.

"Dinner at your mom's, remember? I thought we could go up together. My arm is still a little sore to drive."

"You baby, I would've picked you up. Who drove you here?"

"Audrey. What kind of wine should I get?"

"A dryish red would be nice. You like her, don't you?"

"Who, Audrey? Yeah, I think she's great. If she were a few years older, had a medical degree, knew how to keep me in line, and had your face and body, I might even marry her."

She laughed and blushed. "She's already married."

"Yeah, so are you. And how do *you* know?"

"She wears a ring. Girls?—we notice these things."

I pointed to the exercycle and asked her how many more imaginary miles she planned to rack up and she said she was almost finished. I said I'd wait for her in the bar.

I bought a bottle of Cannonau di Sardegna, sipped a nice glass of Scotch, then Jamie showed up and asked me to drive us up to her mother's house so she could lean back and take a nap: She'd had a tough day (like I hadn't?). Still, I said yes.

Just outside of Rockport I noticed a pair of headlights behind us—keeping a safe two hundred yards or so back. I pointed this fact out to James—who was actually asleep at the time. She woke up and nearly freaked out.

"It's okay." I touched her arm. "It's just Sam Kirby."

She took a deep breath and said, "Oh, Sam. Oh, okay then."

I pulled the car over at the junction of 90 and 17 and the headlights behind us stopped too, well back of the intersection. I let the Jag sit idling.

"What are you doing?"

"I thought I'd stop just to see what he does."

She turned around in her seat and looked back at the headlights. "You're sure it's Sam Kirby?"

"Yeah, he's been following me all day. One of his caution lights is out." She heaved a sigh of relief. I said, "Want me to go beat him up?" I opened my door.

"No," she said, opening hers, "I'll do it. Your arm is too sore, remember?" She got out of the car.

"Then why am I driving? Hey, what are you going to do?"

She leaned through the open door. "I'm just going to go have a talk with him." She turned to go but before she could take three steps the truck peeled off and headed back east, toward Rockport.

Jamie got back in the car and said: "That takes care of that. Let's drive."

I made the right turn onto 17 and we drove.

After a bit I said, "The way you reacted I could've sworn you thought that was Eddie Cole, not Sam Kirby, behind us."

She almost caught her breath, but smoothed it over. "Who?"

"You know who," I said, but she didn't take the bait, so I let it go for the time being.

Laura Cutter made oyster stew, a surprisingly delicious broccoli casserole, and chicken lasagna. I had two helpings of each, which amused Jamie no end and made Laura feel good. There was bright conversation; and some not so bright. I heard the story—for the fifth time—of how Jamie had had her nose broken in the sixth grade and I still managed to laugh in all the right spots and look sad and concerned in the others. We had some more wine, more conversation, then Jamie and I caught Laura up on the investigation and Flynn's background checks on me.

Finally, over coffee, when the table was cleared and after Laura refused any help with the dishes for the third time, and was in the kitchen running some hot water, I took Jamie's hand and popped the big question: "How would you like to perform an illegal autopsy on Richard DeMarco's body tomorrow night?"

She shook her head and smiled at me as if I were a first-grader who'd come home covered in mud. "First of all, tomorrow is the hospital Christmas party—or had you forgotten?"

"I haven't forgotten. In fact, I'm counting on it. I plan on smuggling the body into the morgue while everybody's upstairs in the conference room getting drunk."

"Doctors don't get drunk, we just get—wait a second, why not just do a regular autopsy?"

"Ask your pal Coletti. Or the Virgin Island authorities. Or your boss Dr. Reiner. None of them feels it's necessary."

"You talked to Dr. Reiner?" There was an icy warning sound in her voice.

"Not directly. But everybody seems to think they already know the cause of death. Meanwhile, I have serious doubts, as should you. I think knowing exactly *what* killed Richard De-Marco will help us figure out exactly *who* killed his ex-wife."

She nodded. "I'll talk to Dr. Reiner tomorrow. I have an early meeting with him in the morning anyway. Then I guess if he says no, *and* if there's a John Doe in the morgue tomorrow night, *and* if my idiot boyfriend isn't in jail for—"

"Possession of a stolen corpse?"

"Possession of a stolen corpse, I'll see what I can do. You realize my findings won't be admissible in court?"

"That's okay. It'll never go to court."

"What won't go to court?" Laura asked from the kitchen door, drying her hands on a dish towel.

"Nothing," we said in unison.

I got up from the table and asked if I could use the phone.

"Of course," Laura said, "it's in the hall."

While I checked on Duke and D'Linda, Jamie and Laura retired to the family room, behind the kitchen. Jamie got a fire going and Laura got out some sheet music.

"Everything okay?" Jamie asked after I finished my call and came in to join them.

"Peachy. Was that 'Valse in C Sharp Minor' I just heard?"

"It was. Would you like to hear it again?"

"Every day of my life," I said and sat on the floor in front of the fire next to Jamie.

Laura, sitting at the piano, said, "Good. It always takes me a couple of times through that one to get warmed up."

"It's a toughie," I said.

"Don't tell me you play piano too," Jamie said.

"No. Just tuba, blues harp, xylophone, and flute."

She laughed and punched my kidney. "Jerk."

"Actually," I said, "my mother used to play that. She always had a rough time with it, too. It's my favorite piano piece."

Laura played it again, several times. Then she went on to other pieces from other books—Lizst, Brahms, Gershwin, Kern, and oddly enough, a Tom Waits songbook ("I love his voice," Laura said). Pretty soon, Jamie and I fell asleep in front of the fire, which may have been Laura's idea all along.

"What are you planning to wear to the party?"

It was an hour or so later. Laura had gone upstairs to bed and the fire had dwindled to vermilion coals and white ash. Jamie had her head on my shoulder and had one hand under my shirt, pulling on and then smoothing down the hairs on my chest.

I kissed her forehead. "What would you *like* me to wear?"

She cuddled closer. "Something nice."

I snorted. "That's helpful. What are *you* wearing?"

"I was hoping I could wear my little black Valentino cocktail dress with my grandmother's string of pearls and matching earrings, but I don't suppose you have a tuxedo?"

"Now, why would you suppose that?"

"I don't know," she said, a little peevishly. "I've never seen you in anything but jeans and flannel, with the occasional Irish fisherman's sweater thrown in."

"I'm a dog trainer. And I look good in that sweater."

"Yeah, you do, actually, with your beard and curly hair."

"Thanks. Well, believe it or not, I *do* own a tux."

"You do?" she said, surprised and happy.

"Sure. Every man over the age of twenty-five should own one. Don't you ever read *Esquire*?"

"Does anybody? And are you really going to steal Richard DeMarco's body from the funeral parlor?"

"No, that would be stupid. From the airport loading dock."

She shook her head and moaned helplessly. "Well, please try not to get caught, okay?"

I promised I'd try, then asked her who Eddie Cole was.

"Nobody," she said. I asked her again and she sighed and finally told me: at one point she had become so frustrated about Oren's coke habit that she'd threatened to have his dealer—Eddie Cole—put in jail. She'd never gone through with the threat—she'd just been desperate to do anything she could to get Oren to stop using long enough to get into a treatment program. But oddly enough, a few days later Cole actually *was* arrested for possession with intent. Both Cole and Oren blamed Jamie. Cole had threatened to get even.

"Is he dangerous?" I asked.

"He's just a punk with an attitude." She nestled her head on my shoulder. "Do you have any idea who the father is?"

I said, "Whose father?"

"Of Allison's baby. She was pregnant, remember?"

"Oh, yeah. My theory is that it was either Tim Berry, Sam Kirby, Wade Pierce, Sheriff Flynn, Richard DeMarco, or me."

"Jack! You slept with Allison DeMarco?"

"Hmmmm? Oh, you're right. I would have *had* to in order to be the father, huh? Well, I guess that rules *me* out at least."

"You are such a pain," she said as she kissed me.

Half an hour later—as I was putting my clothes back on— Jamie gave me the keys to her car. She said her mom could drive her down to my place in the morning to pick it up. She walked me to the back door and I said, "Where does Sam Kirby live?"

"Why?"

"I don't know. I thought I might swing by on my way home, if it's not too far, and let all the air out of his tires."

"Oh good," she said, "that'll keep things from escalating."

29

It was a bright cold morning, and the plane ride to Buffalo was uneventful, though Duke didn't seem to enjoy it much. As we took off he gripped the armrests of his seat so hard I thought his knuckles would turn white.

"You know, Leon," I said, after the Cessna reached cruising altitude, "these little commuter jobs rarely crash."

"Rarely, see? That's the word I don't like. And what you be callin' me Leon for?"

"You're not in New York anymore. Up here in Maine you're not the Duke of Juke, you're the Duke of Nothin'. Just another poor black kid in America with no education and no future."

"Man . . . why you be dissin' me like this?"

"That's just the way it is." I recounted some of my conversation with Jill Krempetz and told him that maybe she was right. Maybe he should go back to New York and testify.

"But I like workin' with you and the dogs."

"That's good. But don't you miss your grandma?"

"Yeah, sometimes. But . . ."

"It's okay to be scared, Leon."

"Me? I ain't scared. I ain't scared a nothin'."

I nodded as if I believed him, then caught my breath suddenly, and gripped the armrests like I'd felt the plane do something scary. "We're gonna crash!" I said.

He shuddered, then realized I'd just been playing with

him. He hit me hard on the arm and said, "Very funny. Okay, I am scared a *some* things. But not of going back to New York. Maybe I *will* go back just to get away from *you*."

I smiled. "Well, I'm still trying to arrange it so you don't have to testify before the grand jury. If that works out, you won't *have* to go back unless you want to. But if you decide to stay up here, we'll have to make things legal. You'd have to be my foster kid for real."

"Nah, I don't think so."

"I thought you liked working with me and the dogs."

"That was before you pissed me off."

I laughed. "Well, either way, you've got to go back to high school and graduate. *And* go to college."

"What for?"

"So you can have a decent future."

"Lotta good it did you," he said and almost smiled. "You went to college and now you clean up dog shit for a living."

I laughed. "Maybe so. But it's by choice. If you don't get an education, Leon, you won't have as many choices available to you. And I hate to say this, but your choices are already limited by the fact that you're a black kid living in a white man's world."

"You got that right." He put on his headphones and switched on his portable CD player.

We arrived in Buffalo around ten, and at ten-forty-five I drove through the gates of the Pine Hills Hospital in a rented white Plymouth Breeze. I parked in the visitor's lot and got out, trying to look like a cop on assignment from the NYPD. I was dressed for it. I had on an old suit and tie from the back of my closet. Duke stayed in the car with his CDs.

It was nicer inside the hospital than I'd expected, but not nice enough to make me want to reserve a room. The walls were hospital green and the square floor tiles were industrial gray. The guard out front had asked me my business before letting me drive through the gate and park, and he must've made a call into the front desk because they were expecting me.

"Detective Field, hi. I'm nurse Fielding. You can call me Diana. We almost have the same last name." We shook hands.

"Almost." I stifled my normal impulse to tell her to call me Jack. Detectives don't do that—not while on duty.

She was in her late fifties and had watery blue eyes and nondescript gray-brown hair. Her handshake was firm and her shoulders were big and square, and—like Jamie—she was nearly as tall as I. She walked me toward a reception desk where a young black woman, about twenty or so, was on the phone.

"Where's your partner?" Nurse Fielding asked me.

I wondered what she meant and realized that the guard must have described Leon to her. "Oh, you mean my son. He's waiting in the car. This shouldn't take long."

She gave me a funny look. "So . . . how can we help you?"

I took a photo of Sheriff Flynn out of my jacket pocket and showed it to her. "Do you recognize this man?"

She took the photo, held it at arm's length to look at it, then put on a pair of reading glasses attached to a chain around her neck, looked again, closer this time, and said, "Yes, that's Horace Flynn. Don't tell me you're investigating him."

I ignored her question. "When did you see him last?"

She handed back the photo and said, "He comes here every other weekend to visit one of the patients."

"Was he here last weekend?"

"Yes. What's this all about?"

"Just a routine investigation. Could I speak to Mrs. Kirby?" She gave me a blank look, as if she hadn't understood the question. "Isn't that who Flynn comes to visit?"

She shook her head. "There's no Mrs. Kirby here."

I gave *her* a blank look. I knew from one of Otis Barnes's newspaper articles that Mrs. Kirby was a patient at Pine Hills in Buffalo. "You no longer have a patient named Joan Kirby at your facility?"

"Oh," the light went on in her eyes, "I see what you mean, now. Yes. Her last name *used* to be Kirby. It's been Flynn for several years now. Are you all right?"

"I must be allergic to something in here. Makes my eyes water a little." Maybe Jamie was right about Flynn. Maybe he was a big, blustering softy after all. "You know, I don't think I'll need to speak to her now, but thanks anyway."

I turned to go. The receptionist, who had been listening,

stopped me. She covered the mouthpiece of her phone and said: "Oh, but she loves visitors and she gets so few."

I turned back, scratched my chin. "Just Flynn, huh?"

"And her younger sister comes sometimes."

"I guess I could say hello." The big nurse started to lead me down the hall. "What's the sister's name?"

"Allison DeMarco."

I stopped. I must have been losing my detective's touch. Of course—the clues were all there. Allison had an older half-sister who was institutionalized. Allison's father was Samuel L. Davies and the backs of Wade Pierce's checks were signed by Samuel L. Kirby. Jamie said that Allison had a nephew who'd popped up recently—a nephew I now knew to be Sam Kirby. This might explain how Kirby and Flynn were still so wrapped up in the investigation—or possibly the cover-up—of Allison's murder.

If I hadn't felt it necessary to talk to Joan Kirby before, I certainly did now.

I looked at the nurse. "Allison DeMarco was Joan Kirby's half-sister?"

"That's right, but why do you say *was*? You say it as if—"

I told her about the murder. She and the receptionist were extremely sad to hear the news. The nurse said, "Are you going to tell Mrs. Flynn?" She looked down the hall.

I thought it over. Many's the time I'd had to officially notify someone of a loved one's murder and utter those words. "Sorry for your loss." This just wasn't one of those times.

"I think Sheriff Flynn should discuss that with her doctor first. I don't think she needs to hear it from me."

30

Allison Davies—or, as I knew her, Allison De Marco—and Joan Kirby were half-sisters, even though there was a thirty-year age difference between them. Samuel L. Davies had married young, built a successful real estate business in Portland and Augusta, then divorced and married a much younger woman. His second wife, Doris, was Allison's mother. When he died in the early nineties he was worth almost thirty million dollars. Most of it went to his widow, though he *did* provide for Joan's hospitalization care. Doris moved to Florida where she had a string of three unsuccessful marriages. (Unsuccessful for her, not so unsuccessful for the Cuban gigolos she'd married.) The rest went to Allison, who was twenty at the time. As far as I could tell, none of the old man's money went to Joan's son Sam or to Allison's daughter Tara, which was understandable since Sam Davies never knew about her existence.

This was not easy information to come by, either: Joan Davies Kirby Flynn was not a quick interview. I gleaned what I could by sifting through long, rambling monologues about people I'd never heard of, who had no relation to the case, and in some instances (I suspected) had no relation to reality.

We were in the visitors' room, an almost cheerful space with floor to ceiling windows made of pebbled glass, which let in lots of light but didn't allow the patients to actually look out at the grounds and plan their escape. There was a black spinet piano in one corner of the room, some green armchairs with fading upholstery, and a metal drinking fountain underneath a bulletin board.

Mrs. Flynn—which is what I called her, at her request—was wearing a loose light brown short-sleeved tea-length dress, with a floral pattern of bluebells, daisies, and wild roses. She hadn't put on any make-up but her skin was clear and soft and her blue eyes were large. I might have even thought them beautiful—as I'm sure Horace Flynn did—but they reminded me too much of Sam Kirby's eyes. Nevertheless, until she spoke—which she did with an odd, intermittent twitch of her neck and downward quiver from the left side of her mouth—she seemed as normal as anyone else on the planet.

I hated to bring it up, since I knew it might be painful for her, but I had to confirm my suspicions about Sam Kirby's parentage before I left, so I said, "Does Sam know that Sheriff Flynn is his real father?"

Her face shrank and I thought she was going to cry, but she didn't. I guess it was just one of her little tics. "Sammy mustn't know," she whispered in a voice that made the backs of my arms tingle, "I told Horace from the beginning: 'Even though Walter knows, you must never tell Sam.' And he's always been true to his word." She nodded and smiled at the pebbled glass.

"How about Allison?" I asked. "Does *she* know?"

"What?" She tried to brush back a wayward strand of wispy brownish hair, but it kept falling in front of her eyes. She kept flicking at it until the gesture became compulsive.

I gently took her hand. "Your half-sister, Allison. I know she comes to visit you, doesn't she?"

"Yes. She's been very nice to do that." She started to brush her hair back again, then looked at me and forced her hands to go down into her lap, where they swam and squirmed around for a little while.

"So? Allison. She knew about Sam and Flynn, yes?"

She came back to the real world again and said, "Yes, she knew. We fought about it. She said he had the right to know who his father was. I don't blame her, you see. Not after the way Father treated her. No. I understood the way she felt."

I wasn't sure what that meant and didn't have much time to find out. "Did she and Flynn ever fight about it?"

She nodded like a child and did her crying tic again. "He wouldn't hurt her, though. He didn't mean it. It was just something he said to keep her from telling Sammy."

"What did he say?"

"Oh, it's nothing. She was threatening to let Sammy know and Horace said he'd kill her if she did. He just said it to make her stop. He's much too gentle to really hurt anyone."

"I know he is," I said and patted her hand.

"Yes." She took my hand in both of hers and squeezed it tightly. "He's a perfect gentleman, isn't he?" Then she smiled a smile so deep and passionate it almost made her seem sane.

I signed out at the front desk. The receptionist, who was on another phone call, cupped a hand around the receiver and asked me how my visit had gone. I just shrugged and said, "Well . . ." and she nodded sympathetically, looked sadly down the hall toward the visitors' room, then went back to her conversation.

As Duke and I drove away from the hospital I did something I'd never done before, but probably should have. I put my hand on the back of his neck and told him he was a good kid.

"Now what? You comin' on to me or somethin'?" he said, pulling away. But I could tell he was glad I did it because a few minutes later he turned off his portable CD player, took his headphones off, and relaxed in his seat.

31.

The next stop was the airport coffee shop. I called Lou Kelso in New York. He told me the body had already been diverted at Kennedy and was on its merry way to Portland and should arrive around twelve-thirty. Richard DeMarco's father, meanwhile, was due to arrive in Buffalo any minute with an empty casket. Kelso gave me the flight and gate numbers and I thanked him and hung up. I left Leon in the coffee shop.

The flight from Kennedy was deboarding at gate two. I found a pay phone nearby and had them page Victor De-Marco. A handsome yet overfed man of about sixty or so, with deep tan skin and silvering hair, wearing dark brown trousers and a pastel green sweater, came through the gate, heard the page, handed his carry-on to a beefy guy walking next to him, then went to the counter and picked up the white courtesy phone. The beefy guy was joined by a twin, both wearing blue nylon sweatsuits.

"This is Victor DeMarco." His voice was smooth and his manner was direct.

"I hate to tell you this, sir," I said into the pay phone, "but your son's body is not on the plane."

"What? Who is this?"

I told him who I was—ex-cop, dog trainer, the whole bit. Then I explained that the casket that had been on his flight from Kennedy was empty and that his son's remains were actually on their way to Portland. He made some vague threats, and some not so vague—mostly about suing the airline for negligence, and then, after I explained that the airline was not to blame, that *I* was, the threats became a bit more personal—and anatomical—in nature.

"I understand the way you feel, sir. And I apologize for having to put you through this, but we've got to do an autopsy on your son's body in order to find out who really killed him and his ex-wife."

"My God, she's dead too?"

"Yep. She was murdered the day before Richard was."

"Fucking Island police. They said they had the guy. Some grifter, they said."

"He may have done it, he may not have. But we won't know for sure without an autopsy. Now, if you know of a medical examiner here in Buffalo who'd be willing to do the procedure, I'll be happy to fly back to Portland right now and bring your son's body here."

"What do you mean fly back? Where are you now?"

"I'm in Buffalo, in the airport coffee shop," I lied. "Look, before you decide what to do—"

"You gotta lotta nerve, Field, you know that?"

"I do," I said, then gave him the name of a lawyer known to some of his associates in Little Italy, who would vouch for me, and suggested he call his own lawyer for advice. "Meet me in the coffee shop in fifteen minutes and we can discuss—"

"We ain't discussin' nothin'. You're gonna take me to my boy. Now. You got that? Now!"

He hung up, then started making calls to check my story.

After he found out that the lawyer in New York vouched for me, Victor DeMarco decided that he and his associates would personally escort me and Leon back to Portland and check to make sure his son's remains were where I said they would be. He even booked the five of us a private jet—me, Leon, Slick Vic, and Charlie and Sal (his twin bodyguards).

There was an uncomfortable silence while we waited on the tarmac. DeMarco was thinking things over. Then, as we were about to take off, he turned to me and said, "I don't like it, you did what you did. But I guess you got a point, it bein'

the only way to find out what really happened, and such." He
sighed and looked out the window.

Once we were airborne he said, "So, you trust this ME to
know what he's doing?"

"She," I corrected him. "And yeah, she's the best."

"No slicing open the body, though."

"I hope we won't have to, but—"

"Hope is a four-letter word. No cutting, that's final."

"If you say so. Anyway, I'm glad you understand how important the autopsy is."

He shrugged. "My son was a doctor, remember?"

He was silent again until we were over the White Moun-
tains. He settled back in his seat, looked me over, smiled,
and said, "So you work with dogs, huh? Me, I got a little
Shi-Tzu back home." He shrugged. "The wife's dog, but I
like her."

I nodded. "Good dogs. Terrific disposition."

He smiled. "Yeah, she's sweet, this mutt. Six years old."
He shook his head. "I gotta tell ya, though, I don't care for
the way the wife's always putting ribbons and bows in her
hair. 'She's a dog!' I keep tellin' her, but—"

"I bet you take them out whenever you can, though,
right?"

"What? You mean the bows and shit?" He laughed. "You
got me there. 'Honey,'" he imitated his wife's voice, "'have
you seen Fluffy's hair ribbon?' 'Gee, sweetheart,'" he imitated his own voice, "'I got no idea what coulda happened to
it.'" He laughed heartily.

A limo and a hearse were waiting for us at the Portland
Airport when we arrived around 1:00. A red-faced Carl Staub
was waiting for *me* at the loading platform. I explained a little of what was going on and he flashed his badge at the guy
behind the window, who gave us some papers to sign, and we
were on our way.

"That was easy," Carl said, surprised and relieved.

"Sure. People don't normally expect the police to go
around breaking the law. Where's your wife?"

"She's already on her way home."

"Nice sunburn. I hope *she* used sunblock."

I introduced Carl to Slick Vic and company, and when that was over with I had the hearse driver back up to the loading platform and we loaded Richard DeMarco's casket into the back. Slick Vic insisted on looking inside, just to be sure Richard's body was there, then Sal and the driver got in the front of the hearse while the rest of us—except for Carl, who'd had enough of his association with us for the time being and insisted on following us in a rental car—piled into the limo and made our getaway. It was more like a parade; the limo, followed by the hearse, with Carl in a rented Chevy bringing up the rear.

We took I-95 to the Freeport exit, got on US 1, and arrived at Rockland around 3:30. We drove through town, then turned off the main highway on our way to the hospital in Glen Cove. Slick Vic smiled and patted my knee. "I like you, Field, you know that? You're a pain in the ass, but—hey, what the hell are those? Toby, stop the car, pull over!"

As Toby pulled over I followed DeMarco's gaze. He was looking at a small herd of cows, grazing on some winter hay.

"Belted Galloways," I said. "It's a rare breed of cattle. I'm not a hundred percent sure, but I think they only raise them here in this part of Maine."

It was getting dark, which I suppose made the strange sight of the fat black cows, each with one wide white stripe, seem even stranger. The headlights from the hearse pulled up behind us, followed by the lights from Carl Staub's rental car.

"Looks like a buncha kids got hold of some whitewash and painted a big stripe down the middle of 'em. Sonovabitch! They come that way?" He got out. "Charlie, Toby, come take a look at these cows."

Toby and Charlie got out and did what their boss told them. Leon, who had been trying to act invisible for most of the trip, leaned over to me and said, "If I get outta this alive, I'm definitely going back to New York. I'll be a lot safer with the gangbangers and drug dealers than if I stay here with you. Why'd you have to drag me along on this trip?"

"I thought you'd enjoy a little change of scenery."

"Yeah, that's nice. Ax me how I'd like a change of scenery when I'm sixteen feet under."

"You mean six feet under."

"I wasn't talkin' about no cemetery."

"You really think these guys are killers?"

"Aren't they?"

I pointed out the window at the big lugs gaping at the cows like a bunch of schoolkids gawking at the dinosaurs at the Museum of Natural History. Leon was unconvinced.

Slick Vic and the boys got back inside and we drove off and left the striped cows to chew their cud.

DeMarco sighed and looked out the window. "My kid woulda loved those cows. He was into that kind of shit—always bringing animals home. He woulda rather been a vet than a doc. I was the one insisted that he go to medical school."

We drove for a while. His eyes lost their focus. "I remember he brought a skunk home one time. I beat the shit out of him for doing it. Had to buy all new carpets and drapes." His eyes got moist. "I wish now I hadn't a done it."

I got the feeling there were a lot of things he wished he hadn't a done.

Our little parade came to a grinding halt in the back section of the hospital parking lot around 5:00. We all got out to stretch our legs and discuss our options. There was a small difference of opinion as to the best way to smuggle the body inside. Sal and Charlie's idea—based, one might suppose, on their years of experience hijacking trucks and airline cargo—was to overpower the night guard, tie him up and leave him in a closet until after the autopsy was finished. Slick Vic didn't *mind* the idea, he just thought we should be a little less intrusive, as did Carl and I. Especially Carl. As for Leon, he just wanted to go home.

Finally Slick Vic said, "This is all your idea, Field. What do you think?"

"Let's wait till the last minute to move the body. They're having a party upstairs later. So if someone were to bring the guard a cocktail or a glass of champagne . . ."

"We could even slip him a mickey," said Victor.

I said: "I don't suppose any of you guys has the makings of a mickey on you . . ." Charlie raised his hand. "Well, never mind. Carl and I can handle the guard."

"Speak for yourself," Carl said. "I'm gonna go home and watch TV. I'll look for you guys on the news."

"No, Carl, if you don't want to help with the guard, that's fine. But you're not going home. I need to interview Debbie Sheldon. So you'll have to drive up to Bangor and make up a story—tell her we need her to identify the body. Then bring her down here around nine." To DeMarco I said, "She's the—"

"I know who she is."

"I'm not gonna do it," Carl said. "You got me in enough trouble as it is."

"It's either you or Sal and Charlie. If you do it it's police business, if they do it it's kidnapping."

Finally, we all agreed. Sal and Charlie stayed with the body. Carl drove off, while Toby and Slick Vic dropped me and Leon at the kennel. I told them to meet me around nine at the morgue. He said fine, then asked where he could get a good Italian dinner in town. I told him to try O'Neal's which, come to think of it, is where this whole thing got started in the first place.

32

Jamie looked fabulous in her little black cocktail dress. The word décolletage came to mind. Repeatedly.

In her Jaguar, on the way to the party, she caught me admiring her cleavage for probably the twelfth time and laughed out loud. "Drive the car, Jack. They're just a highly evolved form of sweat-gland squeezed into a push-up bra."

I sighed and looked back at the road. "I wish you hadn't said that. Now, whenever we make love, I won't be able to stop thinking about some fat guy in a Turkish bath."

She laughed. "That's *your* problem."

"So what did Dr. Reiner say?"

"About what?"

"About you doing an autopsy on Richard DeMarco."

"Oh, he said he'd have to think about it. Today is Friday so he probably won't decide till Monday morning."

"Well, the funeral is scheduled for Monday."

"They can reschedule it, can't they? If not, we can always exhume the body, if necessary."

I shook my head. "Victor DeMarco isn't going to like that idea very much. Looks like we'll have to do it on our own." I recounted the events of my day with Slick Vic and company and she listened quietly and sighed.

"I wonder if there'll be any eligible bachelors at the party tonight," she mused.

"Why?"

"I may need to find a new boyfriend."

"Ha, ha," I said. "Try feeding him that line about the sweat glands and see how far it gets you. I like what you did to your hair, by the way."

"Thanks. And don't *you* look spiffy? *Esquire* was right."

I resisted an impulse to tug at my bow tie. When I'd gotten back to the kennel I'd had just enough time before picking up Jamie to shower and shave and press my tux and shirt and slip everything on. I'd tied the bowtie second-to-last, like you do, but I was in a hurry and had tied it too tight.

"And I didn't say that because I want to break up with you, Jack. I was just thinking I should start looking for your replacement, you know, for after the Coast Guard finds your body floating somewhere off Eggemoggin Reach."

"Gesundheit. And if these guys are the real thing, which I'm not so sure they are, the bodies don't float."

I pulled off onto Glen Cove road.

"One question: how come you're chummy enough with a mafia lawyer that he'd vouch for you with Victor DeMarco?"

"There was this case I worked on in New York, but it's a long story. How did your meeting go this morning?"

She smiled proudly. "You're looking at Maine's newest state medical examiner. Still just part-time, though."

"Congratulations."

"Thank you."

"With swollen sweat glands in a push-up bra, no less."

She hit me. "They're not swollen."

"The look swollen to me."

"Your lip is gonna be swollen in a minute."

We pulled into the lot and I parked and switched the engine off. I opened my door and Jamie said, "Let's not go in just yet." She took a deep breath.

I closed the door. "What's the matter? Are you okay?"

She waved her hand in front of her face. "I get really nervous at parties. I don't know why. I need to relax a little before we go in." She looked at me seriously. "Your tux didn't come equipped with a hip flask full of whisky, did it?"

I held her hand. "You really *are* nervous, aren't you?"

"You think I would make this up? And doesn't *Esquire* have anything to say about how all men should own a hip flask?"

"I'll have to check. And don't be nervous—you look great. Trust me, you'll be the center of attention."

She pulled her hands away and began shaking them in front of her to get the tension out. "I don't want to be the center of attention. I don't want anyone noticing me at all."

"Okay, fine, so you have a little social anxiety. Here's what you do—you know that technique where you picture everyone at the party in nothing but their underwear?"

She shook her head and sighed. "I've tried it, Jack. It doesn't work. Just let me catch my breath, okay?"

"Let me finish. You like dogs, right? I mean, you're not a fanatic like me, but you like Frankie and Ginger, right?"

Impatient with me, she said she did.

"Okay. So instead of imagining everyone at the party in their underwear, just imagine that they all have tails."

There was a pause while she tried it out in her mind, and then came a sudden fit of laughter. "And they're wagging them! They're all wagging their tails! How perfect!" She began screaming with laughter, grabbed my hand, and said, "Can I pet their heads and scratch them under the chin?" I said she could. She laughed some more, long and hard and loud until the tension was gone. I gave her my handkerchief and she wiped the tears from her eyes, being careful to stop for the occasional residual spasm so as not to muss her mascara too much. When she was through she handed back my hankie, leaned into me, put her head on my shoulder, a hand on my chest, and we sat like that for a while, peaceful and relaxed with Jamie's pleased giggles periodically bubbling to the surface, then slowly subsiding.

After a while she yawned, stretched, and said, "Okay, cowboy, let's hit the party."

33

The party was held in the conference room, which sits on the fifth, or administrative, floor of the hospital—well above any beds, labs, morgues, or operating rooms. The instant we entered Jamie was the center of attention—not because she tried to be, she just was.

There was an aluminum Christmas tree in one corner, adorned with red and green balls. A band was in the other corner, playing Christmas songs with what sounded like a disco beat. It was a two-man outfit—a sax player/lead singer, and a keyboardist who sang harmony, played bass lines with his left hand and tinkling chords with his right.

To Jamie I said, "That's one helluva band, huh?"

"Shut up and get me some wine."

There was a long folding table at the other end of the room—opposite the band—covered with white linen and decorated with poinsettias. On top of the cloth were glasses of wine—some red, some white—and bottles of Poland Spring, along with an assortment of chips, dips, chicken wings, celery sticks, etc.

"There's Annie Deloit," Jamie said and waved while I got us a couple of glasses of wine—red for me, white for her.

"I thought you said doctors don't get drunk."

"She's a doctor's *wife*."

"Oh, well, that explains it then." I gave Jamie her glass.

She hit me, then took my arm. "Now, look, Jack, if you're gonna—you promised, remember?"

"Promised what?"

She took a quick gulp of wine. "Not to alienate anybody."

"Yeah, but I didn't think that included *you*."

She hit me again. "You're hopeless." She took another gulp then dragged me across the room to meet her friends. "Hi, Darryl. Annie, what a lovely dress."

There were thank-yous and compliments and I exchanged how-are-yous with Darryl, who, other than Leon, was the only black person I think I'd seen since moving to Maine. Slim, with short dreadlocks and wire-rim glasses, he cut a nice figure in a dark blue suit that looked good against his dark skin. I scanned the room and saw that no one else was wearing a tuxedo—just me.

"Don't you look nice?" Annie said to me, sloshing some white wine onto the floor. "Like Cary Grant or something."

"Thanks," I said. "I'm afraid Jamie conned me into wearing this damn thing and now I see that no one else—" I waved my arm at the room and saw Jonas Cutter enter. He had on a tuxedo too. "Well, I guess I'm not the only one after all."

Jamie followed my gaze. "Oh, no. What's he doing here?"

Looking serenely elegant with his white hair and shiny tux, Jonas was surrounded by a crowd of adoring fans, tugging at his sleeve and trying to shake his hand. Being the center of attention runs in the family.

"Didn't you know," Darryl said to Jamie, "he's on the hospital board now. He's leaving Boston General."

"Since when?" Jamie said, draining her glass.

"Since he found out about his heart problem. He didn't tell you?"

"What's wrong with his heart?"

"It's a simple valve replacement. That's all."

"Simple or not, it's still major surgery." She handed me her empty wine glass. Annie did the same.

Darryl looked at the empty glasses and was about to say something like "What are you, a waiter?" but I beat him to it:

"It's the tux," I said. Then, as Jonas caught sight of Jamie and began working his way across the room toward her, I said to Darryl, "Why don't you and me mosey on over to the bar and refill these puppies?"

He caught on that I wanted to give Jamie and her father a little privacy and we crossed to the refreshment table. I had the waiter pour some red wine into Jamie's glass and said, "How's Henry?" referring to Darryl and Annie's pug.

"He's okay." Darryl picked up a glass of white wine, poured half of it into one of the poinsettias, then poured some spring water in the glass to bring the level back up. "I think he may be getting cataracts." He sniffed the glass. "You think she'll notice?"

"Probably, but you've got to try."

I looked across the room and saw Jamie kiss her father on the cheek, then introduce him to Annie. When she was done with that she shot me a hard, what-are-you-doing-over-there kind of look. I gestured with the wine glass and she made a secret motion for me to come back at once. It turned out to be not so secret because Jonas saw it. He looked over at me and nodded.

"How old is Henry again?" I asked Darryl.

"Almost twelve."

"I think I must be a little older than that," a Chinese man said. He and a colleague had just come over for some wine.

"Sorry, Henry. We were talking about my dog."

"Oh, yes. My namesake. The little bulldog, right?"

"Pug," we both corrected him. Darryl introduced me to Dr. Henry Chow and Dr. Ivan Dietrich and they both asked me how the case was going, and did I think the cook and waitress from Peter Ott's had killed Allison DeMarco. I said no, but a certain waiter from O'Neal's and his ex-girlfriend didn't do it. And that's who the police were after.

Dr. Dietrich wasn't listening, though. He was staring across the room at Jamie. "God, she's got great tits," he said, then looked at me, a little embarrassed. "Did I just say that out loud? Must be the wine."

I said nothing.

Darryl told me that Dr. Chow was an internist and that Dr. Dietrich was a gas-passer, meaning anesthesiologist. Then Dr. Chow said, "How many anesthesiologists does it take to screw in a light bulb?" None of us knew the answer so Dr. Chow said, "One hundred . . . ninety-nine . . . ninety-eight . . . ninety-seven . . ." and pretended to fall asleep. Dr. Dietrich made a polite ha-ha while the rest of us managed to contain our hilarity.

Dr. Dietrich had one, aimed at Darryl, a heart surgeon: "How many cardiologists does it take to screw in a light bulb? None, they're too busy screwing in the OR."

Darryl almost chuckled, then told them that I was a dog trainer, that is, when I wasn't working undercover for the Camden PD.

I said, "How many dog trainers does it take to screw in a light bulb? Two. One to screw in the light bulb and the other to tell any onlookers, 'This isn't hurting the dog.'" After the laughs died down I excused myself and Darryl and I made our way back across the room.

As we did I saw Carl Staub standing in the doorway with one hand on the elbow of a tall, thin, fairly attractive blonde with big hair. Neither of them was dressed for the party. Carl was in uniform and Debbie Sheldon—she was the blonde— had on jeans, a turtleneck, and a ski-jacket. I nodded to Carl, he nodded back, then he and Debbie Sheldon went out to the hall.

"Hello, Jack, nice to see you." Jonas Cutter held out his hand for me to shake. I shook it. "Looks like we're the only ones who know how to dress for these shindigs."

"I'll bet you subscribe to *Esquire*."

Jamie hit me, then took her wine glass with the same hand. "He's making a bad joke."

"Speaking of bad jokes," Darryl handed Annie her glass, "we were just trading doctor jokes with Henry and Ivan."

"This doesn't taste right," said Annie. Darryl told her it was probably a bad year. She said, "It sure is," but it didn't sound like she was talking about the wine.

Jonas wanted to know what kind of jokes they'd been telling and Darryl told him. Jonas asked if there were any jokes about brain surgeons and Darryl said there was one, but he felt uncomfortable telling it in front of Jonas.

"Nonsense," Jonas said, with a self-effacing smile. "You don't think I have a sense of humor?"

"Okay, here goes," Darryl said. "How many neurosur-

geons does it take to screw in a light bulb?" We all waited po-
litely. "None. A neurosurgeon never screws in his own light
bulbs. He has his son Jesus do it for him."

Jonas laughed, as did I—it was a good joke. Jamie
laughed too, then took a sip of wine and held my hand. It was
a simple yet completely intimate gesture, which felt much
sexier than whatever her dress and the push-up bra had done
to me earlier.

"Here's a good one," I said, "I have a mafia kingpin and
two of his goons downstairs in the morgue right now waiting
for Jamie to come down and perform an illegal autopsy on
his son's body, which I stole from the airline earlier today."

Annie screamed with delight.

Jonas looked like he wanted to laugh, then said, "You're
not really serious."

Darryl said, "I don't get it. What's the punch line?"

Jamie gripped my hand tighter and finished her wine.
"Don't mind Jack, Dad. He has a surreal sense of humor."
She let go of my hand then let hers slide softly up my pants.

"It's true," I said. "In fact, how many surrealists does it
take to screw in a light bulb? A swordfish."

"Now, that's funny," laughed Jonas. Then he took hold of
my elbow and said, "Would anyone mind if I had a word or
two in private with Jack?"

"Dad!"

"Just for a minute," he said and led me away. I thought
he'd seen his daughter feeling me up and wanted to chastise
me, but it turned out he just wanted to invite me to come with
Jamie on Saturday to his home in Christmas Cove. I think it
was mostly to make sure that Jamie would come. He seemed
worried that she wouldn't. I assured him that we'd already
made plans to come together and were hoping to borrow his
runabout to make a trip out to Monhegan Island. He said that
was fine.

We went back to the group. I whispered something in
Jamie's ear, then we made our apologies to Darryl and Annie,
and told Jonas we'd see him tomorrow and we all shook
hands and Merry Christmassed and left.

Jamie and I went into the hall where Carl Staub and Debbie Sheldon were waiting for us. Miss Sheldon was unhappy

and made her feelings known. "Why do I have to be here?" she said, with a southern accent. "I already identified Richard's body once. I'm not going to do it again. This is not right."

I told her that the Virgin Islands authorities had arrested the wrong man, then asked Carl if the body had been moved yet.

He said it had. Slick Vic had decided it would be much simpler just to bribe the guard.

"Good idea," I said. "Why didn't *I* think of that?"

"What do you mean, they arrested the wrong man?"

"Just what I said." To Carl, I said, "Take her downstairs and wait for us. We'll be right down."

They left. After they were gone I said to Jamie, "Do that thing where you slide your hand up my pants again."

She laughed. "Why, big fella? Did that percolate your hormones?" I said it did—that and seeing her in the dress. She laughed again, took my hand and said, "There's a utility closet just down here," and dragged me down the hall. We went inside and locked the door. After we were done, and she was smoothing her dress, she said, "How's my make-up?"

"Fine," I said, trying to retie my tie without a mirror. "I think you had a little too much on to begin with."

"You're probably right. Here, let me do that." She stood in front of me and tied my tie.

"How'd it go with the wagging tails thing?"

She smiled. "It went pretty well, thanks. The main thing is just getting inside the room. Once I'm at the party . . . Jack, stop that. Keep your hands to yourself. I'm trying to concentrate."

"Me too."

"You're never satisfied, are you?"

"Of course *I'm* satisfied. That should be obvious. I just want to make sure *you* are."

She shivered and said, "Okay," then she hiked up her skirt and I knelt down and started peeling off her pantyhose again.

34

When we got downstairs Charlie said, "What took youse guys?" (He didn't actually say "youse"—I made that up.)

Slick Vic slapped him with the back of his hand.

Sal bugged his eyes at Jamie and said, "Whoa, Cindy Crawford." (He *did* actually say that.)

I introduced "Cindy Crawford" to the guys and she crossed over to take a look at the body. I wished I had a camera. There was Jamie in her cocktail dress, her string of pearls and diamond bracelet, high heels and dark nylons—which I now noticed looked slightly askew—standing next to the body of Richard DeMarco, which lay fully dressed in pink Bermuda shorts, blue, yellow, and pink Madras Topsiders, and a lime green Polo shirt, on the steel examination table. Behind her—somewhat like the three stooges—stood Charlie, Sal, and Vic.

"Jack?"

"Yes, sweetheart?"

Without taking her eyes off the body she said, "I'm cold."

I took off my tuxedo jacket and came over and wrapped it around her shoulders. She leaned forward to take a closer look at Richard DeMarco's face. "Thanks, sweetie," she said, staring into the dead man's eyes. "I can tell you right now, I don't think he died from the stab wound. Who wants to help me get him undressed?"

"This place gives me the creeps," said Slick Vic, as if that answered her question. Neither Sal nor Charlie looked like anything had ever given them the creeps, but they didn't step forward to volunteer, either. I said I'd help, and Victor and the boys conferred for a moment and decided to decamp to the hall to await further developments.

While we were pulling Richard's pants down Carl and Debbie Sheldon came in. "What are you doing?" she said.

"An autopsy," Jamie said. "Jack, get her out of here."

"You got it, sweetie. I'll just have a little talk with her outside if that's okay?"

"Yeah, I'll let you know if I need anything."

Carl and Debbie and I went to the door. I turned and said, "Oh, by the way, Victor says he doesn't want the body cut open."

"Figures," she sighed.

Debbie Sheldon was not happy. Her normally pretty face was closed and hard.

"I'm sorry to put you through this, but—"

"You should be. My God."

"Did anything unusual happen the morning he died?"

"Like what? He got *murdered*. How unusual is that?"

"No, I mean before the murder. Did he receive any unusual phone calls or have any visitors?"

"No. It was just the two of us."

"Okay. Tell me about the last time you saw him alive."

"I told this already to the police down there."

"I know, but it's important that you tell us too."

"Oh, Jesus, okay. It was at breakfast. We were eating and he said he didn't feel well, so he . . . wait a minute . . . there *was* someone. While we were eating he saw someone—a business associate, he said—and he excused himself. Then, when he came back a few minutes later, that's when he said he wasn't feeling too good and I went down to the beach without him."

"Did you see the man or woman he talked to?"

"What makes you think it was a woman? Dickie *loved* me."

"I didn't say it was a woman. I just need to know if—"

"—No, it was a man. I didn't see who it was, but that's what Dickie told me. Who are those guys?"

I glanced over at Slick Vic and company. "The older gentleman is Dickie's father. The other two work for him."

"I guess I should go introduce myself."

She went over to get acquainted. A few minutes later the autopsy door opened and Jamie came out. Everyone gathered around her.

"I took some blood and tissue samples," she said.

"Now, wait a minute," Slick Vic said.

Jamie assured him: "I did it discreetly. We'll see what they tell us. Meanwhile, I can say this—it wasn't the knife wound that killed him. He was dead at least half an hour before he was stabbed."

"What side of the body was the wound on?" I asked.

"The left."

"Aha," I said.

"So what was it?" Slick Vic wanted to know. "What killed him?" He was shaking, and he and Debbie were holding hands like father and daughter. Both were a little teary eyed, too.

"I can't say anything definite without getting the lab results, but there was a needle mark on his right buttock."

"Someone drugged him?" said DeMarco. Jamie said it looked that way. "You'll let me know, though, right?" Jamie said she would. "Thanks. Now, can I take my boy's body home?"

Jamie said, "Of course. Just let us get him dressed first, if you don't mind."

"No, I'd appreciate it." Then he gave Jamie a bear hug and tried to tip her for doing the autopsy. She refused his money, telling him it was her job, after all.

Slick Vic and I shook hands. "I owe you one, Field."

"I may call you on that," I said.

"Feel free, anytime." I was afraid he was going to hug me too but he didn't. He just pointed out that I'd lost a stud.

Then I asked Slick Vic and Debbie Shelton if they'd be willing to come to Allison's house on Sunday, around 2:30, for a confrontation with Allison's killer. They both agreed. Then I asked Charlie if he had some lock-picking tools on him. He said he did.

After we got Richard DeMarco dressed and loaded back onto the hearse we all went our separate ways. Jamie and I went upstairs—she to say goodnight to her father and me to

scour the utility closet for my missing stud. Then we went
out to the parking lot together where Carl Staub was waiting
for me.

"He's on duty tonight," Carl said, "so you should be safe."

"Who's on duty?" Jamie asked.

"That's great, Carl, thanks." I said. "Can you give me a
ride over there?"

"Sure. I mean, I'll drop you off but I'm not coming inside
his house with you."

"Inside whose house?"

"That's fine. I've got a few more bases for you to cover."

"Jack, what's going on?"

"Good night, sweetheart," I said, and gave Jamie a kiss,
then went to Carl's car. "I've got something to do that has to
be done right now. I'll call you later." Carl and I got in and
closed our doors. Jamie banged on my window.

"Jack! Come back here!"

35

Sam Kirby's house—which he'd inherited (Carl told me) when Walter Kirby passed away—was a two-story wood frame, situated toward the end of Bayview Street, about thirty steps from the ocean. In fact, it had its own little dock.

"Try the back door," Carl said. "The latch sticks."

"Sounds like you've broken in before."

He blushed. "Knock it off. Sam had a barbecue here last summer. I noticed it then. I notice things like that, okay?"

"Okay." I gave him the phone number I'd gotten off Wade Pierce's caller ID—the number he'd been calling from to retrieve his messages. I also asked him to look into Debbie Sheldon's background, where she was from, how she'd met Richard DeMarco, what kind of relationship they'd had, etc. Then we arranged to meet at midnight at Gilbert's Publick House—which was only a few blocks away—so he could give me a ride home.

I'd looked through Sam's closet, under his bed, even under his mattress, and was in the process of going through a chest of drawers when I heard a creak coming from the back door. I stopped breathing for a moment and stood very still. There were no lights on, just the faint glow from a distant street light.

"Jack?" I heard Jamie whisper. "Is that you?"

I started breathing again and went to the kitchen just in time to see Jamie, still in her little black cocktail dress, carefully closing the latch. She had her back to me.

"Looking for me?" I said.

She jumped, caught her breath, then ran to my arms. She hugged me for about two seconds, then started punching me in the cummerbund. "Don't ever scare me like that again."

"Sweetheart, I didn't ask you to come here."

"That's another thing—"

"And where did you park? I didn't even hear your car."

"See? I am good at this. I parked down the street. And how about the fact that I figured out where you were going?"

"Yes, dear," I said, going back into the bedroom, "you're an excellent detective."

"Thanks." She followed me. "What are we looking for, exactly?"

"I don't know. Clues, evidence, leftover pizza." She gave me a look. "Hey, they didn't have any real food at that damn party of yours and I'm starving."

She hit me again. "Where have you looked so far?"

"Just in here."

We looked around the bedroom. "What a mess." She was right. The bed looked like it hadn't been made in months, and even in the dark it was clear that the sheets hadn't been laundered in about as long. There were dirty clothes all over the floor and barbells and dumbbells scattered about.

"We'll never find anything in here," Jamie said.

I agreed with her. "What do you suggest?"

She waggled her eyebrows at me. "Upstairs. Walter Kirby's old study." She took my hand and led me up a set of stairs. When we got to the top we found a locked door on the right.

"Interesting," I said. "Have you got a credit card?"

"I left my bag in the car."

"Good thinking. Just in case we get arrested by someone in this county who doesn't know you, you won't have any ID on you to give you away." She hit me again. "Darling, I know you think it's fun to keep hitting me like that, but could you kind of aim your fists away from my sore shoulder next time?"

"Sorry," she said and put her arm around my waist, then kissed my shoulder. "All better?"

"No, but a little better." I got my American Express card

out of my wallet and stuck it between the door-jamb and the latch, just above the lock, then slid it downwards, applying just enough pressure, and wiggling it against the metal. The door popped open.

Jamie said, "Aren't you talented?"

I put the card in my wallet. "Everybody needs a hobby."

We went inside. Jamie said, "Speaking of hobbies . . ."

She was referring to the guns. It was like a gun museum inside. There were guns everywhere, wooden gun racks on either side of the window, two glass-covered gun cases framing the door, various types of guns hanging on all the walls. I mean he had everything: shotguns, rifles, handguns, muskets, even an antique Gatling gun on a special stand in the corner.

"Who decorated the place," I said, looking around, "Charlton Heston?"

Jamie nodded, not in answer to my quip—she had just remembered something. "That's right. I forgot about Chief Kirby's gun collection."

"Quite a collection. Do any of them still work?"

She shook her head. "He took out all the firing pins years ago. Or so they say."

"I just hope Sam hasn't put them back in."

There was an old oak rolltop desk near the window. The cover was down. I tried to open it but it was locked.

"What now, Sherlock?"

"A butter knife would do the trick . . ."

"You're not only talented but versatile."

"Wait here." I ran down to the kitchen, hoping to find a butter knife with a heavy blade. There was no clean cutlery so I settled for a screwdriver I found in a drawer full of odds and ends: shoe polish, speaker wire, twine, rolling papers, condoms, marijuana, and some spare ammunition.

Sam Kirby was a fun date.

The screwdriver did the job. I rolled back the top and we hit the jackpot. The desk was piled high with photos of Allison DeMarco. There were also a couple dozen cassette tapes with crude handwritten labels indicating the date and subject matter being recorded: "Allison and Tim/October 10th," "Allison and Tara/December 1," etc.

"You were right," Jamie said. "Sam was stalking her."

"My theory is that's what Wade Pierce was paying him to do."

"We have to get this to the police."

"Or the DA, but we may not have probable cause for—did you just hear a car drive up?"

"Don't worry, Sam's on patrol tonight, remember?"

"Like Sam Kirby would never punch in and then slack off the rest of the night?" I went to the window and looked out. There was a sloping roof covering the front porch. I couldn't see anything on the street. To the right of the window outside was a brick chimney which blocked my view of the back of the house, the garage, and part of the driveway.

"Jack!" Jamie tugged at my sleeve. "Look what I found!" She held a bottle of prescription eyedrops. The label showed that they belonged to Allison DeMarco.

We both heard a car door slam shut. Jamie and I looked at one another. "Oh, shit," we said in unison. We heard the sound of keys jingling. Then footsteps coming on to the front porch. The keys going into a lock. Then the door opening.

"Okay. Any ideas on the best way out of here?"

We heard the front door close.

"Me?" She could barely breathe.

"See, this is why you should stick to doing autopsies and leave the leg work to me." I looked out the window at the door, then back at Jamie in her little black dress and high heels. She sighed, put a hand on my shoulder, leaned down and took the shoes off.

"I'll put everything back in place. You get the door."

When we'd got the room secured, I put her shoes in the pockets of my tuxedo pants, opened the window, and helped her over the sill and onto the roof, where she did a balancing act on the slanting wooden shingles.

"This is going to ruin my stockings," she whispered.

"Think what a bullet would do to your dress."

I got through the window and closed it behind me just as Sam Kirby unlocked the door and turned on the lights. Jamie and I ducked around the corner, clutching each other and the bricks of the chimney for support. There was a little ice on the roof.

We heard the accordion top roll open, then after a few seconds, we heard it roll closed. Then the study door closed.

"What now?" Jamie asked, clutching my arm.

"We wait up here till he leaves."

"It's cold up here."

I put my arms around her and we waited like that for a while but Kirby didn't leave. Then I saw black smoke coming out of the chimney.

I pointed it out to Jamie. "He's burning the evidence."

A few seconds later we heard the front door open and Kirby came outside, walked to the end of the driveway, got in his Sheriff's Department Jeep, and finally drove off.

Jamie was shivering. "Hang on to the chimney, I'm going to try and get the window open again." I went back to the window, planted my feet, and tried to open it. You may not be aware of this, but it's not as easy opening a window when you're standing at an angle on icy wooden shingles—in patent leather shoes no less—as it is standing on a nice level carpeted floor. I slipped, lost my balance, fell on my face and slid toward the gutter at the edge of the roof. Jamie cried out.

I tried to stop myself but kept sliding right to the edge, and then over the side. Jamie cried out again. Luckily, I managed to grab hold of the rain gutter, which—also luckily—didn't break off. It just bent out and pulled away from the roof. Jamie cried out again. (I think I may have made an utterance of my own at this point.)

Jamie started to get down on her hands and knees to crawl over crabwise to help. "Stay put," I told her, then looked down past my shoes. My shoulder was too sore for me to hang on for very long. "I think I can see a clear spot to land."

I pushed away and prayed.

"Jack? Are you okay?" I could hear her voice, but couldn't see her from my position on the ground. "Yeah," I panted. "I just got the . . . just got the wind knocked out of me a little." I stood up, checked to see if I had broken or sprained anything. I seemed to be all right. "Stay there," I said, walking over to where I could see her. "I'm coming back—ow!"

"What is it?"

I felt a sharp pain in my hip. I pulled a broken shoe out of my pocket. I'd landed on one of Jamie's three-hundred-dollar Manolo Blahniks.

"Sorry," I said. "Maybe I can fix it."

"Forget about the shoe, you idiot, just come save me."

I went to the front door, ran back upstairs, and helped her in through the window. We checked to see if there was any evidence left, but it was all in ashes. We heard another car go by, which scared the crap out of both of us, even though we knew it probably wasn't Kirby coming back. Then we high-tailed it out of there, running all the way back to Jamie's car, laughing like a couple of teenagers.

"God," she said, as I opened the passenger side door for her. "I'm so turned on." I got behind the wheel, feeling the same way but there was no room in the car to do anything so we just drove home. By the time we got there we were too tired so we just went straight to sleep.

Carl Staub called an hour later, wondering why I hadn't showed up at Gilbert's. I hung up on him, I'm afraid.

36

The next morning it was fifteen degrees with a light fog, and on the ride down to Christmas Cove Jamie said, "It's murder out there. Are you sure you want to do this?"

"Pretty sure."

"It feels twice as cold when you get out on the water."

"Well, maybe I'll finally break down and buy a parka." I was wearing my usual flannel shirt and Levi's jacket—the one with the bullet hole in it. Jamie had on long underwear under her ripped jeans. She was also wearing a Nautica ski-jacket.

"Oh, great," she said, "ruin my Christmas present."

"That's what you got me? A new parka?"

"I'm not telling. What did you get me?" She gave up trying to find some decent music on the radio and turned it off.

"How about a CD player for your car?"

"I thought you hated CDs."

"No, I just prefer vinyl. But that's at home. A CD player would make far more sense than a record player in a car."

"Okay, so what *did* you get me?"

"A puppy?"

"Oh, shut up. Why won't you tell me?"

"Because you'll find out on Christmas morning. Besides, you look so beautiful when you pout."

"I look beautiful all the time, according to you."

"Not all the time. Just when I'm looking at you."

She sighed, took my hand, but didn't put her head on my

shoulder, which was a good thing, since she was the one driving—and since there was also a big semi full of "farm-fresh eggs" riding our bumper and waiting for the narrow stretch of US 1 that we were on to widen out so he could finally pass us.

"By the way, there are a few things I didn't tell you about my trip to Buffalo. Things non-'Slick-Vic' related."

"Okay . . ." she said, "what things?"

I told her about Joan Kirby's relationship to Allison De-Marco and Sheriff Flynn. She pulled off to the side of the road, causing the egg truck to swerve hard to the left and miss us by inches. The driver blasted his air horn loud enough to make my testicles vibrate and then go into hiding.

Jamie sat, staring at the windshield. "This case," she said, shaking, "it's almost incestuous."

"You got that right. I'm starting to think that the entire state of Maine is like a small town in the south."

She shook her head. "He really married her?" I confirmed that fact. She sighed. "You probably guessed that I already knew about Sam Kirby being Flynn's illegitimate son."

"I had intimations, yes."

"Flynn told me about it. He needed someone to talk to, I guess. Or to listen. He asked me not to tell anyone, not even Oren, which is why . . ."

"I understand."

Jamie bit her lip. I looked out the window and noticed we were parked across the road from the puppy boot camp where Quentin Peck had had Emma trained. I'd toured the place back when I was looking at kennels, and the proprietor, Kirk Collins—a thick-necked blond Nazi with a choirboy face— had shown me around. He'd even smiled an evil smile as he showed me the baseball bat he used on "hard cases"—a Carl Yastremski model. I'd wanted to try it out on him but didn't.

I looked back at Jamie. "Are you mad at me?"

"No. Why would I be mad at you?"

"For digging around, finding all this out."

"I'd be more angry if you *didn't* find it out." She sighed, leaned back in her seat. "This kind of complicates things, doesn't it?" I nodded. "What are we going to do?"

"I don't know exactly. Take things one step at a time, I

guess. I don't think Flynn had anything to do with Allison's death—"

"That's good—"

"But I'm pretty sure he's been covering up for Sam Kirby. And I think Coletti is covering up for both of them."

"Covering up what?"

"That Sam's been planting evidence. Or in the case of the prescription bottle, hiding it."

She thought it over. "Do you think he killed her?"

"It's possible, though I doubt it. We'll find out for sure tomorrow when I do my little demonstration."

"What demonstration?"

"Pulling an Airedale out of my hat, remember?"

She looked at me. "You're not going to tell me what you've got planned, are you?" I shook my head. "Can you prove that Uncle Horace has been covering up for Sam?"

"I can prove that Kirby planted evidence, but no. I can't prove that Flynn is covering up for him. But then, I don't especially *want* to, either."

"What *do* you want?"

"I want to keep Tim Berry and his girlfriend, and anybody else who isn't guilty of Allison's murder, from getting arrested or shot at or killed. And to do that I'm going to have to solve the case as soon as possible. Then maybe I can have what I *really* want, which is to get back to spending time with you and my dogs."

She flexed her chin, nodded, then turned to look over her shoulder at the oncoming traffic. "Good," she said, "we both want the same things." Then she pulled back onto the road.

37.

We came to Damariscotta, turned left, and drove down the Pemaquid Peninsula. The fog began to lift, though the morning sky was still overcast. When we reached "the gut" at South Bristol, we had to wait at the swing bridge for a couple of lobster boats to pass through the narrow mouth and out to the open water. Jamie used the delay to call her father on the cell phone to tell him where we were. I think she woke him up.

Then, as the bridge swung back and we crossed over to Rutherford Island, it occurred to me that the contrast between the shabby working man's wharf in South Bristol—with its worn wooden buildings and smell of gasoline—and the summer homes of Christmas Cove—with their verdant, immaculate lawns and tidy gardens—was similar to what you find in parts of Manhattan, where rich people live the easy life in one neighborhood while a few blocks away there's aching poverty.

We drove down the narrow one-lane road, with its claustrophobic pines and overgrown hedges, to the end of the island—about a five-minute drive. As we pulled into the asphalt driveway of a stone cottage with wood trim, Jonas Cutter came out to meet us, wearing chinos, a loden coat, and bedroom slippers. At the same moment, the sun came flickering out of hiding and gilded the tops of the trees surrounding the house.

"Have you had breakfast?" Jonas asked, after we'd gotten

out and made our hellos and whatnot. It was still early—not quite nine o'clock—and I noticed some white whiskers on Jonas's jaw and chin.

"No," Jamie said, "we drove straight down."

"Good. I'll have Laurie fix up something." He explained to me, "Laurie's my wife. She takes care of things around here. So, what do you like? Pancakes? Waffles?"

"Either one's fine," I said. "Or both."

"Good, good. Of course, *I* can't have any," he said, leading us inside the house, "bad for the ticker. Dry toast for me. But I can watch you two gobble down the good stuff."

"Dad . . . !" Jamie said, as if she were a teenager and he'd embarrassed her for the gazillionth time.

"What's wrong with that? I need some satisfaction." He led us into the dining room.

There were large double-paned windows looking out over a snow-covered lawn that led down to the rocky beach where an icy floating wooden dock jutted into the lead-gray water. A powerboat, with polished wood panels and brass trim, was tied up with yellow rope. The boat and dock moved up and down together in a kind of rhythmic dance with the tide. The boat was long and sleek, and from what I could tell, had room for six.

"You keep the boat out there all winter?" I asked.

Jonas got a coffee tin out of the cupboard and explained that, no, the boat was kept in a boat shed down at the marina, but since Jamie and I wanted to borrow it, he'd had someone named Hank Waters bring it around early this morning. He measured the coffee into the automatic coffeemaker and said, "I understand you're giving a lecture of some sort this afternoon?"

"I take mine black. And yes, it's about canine behavior and dog training. I guess it would seem pretty silly to you."

"Why?" he said, pouring in the water.

"Well, after all, you must have given thousands of lectures on neurosurgery—at Harvard, no less—and all I do is try to teach people the best way to get their dogs to go to the bathroom outdoors, and to sit and stay and come when called."

He pressed the red button and the machine began to earn its keep. "I see what you're saying, but that doesn't mean I think it's silly. I've spent my whole life focused on just one thing and I think I've paid a price for it. It more or less ruined my first marriage. Now I have a son who's too busy to visit me and a daughter who's mad at me all the time."

"Dad! I am not *mad* at you all the time!"

"See what I mean? Anyway, while the coffee's perking, let me check on Laurie and hop in the shower myself."

After he left I sat down at the dining room table. Jamie went to the refrigerator and opened the door, looked around inside, but didn't find anything to her liking.

"Are you okay?" I said.

She shrugged, closed the door, then came over and sat in my lap and riffled through a copy of the *New Yorker* that was lying there. She put down the magazine and looked at the bright red fingernail polish on one hand. She'd had it done for the party last night. It didn't go so well with her current, more casual attire. She began scratching at her middle finger with the thumbnail of the same hand. "I'm worried about his surgery."

"I'm sure he'll have the best staff money can buy."

"You're right." She almost smiled and gave up trying to get the nail polish off. She ran her fingers through my hair. "If we solve Allison's murder, and my divorce finally goes through, then maybe things will finally get back to normal."

I said that was a nice way to think, then asked, "So, what's Laurie like?"

"Can't you tell by her name? She's a younger, prettier version of my mother."

"Honey, no one is prettier than your mother."

She sighed and kissed me.

"I'm sorry. Am I interrupting?" It was Laurie. She was standing in the doorway, dressed in a yellow terrycloth robe with pink and light blue crocheted flowers tacked on in strategic places. Her hair was still wet from the shower. I could smell the shampoo and conditioner from where I sat.

"No, not really," Jamie said, getting off my lap. "Do you have any polish remover?"

Laurie said she did and went to get it. When she came back she was dressed in blue jeans, a red wool Christmas sweater over a green cotton turtleneck, and ragg-wool socks.

While Jamie sat at the dining room table, undoing her nails, and while Laurie made breakfast, I made small talk. It was true that Laurie was roughly the same size and build as Laura Cutter, though about twenty years younger (which made her my age, more or less). But she was nowhere near as pretty, or as gentle, charming, and self-effacing as Jamie's mom. Whatever similarity, other than the name, that Jamie thought there was between the two was lost on me.

Jonas came back from his shower wearing the same chinos and a tattersal shirt he'd had on earlier and we had breakfast. Pancakes, bacon, waffles and eggs for me, and half a grapefruit and two pieces of dry toast for Jonas. Jamie was hard at work on her fingernails and Laurie was just standing on one leg by the kitchen counter, sipping a Diet Pepsi.

"Don't you two want to eat anything?" I asked.

"In a minute," Jamie said, intent on what she was doing.

"I don't eat breakfast," Laurie said and took another swig of soda from a tall water glass.

"I was thinking," Jonas said, "I'd really like to come hear your lecture." Jamie looked up. Jonas went on, "Why don't we let the girls have the car to go Christmas shopping in Freeport, while you and I take the runabout across the river? We can all meet up later."

"Dad, what are you thinking? You shouldn't be out riding around in a motorboat. Especially not in *this* weather."

Laurie agreed with Jamie. "The reason we're here is so you can rest and relax before the operation, hon."

"It's not a quadruple bypass, for chrissakes, it's a simple valve replacement. And I really want to hear what this young man of Jamie's has to say on the subject of dogs. I like dogs."

"Don't be so sure, Dad. Jack's ideas are a little controversial, to say the least."

"Is that right, Jack? You're a free thinker, out to change the world?"

"I'm afraid so, sir."

"Oh, *please*. Don't call me sir. Call me Jonas. And that makes me want to hear your ideas even more."

I suggested that Jamie and I take the runabout and that he and Laurie take the car but he insisted that would be a waste of time. "Everyone keeps telling me to relax. Well, for my money there's nothing more relaxing than being out on the water."

We couldn't talk him out of it, so we did it his way.

38

It was almost ten when we finished the dishes, and shortly after that the girls—as Jonas called them—took his Benz and left for Freeport. This gave Jonas and me time to get chummy. It was interesting to watch him at work. He tried, he really did, to seem interested in my experiences and my life's journey. He asked all the right questions and actually seemed to listen for a time until it was too much for him and he had to interrupt and tell me how *my* life either did or didn't compare to his. I understood now why Jamie said that her father wasn't interested in anyone but himself. He really wasn't.

Then, a sudden shaft of sunlight streamed through the kitchen window, almost making a golden halo of Jonas's silver hair. His demeanor softened and he said: "You know who you remind me of, Jack? Saint Thomas Aquinas."

"Really? How so?"

"I don't know why exactly. I just get the sense that the way Aquinas felt when he immersed himself in the study of angels must be similar to the way you feel about your dogs."

I was touched for a moment. "Thank you, Jonas. What a lovely thing to say. I don't even think Jamie—"

"Of course, when I was in Catholic school, as a boy . . ." and then he droned on about his own experience and I suddenly realized who the murderer was and why I had neglected to think of him as a suspect, even though he was the most obvious, given the evidence.

After a while, there was a lull in Jonas's monotony—excuse me, I meant mono*logue*—and I finally got him back to earth and asked him, "How would someone go about getting their hands on some epinephrine or PTH?"

He looked startled for a moment and then remembered, "Oh, yes. The murder investigation. Well, let me think. Epinephrine is often prescribed for people with allergies. If someone is highly allergic to bees, for example, a doctor will provide epinephrine in case they get stung. As for the parathyroid hormone, I'd have to ask a colleague. I'm not really sure. You know, if you're going out to Monhegan Island on the open water, you're going to need something warmer than that denim jacket. I may have an old parka you can borrow."

After Jonas found his old parka and gave it to me and I put it on, he said, "Well, time flies. Shall we go?"

I said sure and we went down to the dock and got in the runabout. Jonas started her up and asked me to untie us and I pulled the yellow ropes off their moorings and put them in the back of the boat, then sat down, and we took off.

We got out on the river—which looked more like a wide harbor than a river to me—and Jonas asked me what I thought he could do to get Jamie to stop hating him. I was at a loss for a second, then, shouting to be heard over the roar of the engine and the thump of the water against the hull, I said: "That's a tough one, you know—fathers and daughters . . ."

"But come now," he shouted, "you studied psychology. You're a dog trainer, so you understand behavior modification. Surely there must be something I can do."

"Well," I leaned toward him, "we could set you up on a variable reinforcement schedule with her."

"Good," he shouted. "Tell me what to do."

He seemed so earnest and well intentioned I hated telling him I was making a joke. He looked at me with hurt eyes, then stared out across the water. "Tell you what—I'll share a little secret about dog training that may be applicable. You start by finding out what the dog loves to do most, and then you gear your training around that. I call it 'playing the spoon game' after this dog I once trained."

"The spoon game? What's that?"

We were approaching Boothbay. I waved at Dale Summerhays, who was waiting for us on the dock. "I'll tell you all about it at the lecture," I said.

It was held in a church basement near the minimall. There were about thirty souls in attendance, not counting the dogs. Most of the humans sat on folding chairs, though some sat on the floor with their animals.

Dale Summerhays, a rangy, rawboned woman of sixty or so—who's crazy as a loon and whose grandfather once owned most of the timber rights in northern Maine—started things off by asking for donations, encouraging people to adopt another dog or cat, and reminding them to spay and neuter their pets. When that was out of the way, I was introduced to polite applause.

My opening remarks raised a few eyebrows and kindled a few tempers: "Nearly everything we've been taught about canine behavior is wrong," I said, "and is based on a fallacy called the alpha theory." There was a stunned silence. "In order for a dog to modify his behavior due to the rank status, or authority of the alpha dog, he would have to be capable of abstract, symbolic, or conceptual thinking. And there's no evidence that dogs have such cognitive abilities. In fact, just the opposite."

I also made several other outrageous statements: that dogs have no desire to please their owners; that praise can actually be used sometimes to correct instead of reward a dog; that dogs don't mark their territory—at least not with conscious intent; that dogs don't communicate through body language—again, at least not consciously; and that you can cure aggression in some dogs by playing tug-of-war, as long as you always let the dog win and praise it for winning. These ideas are not only outside the mainstream, they're considered downright mutinous or heretical by most dog trainers.

There was a lot of heated debate and discussion on these topics. I told the group that I understood how they felt since I once believed as they did. "But," I went on, "after I began questioning mainstream ideas—about ten years ago—I began to discover that all the things we've been taught about dogs are wrong. It's a sad fact that the dog is, I think, the most misunderstood animal on the planet. This is why sixty percent of Americans who hire a dog trainer or behaviorist say that the dog's behavior didn't improve and in some cases it even got worse. That's a sixty percent failure rate! Why? Because we've been operating on false or faulty information. This lack of understanding is also a big part—in my opinion—of why our shelters are full of unwanted animals. One reason people get rid of their dogs is because they can't control them. The reason they can't control them is because nobody understands dogs—not even the experts. Especially not the experts. The fact is, dogs are predators, and it's their predatory nature which makes them open to training."

There was more disagreement and dissent, though a few people were amenable to what I was saying. Then I recommended a couple of books that had influenced my way of thinking and a slim, elegant hand was raised in the back.

"What does all this have to do with the spoon game?"

I laughed and introduced Jonas to the group and told them I'd promised to tell him a story about a dog I once trained.

"This will show a practical application of what we've been discussing theoretically—that the key to dog training comes through playing games that stimulate the hunting drive."

As I was saying this Wade Pierce came in. We made eye contact, he took a seat in the back, and then I began telling the story of the spoon game.

Tina was a shy, frightened Jack Russell terrier (an oxymoron, I know) who had been originally trained by an expert—a well-known dominance trainer and the author of half a dozen books on training. At the time I first met Tina I had only worked with four or five dogs myself while this other trainer had worked with hundreds. And I had just *started* training, while he'd been at it for over twenty years.

At any rate, after three sessions with her first trainer, Tina was a mess. Not only would she not obey any of the basic commands, there were actually two command words—down and stay—that caused her to involuntarily evacuate her bowels and hide under the bed every time she heard them. You didn't even have to be speaking directly to her, either. You could be on the phone and say, "I have to *stay down* town," and if Tina were in the room and heard you, she'd shit herself and hide for hours.

One of the first things I asked Tina's owner, after I was hired, was if there was anything the dog really liked to do—something that charged her up, got her riled and feeling spunky. He said there was.

For some reason, if you dropped a spoon on the kitchen floor, Tina became a different dog—confident and aggressive (like a *real* Jack Russell). The sound of the spoon being dropped on the tile caused her to run into the kitchen, grab the spoon in her mouth, and shake her head around as if trying to break its neck. Then she'd take it into the living room, bury it under a sofa cushion, and bark at it until you dug it out and threw it for her to chase. Then she'd go after it, grab it and "break its neck" again, then bring it back to you.

Her owner said he didn't like playing this game with her because she didn't know when to quit (she's sounding more and more like a Jack Russell!)—but I knew, or felt, it was the secret to undoing the terrible harm done to her by her original trainer. So while he was going around telling people about how you have to be alpha and all the rest of that nonsense, I was quietly teaching this frightened animal to obey the same commands that had once scared the shit out of her. And I did it by playing the spoon game.

I started out by lying on my back and letting Tina jump on top of me. This was done to build her confidence. Once we'd done that for about five or ten minutes I started retraining the down command.

Here's how it worked: as soon as she buried the spoon in the sofa cushions, I took it out, teased her with it (this was to build her hunting drive), then suddenly made a downward swoop with my hand, placing it in a position that if Tina wanted to grab hold of it she *could*, but only by lying down first. She instantly went down and grabbed the spoon. As she did I said, "Down!" in a happy voice, even though she'd already "obeyed" the command. The first time I said it, her ears went back, her tail went down, and she dashed out of the room and hid under the bed. I waited a few minutes, then went to the kitchen and dropped the spoon on the floor again.

She came dashing out of the bedroom, grabbed the spoon, "broke its neck," and we repeated the game.

We kept doing this until she stopped running away and would actually lie down, somewhat nervously, when I gave her the command. Then I changed the rules a little: when she obeyed the "down" command I would throw the spoon for her to chase instead of just giving it to her. With this added variation it took almost no time at all to rid her of her fear of the word "down." In fact, she was not only not afraid of it anymore, she actually *loved* hearing it. Why? Because it no longer meant she would be forced to lie down or punished if she didn't, it meant she got to chase the spoon and "kill" it if she did.

As I finished telling this story another part of my brain was wondering if I could use a variation on the spoon game to trap Allison's killer into confessing. Build his confidence, make him feel that I was on his side, and then pow!—nab him.

At any rate, I finished the lecture by saying, "I've found that when you stimulate a dog's hunting drive, you're activating her natural affinity for group cooperation. In fact, in some instances, if you build her drive high enough, you can train a command once—just once—and you never have to repeat it."

"What a load of crap," I heard someone say.

I laughed and said, "Well, that's what I used to think. About *all* the things I'm telling you. At any rate, I think we're about out of time, so—"

"May I say something?" came a woman's voice from the back. "I didn't want to say anything earlier because everyone was beating up on Jack and I thought they might start attacking me too, but my dog was one of the sixty percent he talked about." I recognized her voice. It was Nadia O'Malley. I'd trained her dog, another Jack Russell terrier named Jane. "The trainer at the puppy school we went to said she was too dominant and out of control and couldn't be trained. I was devastated. I thought I was going to have to give her to a shelter. I couldn't stop crying. But luckily, I heard of Jack from Dale Summerhays, and now my dog is obedient and happy. I don't always understand why the things he does work, but they do."

"Thanks, Nadia. Nice to see you. How's Jane?"

She said it was nice to see me too and that Jane was fine and delightful. Then Dale Summerhays stood up, but I interrupted her. "Let me just say one more thing. I just want to thank all of you for your opinions, even if they differ from mine. It helps in my search for understanding the true nature of dogs. So, thank you all for coming and sharing your points of view."

There was some more discussion, here and there, throughout the room as people got up to go. Some came up to me with specific training questions about their dogs. While this was going on, Wade Pierce made his way over. He had the document he wanted me to sign. He handed it *and* a pen to me, the same way he had at the hospital—putting the pen in my left hand with his right, and the document in my right with his left.

"I really do need to have you sign this," he said.

I laughed, switched the pen to my right hand, and signed. "You came all the way out here just for my signature?"

"Well, it's important to, uh, to Allison's estate."

I handed him the document and pen, the way he'd given them to me, as if I were his mirror image—my left to his right—and said, "Listen, I want to apologize for anything I said or did that may have offended you the other day. Jamie has a lot of nice things to say about you, so—"

"Thank you. I, uh, I appreciate that."

"She tells me you're quite a brilliant lawyer and I was wondering if you wouldn't mind being in on something I'm doing."

He made a gesture, as if to say, "Okay, what?"

"Well, I'm planning a little demonstration tomorrow afternoon at Allison's house—a kind of re-enactment of the murder—and I thought you might like to be there. After I leave here I'm hoping to find Tim Berry and his girlfriend and get them to turn themselves in. Once I do that I think I can prove, once and for all, who really killed Allison."

"Really? That's, uh, that's very interesting. Who do you think did it?"

"Well, it may have been Richard DeMarco's girlfriend, framing *him* for it. Then again, it may have been Berry and his girlfriend. Or DeMarco. I need your help to find the truth."

He smiled. "Yes, I think I *would* like to be there. Although, it, uh, it would depend on the time?"

I told him I planned the demonstration for 2:30.

He said, "Okay. Yes, I could, uh, I could probably, uh, fit that into my schedule." And with that he left.

"Fascinating," Jonas said, after we'd retreated from the church and Dale Summerhays had given us a ride back to the marina. "Particularly all the animosity toward your ideas."

"Well," I said, as we walked along the water and looked at the lonely wintertime sailboats, rocking in the water, "there's probably some kind of flaw in my presentation. The ideas are valid. I guess it's just hard for people to give up their beliefs."

"You know, it reminds me of . . ." he said and told me about a cancer researcher who'd been nearly laughed out of medicine twenty years ago because his ideas were considered ridiculous. Now there's a whole branch of medical research and millions of dollars being spent to find a cure based on those same ridiculous ideas.

"That's nice to hear, Jonas, but let's talk about Jamie."

"Yes, you're right." He stopped, leaned his arms against the railing. "So the spoon game means I should start by finding out what she loves, the way you did with that dog, Tina."

"That's right."

"Then what?"

"Then show her you understand it and that you value how important it is to her. Did you know that she's the first volunteer ME in Maine history allowed to perform an autopsy in an ongoing homicide investigation?"

He shook his head angrily. "But she could be doing so much more with her talent than messing around with corpses and criminals! I don't understand why she wants to do that."

"That's just the problem. Homicide is Jamie's spoon game. It's what charges her up, makes her happy; it's what she loves."

He nodded, sighed, and said, "I see that. I see what you're saying. A little less of what I want for her, and a little more of what she wants for herself."

"Maybe a *lot* more, Jonas: you don't heal deep wounds with half measures. As a physician you should know that."

He gave me a look. "Am I being lectured to now by my daughter's boyfriend?"

I gave him a grin and put my palms up in the air. "Hey, you were the one who asked for my help."

He smiled, chagrined. "Yes, I did, didn't I?"

"Just play the spoon game and see what happens."

We had a cup of coffee at the lobster pound—the one that was still open at that time of year—and a little while later Jamie and Laurie showed up with the car, which was brimming with shopping bags and packages.

Jonas took Jamie's arm as we walked down the dock toward the runabout. He said, "Jack tells me you've earned some sort of unique position with the State Medical Examiner's office?"

She looked down at her shoes. "That's right. Though, I don't suppose you'll approve."

"On the contrary, honey. I'm enormously proud of you."

She looked up happily. "Really?"

"Of course. That's quite a feather in your cap. I know I tend to make more of a fuss over Spencer's accomplishments than I do yours, but that's because he's a neurosurgeon. I can relate more to what he does. I just don't know enough about forensics to be able to discuss it very well or to know why it appeals to you so much."

"I'd be happy to tell you about it sometime, Dad. It would really mean a lot to me if I could."

We got into the boat, Jamie gave Jonas a kiss on the cheek.

"Good," Jonas said. "We'll do that tonight, as part of our pre–Christmas Eve gala. Just as soon as you and Jack come back from Monhegan Island."

Unfortunately, things on Monhegan Island didn't go quite as expected—in fact, I was lucky to get out of the experience alive—so we never did have that pre–Christmas Eve gala.

39

"Stop moaning, you big baby," Jamie said, steering us toward the scallop-shaped harbor. We were doing about thirty knots according to the speedometer (or whatever you call it on a boat) and the wind whipped the loose strands of hair around her parka hood. Her cheeks and nose were bright red and her dark eyes were flashing with pleasure.

I was hunched down and miserable in the seat next to her.

"We'll be there in two minutes."

"That's it, yell at me. I didn't get seasick when your father was driving."

"That was just across the river. There's a big difference between a river and an ocean."

"It didn't look like a river to me. That's the problem with people in this state. You call lakes 'ponds,' and oceans 'rivers,' and you probably call that a pebble!"

I pointed to the hulking shape of Monhegan Island. In fact, from a few miles out it *had* looked like a big grayish-brown rock on the horizon. But as you got closer you could begin to make out the tall, dark pines and the rocky sea cliffs, the color of old rusted iron. Here and there you could also spot the sloping roofs and gabled windows of the inns and summer homes of Monhegan natives. Off to the right a sudden green-white plume of spray arched up and nearly doused the abandoned nest of some lonely sea bird.

"Anyway," I said, "I'm not moaning in pain, but pleasure. I feel like I'm in a Winslow Homer painting."

"I didn't know you were an art lover."

"Sure. I used to make the rounds of all the museums in New York—the Frick, the Guggenheim, the Whitney, the Modern, the Met, the Frick . . ."

"You already said the Frick."

"I know. I figure if I keep talking it'll take my mind off my stomach." She laughed. "Besides, I like saying Frick. *Plus* they've got three or four great Vermeers there."

"They have what?" It was hard to make yourself heard over the crash of the waves and the sound of the engine.

"Vermeers!" I shouted. "They have some great Vermeers."

"Oh, *Vermeers*! I thought you said they had some great 'veneers.' Anyway, I'd love to see them."

"Great. I'll take you there sometime. Can you hand me another towel?"

We were close enough by now to see a small group of passengers boarding the big mail boat as it churned the waters of the harbor, making ready for its evening chug back to Port Clyde. There were half a dozen yachts and sailboats moored to the floating docks below the main pier, but no runabouts.

I finished "inspecting the hull" and cleaned my mouth and beard with the towel while Jamie did something with the controls. We slowed down and started drifting toward the docks. "Well, Jack," she said. "That'll teach you not to eat pancakes *and* waffles for breakfast. Not to mention sausages and eggs."

"Oh great, honey, thanks a lot." I lurched starboard for the eleventh time.

"Sorry." She handed me another towel.

I waved my hand as if to say, "No problem," then out loud I said, "but don't dock here. Let's circle the island first."

"Are you crazy? I'm freezing cold! I need some hot cocoa, or better yet, some Irish coffee. And so do you."

"That actually sounds pretty good," I said, realizing it was the first time since we'd left Boothbay Harbor that I hadn't gotten sick at the mention of something to eat or drink. "But the thing is, I want to find Tim Berry's house. It's got its own dock and we can sneak up on him better that way."

"No one said anything to me about sneaking up on anybody," she grumped, but gunned the engine and turned the boat around.

We found the house about ten minutes later. It was on the windward side. There was a long wooden jetty with a floating dock jutting out from a rocky beach. There was another boat—a small cabin cruiser—already tied up there. Jamie cut the engine and expertly nosed us in behind it, just kissing its backside with the nose of the runabout.

I jumped out and began trying to tie us up, but the dock kept swaying in the opposite direction to the rhythm my legs were wobbling in. I kept falling down. I was kneeling on the dock, ready to make another try, when Jamie got out of the boat and took the rope away from me. "Let me do that." She tied the yellow ropes to the iron hook–thingie on the dock.

"Do you hear something?" I said, scanning the ocean behind us. I couldn't see anything except some dark clouds, a flock of gulls, and a fog bank starting to roll in from the open sea.

Jamie had finished tying us up and was looking at the name on the side of the cabin cruiser. *"Saint Joan"* was painted there in red cursive script with gold trim.

"That's odd," she said.

"Yeah?" I said, standing up again. "What is?"

"It's probably nothing. What did you hear?"

We began walking up the narrow dock toward the beach— Jamie holding my arm. "I don't know, maybe my ears haven't adjusted to the quiet, but it sounded to me like a helicopter. Are there any law enforcement agencies around here that use choppers?"

"The State Police. The Coast Guard, maybe. Why?"

We got to the end of the dock and began walking up a long, winding, wooden walkway that led across the rocky beach.

"Are there any regular charter flights?"

"I don't know. There could be, I suppose. But anyone could hire a chopper pilot at the Portland airport. God, I'm cold. I hope there's a fire," she said and shivered.

The wooden walkway gave way to a gravel path with railroad ties for steps. It wound toward the back of the house. The darkling sky loomed over the even darker building. No lights were on inside. I suggested that maybe no one was home and Jamie reminded me that until a few years ago Monhegan Island had no electricity at all and that some of the older homes still weren't wired for it.

"I'll bet you think that sounds like my kind of island."

"Why do you say that?"

"You told Mrs. Murtaugh you thought I was a Luddite, remember?"

She laughed. "Well, you *are*, sort of. You don't own a computer or a cell phone or a CD player."

"First of all, unlike a computer, my filing cabinet never crashes, leaving me without access to my business records. Second, cell phones cause brain tumors."

"No, they don't."

"Yes, they do. And last, to me there's nothing better than the sound of a diamond needle dropping onto virgin vinyl and slowly finding that first groove. Especially if you've got an old McIntosh vacuum tube stereo system, like I do."

"You're hopeless."

We reached the back of the house and found stone steps leading up to the back door, which was framed by a wooden trellis, barren of leaves or vines and badly in need of some fresh paint. There was a glass storm door, and behind that a wooden door, painted green, with three smallish panes in a descending stair-step pattern. I pulled my gloves off with my teeth and reached into the pocket of the parka Jonas had lent me. I pulled out a folded black leather pouch containing Charlie's lockpicking tools and opened it.

"You're planning to break in?"

"Thmthmg wighk thkt," I said and Jamie pulled the gloves out of my mouth. "Something like that," I repeated.

"Why not just knock?"

"The element of surprise, my dear."

I had the tumbler guide in place and feeling around for the second tumbler with the fraction hook when Jamie clutched my arm and said, "Oh, my god. Jack!"

I looked over at her, then followed her gaze up to the door just in time to see a head of blond hair moving away from one of the windows. "Who was it? Tara?"

Her breath came in a burst. "Un-huh. Sorry, I got startled there for a second."

"Well," I said, putting Charlie's kit away, "there goes the element of surprise . . ."

We went through the door and we were standing in front of a long narrow hall, with a high arched open doorway to our left—big enough for a set of double doors. This led to the kitchen. There was a small doorway on the right, with the door standing open. This was a washroom and toilet. At the back end of the hall was a staircase leading upward.

I held the door for Jamie. "Upstairs or down?"

"It's your expedition, Sherlock." She stepped inside.

"Main floor it is, then." I closed the door and we were engulfed in darkness. "Kind of spooky, huh?"

"You could say that." She clutched my arm as we felt our way toward the kitchen. "How's your shoulder doing?"

"Not too bad. Why?"

"It just occurred to me that the last time we saw Tim Berry was when you got shot. I don't suppose you have a flashlight?"

"Sure," I said, feeling my way forward. "I have two of them, in fact. Both back at the kennel." She punched my arm. "There's bound to be some windows once we get into the kitchen."

I was right. There was a bit of dusky light coming in on our left through a row of windows which faced the ocean. There was a slight whooshing noise coming from somewhere to the right. I couldn't make out what it was—a broken radiator? Steam pipes? The noise seemed to rise in pitch and suddenly the room filled with a shrieking sound. Jamie screamed. I think I may have taken the Lord's name in vain. Then I looked over at where the sound was coming from and saw the blue flame.

"Sshhh. It's just a tea kettle, honey."

Then the far door opened, the lights came on, and there stood Tim Berry frozen in the doorway.

After an awkward moment he stammered, "Uh, hi. How did you find me?"

"Easy," I said. "I just looked up Dumbass Fugitive Waiters in the Yellow Pages. You were the only one listed. I hope you don't mind us dropping in like this. It's freezing outside."

With the lights on (the house was wired for electricity after all) we could see that we were in a large spacious room, with long, wide marble counters and what seemed like dozens of cupboards, all painted light blue with royal trim. There was a brick alcove in one wall, which looked to be where the old wood-burning stove had probably stood when the house was first built. There was an old-fashioned gas model in its place now. Tim Berry went to it and turned off the kettle.

"Would you—um—like some tea? You can hang your coats over there by the door." We did that while he got some cups and other tea things out of the cupboards. "My grandmother's English. That's why I take tea over coffee."

Jamie and I sat down at the long kitchen table—made of oak—while Berry brought over the tea things and sat down.

I introduced him to Jamie, then said, "So where'd your friend Tara go?"

"What?" He seemed confused. "Tara's not here."

"Yes, she is. We saw her at the back door not more than a couple minutes ago." He put a metal tea ball into a pale green ceramic pot, then poured hot water in and let it begin to steep. "Look, Tim, you don't need to protect her from us."

"But I'm *not* protecting her. She's been hiding out at her cousin's place while I've been out here trying to get the courage up to turn myself in before things get worse." He put a spoon into the pot and stirred it around a little. "She let me borrow her cousin's boat and I haven't seen her since."

Jamie said, "The '*Saint Joan*'? That's her cousin's boat?"

Berry nodded, and I said: "What?"

"Walter Kirby had a cabin cruiser named after his wife— the '*Saint Joan.*' He left it to Sam when he died."

"Of course," I almost slapped myself in the forehead, "Sam Kirby is Tara's cousin."

"Who's Sam Kirby?"

"A deputy sheriff who has been planting all the evidence the cops have against you." I realized something, looked at Jamie. "Maybe she's in on it, too. Maybe she *did* kill her mother."

"No," Berry said, "I know her. I know how much Allison meant to her. So she couldn't have done it, she just couldn't have." He poured tea into all three cups and said, "You like lemon, or milk and sugar?" We said we both wanted the latter and he obliged.

I blew over the rim. "Then why is she staying with Sam Kirby while he's busy trying to frame you? I think we ought to hold off on our tea party and go talk to her."

"Are you sure she's here?"

"I didn't see her face, but Jamie did." I turned to Jamie. "Right?"

Jamie shook her head. "I *think* it was her. I don't know. Maybe there's someone else in the house?"

"No," Berry said. "No one."

"Well, let's have a look around," I said, and stood up.

"Okay." Berry stood up too.

40

It took us about twenty minutes to look the whole house over—all three stories of it, but there was no sign of Tara and no sign she'd even been there.

"She was probably trying to leave when she saw us at the back door," I said. "Maybe she found another exit."

We went back to the kitchen and Berry made a new pot of tea. After we'd had a few sips, I said, "Maybe you should tell us a few things about you and Tara and Allison."

"Okay," he said, uncertainly. "Like what things?"

"Well, for starters, you said that Allison was Tara's mother, correct?" He nodded. "Who was her father?"

"Um, I don't think she ever told me."

"*Who* never told you? Tara or Allison?"

"Um, neither one, actually. I mean, not that I remember. You like the tea? It's Earl Grey. Some people don't like it."

"Tastes great," I said.

Jamie made a similar comment, then, "Tim, if either one of them told you, you'd remember, don't you think? So who was it?"

He sighed. "I don't know his name. I just know he was some guy Allison knew when she was in high school. I think he was in college. I know he was from Florida. I think—I mean, I got the *feeling*—that Allison's father was some kind of rich, prejudiced bastard who was furious at her for getting pregnant and insisted that she have the baby and then give it up."

"What do you mean, he was prejudiced?"

"Oh. Tara's father was Jewish. Didn't I mention that?"

"No, you didn't," Jamie said, and was about to say something else, but I put a hand to her knee.

"See," Tim took a sip of Earl Grey, "the whole problem with me and Allison was that I used to date Tara back when I was still at Bowdoin. I just knew her as Tara McCullough then. Her mom and dad—her adoptive parents—were really nice. I met them once when they invited me to spend Thanksgiving with them.

"Then, I don't know . . . she was saying she wanted us to get married and all and I wasn't sure, so we broke up. Then I ran out of money and had to come home to Camden, but I really missed her, you know? I couldn't stop thinking about her even though it was over. Then one day Allison came into O'Neal's and even though she was older than me, she reminded me so much of Tara it made my heart hurt. So I asked her out and she said yes. I couldn't believe she said yes."

We all sat quietly for a moment, sipping our tea. "Some people don't like Earl Grey. It's got some kind of spice in it or something. But I still think it's the best." We sipped and nodded and he went on with his story.

"When Allison gave Tara up for adoption, she never knew what happened to her. But after we broke up—me and Tara, that is—Tara saw this thing on *Oprah* about adopted children looking for their biological parents and she decided to find out who her real mother and father were. Mr. and Mrs. McCullough were real nice about it too. And pretty soon she calls me up one day to tell me the identity of her real mom and dad. We were still friends even though we weren't boyfriend/girlfriend anymore.

"So she comes up to Camden to tell me about it, *and* to tell me that her birth mother lives nearby. Of course, at this time Allison and I are seeing each other a lot, hot and heavy like, and when Tara tells me her real mother's name, I was like . . . you know, really weirded out.

"Anyway, I didn't say anything to Tara about me and Allison at first, because I felt sick about it. But then, for some reason, me and Tara slept together that night, like, for old time's sake? And it just slipped out."

I resisted saying something and sipped my tea.

Jamie said, "So you were sleeping with mother and daughter at the same time?"

"I know." He hung his head. "Pretty disgusting, huh? It gets worse, too."

We waited to hear how it got worse.

"So, anyway, Tara freaks out, you know? So the next morning she goes to see Allison for this reunion type thing, just like on *Oprah*, and she tells Allison about me and her, and of course, Allison freaks out also. So now, instead of having like two girlfriends or something, I'm totally out in the cold and feeling like a real pervert when it wasn't my fault. I mean, how was it my fault? *I* didn't know they were related."

"You did when you slept with Tara that night," I said.

He hung his head again. "You're right. I shouldn't have done that. And then, to top things off, Allison calls to tell me she's pregnant and that I'm the father. How sick is that, you know? I'm going to be the father of a baby whose half-sister is my ex-girlfriend."

"And if that weren't enough," I tried to lighten things up, "you had to get a basset hound."

He shook his head. "That dog saved my life, I'm telling you. If it wasn't for him I would've probably killed myself." His eyes started to well up. "I only got the dog so I could sort of practice being a father, you know? Like being responsible for another life and like that? Now, Allison's dead. So is the baby. The police think Tara did it for Allison's money and I'll probably never see Thurston again. What am I going to do, Mr. Field? I don't want to go to jail."

"Well, I can't promise you anything on that score. You *did* shoot at a Camden Police officer."

Jamie touched my hand. "We'll try to help you make the best of it. If we could only speak to Tara and find out what's been going on with her and Sam Kirby, and who her father is—"

"He might be the killer," I said.

"You think so?"

"If he knew about her money and wanted it badly enough . . ."

We all sipped our tea quietly, thinking things over in a very English, Earl Grey sort of way, then there came the sound of shuffling footsteps from the back hallway. Jamie's hand shook, rattling her teacup. The hairs on the back of my neck stood up. We all looked over to the open doorway. A second or two passed and Tara appeared in the open space, a dull look of surprise on her face. She tried to say something, then stumbled over the threshold and fell to the floor. A large hunting knife was sticking out of her back.

We all jumped up and ran over to her. We had just enough time to see that she was still breathing, though her back was covered in blood. Then the lights went out.

The sound of a helicopter filled the air and the sweeping glare of a searchlight stabbed at us through the kitchen windows. The room lights stuttered for a moment, and then came back on. When they did, I saw that Tim Berry was kneeling over the girl's now motionless body, one hand on the knife.

"Don't take it out," Jamie told him. "It could be keeping her alive, believe it or not. Are there any doctors on the island?"

"I don't know. Should I call 911?" Jamie said yes, Berry went to a wall phone by the main door. I ran the other way, heading for the back door.

"Jack, where are you going?"

"To find who did this before they get away."

I went outside and ran down the stone steps just outside the back door, then turned right, toward the front of the house, thinking that was probably the avenue of escape.

I ran across the snow-covered lawn just as a State Police helicopter was setting down on the beach, about sixty yards to my left. I could see the state insignia on the side of the chopper as its blades whipped the cold night air. Then, the blades slowed as the pilot cut the engines and I saw two shadowy figures hop out of the back and begin running, heads and shoulders down, toward the back of the house.

I came around the front and scanned the walkway, which was made of old concrete and stumble stones. It led straight to a dirt road but there were no signs of anyone running away, or anyone riding a bicycle—the most common form of transportation on the island. There were plenty of places to hide—

hedges, a drainage ditch, an old wooden garden shed, even a low rocky wall. I didn't bother with them, though, because it didn't make sense that the attacker would stab Tara and then just hide out on the property.

Once the sound of the chopper died down completely, I heard the sound of another engine stuttering, trying to start up. It came from around back—probably on the dock. I headed back that way and got to the gravel walk in time to see Dan Coletti and a state trooper running toward the back of the house.

Coletti had what looked like an arrest warrant in one hand. "Field," he said, "what are you doing here?"

"Never mind that. Jamie's inside with Tim Berry and the Tara girl. She's just been stabbed in the back. Jamie's taking care of her, but she's going to need your chopper to get her to a hospital. She's badly hurt." The trooper drew his weapon. "Don't worry," I said, "Berry didn't stab her and he isn't armed. In fact, he's ready to turn himself in."

Coletti waved the warrant. "Fine, but it's him *and* the girl we're after now. She broke into Wade Pierce's office and stole a copy of the original will along with some other important files. That makes it pretty clear she's in on it with him."

"Where'd you hear this from, Wade Pierce or Sam Kirby? And who told you Berry was here? I bet that was Kirby, too."

He shook his head. "Just doing my job."

"That'd be a switch." I heard the engine stutter again, turned my back on him and started running for the dock.

"Where are you going?"

"To do *my* job," I shouted over my shoulder. The engine stuttered once more, then caught and began to roar.

"Field, get your ass back here!" I thought I heard the click of the trooper cocking his weapon. My blood froze but I kept running. Then I heard Coletti say, "Let him go," and I started breathing again.

When I reached the dock I saw that the *Saint Joan* was heading out to sea. The fog had rolled in even more so I couldn't see who was at the wheel, though I had a pretty good idea. I untied the ropes on the runabout, jumped in, and looked around for the key. It was in the ignition so I sat behind the wheel and started her up. I wasn't sure if I'd be able to handle the craft—I'd never driven a boat before. But it hadn't seemed that much different from driving a car, the way Jamie and her father had done it—at least, that's what I thought at the time—so I decided to give it a shot. The easy thing about driving a car, though, is that you do it on a marked road on dry land. Roads always lead, eventually, to places with people and phones. There are no road signs, yellow lines, or all-night gas stations on the open sea.

Still, like an idiot, I grabbed hold of the wheel, took a deep breath, and stepped on the gas. The boat took off with a lurch, and the sound of polished wood screeching against the side of the dock. In no time at all I was chasing the disappearing lights of the *Saint Joan* as it cut through the fog and out to the open sea.

41

Two guys on a lobster boat found me a little before sunrise.
I was dead tired, freezing cold, hungry as a wolf, and making
all kinds of crazy bargains with God if only He'd let me die a
painless death (if he was really intent on taking me) or,
please, send somebody to save me so I could get back to
Jamie, Leon, Frankie, and all my dogs. In the end He opted
for the latter proposition. (I think He likes dogs.)

"Ahoy, there!" I'd heard a voice say. "Are you Jack
Field?"

My face had been too numb for me to talk so I'd just nodded.

They got me on board and wrapped me in blankets and
gave me some hot coffee from a thermos, then jerry-rigged
some rope to tow the runabout behind them. The younger one
took the wheel while the older one radioed the Coast Guard,
who'd been out looking for me all night. I heard the lobster-
man agree to meet up with the nearest cutter, located at a
nearby coordinate, then, after he signed off, he smiled at me.
"I'm Roy Anselm," he said, then nodded at the wheel.
"That's my son, Cory."

I nodded and shivered and slurped some more coffee.

"Kind of a dumb thing you did, eh?" said Cory.

"Not the first time," I muttered.

Roy laughed. "No, but it could have been the last."

He was right. It had taken me less than ten minutes to lose
sight of the *Saint Joan*. Once that happened, I realized I had

no idea where I was, where I was headed, or in which direction I ought to go in order to get back to dry land. So I just cut the power and sat in the fog over the deep water, rocking with the waves until I decided that the best course of action—at least, the best *I* could come up with—was to steer the boat in wider and wider circles, hoping at some point on the compass, I'd finally see something to steer toward.

That's how I ran out of gas, thirty miles out at sea.

There wasn't much conversation aboard the lobster boat. I almost fell asleep a couple of times but couldn't manage to do that and shiver at the same time. I was glad to get on board the Coast Guard boat: it had a heated cabin. By the time we got to the docks at Rockland I had actually stopped shivering and had regained most of my motor skills.

There was a crowd of people waiting on the dock, all with binoculars. Jamie was there too, and had an ambulance standing by. "Jack, you idiot," she said as she helped me ashore. "Are you okay?"

"I've been better. But you didn't have to bring the whole town to welcome me home."

She led me toward the ambulance. "What the hell are you talking about?"

"All these people . . ." I said, pointing to the crowd, which I now noticed weren't paying any attention to me at all. They were all staring out at the water through their binoculars.

"They're bird counters, Jack."

"Bird counters? Don't make me lie on that gurney, please."

"Every December they come to count the birds. And you *will* lie down." I obeyed her. "That's right, that's a good boy. I'm going to have you checked out for hypothermia."

"No, I'm fine. I don't need to go to the hosp—"

"Don't give me any of that. If you learned how to act sensibly you wouldn't have to go to the hospital all the time."

"Yes, Mommy." The ambulance driver closed the door on us.

On the way, Jamie told me how *her* night had gone. With the help of Dan Coletti and the state trooper, she'd gotten Tim Berry and Tara onto the police helicopter. Tara had lost a lot of blood, but no vital organs or arteries had been affected.

It had been a rough night, and she was in serious condition, but it looked like she was going to pull through. Tim Berry was in jail and there was a police guard on Tara's room.

After I had been treated for exposure, Jamie took me home. Frankie and Ginger and Leon were almost as glad to see me as I was to see them, but the reunion was necessarily short lived. It was still early Sunday morning, and Jamie and I had both been up all night. Plus we had a little event to attend at Allison's house later in the day and we needed to get some sleep if we were going to trap the killer. So we went upstairs to bed, taking the still-yawning dogs with us.

I turned off the phone and set the alarm for noon. We got undressed, and as we settled under the covers I said a silent prayer, thanking God, not just for my rescue but for creating naked women and long slow Sunday mornings to be naked with them.

Jamie snuggled next to me, all warm and soft in all the right places, and said, "Jack, you do know there's a ship-to-shore radio on the runabout, right?"

"There is?"

"You lunkhead," she sighed. "What am I going to do with you?" A moment or two passed and then she yawned and said, "So do you know who the killer is yet?"

"Mm-hmm."

"Is it who I *think* it is?"

"I don't know. Who do you think it is?"

"Put it this way—am I going to have to start looking around for a new divorce attorney?"

"It wouldn't be a bad idea."

She sighed and said, "I was afraid of that."

42

Jamie and I met Carl Staub at Allison's at 1:30 for our dress-rehearsal. Carl told me he'd checked out the phone number I'd gotten from Pierce's caller ID. It belonged to a doctor's office in Portland. Carl drove down there on Saturday and showed Pierce's photo to the staff and they all remembered seeing him on Thursday, but the doctor who'd treated him wouldn't say for what, citing doctor/client privilege.

Carl also checked out Pierce's alibi. He'd been at home alone, he'd told Carl, watching a Pats game when the murder took place. He told Carl he had taken one phone call during the game. It lasted about thirty minutes (the call). Carl checked the LUDs and verified that a call had come to Pierce's home line from a cell phone belonging to Robert Erickson, who was on-staff with the marina project. Carl was unable to get corroboration from Erickson. He was out of town for the holidays.

I asked Carl if he was ready for our little trick and he said he was and demonstrated as much with Ginger. She performed just as I'd trained her to do.

We were ready for the show.

Everyone but Tara McCullough was there. The party included Rockland County Sheriff Horace Flynn, Camden Police Lieutenant Dan Coletti, ace reporter Otis Barnes, waiter and murder suspect Tim Berry, Camden Police Officer Carl Staub, college student Audrey Stafford, attorney and developer Wade Pierce, Sheriff's Deputies Sam Kirby and Quentin Peck, Buffalo Carting and Hauling tycoon Victor DeMarco, ex-model Debbie Sheldon, Assistant State Medical Examiner Dr. Jamie Cutter, cardiologist Dr. Darryl Deloit, and me—I'm a dog trainer. Oh, and Ginger, too, of course—the Airedale Heiress. She was the star of the show.

"What's all this about?" Flynn demanded, after I'd gathered everyone in the dining room. Everyone but Audrey, that is. She was upstairs, changing. "And who's the girl upstairs?"

"That's Audrey Stafford," I explained. "She's going to play the murder victim in our little production. She's in Allison's bedroom, changing into some of Allison's clothes."

"Why is *she* playing the victim?" Coletti wanted to know.

"Because she's three months pregnant, just as Allison was at the time of the murder." (Audrey had announced her condition to her family and had given me permission to discuss it.) "This is important because her body is giving off pheromones that the dog responds to. Plus, she's about the same general size as Allison, though a little skinnier. Besides," I scratched Ginger's neck, "the dog likes her."

"What does the dog got to do with it?" Flynn asked.

"Everything. She witnessed Allison's murder and she's going to help us identify the killer—through her exceptional sense of smell. But more about that later."

There was a bit of a hubbub over that.

"Look, here's how it's going to work. We're going to stage the murder the way I think it happened. Audrey will be at the computer, putting eyedrops in one eye then mimic the effects of a heart attack, which is how Allison died. As she does this, one of our possible suspects will come through the kitchen door. When each suspect enters, Audrey will jump up, stagger to the kitchen counter, pretend to pull a knife out of the knife block, and the potential killer will come toward her. Ginger, meanwhile, will be lying by the heating duct next to the downstairs bathroom—her favorite spot. If she simply lies there and watches the action, or if she gets up but wags her tail happily, we'll know that that particular suspect is not guilty. But if she growls and barks, we'll know who the killer is."

Wade Pierce said, "This is ridiculous. This is not a proper, nor a, uh, legal form of inquiry."

"Not admissible. Exactly true, counselor. However, everyone should know that this is unofficial and has no bearing on any possible arrest or future court proceeding. I am not an agent of the police—just a private citizen conducting an experiment. Everyone is free to leave at any time."

"Fine by me," said Pierce, making to leave.

"That's okay," I said. "You're not one of our potential suspects anyway, so if you want to go—" I deliberately stopped in mid-sentence. "Wait a second, Carl? Does Mr. Pierce have an alibi for the time of the murder?"

Carl pretended to leaf through a steno pad. "Uh, yeah. Sort of. He was home alone, watching a football game. But he did receive a phone call. It lasted about thirty minutes, which wouldn't have given him time to drive from his place in Owl's Head to Hobb's Pond, so I guess he's in the clear."

"There you go," I told Pierce. "You're not a suspect. I just thought that as her close personal friend and as executor to her estate, you might like to be here to help us better understand Allison's daily routines as well as her business dealings and the nature of her will. But if you want to go . . ."

He shrugged and stayed put.

"So who all is suspects?" said Sam Kirby.

"Besides you, Sam?" I said. "Tim Berry, Tara McCullough, Sheriff Flynn, Debbie Sheldon, and Richard De-Marco."

Everyone reacted. Victor DeMarco said, "Now, wait a minute . . ." but then remembered his lines. "Well, since I know my boy ain't guilty, that's okay, I guess."

"You're saying *I'm* a suspect?" Flynn said, incredulous.

"Of course you are. I'm not going to go into the personal details, out of courtesy to a certain woman who lives in upstate New York, but you had a close family relationship with the deceased. This same woman in New York told me personally that you threatened to kill Allison if she ever revealed certain secrets about your past. Maybe Allison did just that and you made good on your threat."

Flynn's face went red and he looked over at Coletti, who shook his head.

"You see, Sheriff," I said, "you've been nosing around in this investigation from the beginning and doing it in a way

that casts some suspicion on your motives. I don't personally think you had anything to do with the murder, but I
wouldn't be very thorough if I didn't include you in the list
of suspects."

His face got even redder and I thought for a second he
might walk out, but I knew he wouldn't. Curiosity: that's
what kept us all in that room. All except Ginger.

I looked over at Pierce as if seeking his approval. He gave
me a deferential nod.

"Sure, okay, include me," Flynn said. "But you're gonna
regret this afterward, Field. And I mean a lot."

"Now, wait a minute," Coletti said. "Clue me in on something here. What about Tara McCullough and Richard De-
Marco? One's in the hospital and the other's dead. How are
they going to participate?"

"Well, like I said before, Ginger is going to identify the
killer through her sense of smell—a dog's most important
faculty. The law holds, for instance, that a bloodhound's behavior while tracking a suspect is as admissible in court as
the testimony of an eyewitness. We've already conceded that
the outcome of this demonstration won't be admissible or legal evidence. But for today's purposes we'll have to settle for
what we can get. That's why Audrey is upstairs putting on
Allison's clothes. They bear her scent. The same thing with
Tara McCullough's clothes. Since she and Jamie are roughly
the same size, I had Jamie put on some of Tara's things, as
well as a touch of her perfume, before we came over here."

"I was wondering what happened to your classy sense of
style," Coletti said, looking at the black jeans, motorcycle
boots and leather jacket Jamie was wearing.

"Thanks, Dan. But I kinda *like* this look."

"What difference does it make if she wears the killer's
clothes?" Flynn said. "The dog knows it's not her."

He was right, of course. But since no one else there knew
enough about dogs to argue, I figured I could get away with
my argument—as long as I cloaked it in jargon. "It's a well-
known scientific fact that a dog's visual acuity is thirty to
forty times less precise than that of a human, while the canine
olfactory capacity can be up to a million times more powerful. So, to a dog, a scent ID can be a million times more ac-

curate than a visual ID. If you want, we can even blindfold
Ginger to prove that she's making her ID based on scent
only."

People seemed impressed. Coletti said, "Okay, so Jamie's
wearing Tara McCullough's clothes and perfume. What
about Richard DeMarco? You yourself said he looked like the
best suspect. How are we going to—"

"I had Carl Staub pick up some of his clothes from his
hamper in Bangor. As with Tara's clothes, they smell like
him. We also have some of his cologne. Since DeMarco's
clothes will fit me the best of anyone here, I'll go last, playing him."

"My boy didn't kill nobody," said Slick Vic, right on cue.

"Well, we'll see," I said.

"All right, then, let's get on with it," Coletti said. "But I can
tell you right now, if this damn talent show works at all, it's
gonna prove that Tara McCullough killed Allison DeMarco."

"I have no problem with that, if that's what Ginger's nose
has to tell us. Believe me, I'm just looking for the truth."

Audrey came downstairs just then, wearing a baggy pair
of Allison's sweat pants, an old T-shirt, and the same calico
apron Allison had been wearing when she died.

"Okay, Audrey, you ready?"

She nodded. "What do I do?"

I pointed to the computer. "Sit there." I turned to everyone
else, trying not to let my feelings of foolishness and deceit
show through my professional demeanor. "Okay, Tim Berry
goes first. Everybody else has to stay in the dining room so as
not to distract Ginger. Carl you stand next to her and hold the
leash, just in case she gets a little too excited by the demonstration." Everyone got in place, some shaking their heads
and muttering. "Quent, you go outside with Tim just to make
sure he doesn't make another run for it."

"I'm not gonna run off again, Mr. Field. I mean, Jack."

"Yeah, well, I think Lieutenant Coletti would be a lot happier if you weren't left to your own devices just now." Berry
nodded sadly.

"Okay now, Tim, you watch through the door to see when
Audrey puts the eyedrops in her eyes, then come inside."

I took Ginger over to the heating duct and told her to lie

down and stay, which she did, then gave the leash to Carl. I went into the dining room to join the others.

"What's the deal with the eyedrops, anyway?" Coletti said.

Jamie said, "Her body had elevated levels of epinephrine, renin—an enzyme—and PTH, or parathyroid hormone—along with naturally high-occurring levels of estrogen due to her pregnant condition. The estrogen further elevated the normal levels of renin substrate and angiotensin II. That, along with the large doses of calcium and iodine supplements she was taking, brought on what we call v-tach—an abnormally rapid heartbeat—which initiated a condition known as calcium rigor, where the heart is arrested during systole. This process took a maximum of about thirty seconds, and *Bang*, her heart just stopped."

Everyone was silent for a moment. Finally Dan Coletti said, "How do you know the chemicals were in her eyedrops?"

"They were hormones, Dan, not chemicals. And we don't know that for sure. But it's the only explanation which accounts for the elevated levels found in the blood at the time of death, and the blown right pupil, and the fact that there were no needle marks on her body. Okay?"

"Okay," Coletti thought it over. "I don't understand it, but if you say that's what happened I'll take your word. So let me get this straight—she puts the eyedrops in one eye and all those chemicals you mentioned—"

"Hormones," Jamie corrected him again.

"Yeah, all those hormones take effect, the killer comes through the door, she starts to fibrillate, or whatever you call it, she grabs a knife, and then what?"

I said, "This is all a hypothetical re-creation, based on the forensic evidence, but at the point the killer comes through the door, either Allison stabs him intentionally because she realizes what he's done, or the dog jumps up on his back and pushes him into the knife she's threatening him with. Allison then falls to the floor, in cardiac arrest. She's dead. Meanwhile, the killer is bleeding from a stab wound to his abdomen. He somehow gets the dog under control and ties her up out back. Then he comes back inside and cleans up the blood on the knife and on the floor, but at this point he isn't sure whether to get rid of the knife or leave it. He's very clever, you see. He realizes that if he leaves the knife at the scene, there may be traces of his blood that he can't get rid of, so it's better to get rid of it. But then he thinks, what if someone knows the knife is missing? So he cleans up the blood the best he can, slices a tomato on the cutting board to explain why she had a knife, and he puts it back in her hand."

"Well," said Wade Pierce, "it seems pretty clear that the murderer is—"

"Hang on a second, Wade. Let's not get ahead of ourselves, okay?"

He put his hands in the air. "All right. It's your show."

Coletti said, "Okay, then what?"

"After the killer plants the knife, he cleans the floor and notices some blood on Allison's slippers, so he takes them off and hides them in the bedroom closet, upstairs."

Coletti looked at Jamie. She said, "The blood on the slippers matches a minute trace found on the knife. Neither is Allison DeMarco's blood type. We're running PCR on them now."

"Why hide the slippers at all? Why not just get rid of them?"

"Because," I explained, "he's smart but he's also cocky. Too cocky for his own good."

"Okay, go on."

"Then he sits down at the computer and makes some changes to Allison's new will. Only he's smart, like I said. So he doesn't do anything stupid like leave himself all the money. He just makes enough changes to ensure that the new will can be contested in court, which will cause the estate to revert back to the old will, benefiting him.

"Once he's done with all that, he exits, leaving the back door open and the dog tied up outside."

Sam Kirby was eyeing the door, but I don't think he was trying to picture the scene in his mind. It looked to me like he was getting ready to bolt.

Flynn wiggled his mustache twice and smiled. "Well, if

that's really the way it happened, we can eliminate Sam and me as suspects. Tim Berry too, for that matter, since as far as I know, none of us has been stabbed recently."

Kirby laughed and said, "Hah. That's right, wise guy."

I agreed. "Tim Berry doesn't make a good suspect as the actual killer anyway since he has an airtight alibi. He came on shift at the restaurant at two."

"Hey," said Flynn, "I got an alibi too."

"That doesn't count. We know you were in Buffalo on Saturday and that your name was on the passenger list of a flight back to Portland Sunday evening. But we have no corroboration that you were actually on the plane."

"Well, I was. Sam can tell you that."

Sam confirmed that he'd picked the sheriff up around six.

"But Sam didn't see you get off the plane, Sheriff. He was waiting for you in the car, not at the boarding gate. But all that aside, let's agree that you and Sam aren't suspects. As long as you both show us your torsos."

"What?" Flynn was outraged. "No frickin' way."

Kirby immediately pulled his shirt up for all to see. He was very proud of his killer abs. There was no knife wound.

I looked at Flynn, then at Coletti. Coletti looked at Flynn, kind of sadly, and said, "Horace?"

"Ah, jeez," and began pulling his shirt out of his pants. "You're gonna pay for this, Field. Trust me."

He got his shirttails out, unbuttoned the uniform shirt, then pulled it and a T-shirt up so we could see his beer belly. He had no knife wound either.

I called out to the porch and had Tim Berry come back inside and show us his torso. He was in the clear.

"Well," I said, that leaves just me and Jamie to do the demonstration with the dog. She as Tara, and me as Richard DeMarco. We know *he* had a knife wound because that's what he died of." (That's *not* what he died of, of course—not according to Jamie—but I didn't want the killer to know that.)

Jamie went to the porch, everyone else took their places in the dining room. I told Audrey to sit at the computer. She sat down and pretended to put eyedrops in her right eye. She then pretended to have a heart attack as Jamie came through the door. Audrey got a wooden spoon from the kitchen counter, near the knife block (which we'd emptied of knives for security reasons). She warned Jamie away, calling her "Tara." Ginger just watched the little skit and yawned.

"Look," said Flynn, "the dog's as bored as we are with all this crap." There were a few chuckles.

(The dog wasn't bored—dogs don't yawn out of boredom but as a way of—oh, never mind. Let me get back to the story.)

Coletti said, "Look, unless that dog goes nuts when someone else comes through that door, I'm not releasing the McCullough girl from custody just because Ginger didn't bark at Jamie."

"No reason you should, Lieutenant. Who's next?"

Jamie said, "Uh, that would be you, Jack. Remember? This is your little farce, after all."

"Thank you, sweetheart." To everyone else I said, "We know that a man named Richard DeMarco flew from Portland to the Virgin Islands the night of the murder. We also know that he was stabbed to death. So let's see what Ginger does when I put on DeMarco's clothes."

Victor DeMarco stepped forward. "Wait just a second, here. Ain't you the one that trained this dog?"

I said I was.

"So what's to say you ain't got some kind of hidden signal to make her go nuts and bark when you come through the door?"

"Actually," Carl said, "it's more likely she *won't* bark because she knows Jack."

"What do you mean?" said DeMarco

"You should see how dogs act around him," he explained to DeMarco and the others. "My sister's dog goes nuts whenever she sees him, but in a good way."

I acted stumped. "I hadn't thought of that." I looked around and my eye happened to fall on Wade Pierce.

He shook his head. "Un-uh," he said. "No way."

I took him aside, into the living room, so we could speak privately. "Look, this is kind of awkward. I really need you to go along with this—"

"No way."

"But why not? You're not a suspect. Besides," I lowered my voice, "I already tested out Richard DeMarco's clothes on Ginger. The minute she smelled them she started growling."

He pulled his neck back. Now he was interested. "Really?"

"Yeah, and if you refuse to do it . . ." I looked back over my shoulder at Coletti and Flynn ". . . it's gonna raise some doubts."

"Oh, all right." He took the clothes from me. "Where do I change?"

I pointed to a half-bath under the stairs near the dining room and he went inside and locked the door. I took Ginger into the living room and waited for him to come out. When he did, he was wearing a bright pink Polo shirt and a pair of blue slacks. He was also wearing a slightly smug look on his face.

"Let's do it," he said and smiled.

Little did he know what he was in for.

43

"Thanks a lot, Wade," I said, "I appreciate your help."

He went out to the porch. I handed Ginger's leash to Carl and we took her over to her spot by the kitchen heating vent. I told her to lie down, but didn't tell her to stay, hoping no one would notice. Then I looked at Slick Vic and said, "Since there's some speculation that I have a hidden signal to make the dog 'go nuts,' I'm going to stay back in the living room, where she can't see me. Is that all right with everyone?"

It was, so Audrey sat down at the computer and we did our little reenactment again. Audrey mimed putting in the eye-drops, then the heart attack, and Wade Pierce came through the kitchen door. As he did, Carl Staub put his hand to his mouth and coughed. Ginger leapt up off the floor and began barking furiously. No one noticed that she wasn't actually barking *at* Pierce, they just assumed she was—especially Pierce, who started to back slowly out the door. I came over to the dog, said, "Okay, quiet!" and she stopped barking. Then I took the leash from Carl and led her back to the dining room.

As I did this, Coletti said, "Well, I don't know if that's proof of anything, but it sure casts reasonable doubt on the McCullough girl's guilt."

"It sure does," I said, and tied Ginger to the banister.

Victor said, "My boy wouldn't a done it. You rigged this whole shebang."

"Well, uh, I don't know," said Pierce. "I was, uh, I was

skeptical about this at first myself. But, boy, the way she was barking sure convinced me. It may not be admissible in a court of law but there's no doubt in *my* mind that—"

"Just one other thing, though," I said, acting a little confused. "Jamie, could you . . . ?" I motioned for her to come to me, which she did. We pretended to whisper things about the case to one another, but we didn't. I won't bore you with the details of our conversation, but it had more to do with the bedroom than the courtroom. Once we'd finished our charade, she walked away and I said to Audrey, "Stand over here," and I positioned her in front of Pierce, directly facing him.

"What's going on?" Pierce said.

"Well, there's just one thing that's not clear about how Allison stabbed her ex-husband, so I just want to clear that up. It'll only take a second." I kept looking back and forth between the two of them, shaking my head like something didn't fit. Audrey was holding the spoon in her right hand. I looked down at the spoon and waved my right index finger at it.

"Does this look right to you, Mr. Pierce?" He gave me a blank look, put his hands in the air. "I mean, you knew Allison pretty well. You've been to her house, you've seen her hold a coffee cup or a bottle of Poland Spring. She's been to your office and signed documents, correct?"

"What are you getting at?"

"Well, was she right-handed or left-handed?"

He made a nervous, self-deprecating huffing sound. "You know, it's funny. I've never been very good at that sort of thing. Noticing who's right-handed and who's left-handed." He looked back at the others. "I, uh, I don't know why."

"Well, just try to picture it in your mind. If she were about to stab Richard DeMarco—and by the way, you're still standing in for him at this point—" He nodded, then began picturing it in his head. "Would Allison have been holding the knife . . ." I pointed to the spoon in Audrey's right hand ". . . in her left hand, the way Audrey is doing? Or would she have been holding it in her right?" I pointed to Audrey's left hand.

Pierce nodded and smiled. "You know, come to think of it, you're right. She would've been holding it in that hand." He pointed to Audrey's left hand and said, "Her right hand. So I guess she *was* right-handed."

"Huh. Because . . ." I pivoted Audrey so that she was standing next to Pierce, parallel with him. ". . . Audrey is actually holding the spoon in her *left* hand, not her right."

Pierce was genuinely confused. "I, I, I don't get it."

"That's because you have a psychological disorder called ·reverse reflective dystopia. Don't worry, it's just a little glitch in how your brain perceives others as if they were mirror images of yourself. That's why, when Allison stabbed you—"

"Wait a second, wait, wait." He was really pissed off. "Are you saying now that *I* killed her?"

"Well, of course you did."

He huffed in disbelief. "What about the dog? She was barking at DeMarco's scent in these clothes, wasn't she?"

I turned to Carl. "Carl, did you get the clothes Mr. Pierce is wearing from Richard DeMarco's hamper, like I asked?"

"Uh, no sir. I bought those yesterday and had them washed a few times to make them look as if they'd been worn."

I gave Pierce a sad, apologetic face. "I'm sorry. It wasn't the *clothes* she was barking at, it was *you*. You killed Allison and the dog knows it. And so does everyone else here."

Pierce was fuming. All eyes were riveted on us.

I stood directly in front of him. "You see, I think Allison stabbed you with her left hand, leaving a wound on your right side." I reached out to touch him and he backed away slightly. "Not very deep, just deep enough to draw blood and a few days later, after it got infected, to force you to make up lies about why you were sweating and in pain. Did you know that the squash courts at the Samoset have been closed for a couple of weeks?" He rolled his eyes but said nothing. "I admit you were clever, Pierce. You set up the murder to look like a heart attack, but knowing about modern forensics you also had to have a back-up plan, in case the medical examiner on the case was smarter than you, which she was." I said this mostly to piss him off, but also to make Jamie feel good and to *look* good in front of Flynn and Coletti. "So—knowing her ex-husband was an endocrinologist—you decided to kill Allison using hormones, something you're familiar with yourself, since you have a prescription for epinephrine." I nodded at Carl, who opened a file folder and showed Pierce a prescription form. "Your doctor wouldn't tell us what it's for, but I'm guessing you're allergic to bee stings?"

"Shellfish," he said with a snotty tone.

"Shellfish, okay. My mistake. But when Allison stabbed you, you had to get even more clever, so you came up with a new plan to really cash in. You flew to the Virgin Islands under the name of Richard DeMarco, found him at his hotel, went to his room, and injected another dose of epi—into his butt this time—and then stabbed him, trying to re-create in your mind the exact way Allison had stabbed you. You know, to make it look real. And that's where that little brain malfunction of yours screwed you up. Since you see everyone else as a mirror image of yourself, you narcissistic sonovabitch, you stabbed DeMarco the way you thought Allison had stabbed you—with her right hand. That's why the wound is on the left side of Richard DeMarco's body. But since everyone who knew Allison knows that she was left-handed—everyone except you, that is—it means that if she *did* stab someone stupid enough to leave the knife at the scene, the wound would be on the right side of *his* torso." I jabbed at him with my index finger but he stepped back. "Care to pull up that pretty pink Polo shirt and show us your tummy, counselor?"

He sighed, hung his head. "I want a lawyer."

I put my hands in the air, acting puzzled. "You don't need a lawyer. You're not under arrest." I turned to Flynn and Coletti. "Is he under arrest?" They shook their heads. "You're not under arrest. I'm not a cop. I'm just a private citizen having a private conversation with you, that's all."

"I'm not saying anything else until I talk to a lawyer."

"Fine. Let's add up a few things, though. Your DNA on the slipper, your visit to a clinic in Portland to have your wound mended, your fake alibi using a cell phone you borrowed or stole from someone named Robert Erickson to make a call from Allison's kitchen to your own answering machine while you worked at her computer, revising the new will that Tim Berry wrote . . ."

He huffed. "What a joke. That will was such a piece of crap. That kid is an idiot."

"You're right—he's not as smart as you. But then, he won't be spending the rest of his life in prison either, will he?"

"I told you I want a lawyer. Anything I say after that is inadmissible."

"It doesn't matter because you're going to confess."

"Hah."

"Oh, yes, you are. You killed two people in cold blood. You planned it and you executed them. So you're going to confess to two counts of first-degree murder and you're going to serve twenty-five to life at a nice safe prison in Maine, where you'll be kept apart from the general population, just in case Richard DeMarco's father develops any ideas about getting even."

Slick Vic did his best to look menacing.

"Now, Mr. Sinclair, here . . ." I nodded at Darryl Deloit, who was standing to one side ". . . has a different outcome in mind. He's from the Virgin Islands, where they still enforce the death penalty." Darryl took a legal document from a briefcase. Standing there, with his dark skin, smooth manner, and short dreadlocks, he looked like he really could have been a government official from somewhere in the Caribbean. "He wants to extradite you and prosecute you for a murder in his territory. And you will be *convicted* there and you will be *executed* there, unless you confess right here and right now!"

Pierce made an angry, frustrated sound. He knew the jig was up (whatever a jig is). "That stupid *bitch*!" he said.

"Oh, it's still her fault, huh?" I almost laughed.

"It's *all* her fault! If she'd just signed over the property, none of this would've happened. She would've even *made* money once the project was up and running."

"Well, if you're a good boy, Wade, you might get out in twenty years. Maybe by that time it *will* be. Carl? Take Mr. Pierce's confession, would you please?"

Carl came over and shook my hand, secretly giving back the silent dog whistle I'd given him earlier. (Remember I said that Carl coughed into his hand when Wade Pierce came through the door? He wasn't just coughing, he was also blowing on the whistle. I'd spent a little time with Ginger earlier in the week, training her to bark madly whenever she heard it.)

Carl took Pierce into custody and he made a full confession. I found out later that my story was pretty accurate, except that Pierce hadn't been outside when the murder took place—he was already in the kitchen. Allison had e-mailed him a copy of her new will. He called and told her it wouldn't hold up in court and offered to come over that afternoon and help her make some changes. While she wasn't looking, he injected the epinephrine into her eyedrops, knowing that she used them whenever she was on the computer. She turned on the computer and put the eyedrops in her right eye, and her heart immediately started racing. He laughed and told her he was killing her because she wouldn't let him use her property at Owl's Head. She was in a panic, got up, and reached for the knife, screaming bloody murder. Ginger—who wasn't by the heating vent, but in the bathroom, drinking from the toilet—came running in and jumped up against Pierce from behind, pushing him onto the knife blade. (It was nice to know that Allison, even though she was dying, hadn't intended to stab her murderer.) As for the rest of it, it was pretty much the way I'd explained things.

As Carl and Dan Coletti took Pierce away, Audrey went back upstairs to change and Quentin Peck came over to shake my hand. He had Tim Berry in custody (the kid would still have to face charges of shooting at a police officer). Peck said that Emma, his chocolate lab, was no longer eating everything in sight and thanked me for my help. Then he left, taking Berry, who said, "Thanks, Jack. Take good care of Thurston for me."

Jamie brought Flynn over and made us apologize to one another. We did and shook hands. "I guess you'll be making a trip to Buffalo now." He sighed and said yeah. "She's a lovely lady, Sheriff—though kind of fragile. But I guess you know that. I'm sorry you have to tell her about her sister's death."

"Yeah, me too." He and Jamie went and sat down in the living room for a bit. She was holding his hand.

Otis Barnes came over and I said, "Well, Otis, did I come through for you like I said I would?"

"Oh, yeah." He smiled.

"But you'll leave me out of it, right? Make it sound like Carl Staub solved the case on his own?"

He shook his head. "I can't do that. But I can get away with simply referring to you as a police consultant, with no mention of your name. How's that strike you?"

I said it struck me just right.

Audrey Stafford came back downstairs, and got ready to go. I stopped her. "Audrey! Aren't you forgetting something?"

She looked around, frightened by my tone. "What?"

"Your dog." I pointed to Ginger, who was still tied to the banister, staring at her and whining.

She gasped, stared at me, put her hands to her heart, then actually started to cry. "Do you mean it? She's mine for *real*?"

"Yes, ma'am. Merry Christmas."

She thanked me and hugged me and kissed me and then went running over to get Ginger, who—at least as far as I could tell—was just as happy with the arrangement as *she* was.

Flynn and Kirby left and Jamie came back over with Darryl Deloit. I thanked him for the masquerade and he said it was no problem and that he actually enjoyed himself. "You guys are a fun couple," he said, smiling. "We should go out sometime—you, Jack, me, and Annie. Maybe play a little pool or go dancing?"

Jamie hugged me and looked up hopefully, and so I told Darryl I thought that sounded like a great idea and to count us in.

After he left Jamie said, "Congratulations, Sherlock."

"Thanks. I would've had him in my sights sooner, but I got it stuck in my mind that the killer had to be from a warmer climate, you know, because of the slippers. Once I realized we were dealing with a fairly severe case of narcissism—which I finally did during my conversation with your dad, not that he's as bad as Pierce, but he *is* a little self-absorbed—I also realized that a narcissist wouldn't necessarily take notice of someone else's slippers."

"How did you know he had that strange brain disorder?"

"What brain disorder, you mean reverse reflective dystopia? I just made that up—even the name—couldn't you tell?"

She hit me. "You didn't."

"Of course I did." (I found out later there really is such a disorder, though that's not what it's called.) "I made up most of what I said here today, except for the stuff about dogs, of course. In fact, I have no idea if the penal system on the Virgin Islands still calls for the death penalty or not."

"No!"

"Yep. It was all just to break him down so he'd confess. And how about you, brown eyes? What was that you said— renin substrate and angio-something II? Where did you get that?"

"Off this thing called the Internet," she laughed. "You should look into it sometime."

"The Internet? I don't know," I acted nervous, "it doesn't involve . . . computers, does it?"

She laughed. "You bonehead. So, Jack," she took my hand and we walked through the kitchen, "now that the case is solved maybe you can get some rest for a change—doctor's orders?"

"Sure, so long as the doctor comes with."

"Well, I don't usually make house calls," she smiled, "but I suppose in your case . . . plus, I think you may need this new form of therapy I've been wanting to try."

"Oh, really? What's that?"

She whispered in my ear, "I am going to percolate your hormones, cowboy." She took me home and did just that.

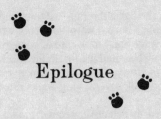

Epilogue

The view of the park and the skyline looked terrific from our suite at the Plaza. It almost made me wish I still lived in New York, the greatest city in the world.

Jamie said, "Thinking about moving back?"

It was a week after Pierce's forced confession. I'd spent Christmas Eve and Christmas morning at Laura Cutter's home. Jamie gave me a down parka and a cell phone for Christmas. I gave her the weekend in New York and the trip to the Bahamas. Since I got to go on the vacation *with* her, I also gave her a pair of diamond earrings and a brand of men's cologne she likes (she's allergic to perfume but still likes to smell nice).

Frankie and I had to leave early on Christmas morning—about ten—and Laura seemed hurt so Jamie pleaded with me, "Jack, can't I *please* tell her where you're going?"

I gave in and said she could.

She smiled and told her mother, "Frankie's a therapy dog! He and Jack visit the pediatric ward every Monday at noon. The kids love him. Though I think today," her eyes sparkled at me, "is a bit more special than usual. Right, Jack?"

"What do you mean?" I gave her a blank look.

She hit me. "It's Christmas! You want those kids to have a special visit from Frankie on Christmas morning, right?"

It was true. Call me sentimental, but I had even bought him a Santa hat to wear. The kids went nuts, of course.

Later that week Jamie flew down to Boston to be with her

father during his operation (he came through just fine) and on Friday I joined her there and then we flew to New York where Jamie went on a shopping spree and I took care of some business and legal matters. We also visited the Frick, the Modern, and the Met, took in a Broadway show, went dancing, listened to some live jazz, and took several long walks through Central Park.

Carl Staub got promoted to detective, second grade. He called me as soon as the word came down. But no matter what I said or did, neither Dan Coletti nor the district attorney would drop the charges against Tim Berry.

"He fired at a police officer," Coletti said. "What kind of message does it send if we don't prosecute him for that?"

He was right. But then, so was I. I just hoped that Tim would get off with a light sentence. Meanwhile, he was out on bail, waiting tables, interning for Jill Krempetz (at the request of one of her longtime clients—namely me), and taking care of his puppy dog, the one-and-only Thurston. He and Tara, who'd recovered from her injuries, were still good friends.

I had lunch with Lou Kelso at the coffee shop in the lobby of the Fisk Building, which is where he keeps his office—as he likes to say. It was a snowy afternoon. Jamie was out shopping on Madison Avenue. He'd gotten a little older—Kelso had—and a little fatter. It was mostly the whisky, he told me. That and the fact that he'd finally given up cocaine. The whisky? Well, he was still working on that one.

He'd convinced the judge in the case against the scumbags who'd killed Leon's family to reverse his decision and let the evidence we'd gathered—two years earlier—to be brought to trial. After the decision came down, the gang bangers fell all over themselves trying to sell each other out. Leon and I were off the hook. I didn't ask Kelso how he'd convinced the judge, and he didn't say. Still, I was grateful.

"I owe you big time, buddy."

"Yeah," he'd said, lighting a French cigarette—or frog butt, as he likes to call it, "send me a basket of blueberries next summer. Or better yet, make it a nice bottle of Scotch."

"Jack? Are you listening to me?"

"What, honey?"

"I said, are you thinking of moving back here?"

"Not really. It's just been nice to see it all again."

"You miss it, though, I can tell."

"I miss some things. The Vermeers at the Frick."

"Weren't they beautiful?"

"And Central Park."

"Mmm-hmm."

"And the architecture, the lights, the rhythm."

She led me to the bed. "What was the name of that singer you took me to hear?"

"Mary Cleere Haran," I said, getting under the covers with her. "She's good, huh?" She nodded. "But I don't miss what it can do to some people. It's a double-edged sword, I guess." I was thinking of Leon and Lou Kelso and maybe a few dozen more souls I knew who'd been battered and almost beaten by the city.

She snuggled up to me. "Or the dogs, I guess?"

I turned on my side and faced her. "Oh no, it's a *great* place for dogs, honey. Are you kidding? In fact, I wish we could have brought Frankie with us. There are a lot of dog runs and parks. And, unlike what you might read in most books about dog behavior, a city can be a great place for—"

"Sshhh, Jack," she put her hand over my lips, "we had a deal, remember? No talking about dogs on this trip."

"I know, honey, but let me just tell you this one thing—"

"Is it worth sleeping in the other room for?"

Honestly? I had to think it over before I said no, and by then it was too late.

Suggested Reading

Play Training Your Dog, Patricia Gail Burnham. St. Martin's Press, 1986. (Shows the importance of tug-of-war and teaching a dog to jump up on command.)

Shutzhund Theory and Training Methods, Susan Barwig and Stewart Hilliard. John Wiley and Sons, 1991.

Natural Dog Training, Kevin Behan. William Morrow and Company, 1992. (The best dog training book ever written.)

Behavior Problems in Dogs, William Campbell. Alpine Publishers, 1999. (Although I find that some of Campbell's techniques don't work, it's still a breakthrough book.)

Dogs That Know When Their Owners Are Coming Home: And Other Unexplained Powers of Animals, Rupert Sheldrake. Three Rivers Press, 2000.

Emergence, Steven Johnson. Scribners, 2001. (This book has nothing to do with dogs but may provide thoughtful owners a new way of looking at pack behavior.)